THE
THIRD GAMBIT

ORDER'S LAST PLAY

BOOK TWO

E. ARDELL

ISBN: 978-1-937546-83-0

To my sister, Candice, who kept asking
"When are you going to get back to writing
about the Lauduethes?"

THE
THIRD GAMBIT

CHAPTER 1

DEVON

A LONG, CURVED BLADE SLASHES the air an inch above my head. I give ground, stumbling backward and swinging my five-foot titanium staff upward to catch the heavy blows aiming to cleave me in two. The sword leaves notches in my weapon. Sweat burns my eyes. I can't blink it out for fear of blindness, even for a second. I can't wipe it, because both hands are frantically trying to keep this woman from killing me.

"Stop retreating!" Desiri Lilias snarls, her voice hot with venom as she rears the blade to strike again.

I jump to avoid it, boots clanking against the gray, metal floor of the ship's practice room. My arms and back ache from taking Desiri's hits. I want to attack, but when I do, she kicks my legs out from under me and I end up rolling out of the way of a death blow.

"I'll stop, if you stop trying to kill me!" I shout and cringe, my voice cracks on the last word like I'm twelve instead of seventeen.

"*Fahat*! If I wanted to kill you, I wouldn't use this!"

She shakes her slasher-film-worthy weapon for emphasis, before swinging it at me again.

I dodge and trip over my own foot. My legs feel like Jell-O. This is worse than football, track and basketball training combined. In fact, I'd pay big money to be transported back to my old high school, where I hid my powers and pretended to be normal instead of combat training with a bloodthirsty battle-mage.

"She's telling the truth," a smooth voice says. I chance a look at my older brother, Evan, who sits on the sideline watching us.

I'm punished for my distraction. Pain explodes from the right side of my ribcage, and I'm airborne for a second. I crumple to the ground, staff clanging against the floor. Bright spots swim in my field of vision as I wheeze, trying to get my breath back. Damn. I think she broke one of my ribs. I make a fist and pound the floor as agony washes over me. My pitiful life flashes before my eyes, void of a senior prom and a college-aged girlfriend kissing me stupid, and I swear I see the face of God in a glowing white cloud.

Then reality smacks me harder than the blunt side of Desiri's sword. There is no one God. There are lots of them, petty and jealous, and into ruining people's lives. The memory of a goddess with four boobs, black holes for eyes and lightning for hair makes me yelp and sit up. The right side of my chest screams as I whip my head around the room looking for Her, Goddess Order, to say, "Hell no, take your stupid gift and shove it up your ass!" I don't want to be anybody's leader, fight anyone's war, or allow any decision of mine to be the reason people die. But it's the job I've been cursed with, to end Order's war with my choices. And I won't even know which choices count.

"Are you all right?" Evan calls.

My vision clears and the work room comes back into focus. It's oval-shaped and made completely of silver-colored metal, like everything else aboard the ship. Weapon racks sit against the curved walls. The ceiling is glass and the floor above it has theater seating so anyone up there can look down into the fishbowl and watch me getting my butt kicked.

I groan and cradle my ribs. I want to milk it, but everyone knows my body will heal itself in a matter of hours. I didn't used to heal this fast. I never needed to, until now.

A hand rests on my shoulder and Evan kneels in front of me. The grin on his face makes him look about thirteen, though he's eighteen, older than me by eleven months, but nobody would ever guess that.

"Need a break?" he asks.

"Yeah." I needed a break two hours ago.

An annoyed growl comes from one side of the room. I look over at Desiri, who's putting her sword back on a rack.

She glowers at me. "We've still got more practice time on the schedule. I booked this room for—"

"Good!" Evan says. His voice is light and melodic. He always sounds like he's singing. "I need some exercise." He stands, stretching his right hand down to me.

I grab it, letting him help me up.

He unbuttons his green jacket and shrugs it to the floor. Standing in a black, sleeveless tank, he rolls his left shoulder and pats the flesh-colored healing membrane encasing it from collarbone to elbow. Worry shifts through me.

"Hey, are you sure that thing's up for fighting with…" I feel Desiri's glare on my neck. I whirl and raise my hands as she comes near. She's tall and slim-muscled. Her tawny skin dewy with sweat from thrashing me. I'm bigger than her, broad shoulders, muscles, and over six feet tall, but this girl scares me. She's like Starfire and Storm together, gorgeous and deadly, except her eyes don't glow.

"I'll go easy," Desiri purrs, gold eyes tracking Evan as she adjusts the hairpins holding her huge, curly copper-colored bun in place.

Evan smirks and picks up my abandoned staff like it's a broomstick. The thing has to weigh over a hundred pounds. It doesn't unbalance me, but my pipsqueak older brother should at least grunt. I'll never get over how friggin' strong he is. Not stronger than me, but he kicked a damn hole through one of the ship walls when someone pissed him off. No effort, just pow. Healers say my powers are the result of a raging adrenal gland in a souped-up body adapted to put extra adrenaline to good use. A great birth defect for superheroes, I guess. Evan says his strength comes from the Tinkerbell DNA floating around in our gene pool, a side effect of our ancient Lauduethe ancestors sleeping around with faerie people. But he's the only one of us to show any physical signs of that heritage and to receive any active magic from it. He sings to nature and works spells, like a fairytale character with soft, rounded features who'll probably never look older than he is now.

Evan spins the long staff like a baton.

"Your shoulder's not all healed up yet," I say. Not even twelve weeks ago, he'd almost died after a bad guy tried to rip his shoulder off and left him for dead on a foreign planet. There's no way that shoulder is ready for a fight.

"No, but I want full range of motion back, so I should exercise. Now get out of the way, unless you want to join in."

Panic flares as I shoot a look over at Desiri who pulls a staff off the weapon rack to match Evan's. Oh hell no. I scramble off the floor, my wobbly legs gaining strength as I make it to the sideline and plop down to watch.

Desiri seems to have the advantage, because she's taller with better reach, but Evan is fast and agile. He matches her blow for blow and then goes on the attack, pushing her back a few steps then striking so quick he blurs. Desiri spins and tries to kick Evan in the shins. She misses. He's behind her, beside her, in front of her, all in the blink of an eye.

He's going to win.

Desiri grins and breaks her staff in two. She wields the halves like something out of *Mortal Kombat*. She catches Evan's strike with one piece and stabs out with the other. Evan does a back flip and then helicopters his staff. Desiri laughs and dances out of the way. Evan grins and they circle each other like monsters in a cage.

Chills creep up my spine at how much fun they're having. I grab a nearby towel and rub the sweat off my face. These guys grew up with weapons, fighting, aliens....

No, not aliens. I have to stop saying that. It pisses people off. But hell, months ago, before prophecies and visions, they were just aliens: Visitors. Strangers that had nothing to do with me. Months ago, I was just a really strong kid from Houston with a psychotically hyper little brother and a moody twin brother. The only thing I worried about was not being normal enough to trick my classmates into thinking I was as human as they are.

A sound like fire igniting in a hot air balloon brings my focus to the match again. Evan's staff burns like a torch. He draws a circle of flame in the air. The ring of fire hovers in front of him. He tosses the staff to the side with a clatter. Desiri beats her sticks together like a kid in music class. Sparks fly from the tips.

"Cheater," Desiri says, a Crest smile on her face.

"You never said no magic," Evan says and blows on his fire ring like a birthday candle. The flames ripple and spin toward Desiri.

Desiri's eyes widen. "*Iska!*" The flames surround her, snuffing out the fire on the ends of her double staffs. "*Gak mopi*! Encapsulate?"

"If you can't break it, I win," Evan sing-songs.

Desiri sneers and starts mouthing magic words. The air around her shudders and she breathes out mist. She stretches a hand toward the flames, stopping before her fingers are burned. "Ah!" She pulls back and narrows her eyes. "Yield."

Evan sucks in a breath and the ring of fire puffs out, wisps of smoke coiling around Desiri like rope. She waves one hand and the smoke vanishes.

"Hand to hand, no magic," she says. "Right now."

Evan shakes his head. "Next time." He rolls his injured shoulder. "That staff was too heavy."

Desiri snorts and throws her weapons to the side. "Excuses." But she doesn't seem mad. She approaches Evan and corrects his technique for fighting right-handed with a long weapon.

They're so easy with each other. They've got a de-

cade of history together. It's like Evan is related to Desiri, and not me. Guess spending two months trapped on a
spaceship with the guy doesn't make up for the ten years
we spent apart. I wasn't expecting to care so much, but it
kind of hurts watching him goof around with his friends
the way he would have goofed around with me had we
been raised on the same planet.

"I reserved the room for later on this evening,"
Evan says. "Rematch then?"

"No magic," Desiri says.

Evan shrugs his jacket back on and rolls his left
shoulder again. Then he claps Desiri's bicep and walks
over to me.

The weapon rack rattles against the wall. Desiri
pulls down two long, straight swords and takes a wicked
fighting stance in the middle of the floor.

Evan grimaces. "She's going to kill you during your
next combat session."

"Look, I can't help it if I suck!" Frustration makes
me sound like a punk. "She's like a ninja, kung fu master
with friggin' magic! I can't keep up." I'm not cut out to
be a warrior.

Evan snorts. "Nobody expects you to keep up.
You're a novice. But here is what she won't tell you:
you're actually doing pretty good."

He kicks my leg and nods for me to stand up. I obey,
legs groaning in protest. I follow him as he heads for the
oval doors.

"Where're we going?" I ask.

"Upstairs," he says. "I stop in to watch all of you
guys' training sessions when I can."

We enter a bare silver corridor. The metal floor
echoes under our boots. Two soldiers in tan jumpsuits

round a corner, laughing and punching each other. They halt in front of us and give split-second salutes, tapping two fingers to their chests and then right temples. Their eyes glitter with respect as they look at Evan. Their interest dulls when it comes to me. They go back to laughing as they pass us, muttering to each other in another language. It sounds kind of Nordic, so maybe it's Remasian. It's got the same lilt that accents Evan's otherwise perfect English.

Out of the corner of my eye, Evan smirks.

I snarl. "Are they talking about me?"

"Yes."

"What the hell, man? They can't make fun of me! I'm one of their reincarnated, prophesized leaders come to save the world as they know it." There are four of us— Evan, Lyle, Lawrie and me—so we're not a Holy Trinity. "We're a Holy Quartet!" I stop and whirl around. I can't kick Desiri's ass, but if I hit one of those guys in the face, they'll feel it for a month.

Evan tosses his head back and laughs. God, that noise grates on my spine. When he really gets going, he sounds like the Joker on helium.

"They like your shirt," he says, still laughing, and leaving me behind.

I scowl down at the Batman logo on my T-shirt. Nobody cares what I wear under my training clothes. But who would have thought alien—no, Visitor—no, REMASIAN—soldiers would be into superhero junk?

"They wouldn't dare say bad things about you where I might hear it." Evan sounds   amused.

My boots scuff the floor as I jog to catch up to him before he reaches the Tube. I glance at him. Aside from having the same almond brown skin and green eyes, we've got nothing in common look-wise. He's got dark blond curls down his back and features that would make old ladies pinch his cheeks and feed him cookies. I wonder how many people fall into that innocent trap before he stomps the hell out of them. I fell into it. Thought I'd gotten a big brother I would have to protect as much as I do my little ones, then he punched me in the spleen for making a crack about the dumb braid he wears his hair in.

"You're scary, man."

He gives me a sideways look. "You have no idea."

The door to the Tube glows blue and slides upward. We step inside.

Evan gives a command in Remasian as the door snaps shut.

The Tube shuttle snakes through various floors and hallways like Willy Wonka's glass elevator. The best part is that the walls are opaque, so I don't have to be scared crap-less as we move.

I tap my fingers against the wall and clear my throat as Evan hums.

He glances at me. "We're a day away from landing on Lenore. After The Maidens read your Mark, your court will be selected, and you'll go on a quest for your Stone."

The Maidens: three more Champions of Order who happen to be immortal, reclusive alien queens of a planet nobody but natives have been on for over a hundred years. Can't wait to have dinner with them.

"Finding your Stone should be easy," Evan continues. "You don't have to worry so much about being really good with your powers. You just need to be good enough to protect yourself."

"It's the needing to protect myself that worries me. And I don't want my Stone." An image of a ruby the size of my hand flits through my thoughts—Order's Gift. It calls to me and feelings of need churn in my gut. I make a fist at my side.

I. Don't. Want. It.

Evan wrinkles his nose. "And you think I want mine?"

He scratches his left palm, seemingly lost in thought. I call it Stone-Zoning. It's like his brain goes to another dimension when the emerald he had nearly been buried with occupies his mind.

"I hate that it's on board the ship," Evan says. "I feel it under my skin. It's poisonous."

"And Lyle, Lawrie and I are going to go out to find three more of them," I snort, my heart a brick in my chest.

We're all going to end up like Gollum, cracked out on the One Ring in the form of toxic gemstones. Forget power and infamy, because I can't forget that the last guys who owned those things all died bloody. Then, hundreds of years later, my brothers and I inherited their crap-jobs because, surprise, we're their reincarnations.

"How's the war stuff going?" I ask.

Evan's been an official leader for three years and was trained to do the job for years before that. He's kept in the know when it comes to the riots and battles and death tolls. The only thing I really cared to know about is that our mom, who'd joined us on this ship for a little while, made it back to Earth safely.

Evan sighs. "The Allegiances have lost territory and we've lost communications with Sector 11. Sector 10 has become pirate space. Undocumented vessels are looting Allegiance and private cargo ships." He rubs his eyes, and I notice the dark circles for the first time. "But none of that is your concern. You just—"

The shuttle rocks and the lights go out. I stagger into a wall and catch Evan as he bumps into me. Sirens blare.

"*Fip*," Evan breathes. A small blue and orange flame blooms in front of him, lighting the shuttle.

A disembodied voice drifts through the walls, and damn it all, it speaks in Remasian.

"What's it saying?" I ask. "What's wrong with the Tube?" I pound on the door.

Evan grabs my wrist and squeezes hard. "Shut up!" His militant bark practically screams 'Houston, we have a problem.' The mood in the shuttle shifts from inconvenienced to 'we're going to die' in thirty seconds.

My heart pumps. "Are we under attack or something?"

Evan clamps a hand over my mouth. His eyes narrow as the announcement continues on in Remasian.

What's it saying? Why didn't he answer me? How bad is this?

My hands shake. Is this the part in the movie where the bad guys blow us up? People don't survive being blown up in space. My knees give out. Evan sinks to the floor with me and removes his hand from my mouth.

"Breathe slower. There's a panel in the floor. I'm going to pull it out and open the trap. Stay close to me." The flame he'd created dips low to illuminate the ground. Evan's swift fingers locate a latch and a patch of floor opens to reveal a tablet-like device. Evan runs a thumb over it in a series of patterns and the shuttle door trembles.

"We're between passageways. The safety won't let

us open the trap. I'll have to do it."

"Between passageways?" I ask. "Like in an elevator shaft?"

Evan gives me a strange look. "Just do what I say."

"Are we under attack?" I ask, my voice a whisper.

He grabs me by the shoulders and stares me down, nose an inch from my face, eyes serious. "Yes."

Panic makes the world spin. Ohshitohshitohshit....

Evan's fingers dig into my collarbone. "We need to get to the bridge. The next Tube platform is two floors up and over. Hope you're not afraid of heights."

He lets go of me and crawls to the door, extracting a small knife from his pocket and wedging it under the metal trap. He grunts as he pulls up on the knife handle, using it as a lever. The door screeches and lifts off the floor a crack. Then, he works his fingers into the gap and tugs.

"Some help!" he barks.

"Oh." I join him. My hands are larger than his. I can't get a decent grip, but after a minute, the door rumbles up a few feet. Good enough to crawl through. Evan's tiny flame floats out into the dark space, lighting the passageway and showing me a black hole-like drop. As the shuttle quakes and sirens blare, Evan boosts himself into the darkness, calling for me to follow.

2
LAWRENCE

GLOWING STRIPS LINING THE FLOORS are the only lights in the dark corridors. The shrieking siren overhead and the pounding of feet around me make my blood bubble with excitement. I laugh as I'm practically dragged by my trainer, who could outrun an Olympic gold medalist. My legs are about to fall off from trying to keep up.

Every now and again, the siren stops and a lady's voice drones with reports of damages to the ship. I've picked up some Remasian in the past few weeks—common phrases, simple sentences, lots of cuss words. I can pick out words like 'damage' and 'puncture.' I grin as adrenaline shoots through my system like an intravenous hit of Mountain Dew. I friggin' love danger. 'Gotta do something,' a crazy hormone that makes it impossible for me to stay still, is ready to bust loose. And now is finally the time to make up for everything I couldn't do months before.

The whole place rocks and the floor lights flicker.

My sneakers lose traction as I stagger to the left then get jerked hard to my right by Adonis who never lets go of my arm. Soldiers and whoever else is in the hall around us cuss. The sound of stumbling steps and thudding bodies echo through the hall as the place continues to tremor. I smack into Adonis, who's slowed down.

The lady on the speaker is talking again. 'Calm,' 'bridge,' 'leaders,' 'evacuate.'

"I need to carry you." Adonis's voice is deep and passionless as ever. It's like he's eternally bored. He releases my arm and I feel him turn to face me.

"Wait. What? Whaa!" I'm airborne then winded as my gut smashes into Adonis's shoulder blade. He grips the backs of my knees.

And it's like I'm riding Pegasus! I'm flying through the corridor, arms and legs bumping into random soldiers as we speed past. This isn't so bad. Just wish the lights would come back on so I can see the expressions on people's faces. Somebody else has got to be stoked about breaking out of this training prison and getting some real action.

I've had two months of nothing but lessons on meditation and feeling the rhythms of my body from Adonis, who I couldn't take seriously at first, on account of his name. Two whole months of lectures on how to behave at political functions from Councilor Theorne, the slimy bastard who, together with Councilor Viveen, stuffed my mom in a spaceship bound for home and banned all communication with family and friends on Earth.

Adonis whips around a corner and slides me off his shoulders. We stand uncomfortably close, my face directly in his. Enough light shines up from the floor for me to distinguish his features. His lips are downturned and his gray eyes look black.

"What's up?" Can't be good if this guy's making facial expressions.

"I need to take you to Deck Two."

"Is it hard to get to?" I ask.

"It is five levels down from the main bridge. If I take you there, I won't be able to come back up."

"So?"

He sighs. He's not a guy who talks much, so I'm sure he's straining himself dealing with me. "The orders are to evacuate the councilors and leaders. You are to be sent out in an escape vessel surrounded by honor guard."

"You're an honor guard," I say. Well, he's one of Evan's three special honor guards. People around here call them a court. All Remasian leaders get one. I kind of think of them as the mini-bosses video game heroes have to fight before they can take down the big boss or Champion—which would be me. I'm supposed to get a court after we land on Lenore for the Reading Ceremony. Order's Mark on my back, an involuntary tattoo that starts at the top of my neck and trails down my spine, that brands me as a leader of Rema, itches like it knows I'm thinking about it.

"Evan won't follow orders and won't go to Deck Two," Adonis says. "He'll go to the main bridge."

Ah. "And you want to go where he's going." Adonis doesn't seem the type to care much about anything, but he loves Evan like a brother and he's still feeling mad guilty about Evan almost dying on his watch.

"Then let's go to the bridge!" I clap. "Pick me up again and let's run."

"It'll put you in danger. If the Ievisara can't be salvaged and we can't defeat the attacking vessels—"

"Oh please, if this ship loses, the bad guys will come after our escape ships. What chances will those things have?" Actually, escape vessels are more like pods armed with combustion canons that'd give a nuke nightmares. They'd be safer than the ship.

Adonis sighs again. "Technically, with no other superior present, you're in charge, Leader Four. What are your orders?"

He had to make it awkward. Leader Four. My new title. After the deaths of the First Four of Rema, the planet only had one Marked leader, and maybe an heir apparent, about every twenty years or so. A few months ago, Evan was the only Marked leader of Rema, then he found the Stone of Magic, woke Order's prophecy, and poof, Devon, Lyle, and I got Marks too. Before us, everyone called Evan Leader Lauduethe. Now, there are four Leader Lauduethes and the super creative Remasian Council, a parliament of twelve, ten I haven't met, decided on the numbering system, like they were afraid we'd name ourselves something lamer than the second coming of the Four of Rema.

I bite my lip. Okay, my first order as Leader Four. "Take me to the bridge." I sound like Captain Kirk, and energy swells inside me. Adonis tilts his head and studies me. It's creepy. He's like an Abercrombie poster that blinks every few hours, and yeah, that look is why I'd thought his name was a joke at first. But, as it turns out, many Earth mythologies stem from other planets and 'Adonis' is a popular boys' name. Kind of like James, for aliens. Though, I'd sure hate to be fugly and called Adonis.

"All right," Adonis says after a moment and steps toward me.

"Ah-ah, second order. Piggy-back." I laugh at his confused stare. "Turn around." I glomp onto his back and he catches on right away.

The traffic in the halls is divided. Some soldiers rush up and some down and I wonder how many are going to fight whatever's trying to blow us up as Adonis weaves through soldiers who'd probably part for him if they could tell who he was in the dark. He heads for the ramps that will take us up three levels.

Another thought hits me as I hang onto Adonis's shoulders. I wonder if Devon and Lyle are being taken to Deck Two or if I'm gonna see them on the bridge. Warring emotions fight it out in my stomach—excitement, because I want us all to be awesome together, and fear, because if this ship really blows up, all of us could die.

But the fear's short-lived. 'Gotta do something' doesn't have much use for it or the accompanying anxiety. Lately, though, fear and anxiety have been a little more common in my daily diet of emotions. Science says those kinds of things keep you alive, survival instincts and all. Guess something in me wants to live.

Adonis shrugs me off. My feet clump to the ground as we near the open space of the main bridge. It's a half circle of a room that looks out into the space in front of the ship with back-up and side-view cameras. The white lights in the ceiling are on. Glittering navigation equipment spans two walls. A wide screen upfront shows us an ocean of fathomless space, spotted with rapidly zigzagging red and orange patterns.

A cacophony of voices speaking in a foreign language swarms through a room buzzing with life. About ten soldiers in tan jumpsuits with cargo pockets man various stations. Some gather around the navigation board.

Two *strategosi* stare out into the wide screen, fingers tapping the gauze-like material covering it and manipulating the zags. It's Battleship with real players in the water.

Adonis glides into the room like he owns the place. I feel like some kind of groupie beside him, though it should be the other way around. A six-foot lady with light blue skin and an inky black ponytail, so tight her eyes look squinty, plants herself in front of us. Adonis does that unnerving stare-thing of his and the lady raises her chin, matching his gaze. They're the same height and I feel fun-sized as I lift my head to observe them.

"Honorable Mauve, why is Leader Four here?" The lady's voice is cold.

An orange pin glows on the lapel of her tan jumpsuit—a translator. Most of the soldiers and crew wear them. Evan's the only person onboard, besides Dev, Lyle and me, who speaks English.

"His orders." Adonis looks away from her and moves on by, glancing around the room.

I smile at the lady and look around too. None of my brothers are here.

Adonis turns back to the woman. "Chelate, any word from Leader One?"

"The compal network onboard has been compromised," Chelate says. "No internal messages are coming through other than what's being relayed on the Sil-Al Net." Her hard, yellow stare falls on me. "Leader Four, I must stress your importance to society and insist that you allow yourself to be escorted to Deck Two."

The ship rocks again, making us all stumble a few steps. Well, all of us but Adonis. Stumbling is probably too plebian for him.

"Yeah," I say to Chelate, running a hand through my tangled curls. "I'm important, I got it. But uh…" Well, hell, what can I really do to help out? I don't know how to fly the ship or work the weapons.

"*Navai ma!*" A voice like a pop star calling his screaming fan-girl audience to attention has heads turning. Evan strides onto the bridge, Devon struggling to keep up behind him. Adonis dumps me like an ugly ex and makes his way to Evan's side, passing Devon as he walks toward me.

"Hey." Dev's voice is as rough as he looks. His dark skin is flushed like he's been running laps and climbing mountains. He's got black grease on his hands and clothes.

"Looks like you've been having fun without me," I crack and dodge the punch he aims my way. Dev is superhero strong, but doesn't always pull his punches when he's mad or emo.

"Big brother had us climbing elevator shafts and kicking in doors." Dev's eyes travel around the room. "What are they doing?"

"Looks like they're setting attack sequences for the fighter ships." I stare at the wide-screen and frown as a few of the zigzags disappear, indicating that the fighter ship is no longer in service. I flinch. People are dying. Wonder if I know them…knew them. There are a lot of soldiers and crew aboard the Ievisara. My memory's great, but not exactly photographic for things that aren't awesomely nerdy. I don't remember everyone I meet.

'Gotta do something' taps its toes and I shake my head. I need to be closer. Evan and Adonis stand next to the *strategosi* guiding the fighters on screen. I start in their direction, but Devon grabs me by my shirt collar.

I gag and turn to find him glaring at me.

"Have you seen Lyle?"

"No. Maybe he's on his way. Or maybe he got put in an escape vessel. That's where we're supposed to be."

"We're supposed to be escaping?" Devon frowns. "Who says?"

"The instructions were for leaders, us, to evacuate. Adonis didn't think Evan would, so he wanted to come here, and hey-hey! So did I."

"That little jerk!" Devon makes a fist. "He wouldn't tell me what the announcements were saying!"

I cackle. "You got played?"

Devon's face goes from friggin' wazzed to exasperated to wazzed again. He growls and pantomimes choking the air in front of him, glowering in Evan's direction, but he moves no closer. It's funny. Devon would have wrestled me to the ground. He would have cussed Lyle out. But Evan? None of that. Yeah, Evan's kind of new to us, but he's not a stranger anymore. By all means, Devon should be ready to get in Evan's face about shizz not being fair to him, but I think he's scared.

I pat Dev's shoulder. "Well, we're here now. Might as well see what's going on, huh?" I jog past him to Evan and Adonis.

New zigzags join the on-screen patterns.

"Fresh troops?" I nod at the screen.

"Yes," Evan says, sounding distracted. "Sending them out in odd intervals. A few are going to drop from Deck Seven when the escape shuttles go out. We just need to get a little closer to Madunat's pull. This force here," Evan points to a mass of zigzags, "is engaging and will hopefully draw and lead the enemy fighters out of Sector 2 and into Cold Space."

I didn't know we were already in Sector 2, the Le-noran Stellar System. "Madunat's not a populated plan-et, is it?" I don't remember seeing any information about its peoples.

"It's all greenery," Evan says, "but there are a few outposts for naturalists. So, the escape vessels can land safely."

"What's Cold Space?" Devon asks and I palm my forehead. I swear if it doesn't have to do with his hair or something emo, Dev is a brick of stupid.

Even Evan curls his upper lip while I groan. At least I'm not the only one being tormented with Devon's unique brand of special right now.

"Cold Space is the area within a Cold Zone territory not owned by a planetary allegiance or alliance." I reach up to pat Devon's spiky hair. He smacks the shizz out of my hand. My fingers throb, but that doesn't keep a smile off my face.

"What are these guys doing?" I point to circular patterns that the *strategosi* seem to be ignoring. I stick my face between the two short men controlling the fight-ers and receive two heated glares. I pull back, hoping I wasn't asking stupid questions too.

Evan points to the circular patterns. "This unit is what is known as a home guard. They're defending the Ievisara."

"Why so few?" I ask.

"Because this ship is meant to be a sacrifice," Evan says. "All of the important officers should be abandon-ing the premise. The only people left behind should be simple soldiers and crew—the last defense."

"So, why are *we* here instead of getting out?" Dev-on asks and then cringes as the 'simple' soldiers in the room shoot him nasty, 'sleep with one eye open' looks.

"Because I'm choosing," Evan draws out the word, "to not lose the eighty people stuck on this ship, because Councilors Theorne and Viveen got twitchy. We save the Ievisara and protect Lenoran space."

Spoken like a kick-ass general. He's inches shorter than me, but I look up to Evan. Hell. I need to be like him, soon, and I'm still just learning where to start. This war isn't gonna wait for me to be ready. I'm prophesized to help end the war, and the people in charge want this war over yesterday.

'Gotta do something' gives way to a feeling of thick-bodied bugs crawling in my chest and batting their wings against my ribcage, my anxiety locusts. Thought I'd evicted these things weeks ago, but they're worse than roaches.

"Sorry." Devon gives off a kicked puppy vibe, ducking his head. A few people are still tossing him dirty looks and hissing in Remasian. In a more subdued voice, he asks, "Has anybody heard from Lyle?"

"I'm here."

I whirl around, locusts retreating at the distraction, and wave at my older brother Lyle. He enters the room with Jalee Orcharest, another member of Evan's court, at his side. Lyle's dark skin is gray, his green eyes bright, like he's sick or something. He's looked like that a lot lately—less CW more HDTV that shows flaws in the complexion. If he keeps that up, people might stop accusing him and Devon of being twins.

"Ly!" Devon sounds like a starving man being handed a twelve-pack of tacos.

Lyle and Jalee make their way to us. Lyle takes his place next to Dev and Jalee goes over to stand by Adonis.

Jalee, Adonis and Evan speak to each other in Remasian. I follow the cadence of their words and pick out some of the meanings. They're worried about how many enemy fighters are out there. And I think there's something funky going on with the enemy's shields. They're absorbing energy, when they should probably be blown to bits instead.

"You okay?" Devon asks Lyle, touching his shoulder.

Lyle takes a deep breath and massages the bridge of his nose. "Headache."

There are no psychics on board the ship to teach Lyle, so Jalee stepped in to run Lyle through textbook psychic exercises, working on his telepathy and telekinesis. Lyle says she's a witch, literally. She specializes in potions and spellcasting which apparently take a lot of concentration and inner peace and equate well with what Lyle needs right now. She teaches him about protecting his mind from outside thoughts through meditation.

"How's it going?" Devon asks, worry tainting his voice.

"I still have to take the drugs, Devon." Lyle's words are clipped.

"Oh." Devon sounds disappointed.

"Leave him alone." I don't see what the deal is about Lyle needing psychic Tylenol to help him turn down outside voices. The way I see it, he's a lot saner when he's had his candy. He'll wean off it when he gets more lessons.

"Shut the f—" Devon starts.

"*Iska!*" Several cusses fill the room, from navigation and the *strategosi*.

I look back at the screen to see a cluster of zigzags

disappear from action.

Evan barks out an order and the screen divides itself into two viewing windows. One window still shows black space filled with patterns, the other shows real-time space loaded with ship debris and hazy with energy residue. Outlines of small double fighter ships flare as they approach.

"What model of ship is that?" Jalee asks. "Focus the image."

Evan yells something else in Remasian and the vid reel goes into freeze frame then zeroes in on a single ship, enlarging it until it fills part of the screen.

"It looks like a Manasta model," Evan says, "but look at the shape of the hull."

A blast of orange energy slams into an invisible wall around the ship. The energy shudders then gets slurped into the ship's exterior like Sunny Delight going down a drain.

"Is it supposed to do that?" Devon asks. Lyle stomps on Devon's foot and Devon yowls.

I study Evan's face. His eyes are wide and his mouth is slightly open. He gives another command and the view on the screen expands again, showing more of the space battle. All of the enemy ships are sucking up our attacks. My anxiety locusts make a comeback. If we can't stop those ships, game over.

"What about the canons on the escape vessels?" I ask. "Those things—"

"Are the same canons on the Gha squad ships," Jalee says.

"Who's the Gha squad?" I squint at the zags on the other screen. The *strategosi* move patterns around the board in a flurry.

"The ones out there getting destroyed," Evan says. "Chelate," he calls over his shoulder. "Pull up all of the latest information on Manasta models. Maybe there's an update in there about these things."

Manasta models. Mental schematics of random versions of the Ruj ships fan out in my head. What's the closest blueprint to the things on screen? Model 133479. But that model is only a prototype, something I randomly saw in a file full of stolen Ruj plans on Evan's compal. The Ruj are months away from coming up with a version that won't overheat in deep space, or so I thought.

"I know what they are!" I blurt.

All eyes are on me.

"They're those new models that haven't passed inspection yet. They have conversion shields that deconstruct v-wave energy and alters it into neutral fuels that the ships can absorb and get a boost from. Guess our information was false."

"All of our canons fire v-waves," Adonis says.

"Contact with Lenore is nil," one of the *strategosi* says, leaving the zags for the other guy to control. He sounds resigned. "Lenore does not have fighter ships, but the Majesty Harliels landed planet-side *cycles* ago with some of their military. They might have been able to send aide."

My stomach flips at the realization that all three sets of Order's Champions—the current three monarchs of Zare sometimes called The Majesty Harliels, The Maidens and The Leaders—are soon to be in the same place. If this ship doesn't blow up.

The soldiers around the navigation walls are quiet. The *strategosi* stare at Evan. I bite my lip. They're waiting for orders. My body runs cold as I watch Evan struggle with the decision to abandon ship and leave these guys to kamikaze for us.

Evan cracks his knuckles, a nervous habit all of my big brothers share.

'Gotta do something' sparks. Firecrackers replace the locusts. "Wait-wait-wait!" I clap my hands. Oh, hell yeah, I think I got something. "Okay, all right, so Models 133479 have converters for energy blasts, but their shields can only defend against canons and other projectile-busters that fire energy waves."

"Which is the entirety of the weapons' systems aboard our ships." Evan's green eyes are murky as they meet mine.

"So," a smile stretches across my face, "let's not shoot at them anymore. If there's no energy to block, the conversion shields are just...there."

"Are you proposing we throw things at them?" Jalee quirks a brow, her cinnamon-colored eyes amused. She's a half inch shorter than me with medium brown skin and coffee black hair. This really isn't the time for me to stare at how pretty she is, but she's like 'hey, I'm Victoria's big secret!'

"Ah, uh, no, maybe," I stutter, shaking my head. "But we can—"

"Crash into them?" Adonis asks. "We have extra fighters and they do not have to be manned."

"But it's not enough," Evan says. "We've got a lot of cargo that can be jettisoned as projectiles, but we need something bigger. Something to keep them off us and Lenore. What can we use to win?"

Tick-tick-tick. I feel my brain clicking.

"*Rasi-va!*" Desiri stomps onto the bridge holding something that looks like a Dungeons and Dragons style mace. "Do you know how hard it is to get to this place with the Tubes down?"

"It's about time, Desiri." Jalee's tone is dry.

"I'm only embarrassed that you beat me here, Priestess." Desiri sneers as she joins us. "Somebody give me a report."

The ship rocks and metal groans. The lights on the bridge flicker. For a few seconds, everything's black, then the power comes back on. Adonis touches Desiri's shoulder and leans toward her ear, lips moving, probably filling her in.

Tick-tick-tick. I stare at Adonis, the stoic, super-fast magic user teaching me to control water as an element. He's one-fourth naiad, a Magic Breed with an affinity to water, and a master of water magic. He takes me up to the ship's reservoir once a day and has me sit and watch the sterilized liquid swaying in its tank, breathing and analyzing its molecular structure of hydrogen and oxygen.

Water. Released in space it'd freeze hard as shizz… and a mass of it the size of an Olympic swimming pool could become a block of death. "Adonis!" I shout.

Everyone jumps. Everyone but Adonis, because jumping is for chumps.

"I have an idea!" I look at Evan to find him gazing back at me. Do I need to ask his permission to discuss a plan/ proposal/ pipe dream?

The whole room's quiet. All attention is on me again.

Evan nods and waves a hand at me. "Talk. Fast."

The ship quakes and the lights waver. Locusts and 'gotta do something' puff up in my chest and the bean and cheese soup I'd had for lunch touches the back of my throat. If these guys take me seriously, I'll be implementing a military plan, and putting the lives of about eighty other people in my hands.

I take a deep breath, cough to clear my throat, and begin.

"I SHOULD CHARGE YOU A transportation fee," Adonis says.

I laugh. Adonis made a joke! "You should be honored to carry me!" But seriously, if he charged a piggyback fee, I'd pay it. He's better than the Tube as he races through hallways and up inclines, cutting corners and taking shortcuts. We're to Reservoir Level in about forty-five seconds. He drops me when we get to the thick metal door and studies the panel beside it.

The mounted tablet is dark, no power.

Damn. I try to recall instruction files for a manual override. "Maybe…"

Adonis reaches out with both hands and rips the tablet from the wall. Metal shrieks and wires tumble from the hole it makes. Adonis grabs the wires like he's wringing a cobra's neck and tugs. Fiber as strong as steel snaps like dental floss. He tosses the tablet and wires aside, then presses the heel of his boot against the door and kicks it out.

The door crashes to the ground and vibrates the floor under my feet.

Holy shiggity. Don't think I'll be pissing this guy off ever.

Adonis slaps dust from his hands. "After you."

Oh yeah. "Sure." As I enter the room, I immediately notice that it's too warm. The insulated black walls of the octagon-shaped room keep this place just under sixty degrees. Right now, it feels like eighty. The scent of rust spices the air. The Olympic-sized tank holds about 4.5 mega-liters of water that needs to stay tooth-numbing cold or it becomes bacteria soup. Good thing we won't need this stuff anymore.

I press my hand against the clear membrane that makes up the tank. It's slick with sweat, but the water pushing against it feels cool.

Breathe.

"Remember your rhythms," Adonis says softly. "Focus on your heartbeat."

I nod and close my eyes, forcing everything else in the room out of mind. Thump-thump. My heart pounds like a kick drum at a rave. It hypes me up. I bounce to the beat, super aware of the blood racing through my veins.

Thump-thump.

Canned, recycled air from a machine fizzes around me. Its life force is dull, but it still rustles my senses. I breathe in its energy and extend my consciousness. I feel the hollowness of the metal floors and walls around me. The individual elements making up the compounds within my surroundings pulse. More power for the taking, but it's like trying to pick a well-woven thread out of a heavy quilt.

A whisper ghosts over my flesh. I shiver as the tingling flow of life force from pure water ripe with bubbly minerals greets me. I open my eyes, staring at the water behind the membrane walls.

"Are you ready?" Adonis asks.

"Yeah." I feel so calm. The water has no worries. It's infinite and strong. *Ly?* I think my brother's name like I'm calling him from across a field. Can he hear me?

/You don't have to shout, Lawrie. I hear you./ Lyle's mental voice sounds annoyed.

E*verybody hears you.*

I jump at the sound of Evan's voice in my head and feel my connection with the water slip. Shizz. I focus on my heartbeat again. Damn, that was close, but it's freaky enough just having Lyle in my head without him linking me to various other people onboard as well. It's like having a radio in my brain.

O*kay*, I think. *We're about to tear the membrane and release the water. Are you sure the halls are clear?*

Everything's set, Desiri's rough voice cuts in. *Cargo Bays 3 and 15 are ready.*

Decoy ships have been released, Jalee adds.

L*et it out,* Evan orders. *The* strategosi *think they can give you a three-and-a-half-minute window. Good luck.*

I turn my head to meet Adonis's shiny gray eyes. "Let's do this!"

"Follow my lead." Adonis touches his hand to the membrane.

I feel the sensation of lukewarm water running over my back, though I'm not wet. The membrane quivers under my palm. I take a deep breath, energy swiveling in through my nostrils, and pull the power within the water toward me.

The liquid whirlpools and the membrane thins, straining to its popping point.

"Steady, Lawrence," Adonis says.

I'm....

The membrane bursts and over two thousand tons

of water sloshes centimeters from my body, restrained only by my power and Adonis's. Now I kind of know how Atlas must have felt. I feel like I'm carrying a loaded cement truck on my back.

Oh God.

/You've got this, Lawrie./ Lyle's voice is soft and assuring, a weird tone for Lyle, but it's kind of comforting. Warmth fills me. Is Lyle sending me good juju?

I pant, sweat burning my eyes and trickling down my nose. *Thanks, Ly.*

Adonis touches my shoulder.

"Let the power roll through you," he says. "Move the water like you would your legs. Guide it, but keep it behind you. And don't forget that I'm next to you."

"Y-yeah." Thump-thump-thump-thump. My heart's in my throat as I reach for the water again, pulling it.

I glimpse Adonis out of the corner of my eye, heading for the broken door. I follow him, a small ocean rippling behind us.

"Three minutes," I say.

"Are you acclimated?" Adonis asks.

I hear water splashing in my ears like toddlers in a tub. I feel like I'm floating in a pool of energy. The power caresses me. "I got this."

Adonis moves in front of me and I glomp his back again.

Silver walls blur as Adonis flashes through the corridors. I choke a few times, breath catching in my throat. Slaps of water splash from the tidal-waving mass behind us. Metal whines as it yields to the weight of the reservoir.

"Approaching Bay 12," Adonis says. "Lawrie, get ready to jump."

Here comes the harder stuff: parting the sea. I nod, preparing my muscles.

"Now."

I shove off Adonis's shoulders, throwing myself sideways. I rebound off a wall and my boots clump onto the damp floor. The tough soles of my shoes squeal as I lose my balance, then right myself. I turn to the reservoir, pushing it back and watching my command slice through it like a stone in a river. There's a fork in the hall, one corridor dipping down to the lower levels while one stays on track, heading out to Bay 12.

Footsteps behind me.

"Good job guys." Evan's voice makes me yelp. I knew he'd be here, but I'd gotten so used to it being just me, Adonis, and the surging power of the tide that Evan seems alien.

"Lawrence," Adonis says as he sidesteps toward the opposite hallway, "follow my lead again. I'm going to pull half of the water towards me. You focus on holding the pool still."

I groan as the strength of the tide divides, like an amoeba becoming two separate entities. I push as the energy tingles through my legs. Stand strong, stand still. Oh shizz. I want to take a picture of this. Adonis is friggin' water-bending. He can kick an avatar's butt. The water rises up like a waterfall in reverse, funneling toward him as he backs down the hall.

"Good luck," Adonis says. And he's gone, taking his tide down to flood Bay 3.

"This is going to feel strange." Evan breathes in my ear, hand on my shoulder. He sings a soft song with no words, the notes legato with mild vibrato.

My heart shudders in my chest as the pool's life

force shivers in reaction to Evan's song. It's Kool-Aid mixing in a pitcher. Evan's magic doesn't feel wrong, but it's not an original part of us—the water and me.

"Don't fight me." Evan's words are light. "If you do, the water won't listen and I can't help you guide it."

Right. I'm the king. The success of Evan's magic depends on the courtesy of the elements. Magic users need spells, rituals and gimmicks to borrow or invoke natural powers, while people like me simply command the elements because we interact with them on a molecular level. It's not magic, it's god-level science. And this is the first time since I found out I'm an elemental that I actually feel like one.

"Aooooooooooo!" I howl. 'Gotta do something' bombs my body with excitement. Water rocks from side to side against the walls. Oh snap. I push back, reining 'gotta do something' in.

"Focus!" Evan hisses.

"Sorry." I take a deep breath, the tang of rust heavy in the air. Thump-thump-thump. Pull. "Do your thing, Big Brother."

Evan keeps a hand on my shoulder as he hums, voice rising above the crashing waves behind us. My heartbeat slows as some of the pulsing pressure of holding back the tide is relieved. I follow as Evan leads us into Bay 12 like a pied piper. I'm the band, he's the conductor.

Bay 12 is four stories high, a half story taller than the reservoir. Long silver beams suspend from the ceiling.

"I'm going to let go now. You have to hold the water on your own."

It's easier to hold the pool by myself since Adonis took half, but stopping it is like fencing in the ocean. I grit my teeth. My body's wet with sweat, my T-shirt and soldier cargos are glued to me.

"Good. Maintain your focus."

Does he sound nervous? No, he can't. He eats danger for breakfast, lunch and dinner. But...

"I don't do this with other people. Close your eyes if you want." He hums an arrangement of notes that sounds like 'Hey Diddle-Diddle.' I feel a tug and let out an 'oof' as Evan grabs me around the waist. My feet leave the ground; I dangle from Evan's arms as we rise.

Some water escapes my hold and leaks from the water-wall like a bad yolk from a cracked egg. The dam's breaking.

Push. My vision's blurry. I wipe perspiration from my face, rubbing sweat into my eyes. I suck in a breath as the whole first story of the bay floods and more water ruptures through my hold.

Evan speeds up the song. My ears pop as we spiral upward toward the beams. Too fast. Much too fast. Thump-thump-thump. My hold slips completely and the tidal wave crashes down. The second story floods. Water laps at my heels. I kick at it as we fly higher.

"Grab a beam." Evan's voice is urgent.

I reach out for one, wet fingers squeaking across a beam, before I get a good grip. My skin screams as the metal cuts into my palms. I hear Evan's flesh slap against steel and watch him swing himself up on a shaft like an acrobat. He grabs my wrist and yanks me up to sit beside him.

I gaze at the ocean beneath us filling up the bay. Random ship parts, crates, and machinery bob in the sea, clanking against each other. Small waves crash together as the water writhes.

Laughter bubbles inside me and I let it rip. "We friggin' owned that piece!"

Evan grins at me. *Jalee, Bay 12 is flooded.*

Bay 3 is ready as well, Adonis thinks.

Secure yourselves. Jalee's mental voice is calm. *Inner bay doors will open in forty-seven wisps.*

The beam bounces as Evan stands on his toes, rapping his knuckles against the metal-patchwork ceiling. He hums off-key and I raise a brow. That's different.

I'm probing for empty space, cratch, Evan thinks. *There's a half-level for storage up here.* Evan stops humming and places a flat palm against a ceiling square and smiles. "Put your hand here."

"Uh." I don't have the balance that he does, but you know what? I slowly shift into a crouch and stand. Evan catches my wrist when I wobble and lets go so I can slap my palm next to his.

"Can you feel the elements making up the metal?" Evan asks.

Focus. Thump-thump-thump. Breathe and extend my awareness. The metal's basically steel: carbon, sulfur, nickel, manganese, and iron glow in my mind, burning with life force. They're blended with artificial elements I don't recognize. They're dull and cold in comparison to the naturally occurring ones. They're a beast to work around as I shift the living elements, creating cracks in the patches.

"Twenty-eight *wisps* left," Evan says.

Thump-thump-thump. The fissures in the metal widen until I see the dark space above.

Evan blows on an index finger like a birthday candle and a skinny spire of fire shoots up into the dark space and becomes a mini-sphere of light. "Move your hand." He makes a fist and punches the broken ceiling tiles. Fragments of steel rain down on our heads.

The beam under my feet shakes again as Evan reaches for the jagged edges of the hole he's made and drags himself up. I watch him disappear for a second, then he's back, stretching his arms down to me. Ragged metal scratches at my legs through the cargos, as he hauls me up, but I don't feel my skin tear. I scramble to get my legs and feet the rest of the way in as Evan scoots back.

"Fifteen *wisps*." Evan shrugs off his jacket and drapes it over our entrance hole. The fabric barely covers the area. He runs his fingers along the edges of the jacket. I feel the frenetic vigor of fire in his fingertips, fusing the jacket's coarse material to the floor.

Leader One, Leader Four, Honorable Maeve, are you in place? Chelate's voice.

Yes, Adonis thinks.

Do it, Evan's mental voice is weak.

*Outer bay doors opening in…*thinks Chelate.

The nightmarish roar of a tornado and a hurricane crashing around like King Kong in a rage keeps me on my knees with my hands over my ears. The foundation rattles worse than a wooden rollercoaster with a car full of Sumo wrestlers hitting the track at a 90-degree angle. I'm thrown onto my side and my body rolls over the floor, crashing into a large metal bin. My ribs cry out and I flop onto my back, feeling the rhythm of quaking metal under my spine. Squeezing my eyes shut, I envision the path of the reservoir below as the water rumbles through the airlocks and out into space where it becomes a titanic block of solid, black ice.

I wheeze, chest aching, body spent, soaked through with sweat. Dammit, that felt good. I sit up, abdominal muscles twinging like I did a thousand sit-ups.

Status? Evan's thought is a whisper. Concern for him prickles under my ribs. I look for my brother and find him hunched over his jacket. The little ball of fire still burns.

Herding maneuver successful. Seventy-five percent of the Ruj models were destroyed by the double trap. Another twelve percent downed by the decoy fighter—De-siri. A supplemental team from Lenore has detained one percent, and the rest fled.

Adonis, status? Evan asks.

Clear.

"Are you okay?" I crawl toward Evan. The storage level's ceiling is high enough for me to stand, but my legs are ten-ton weights. I better be ripped after this. Clark Kent should have nothing on me.

Evan huffs like an asthmatic and clutches his left shoulder like he's holding it together. Shizz, his arm. The flesh-colored membrane over his injury bleeds red.

"What can I do?" I reach him, hands hovering, and touch his other shoulder. His skin's fever hot and his eyes are glazed, but he raises his head and gives me a crooked grin.

"Good job," he breathes. "Couldn't have asked for better on your first assignment."

"Th-thanks. Your arm though."

"I'll live," he says, closing his eyes.

/Lawrie, you guys all right?/ Lyle sounds freaked.

You're not dead, are you? Devon speaks up for the first time.

We're okay, I think. You?

/We're good./

You two strap down on the bridge. Don't go any-

where. Evan's eyes stay closed. *Bay Door 12 locked down?*

Yes, sir, thinks Chelate.

Evan sighs, and I catch him as he slumps into me. "Whoa-whoa! H-hey!" I struggle to turn him over and get him lying on his back, head in my lap.

Hey, we need a medic. We're in the storage level above Bay 12.

Evan stares up at me, eyes bright. He seems pleased. *Jalee, send the battle record to the Silver and Gold Allegiance Councils. Recommend enhanced patrols of Sector 2. Desiri request a shuttle pick-up on Madunat, so the councilors and their guards can join us later.*

Doing it now, Jalee says.

I'm on it—Desiri.

Evan lets out a slow breath, then chuckles, eyes still on me. "How do you feel about all that down there, little brother? What was it you said before? 'We friggin' owned that piece'?"

I laugh, hysteria and 'gotta do something' hand in hand. "Yeah! We were awesome! Batman and Nightwing with superpowers!"

It's what other people needed me to do for them, and I did it. I helped save eighty people. I helped protect Lenore. I did what I couldn't do back on Earth, even after I'd found out I had powers and a destiny. And this is only some of what I'll be able to do. The rest is yet to come when I'm officially Leader Four, one of Order's Ten Champions.

Evan chuckles again, the sound hoarse and exhausted. He raises a shaky fist and I tap it with my own. I've only known this brother for a little while, but I think we're friends. It's not quite like what I have with Dev and Ly, but maybe we'll get there. Especially if we keep being kickass together.

Strategos Vimraz, resume Ievisara's course to Lenore. Evan winks at me. *We've got some new leaders to introduce.*

CHAPTER 3
LYLE

IT TAKES TWO MORE HOURS to get to Lenore.

I sit with my head in my hands, pretending to be asleep. The constant buzz of the crew's thoughts makes me want to hurl myself out of an airlock. I can keep their direct thoughts out of my head, but I'm always aware of them. It's like listening to the beat of a popular song, without the melody. Drives me crazy.

I'm not sure that I'd rather hear their actual thoughts instead, though. I mean, I can hear them if I want to, if I force my way in. I don't know Remasian. Can't even guess what most of the soldiers are saying, but when it comes to their thoughts? My brain translates those into messages I understand. Guess meanings transcend language.

"Preparing to enter the atmosphere," Chelate says. Her words have the generic accent of someone speaking through a translator. "Secure your harnesses."

I'd strapped in hours ago, not trusting that there wouldn't be another attack. I pull my face out of my hands, observing everyone from an almost throne in the center of the room, surrounded by wall-high computers and big screen visuals of outer space. Devon's strapped in next to me, his misery is almost tangible. The need to talk drips from his aura like sweat and I feel guilty. I know he'd love to talk to me, but after two months of trying to be open with each other, as we'd been when we were kids, I learned how different we've become.

I would have stayed with Lawrie and Evan in the med unit, but I'd almost puked watching the medic cut the membrane from Evan's arm. The smell of roasting, human meat was gag-inducing. Lawrie had covered his nose with both hands. Devon threw up in a sink. After that, Dev and I had been dismissed to 'supervise' the crew on the bridge.

I mentally snort. Nobody here needs supervision, and if they do, Adonis, Desiri, and Jalee have it covered. The ship gives a slow, full body shudder and a slight falling sensation tickles my stomach. Devon moans next to me and I roll my eyes. /Are you going to be sick again?/

No. He sounds awful.

/You sure? I swear, if you throw up on me..../

Ly, I can't do this. I trained and worked out and, even though Evan says I'm doing good, I'm still useless. Devon puts his head in his hands, copying my earlier position. *Lawrie was awesome, and you, you linked everybody together. They couldn't have pulled this whole thing off without you doing your thing. I just...I sat and watched you.*

I sigh. /Dev, we didn't need your power. A lot of people sat back./

The simple soldiers sat back, Devon grouches. *The grunts the council left to go down with the ship. I'm let-*

ting everybody down.

/You didn't let me, Lawrie or Evan down, and we're the ones who matter. Evan said you were doing well. You know he doesn't lie./ Because he can't. Damndest thing. He claims it has something to do with his magic.

Devon takes his head out of his hands and shoots me a look. *Why can't I be like you and just not give a crap? Must be nice.*

I push back a small sting of hurt. A few months ago, I might not have cared about what he said. /Screw you./

His green eyes shine with apology. *I'm sorry. I'm just mad. I don't want to be here, but I'm stuck, so I need to be better. I don't want to find that damn Stone, but it'll make me stronger, right?*

And he had to bring up the Stones.

A square-cut, palm-sized sapphire shimmers in my mind along with a hunger that gnaws at the edges of my brain. My powers are bigger than me. I can't hold them in. On Earth, I was losing it. I hurt somebody, using their feelings as psychic ibuprofen to hold my mind together. Thoughts and emotions are so loud. They bash at my awareness like sledgehammers wielded by friggin' Wreck-It Ralph. Pleasure feedback works like Band-Aids. It dulls pain and makes being around people bearable. But it's a temporary fix, like the psycho-active drugs I've been shooting up. People keep saying the more I train, the less I'll need the drugs. So far, I don't see it.

Lyle?

When I'd held my Stone in Order's lair, even though it was just an old memory of a past life long gone, it'd been like holding a cure. There was no pain, no outside noise, my thoughts were my own. I want peace.

"Lyle!"

Devon's real voice shakes me. "Where were you, man?"

I shrug and purposefully turn my attention away from Devon to the big screens in front of me. Through them, I see swirling pink and green atmosphere, shot through with blue, like cotton candy. I shut my eyes, concentrating on the sensation of the world toppling down as the ship touches ground. The Ievisara takes a couple of hops in its landing, a gymnast with a terrible dismount. The ship doesn't break, so maybe it's supposed to do that. We stop moving and the big screens go blank, turning as silver as the walls around them.

I wait for Chelate to make some kind of announcement, Captains do that stuff on planes, but she sits in her piloting chair, face still, nodding as if she's listening. The translation devices also serve as two-way radios connected to alien Wi-Fi that send signals through the auditory nerve to the brain. I frown as her eyes go bright.

Devon grabs my arm. "What's she doing?"

"Something's wrong." I reach for Chelate's mind. The prickle of premonition that tells me to go right instead of left touches the base of my skull. She's got mental shields, meaning she'll feel me enter her thoughts. So, I shouldn't. But....

Her voice comes over the loudspeaker: "Attention crew, we have landed on Lenore. You may unstrap, but please remain in your quadrants, unless you have been given permission to do otherwise." The crew on the bridge whisper; they know something's off.

I unstrap from my chair, getting to my feet, not waiting for Devon. I come face-to-face with Chelate who's in the process of coming to us. Her gaze is grim.

"Leader One's injury ruptured. The bleeding can't be stopped with what we have onboard. He's being prepared for emergency vehicle transport on ground. You need to meet the gurney-cart on Base Deck. I'll take you now."

My stomach drops as I picture Evan's arm, recalling the stink of human meat and seeing a waterfall of blood. I barely register Devon's grip on my arm as he drags me after Chelate, making me run to keep up.

LENORE DOESN'T HAVE A TRAVEL-PORT for large ships. The Ievisara landed in a massive outdoor auditorium. The white pebbles that make up the circular landing pad crunch under our boots as Devon, Lawrie and I chase Evan's evac-cart.

I catch a glimpse of his face as the cart flies by. He's still as a corpse and his lips are blue. I flashback to his body face-down in a pond, dead, but not. He's not dead. He wouldn't die now, not after all we've been through.

Several feet away from where the ship landed, a tall square vehicle hovers inches above ground. The back doors open and Evan's cart is lifted inside. Adonis, Jalee and Desiri jump in after it, along with the Ievisara's medic. The doors close by themselves and the car zips off, giving me a clear view of what looks like a horse-pulled purple and black carriage with a tall woman waiting beside it.

That's our ride to the palace? A wagon is supposed

to keep up with a car?

Devon runs to the carriage, Lawrie hot on his heels, both of them in better shape than I am. The woman moves to intercept us, her long violet hair and white skirts blow in the wind. Her skin is a pale, leaf green and her black eyes have no lids or whites. Devon stops in front of her, Lawrie crashes into his back. I double over behind them, hands on my knees, huffing.

"Greetings, leaders. You will be riding with me," she says in unaccented English. Her voice is throaty, like she sings the Blues for a living, her expression grave.

"To where our brother's going, right?" Devon says.

"Yes," the woman says. "We are going to the palace."

But her answer sounds hollow. I run my power along the edges of her mind, finding the black wall around her thoughts impenetrable.

Her dark eyes glitter in my direction, then she gestures toward the carriage. The wagon lowers itself to the ground, like a horse kneeling to let on a short rider. Devon and Lawrie step into the thing, taking seats in front.

"Leader." The woman gazes at me, waiting for me to get in.

The prickle is back, but it doesn't tell me not to go with her. I climb into the carriage. There are four purple couches set in rows with aisles on either side. The driver's seat is a plush armchair. Two huge, gray and black animals that look like bears with long legs and taloned four-fingered paws prance and pull at black bridles.

The woman climbs into the driver's seat, grabbing up black reins, and the carriage bucks like it's got hydraulics, raising back up to sit on top of its large, spoked wheels. The animals give lion-like roars and do a one-eighty, pulling the cart in a half circle, then charging in the direction the emergency vehicle had gone. My neck jerks and I nearly fall out of the seat. I grip the chair in front of me, glaring at the back of the woman's head.

"My name is Persehain," the woman says over the noise of the carriage wheels and the pounding feet of the animals. We hurtle over a cleared pebble path under an umbrella of parachute-leaved trees. "I will be your palace guide as well."

"So, you'll show us to the hospital wing," Devon tries to confirm. His mind can be so one-track. I watch him pull on his knuckles and chew his lower lip. I don't have to tap his mind to know he's struggling to stay calm.

"There was blood everywhere," Lawrie says. He looks at me, and for the first time, I notice the blood under his nails. "Everything was fine and then the lancet went in too deep, popped the wrong stitch, and blood just…" He shakes his head. "Adonis had to freeze it, but Evan's body can't handle cold like that. He started seizing and blood went everywhere again."

I squeeze Lawrie's shoulder, surprised to find him shaking. Lawrie doesn't freak out about much. I glimpse a room that looks like a murder scene in his head. So much blood. I shake off his thoughts as my head starts to ache.

"He'll be fine," I say, because it's what I'm supposed to do. People expect you to utter words of comfort, even when you don't feel them. They mistake conforming to social norms for empathy.

Lawrie gives me a dark look, then gazes at the back of Persehain's head, eyes narrowing. "Did she actually say she's going to take us to Evan when we get to the palace?"

I stare at Persehain again. Her back is straight, head high, shoulders tense. And that prickle travels up my neck.

"No."

I sink back in my seat, stomach churning with unease as the carriage emerges from a forest into a dusky clearing. A red sun rides low in a purple sky so dark the growing outline of a city seems to glimmer as we race toward it.

In what feels like ten or fifteen minutes, the rock pathways turn into cobblestone roads. One and two-story buildings shaped like massive trees made of green and brown wood line the streets. Vines twined with glittering prism-bulbs hang from leafy roofs.

We pass through a maze of similar buildings until we reach an open courtyard with an honest to God castle at its center. I blink up at the tall steeples and flying buttresses. This is straight out of Camelot, only there's no drawbridge. Persehain pulls the reins and the carriage slows. The monsters pulling us trot to an arched doorway that's as big as an entrance to a two-car garage.

Persehain rises from her seat, turning to us. "Follow me, leaders."

The carriage dips, putting us at ground level again. Persehain steps out, Devon close behind her. He'd been so quiet on the way here, ignoring Lawrie's stupid noises of amazement as we whizzed through town, and not meeting my eyes.

Lawrie touches my arm before I stand up, a look passing between us, before we jump out of the carriage and join the group. Persehain glides to the castle's door and spreads her arms wide. The door splits into two, swinging open to reveal an indoor garden. We enter, soft green grass squishing under my shoes. The foyer breaks into ten corridors and eight staircases, four spiraling up, and four spiraling down, all coated in grass and brown flowers with furled petals. The sickly-sweet smell of tree sap burns my nose. More prism-bulbs glitter, hanging from orifices in the ceiling and bathing the room in splintered disco ball light.

"How do we get to wherever it is they do surgery?" Devon asks, looking around as if he's going to see someone he knows. "Does your translator-thing work like a radio too? Did you let anyone know we're here?"

"The Maidens know that you have arrived," Persehain says. "We anticipate the complete occupation of this Sector by Nazflit and Su forces in five *cycle*s, and you three must be gone before this happens. The Maidens will read your Marks now, so that your quests can be mapped immediately."

"You act like you're throwing us out tonight," Lawrie says. "How long will it take to Read the Marks and make the maps? I thought our court trials still needed to happen."

"They are happening now," Persehain says. "Your honor guards will be fully selected by tomorrow's first moon."

"Let us see our brother first!" Devon squares up to her, hands curling into fists. "I'm not going anywhere until I see him! You better call somebody."

Persehain's dark eyes are blank as she studies Devon. Her voice is steady, unbothered. "Leader One is in skilled hands. If he does not survive, there is and was nothing you can do about it. Your presence will mean nothing." Devon growls as she continues, "But his sacrifice to get you here will mean something. The sooner the Reading, the sooner you can be with your brother."

Dead or alive. She doesn't say it, and even if I could, I don't need to read it off her. I hate Persehain. I choke down fear and reach for Devon's bicep. "Come on." He jerks back, glaring. "But…"

"We don't have a choice," I say. "We'll see Evan later." And if he's not okay, does it really matter when we find out? My throat tightens. It's hard to swallow. And my twin turns away from me.

Lawrie's shoulder brushes mine. "This high-key sucks," he says and I agree.

Persehain gestures to one of the staircases that goes up. "Stay a few paces behind me and stop when we approach the waiting room. I must announce you before you are allowed into the presence of Our Maidens." She says 'Our Maidens' like a fanatic sighing over talentless celebrities, but at least these ones were handpicked by a goddess once upon a time. She takes a deep breath, seeming to savor the cloying smell of sap, and drifts up the stairs, long skirts dragging over the steps.

The staircase spirals up into a square gap in a vaulted ceiling veined with long vines. We pass through the gap, and Devon goes wide-eyed and Lawrie whistles.

We're in another garden. A mile of dark green grass spreads across the floor. Fruit trees full of red, green and silver apples dot the area. A few silver apples lay in the grass. Butterflies with purple, blue and green wings as big as the splayed width of my hands flutter from tree to tree. A stream of bluish green water trickles down from one wall, flowing toward the center of the room into a small pond lined with translucent silver and blue rocks.

"Remain here," Persehain says, then ventures through the garden, past the pond and through an open archway made of fat, greenish-brown tree roots twined together like a bracelet.

"No problem." Lawrie sounds preoccupied. He crosses the grass to the pond, peering down into it. After a beat, I go too, and hear Devon behind me. I hesitate, taking a deep breath before I kneel beside Lawrie. The last time I looked into a pond on an alien world, I'd seen a vision of our past life. We'd been the Peredil brothers meeting Order for the first time. I'd gotten pulled in. I gaze down into the water now and see Dev, Lawrie and me, three rumpled Earth teenagers, surrounded by an alien fantasy garden...but then the water ripples.

I blink at our reflections and frown. It's us, but my eyes are darker, heavier, and Dev's face is thinner, his shoulders broader. Lawrie's wild, chin-length curls are cropped close to his scalp.

That's not us. It's Jain, Padain, and Aman Peredil.

I was Jain, Devon Padain, and Lawrie Aman.

I reach into the pond, hand breaking the surface of the water, and feel smooth fingers brush my own. I wait for something to grab my wrist and pull me in, like months before, when I'd crashed Evan's unconscious mind for the first time. There's no pull. The guy, the one who looks like me with sad eyes, gives a melancholy smile.

Take care, young one. His mental voice sounds like mine. *Make wiser choices.*

I feel his mental presence fading. Curiosity cyclones inside me. /What choices did you make?/

The smile dissipates. His eyes are dead.

/What happened to you?/

No answer.

The image of the Peredil brothers vanishes, leaving

Devon, Lawrie and me behind.

Lawrie turns to me. "Are you okay?"

No. But I nod anyway and take my hand out of the water, shaking it dry. What had made Jain's eyes so dead? Will it happen to me? The fear I choked down earlier resurfaces, but with a new taste. What makes people die on the inside?

Death on the outside. Corin Peredil wasn't in the reflection, because he—

"Leaders," Persehain calls. We turn to her. Her face is reverent. "Our Maidens wait for you."

Lawrie and Devon get up, but I stay down, willing Corin Peredil's image to appear in the water. Lawrie taps my shoulder and I tear my gaze from the pond. His mouth starts to open, but I stand before he can ask if I'm okay. Devon walks past us, going to Persehain. After a beat, Lawrie and I follow. When we reach her, she steps aside and signals, with a sweeping gesture of her hand, for us to pass her and enter The Maidens' chamber. I half expect to hear trumpet fanfare, but there's no music as we cross the threshold, only a strange feeling of changing air pressure that makes my ears pop.

Three women, or maybe two women and a girl, sit on mattress-sized red pillows on the hardwood floor. They're green-skinned and black-eyed like Persehain, but there's a radiance, an inner light about them, that's almost holy. They all rise to their feet. Their long skirts touch the floor. The tallest woman has dark red hair that falls over her shoulders in small twists corded with black ribbon. The other woman has blond hair streaked with princess pink piled in a big ball on top of her head. Her thin neck looks ready to snap from the weight. The girl—or maybe she's an adult, her fierce expression doesn't belong on a kid's face—can't be more than five feet tall. She's built like a prepubescent girl, with a waterfall of pitch-black hair down her back.

"Come closer," the red-haired woman says. "We will not eat you." She speaks with a heavy, almost-French accent which means she's not using a translator.

Devon snorts and the redhead narrows her black eyes.

"Introduce yourselves as you would on your home planet," she says. The other two stand on either side of her, silently watching. Red must be the head Maiden.

"I'm Lawrence Ladreth—Lauduethe," Lawrie says, sticking out a hand. "Shake? That's what we do at home."

I bite back an urge to laugh at the way Red's face twists. I'm guessing she's mortified. The tiny Maiden smirks lightly. Lawrie wiggles the fingers of his outstretched hand and gives Red a wide-eyed look.

Red lets Lawrie's hand hang. "I am Hellene. These are my sisters, Nialiah," the blond curtseys, "and Imari." The short one moves forward to stand with Hellene. With a broad smile, Imari extends a hand to Lawrie who shakes it.

"Welcome, fellow Champions," Imari says.

Hellene shoots Imari a vinegar look and lets that saltiness drain into the gaze she turns on Devon and me. "Your names?" she asks.

"I'm Devon." He gives a quick bow, probably recalling Councilor Theorne's crash- course in diplomacy and customs. We'd all been drowned in information, but damned if I remember more than bow, smile, and keep in mind that if I can't say anything nice, don't say anything at all. Theorne assured us that he or another council member would do our talking for us. There's no need for us to worry about politics, he'd said, casting a shady look at Evan in particular.

"And you?" Hellene presses. All three of The Maidens stare at me.

"I'm Lyle."

"The psychic," Nialiah sighs, sounding pleased. "You were once called Jain. You look like him. It is amazing how handsomeness can be inherited through a bloodline. Though, you might be a little prettier."

I don't like the hungry look in her eyes. Had she and Jain…?

"You guys were around to know the first Four." Lawrie directs his statement at Imari. "What were they like?"

Nialiah smiles at me. "Scintillating."

"Disappointing." Hellene's eyes cut to Imari who seems to be studying the space behind us. "But we will see to it that the same mistakes do not happen twice. Right, Imari?"

Imari's mouth tightens.

Devon bumps my elbow. *Is something going on between them?*

/I'm not reading them./ I reach out to Imari and rebound off a wall of white noise.

Her black eyes meet mine. Her mouth stays tight.

I look away.

Hellene snaps her fingers and the wall behind their fat pillow-seats parts like a stage curtain, revealing a small, half sunken room. We trail behind The Maidens as they descend a short staircase onto a grassy floor. Three lawn chairs carved into the base of a large fruit tree sit against the rear wall.

Hellene removes what looks like a pitch pipe from

the folds of her skirt and trills five notes in an unfinished scale. The tree's roots arch out of the ground and push the chairs into the middle of the room. The mutant butterflies drop down from the tree, one perches on the arm of a chair.

"You may sit," Hellene says.

We each take a chair. The bark under my body is leathery and tough. I scrub my hand along the armrest, scowling as brown scales flake off on my palm. I turn my hand over, inhaling the sharp, sweet tang of sap and get a Lawrie-like urge to taste it.

"Sit up straight," Hellene commands.

I stifle a yell as the back of the chair collapses with a loud snap.

"Remove your tunics," Nialiah says with a soft grin.

Her eyes rest on me as I unbutton my shirt and shrug out of the sleeves. Lawrie chuckles to my right.

Lyle's got a girlfriend—the original cougar. Bet she ovulates sand, brah, Lawrie sings, all seriousness gone from his demeanor.

/Shut up./

The Maidens ripple toward us. Nialiah floats in my direction, but Imari pushes her over to Devon. Imari stands in front of my chair. I tilt my chin. She looks impassive, but she'd made sure she got me. Why? I skim over the white noise in her head; feels like quivering peach fuzz.

Hellene plays a long note on her pitch pipe and the tree roots arch again, spinning the chairs and putting our backs to The Maidens. Imari's hands are warm on my flesh as she kneads them along the length of my spine.

Brace yourself, Lyle Lauduethe, Imari's voice slips through my barrier, easy as breathing.

/How did you—?/

Ice inches its way up my spinal cord. My body seizes. Pain rips through my tongue as I bite it. The twang of copper fills my mouth. I cough out blood, then lock my jaw to stop my teeth from chattering. The seizing stops, but the cold spreads through my arms and legs, stabbing into my fingers and toes. My head reels, brain a melting popsicle ready to ooze from my ears.

Images scroll through my mind like a badly exposed movie; pictures crackle and flicker, the sound is distorted. I see three people—the Peredil brothers: Jain, Padain, Aman. Their faces are gaunt, their expressions are grave.

They sit around a stained wooden table staring at three, square-cut chunks of gray rock. Aman touches the rock in front of him and it shifts, gray color glittering until it's a clear diamond. Jain and Padain watch, then reach for the other rocks. Padain's glistens red, and Jain's— mine—shimmers blue. A sensation of need pulses in my gut. I try to move forward, to take the Stone from Jain, but I have no body.

"The Stone of Magic really just disappeared?" Padain asks. His voice has Devon's timbre.

Aman grimaces, eyes prematurely lined. "When Corin…when he…. When I found him, it was gone from the chain he'd been wearing it on."

Jain rubs at his puffy red eyes. "I-I should have sensed it. I should have known when he left."

"You *should* have sensed it," Padain growls. "But you were too busy playing with that damned Maiden."

"And where were you?" Jain shouts, slamming the table with his fist. The sapphire's light intensifies and he quiets, staring at it, then stroking it. The glow dims.

"I'm not the psychic!" Padain says. He snatches up the ruby. "How do we get rid of these things?"

"I think," Aman says slowly, "they vanish when we die. I read something."

"You're always reading something," Padain grumbles, but without bite. He shoots Aman an affectionate glance.

"I don't think the war will end before we die," Aman says. "Not without Corin's power. But you know She won't let it go. Someone has to end it. I think Corin's Stone went to someone else."

"Who?" Jain and Padain demand.

Aman shrugs. "There's no telling. Could be someone close by. Could be..." He looks distant. "Gods are immortal. Wars can span across lifetimes."

My stomach tenses. Had the prophecy about us turning the tide of the war with our choices not been written in their time? Hell, why would it be written if these guys were still alive? It had to have come into play after they failed.

"Maybe whoever gets the Stone next hasn't been born yet," Aman says.

"What are you—" Jain begins.

"She's losing ground," Aman says. "Things aren't working out like She wanted. Majesty Yarhin's dead. C-Corin's dead! Order's smart. She's a strategist. What would you do, if you were Her?"

"Go to ground and regroup," Padain says.

Aman nods and rolls the fist-sized diamond over in his hands. "We're going to die."

"When we're old," Padain says. "Let's bury these things. We'll desert, go into hiding."

"Don't you think that's what Corin wanted to do?"

Aman asks. "He said—"

"He was crazy!" Padain shouts.

No. No, he wasn't. Not really. I pull back my memories of Corin Peredil, when I'd been in the cave with Evan sharing his coma-dream. Corin had said he'd found something out, that he was about to make a choice that Order wouldn't have approved of. That she'd cursed him with madness. He told us to take the Stones, to use them, that the choices of the Four of Rema really would determine the outcome of the Sector War. And he'd warned us not to let anyone take our choices away. Not even Order.

I shut my eyes on the scene in front of me, remembering the scars on Corin's wrists.

Crap.

When I open my eyes, the scene has changed. Padain is gone. Jain and Aman stand next to each other outside of a small house in the woods. Jain sobs and falls to his knees. Aman sits beside him, hugging him tight.

"You're all I have," Aman whispers. "Please."

The scene blurs until only Aman is in it. He sits cross-legged in front of a fireplace, gazing at his diamond. The walls of the house rumble, books fall off shelves, ornaments crash to the floor. Outside the window, fire and lightning streak across a black and red sky. Aman looks up, his face damp with tears, eyes closed. He holds the Stone toward the ceiling, and the entire room bathes in white light.

And there's nothing. Black on black. Then fragments of consciousness; shards of gems. Sapphire blue flares like a bulb before it blows out, tumbling, like a falling star, heading for—

White noise. My thoughts swim, my melted brain oozes. My ears are damp, wetness leaks from them, rolling down my jawbone.

Take care, Lyle Lauduethe. It is over now. Imari.

I lie flat on my back. I open my eyes and stare at the mutant butterflies attaching at the butt like love-bugs and playing tug-of-war. My head pounds, my body thaws. I dip my finger in the goo pooling in my left ear and pull it out, bringing it to my face. Blood.

Around me, I hear my brothers groaning.

What had that been? Confusion makes my head heavier. I need my medicine again. Something to make the pain stop.

Imari said it was over now.

But the pain isn't over. What was she talking about? What's over?

"Contact the Allegiances." Hellene's voice is like a grenade behind my eyes. "Tell them we have the locations of the Stones and we will have the maps drawn immediately."

Another voice responds. Maybe Nialiah's. I don't know.

The mutant butterflies rip themselves apart. Their bodies fly in opposite directions, scattering across the room, as the Stones had across a galaxy.

Blackness flecks my vision.

"He's hemorrhaging!" Imari.

Warm hands on either side of my face, and black eyes. *I'm going to take care of him this time, Jain Peredil.*

Take care of who? I want to ask, but I can't export the thought. Imari's hands are the last thing I feel before I give into the dark.

CHAPTER 4

EVAN

"YOU ARE A FOOL," SHE HISSES into my neck as I hold her small body against mine. Her skin is cool like she's been outside after dark on a desert planet.

"I'll be fine." I kiss her temple and run my fingers through her glossy, blue-black hair.

She pushes away from me and turns her back, shoulders heaving.

Hurt and uncertainty flood me and I move, wrapping my arms around her from behind and pulling her against me again. She doesn't struggle.

"Corin," she says. "Be careful."

"I—"

"You are never careful!" she moans. "She will kill you!"

"Nonsense." I kiss her right earlobe and she sucks in a sharp breath. Her tiny hand fists my hair, holding me in place. I kiss her again and she tilts her head, giving me access to her neck.

She moans. "You are impossible."

"So you say." I kiss her collarbone.

"I mean it." She releases my hair and grips my hands locked around her waist. *"Stay here."* Frustration and the spark of a fire building inside makes me push her away. *"You don't experience emotions the way I do."*

She's cold.

"But I love you," she says, turning and taking a step toward me as I move back.

"Do you know why?" My voice is hard, and the mounting anger is gone. Suddenly, I'm tired, bone weary, like an ancient ready to cross the Night Bridge. But I don't want to die.

She stiffens. *"If you still need to ask me that, then you do not deserve my feelings."*

So tired. So cold. But the sight of her, beautiful and regal, standing with her arms at her sides glaring at me, makes my heart pound. Maybe I don't know why she loves me, but I love her.

"She will kill you, Corin," she whispers. *"She will not let you ruin Her victory. She will make you choose, and then you will die. Gods do not have favorites, they have servants. She will save the loyal."*

"She'll save no one," I say, *"but you and yours."*

"And you too. Because I love you, and for now, you are loyal," she says. *"Do not do this."*

I say nothing.

"Then," she looks away, *"for Niobe's sake, take care."*

I open my mouth to say something smart, but nothing comes out. Instead, I place myself in front of her. Her large black eyes are closed, tears stream down her cheeks. I brush my fingers along her jawline then press *my lips against her forehead.*

"I will, Imari."

I leave her chambers, wondering if I'll see her again.

BEING CONSCIOUS AND BEING AWAKE are two different things.

I snatch at the fading tendrils of the dream world. The softness of the girl's skin, the curve of her cheek, the sheen of her hair. The feelings that stirred when I'd looked at her.

…but she'd called me Corin.

"You are awake," a girl's voice says.

The last fiber of the dream world vanishes and the real world sharpens into focus at the sound. I know that voice. I orient my head toward it. My neck muscles pop, a dull ache spreading from chin to collarbone. I groan. *Niobe-va*, how long have I been lying in this position?

"Careful. Let me help you," the girl says.

My eyes adjust to the dark. I sense a tiny, flickering pulse of fire, before I notice an old-fashioned lantern: a clear shallow bowl half-filled with thick yellow syrup. The fire burning over the liquid leaps with excitement, its little pulse racing, acknowledging me as a fire-user. My core magic sputters, its inner flame burned down to the base, barely alive. I shiver at the chill.

My left arm is heavy. Memories flash through my mind: my shoulder shredded to the bone, blood painting the ground leaving a thick trail for enemies to follow.

I look at that shoulder now, whole and unscarred.

"Do not try to move it," the girl says. "Hold still." Fine-boned fingers touch my cheek and liquid black eyes, bright in the firelight, come into view. Blue-black hair spills over a green-skinned, heart-shaped face.

By the *Vale*.

"Imari." The girl from my dream.

She removes her hand. "You know me?"

"I...yes," I croak, then cough.

Imari vanishes from view and returns with a wide-brimmed cup. "Sip slowly," she says as she lifts it to my lips.

I try to turn my head away, but she touches my cheek again.

"It is water with melaine," Imari says. "It will help your throat."

The notes in her voice ring clear with no false undertones. She's telling the truth.

I sip the lukewarm water, savoring the subtle sweetness from the flower. I sigh after the first mouthful, throat loosening, and drink until the water is gone.

Imari pulls the cup away, watching me, expression faraway. "He was a full head taller than you, and his face was thinner."

I see a past flicker of Imari with tears running down her cheeks. "He?" I ask.

"Your former. Corin Peredil. I knew him well."

Maybe too well. I shrink away when her hand reaches for my left shoulder, and she stops, hand hovering over my bare skin. Bare skin. Am I naked? A gossamer sheet covers me from the waist down. I balk, grabbing the sheet and pulling it up to my chest.

A small smile twitches across Imari's lips. "Cold?"

I blink, her familiarity sets me on edge. I pinch the bridge of my nose, trying to bring back the dream, or rather Corin's memory of her, what they'd talked about, but the memory—my memory—is fuzzy. I feel like it was important, like something I need to know…then a heavy realization hits me in the face, and I let everything else go.

"Imari." I stare at her. Tiny and pretty. She looks like a teenager in her over-sized tunic and baggy trousers. Nothing like I'd imagined. "You're *Maiden* Imari."

Thick webs clear from my brain. If she's a Maiden, then I'm on Lenore. When…?

Niobe-va. The battle. My brothers. The Mark-reading.

I fling the sheet back and push myself into a sitting position. The room reels. My vision doubles and my ears ring. The effort of being upright causes me to break into a cold sweat. I can't let that stop me, but my body locks when I try to move again, stomach cramping.

"Are you all right?" Imari asks. I feel her small, warm hand on my back, and I flinch away.

"No." Why do people ask that when they know the obvious? It's irritating, more irritating than not being all right. I have to be in control—a fatal flaw of mine. "My brothers? The Mark-reading? The captured Ruj pilots from the fight? The scope of the Sector?"

Knowledge is control. Data calms me.

Imari moves away from me, looking hurt. "Your brothers are fine. Their Marks have been read, the maps to all of their Stones are just about complete, and their honor guards have been selected. They will leave on their quests in the morning. The Ruj prisoners are below and not to be worried about, for they will be executed tonight."

I start, blinking. "Executed?" Maybe I didn't hear that right. "I haven't questioned them. They can't be executed until then." It's the way we do things on Rema.

Imari frowns. "What difference will it make if you talk to the prisoners? Do you think we would not have learned everything they know, before making the decision? We have worthy methods of extracting truth from the unwilling." She doesn't sound insulted, just curious, and strangely, that tone keeps my temper in check. She's just asking a question.

"I don't think anything about your methods," I say. "But your methods aren't mine, and those prisoners are. My trap caught them. It's my right to question them." Another fatal flaw: I hate not finishing what I start. It screams at me until I go after it. Jalee calls it obsession. Desiri and Adonis call it crazy.

"How long have I been out?"

"Almost a complete *cycle*. You woke up sooner than expected and should still be resting. You almost lost your arm."

"I'll rest when I'm dead," I mutter. "Are my clothes in here? Is my court nearby?"

"You are not leaving this room," Imari says, hands on her hips. "You can barely sit up." I force my spine straight and swing my legs over the side of the bed, battling nausea and dark spots in my vision. "You say the soldiers are going to be killed tonight. Not before I see them."

"Just what do you think you are going to accomplish, staggering out of here half-dead? You will not learn anything we have not from those prisoners. You do not even know where they are, and no one will take you to them. Now, lie down. I will send for food."

I set my feet on the ground, ready to push off the bed and try to stand. Imari makes a soft noise and actually pushes me back. I flounder, but steady myself, standing heads taller than she is. The room spins again, but not as fast. My stomach calms. A spark from my core magic sends energy through my body, helping me focus.

"Do what you want, I'm leaving," I say, tying the sheet around my waist like a skirt.

"Your councilors gave instructions for the healers to alert them when you woke up. If you are really ready to leave this room, then you are ready to see them. I will have them summoned."

That stops me cold. "No!"

They'll punish me for the Ievisara, and I'll be useless for another *cycle*. I might even miss my brothers leaving. I grab her arms, careful not to squeeze. I'm bigger and stronger than her, and as far as I know, she's not an enemy. Not yet.

Her black eyes glitter as they drink me in. Her skin is smooth, soft, her fierce expression reminds me too much of the girl—the Maiden—that Corin had cared for. I let her go, but she doesn't jump away from me. If anything, she steps closer. Her breathing deepens, her voice comes out husky.

"Do they hurt you?"

She must take my silence for an answer, because she sneers, but I don't think the expression is meant for me. "I have always hated Theorne and Viveen." She raises a hand, letting it hover near my cheek, before pulling it back.

I wait for her next move. What's she going to do? Call Theorne and Viveen anyway? Cast a spell to keep me here?

But the way she looks at me....

"There are clothes in the wardrobe behind me. Your court is near. They haven't left the Healing Floor since you arrived. Healers come in to check on you every few *jewels*. They would come more often if I was not seeing to you as well. You have a *jewel* before they return, and they will report to Theorne and Viveen if you are not here. I suggest you move fast. I'll convince others in the palace to causally not notice you moving about, but you're on your own beyond that."

"Thank you." I don't flinch from the hand she brings back up, and this time, her fingers brush my chin, traveling up my cheekbone.

"You are so like him," she says. "Nothing was ever good enough unless he did it himself. Only then could he sleep."

I don't know what to say to that.

"The next people to enter your room will be your friends. Wait five *facets* after that, then you and your friends may leave the room, and I can assure you safe passage from the Healing Floor."

Her smile is mischievous; makes me wonder what the other Maidens are like. If they're all into breaking rules and sneaking around, we'll get along fine. Had they all gotten on well with the Peredils, been true allies? I open my mouth to ask, but Imari nods her head toward the lavender-wood wardrobe. "Get changed."

She slips from the room without another sound.

N*iobe-va*. I watch the door close, then go to the wardrobe and dress in the soft blue tunic and pants I find inside. I'm tightening a drawstring at my waist when the door to the chamber reopens and I whirl around as Jalee,

Desiri and Adonis enter. At first glance, they look apprehensive, then they see me.

Adonis is by my side in a half-blink, invading my personal space and looking me up and down. "How does it feel?" His fingers hover over my left shoulder.

"Better," I say, and he stares at me. Adonis doesn't talk much, hadn't even when we were kids, but he doesn't need to, not with me. The fact that he's still standing so close tells me I scared him, again.

"It's not your fault." Because he can't be everywhere, especially when I order him away. It's hard to draw the line between being a superior and being a friend. He rests a hand on my shoulder, eyes half-closing. I hear his life song, full of chimes, runs and arpeggios, a lively tune no one capable of hearing the musical scores that define most living things—The Movement—would expect from him, because he acts so stoic. Life songs embody the essence of their owners, and Adonis's song is bold.

"Your core magic is weak," Adonis says, letting his hand fall off my shoulder. I fully sense his magic and its connection to Lenore. It basks in the extra energy. He probably suffers more than I do on extended space voyages.

Jalee joins us, leaving Desiri to close the door. The mage leans on it, ear against the wood. "That Maiden said wait five minutes, then we can hunt some Ruj prisoners. I bet Jalee my new knife that you'd burn this place down if those *cratches* got splattered before you woke up."

"Those prisoners really don't seem to know much." Jalee rolls up the sleeve of my tunic, callused fingers tracing my unblemished shoulder. I lean into her nutty, cinnamon smell. The same elegant features I've known since I was little are different to me lately and her eyes seem more hazel than brown. She frowns at me. "You should stay here."

"I think they know plenty." Desiri gazes at a crystal time piece she keeps in her belt gear. "The way they acted when they got dragged into interrogation? That's a standard mage-tactic when captured. I told them that, but Lenorans don't listen to mages." Her tone is sardonic, her eyes go to Jalee who purposefully keeps her attention on me.

"Perhaps, if mages behaved with a bit more honor, people who aren't paying them for information or murder would listen," Jalee says quietly and rolls down my sleeve.

Desiri mimes strangling Jalee and turns her attention back to the door and her time piece. "Careful, Priestess. It's a mage who watches your back."

"Stop it," I say. Ten *revs* of working together hasn't made them friends. The blood-hate between witches and mages runs too deep. But they do trust one another. Too many battles and close calls keep them bonded in a way no one who hears them argue can believe. I level a look at Jalee. "You know it's my job."

"Your self-appointed job. No one asked you to..." She stops and sighs. "Fine. But do you have a plan? The Ruj are in the dungeons beneath the castle, but we don't know what tunnels to take or how to get to them. They're hidden from everybody, but—"

"Leave that part to me, Priestess." Desiri taps her timepiece. "Two more minutes to go, by the way. You need shoes, or anything, leader mine?"

I shake my head. My bare feet are steady and swift.

I move better this way, especially when I'm off-balance.

"Theorne and Viveen are livid, Evan." Jalee's voice is low with warning. "They have healers reporting to them constantly about when they think you'll wake up. If they find out you left this room—"

"They won't find out. We'll be back before then, and if not, it's because we found something, and maybe they'll forgive me for it." They won't. They never do. I learned that at thirteen and keep re-learning it when the council thinks I forget.

Jalee reaches out, gathering my hair in one hand. The braid's loose. She unplaits it quickly and redoes it with practiced skill and a soft smile. "Time, Desiri?"

The mage opens the door. "Let's go."

We leave my chamber, creeping out onto the main Healing Floor. The place seems empty. Imari's distraction? The grassy carpet from my chamber continues through an indoor forest contained by wooden, vine-coated walls. I tilt my head back to take in the vaulted ceiling made of a transparent fiber that reveals the blended pink and purple sky.

"What time is it?" I ask.

"Late evening," Desiri says. "You missed dinner. It was great."

"Much appreciated detail," I say. We move fast.

Adonis hovers near me, ready to throw himself over me if anything suddenly pops onto our path. He'll stay on high alert for another few *cycles* before he calms down. I nudge him with my elbow. "What did you hear about the prisoners?"

Adonis's gaze is cool. "They won't take food or water. The healers wrapped up their injuries just enough to preserve them. They have an elixir that siphons truth from the brain, however…"

"Strong beliefs can taint truth," I say. "Zealots?"

"I don't think so," Adonis says. "The reports say the pilots didn't try to suicide before capture. And they didn't talk anymore after their initial threats."

"They're too quiet," Desiri grumbles. "If they'd just given me a *jewel* with them…"

As we pass through the doorway that leads to a staircase, I blink. *Vati fip.* "Desiri, do you know how to get to the dungeons?"

She laughs, pausing on the first step down and turning to me. "Now, you ask. No, I don't. But I know who does and where he is."

Her grin turns feral as her eyes gleam with an unholy light that tells me who we're meeting. I hope His Majesty is in a good mood.

CHAPTER 5

EVAN

DESIRI LEADS US TO BLACK double-doors with winged dragons carved into the wood. She pushes it open without knocking to reveal a green, indoor tournament field...and my little brother getting the *pidge* smashed out of him by Xijure Harliel.

"My, my, Majesty, you're in fine form this evening," Desiri calls.

Xijure whips around to stare at her. Behind him, Devon gets to his feet and takes a fighting stance. He clips Xijure's ear with an open fist and Xijure drops into a spin kick that Devon jumps over. He grabs Xijure under the shoulders and flips the king over his head.

My laugh echoes around the tourney yard. "Excellent!"

Desiri scowls as Xijure springs back up and tackles Devon. They roll, both trying to end up on top. "Keep a knee up!" she shouts. "Get space between you! Use your *fipping* elbow!"

I groan. "Don't tell his *cratchiness* what my brother's going to—*oi vati pidge!*"

Dev somehow gets enough room to kick out. Xijure yelps as he sails backwards through the air, flailing his arms and legs for a split *wisp*, before he crashes into a set of tall bushes, falls through the foliage and hits the ground with a loud thud. Devon does a kick up to his feet, eyes and mouth open wide, horror clear.

"Oh my God! I'm sorry!" Devon runs to where Xijure's sprawled on the ground at the base of the bushes.

I howl with laughter as Desiri walks over to help Dev stand Xijure up.

"*Shasae-va*, you've been holding out on me!" Desiri crows at Devon, letting go of Xijure as soon as he's upright, and smacking Dev's shoulder.

Devon blushes, looking sheepish. "Ah…" He grimaces and turns his attention back on Xijure who's shaking his head, expression dazed.

"Are you okay?" Devon asks. "I didn't mean to. I mean, I was just trying to get you off me. But are you okay?"

Tears roll down my cheeks as I continue to laugh. *Niobe-va*, this feels good. Adonis and Jalee move to stand on either side of me. Jalee's shoulder brushes mine as we watch Devon, Xijure and Desiri make their way over to us. Xijure's top lip is bleeding. He wipes the blood away with his thumb and gives Devon a big grin.

"Like that, Devon!" he says. "I want it just like *that* every time!"

They stop in front of us, both Desiri and Xijure beaming like proud parents, though neither of them is more than a *rev* or two older than Devon. Devon seems conflicted, like he doesn't know if he should celebrate or keep apologizing like a *danderpris*.

I stifle laughter, rubbing my eyes, and wheeze out, "*F-i-i-p*, Majesty. That was a hard fall. You okay?"

Xijure snorts, copper eyes glittering with good humor. "I should ask you that. Had a good nap I see."

"The best," I say and gaze around the green, glad that it's empty aside from us. "No spectators?"

"They got bored," Devon says. "I've been training a lot with Xijure."

"And I'm impressed," Xijure says. "For a non-fighter, you've got good reflexes and you're picking up combat technique nicely. Next time we fight, I'll use my Haribu."

Devon makes a face. "Your what?"

"His big ass sword," Desiri says. "His gift from Order."

Xijure rolls his eyes. "A gift from my father, who got it from his father, who got it from his mother."

"And so on, and so on, until you get to the original Zaran monarchs, Order and Her Table," Desiri says. Xijure growls at her, but his eyes are alight. They stand close, Desiri practically leaning against Xijure's body. Xijure sucks in a breath, looking ready to wrap his arms around Desiri's waist and take a bite of her.

Jalee sighs through her nose. "If you two want to go make out somewhere, do it later. We have more important business right now."

Desiri's eyes flash, but she snaps to attention, turning around to face a disappointed king. He leans down as Desiri talks to him, face going serious. I sober up at his expression. We're not here for fun, even if laughing at my brother makes me feel like a full-fledged member of the living again.

Devon frowns at Xijure and Desiri, then at me. He

comes closer, arms twitching at his sides like he wants to hug me. "How are you doing? Last time I saw you, you were sleeping off anesthesia in that healing room. You look okay, but uh..."

"I'm better. I won't break if you touch me." I can't resist a smile as he closes the distance between us and wraps his arms around me. The embrace is quick and light, because he probably does think I might shatter if he's too rough. I hate being handled like an invalid. I punch his shoulder a little too hard, watch him flinch. How's that for weak?

My smile at him widens. "Good job destroying His Majesty over there. Too bad the other majesties weren't here to see it, or Lyle and Lawrie. Where are they?"

Whenever I remember Lyle and Devon as kids, it's as a unit. They were always together. It's not that way now, and I don't know if it's just from them growing up and apart, or if something happened. I should probably ask. A good big brother would ask, or just know, right?

Devon runs a hand through his sweat-spiked brown hair. "Lawrie's probably messing around somewhere, and Lyle's with one of the green lady healers. She's doing some kind of mind-healing. When the Maidens read our Marks, his brain couldn't handle it and he popped a vessel."

Pidge. "Is he okay?"

"He's good," Devon says. "They fixed it right when it happened, but they still have him visiting a healer twice a day for check-ups."

"Are they afraid it'll happen again?"

"I don't think so, but I think they want to play it safe."

I mentally note that I should go see Lyle and talk

to his healers. It's not uncommon for psychics to burst blood vessels, but it signifies that their powers are over-taxed.

Devon avoids my eyes and scratches the inside of his elbow. An awkward moment of silence passes between us. I don't know what he needs me to say now. I get the sense that this brother doesn't like to talk about feelings.

He frowns. "Lyle thinks Theorne and Viveen are pissed at you. Have you talked to them yet?" He looks up, seeming hopeful.

I shake my head and his face falls. "What's the matter?"

"I wanted to hear that you guys already met up and that you didn't get in trouble or anything. They're acting all smug, like they're going to do some kind of martial punishment. Can they hurt you? Are they strong? I mean, do they have some kind of power?" Devon cracks skinned knuckles and winces as if he's forgotten the skin is missing. He flexes his fingers and blows on his knuckles.

I chuckle at him, then sigh, not wanting to think about Theorne and Viveen. "They're not strong and they don't have power." Not of their own anyway. What they have is worse.

"But—" Devon begins. Xijure's shout cuts him off. "You want to what?"

Desiri clamps a hand over his mouth and yelps when he bites her.

"Are you crazy? Never mind." Xijure gazes at the entire group, his eyes finally settling on me. "Those prisoners are being executed in a few *jewels*."

"Yes, but before that I'm going to talk to them. Desiri told you what we need?"

Xijure huffs. "For me to take you underground. Why can't you ever just let things happen as planned? You're not going to get anything more from those *sludges*. Why risk the wrath of the councils?"

"Because a mage told me the sparkly way the Maidens' interrogation specialists do their questioning isn't as good as mine." I smile.

"You really need to talk to a professional about your constant need to intimidate people." Xijure mimes petting my head and I snort a thin wreath of flame from my nose, letting it spiral between us.

Xijure belly-laughs. "If you stretched yourself a head taller, maybe you wouldn't have to compensate for so much." He winks. His way of showing he's joking, but not really. Xijure's a big guy. He's taller than Devon and almost twice as broad. When he enters a room, people look up and step back.

"So?" I press.

Xijure shoots a hooded glance at Desiri who stands with her arms folded over her chest. "Well…" he drawls, his eyes glitter. "Maybe I want to see if you can get something extra out of them too. Those *cratches* killed two of mine, before we got them grounded."

"I don't suppose you'd want to stay here and keep working on your form?"

Devon blinks, confusion making him look younger than me for a change. "I don't even know what you guys are talking about."

"We're going to get some answers out of the Ruj *spuccum*, before the councils kill them off," Desiri says. "If you aren't coming, you're keeping your mouth shut." Her smile's as poisonous as the blue barrettes pinning her bangs back from her face.

Devon gulps. "But why—"

"Coming or staying?" Desiri snarls.

"Stay," I say, giving him an out. He's scared. He doesn't need to be a part of this. He'll see more real action versus politics in play soon enough. Why rush it?

"Coming." Devon straightens his shoulders. "I want to come." He tries to put himself at my side, but Adonis steps closer to me, quirking an eyebrow at Devon.

I smirk. Adonis has been at my right since I was five, fresh from Earth and new to everything. Nobody's taking his spot any time soon, not even a little brother.

Xijure scowls at us. "Line up, children, and don't fall behind. It's dark down there."

He strides to the doors we'd come through and leads the way to the dungeon.

"SINCE MY SOLDIERS WERE THE ones who captured them," Xijure says, "we were given the honor of locking the prisoners up ourselves." His chest puffs with pride, or *pidge*. Xijure loves talking about his accomplishments like he's the only one responsible for victories.

"Only your soldiers?" I ask. "I thought Caea had reign over the aerial troops."

Xijure sniffs. "My ground troops were the ones who salvaged the scum from the wreckage and got them here."

"Ah," I say, laughing when Desiri swats me.

"Your sister's really cool," Devon says to Xijure in a goofy tone of voice.

I laugh. "You sweeting on Caea, brother?"

Devon's face flushes. "No! I mean, shut up! She's a friggin' queen!"

"And you're Two of Four," Desiri teases. "You're all Order's Chosen. I think you're on her level, kid."

"I don't—" Devon bites his lip. "I have a girlfriend." His voice climbs an octave before he cuts himself off.

I pat his back, feeling a rush of warmth for him. He's bigger than me, yeah, but this is my kid brother. More foggy memories crowd my mind: giggling and pouring multicolored toy blocks down a drain with two other tiny people; boxes of sand with toy cars and a shoe buried somewhere inside; a tiny Devon crying about his missing shoe and me not being able to say I didn't know where it was, because I never could lie. Feelings of loss crawl into my chest. I missed out on teasing Devon and learning what else makes him squirm. Perhaps we'd have been close. Maybe we'd have hated each other. Neither of us will ever know. I catch him looking at me, his face seems solemn, reflective. Wonder if he's thinking about the same thing I am.

We take a long stairway into the bowels of the palace. The texture of the stairs changes from grass to dirt as we descend into the earth. The smell shifts from sharp greens to moist, nutty soil. The walls become gnarled root woven into a tapestry. I graze my fingers along them, hearing life melodies made up of string instruments plucking staccato chords.

As we near the final floor, the chords become single notes that fade into gray silence. Healthy brown roots become black, the tight tapestry from above has unraveled ends. The air turns stale and heavy, the dirt floor cracked and brittle.

"This is a tomb." A fitting place for criminals waiting to be executed, but hard to believe that something like this would be located under The Maidens' castle.

"The music ends here," Adonis says softly.

I glance at him. His dark skin's ashen, body tense. I want to kick myself for being such an idiot. He doesn't tolerate being completely cut off from The Movement well. He thrives on hearing life songs and pulling water chords from any element. I listen hard. There is no water here, not even for the prisoners.

"You can go back up, if you need to. Watch the entrance for us." I pitch my voice so only he can hear me.

He looks tempted to bolt back up the stairs, but he shakes his head. His eyes close and he takes shallow breaths. "I'll manage."

"I'll be quick," I promise. I have to be anyway.

We reach the ground floor. The dying walls of this place siphon vitality from the air. My lungs hurt. Each step across the cracked earth scrapes the soles of my feet. My limbs start to feel as heavy as they had when I'd first awoken.

Xijure presses panels against the wall and hanging circles of light buzz, bathing the tomb in pale orange. "The magic orbs won't travel down here. This is the only place in the castle where they use artificial light." He shudders like being in the tomb bothers him too, but Xijure can't sense magic to know what this place truly is: a dead tempo.

How can a planet with a magical core have barren spots?

"Are you two okay?" Jalee steps between Adonis

and me. Jalee can't hear or see magic. Neither can Desiri, or most others without active Magic Breed genes for that matter.

"Surviving." I hate that she draws attention to us.

Devon touches my left shoulder. He walks behind the group. I almost growl at him but hold back. He's touching my left shoulder, a feather light touch with no real grip, but it's a positive step toward him not treating me like I'll break. I pat his hand, then flick it off.

"I'll live," I say, not bothering to check with Adonis. He hates concern more than I do.

The open foyer of the prison narrows into a hallway.

We reach a large brass door with a horned Dakshin carved into it; a large keyhole centered in its right eye. Xijure pulls an old-fashioned key, metal with multiple grooves, out of his back pocket and fits it into the lock. Gears clink and grind before clicking, and Xijure shoulders the door open.

"*Niobe-va!*" I cover my mouth and nose as the drowning reek of unwashed bodies, excrement, urine, blood and vomit floods out to say 'hello.' My eyes water and I retch.

Jalee ties a cloth around my neck. Grateful, I pull it up over my nose and suck in a breath, inhaling the clean scent of kiani and leaf-soap, the tidal wave of unholy stench blocked. Bless the witch who invented odor canceling brews. I blink tears from my eyes and touch my index and middle finger to my chest to salute Jalee for always being prepared.

Everyone ties on a kiani cloth except Xijure and Desiri. They sneer at us and grin at each other in a way that makes me want to curse the *pidge* out of them. I march forward, shoving myself between both of them and gri-

macing as I step onto cold slushy earth, damp with something I don't want to think about. I should have grabbed
some shoes after all. Ugh. I surge on to the end of the
dank corridor toward a grated cell and halt an *iut* from
the silt-crusted metal bars. I peer in at two people sitting
hunched on a dark, stained floor.

"Devon." I look over my shoulder, glad to see my
brother pacing behind Adonis, Jalee, Desiri and Xijure.
He looks at me and then tries to look beyond. I give a
brief hand signal, and Desiri grabs Devon by the neck
and spins him around.

"Hey!" Devon shouts.

"Guard the door for us," I say.

"But—" He hisses as Desiri applies pressure. "Yeah,
okay," he grumbles.

I watch him disappear down the corridor, before I
turn my attention to the prisoners. They're filthy, covered
in soot and ash hardened by sweat and blood. "Looks like
we get to greet each other properly this time. I'm Evan
Lauduethe. You met some of my soldiers a few days ago,
but I bet you really wanted to meet my brothers and me."

They stare at me, the slit-pupils in their red irises
dilating. One presses his/her face against the bars. I can't
decipher gender in the state they're in.

The prisoner laughs, the sound broken and gurgling.
A slow, crooked grin full of blood-stained pointy teeth
stretches across the blackened face. "We were beginning
to think you wouldn't come to us."

I blink. They were waiting for me? Good, a person-
alized message from the enemy. Even if it's just a threat
of future doom, I bet I can finagle some useful information out of them. I wonder if I'm the only person they'll
talk to, or would they speak to my brothers as well?

The prisoner squints. "So, *you're* Evan Lauduethe. Where's the rest of you?"

I laugh with the prisoner, like we're old friends. Then I roll down the kiani cloth and pull from my core, filling my lungs with flame and blowing it out. Fire traces the lattice of the bars, burning orange then blue as the heat intensifies. The prisoner sprawls back on his hands, eyes wild. The air shimmers with heat. Tongues of flame lick through the bars into the cell, stretching toward the prisoner, teasing but not touching. The ground crunches behind me. I chance a look over my shoulder to see Desiri, Adonis, Jalee and Xijure giving ground as the temperature in the room rises.

"What's your name, Funny One?" I still don't know if I'm talking to a male or female. The voice had been rough; could be a man or a dehydrated woman.

"What do you care, Death Bringer?" the other prisoner growls, then coughs like his/her windpipe is clogged with sand. "Going to chisel names on our death plates?"

"Death Bringer." I roll the title over my tongue and re-secure the kiani cloth over my mouth and nose. "I like the taste of that. Is that what your people call me?"

"It's what everyone calls you." The prisoner coughs again.

"So, your leader wanted revenge on the Death Bringer?" I ask. "Revenge for some battle they lost against me. Let me point out the hypocrisy in this. I'm very sure your leader brought a little death too. Perhaps we should share the title."

"Slave of Order," the one who'd pressed themself against the bars spits. "Do not seek to compare yourself to our honorable general."

I narrow my eyes. "Who's a slave?"

The prisoner spits again. "You serve without question."

"Says who?" I press.

The prisoner bares his teeth. "You'll die, and this time you won't come back. This war will end. Your Goddess will fade and your planets will be devoured. Kahine will flush Kahanna's taint and create balance in this world."

Oh, perfect. "Adonis, I thought you said they weren't zealots."

"My mistake."

"Who's your general?" I ask, ready for tight lips, but the prisoner laughs.

"You know him," he rumbles. "You scarred him and then dishonored him by not taking your warrior's kill. You deemed our general unworthy."

"I'm not following you. Be more specific."

The prisoner's voice drops an octave. "At your request."

My vision dims as the fire is sucked out of my lungs. The flames on the bars puff out. My face goes numb with cold as my ears ring. The prisoner's craggy hand reaches out, gripping my braid and yanking me forward. My forehead clangs against metal, rust and soil scratching my cheek.

Angry shouts. A tornado of arctic air whips pasts me. Then there's silence as a wall of magic slams down around the prisoners and me. The wall is opaque. I can't see or hear anything on the other side or through it. *Fip.* I stare into the enemy's red eyes. A ward. Where did this *cratch* get the magic to throw up a ward like this, and how did I not sense it?

The other captive staggers to the bars and leans

against the one holding my hair.

Their bodies sizzle with frost, cold smoke billows from their ragged clothing. They smile, mouths stretching across their faces until the skin cracks and rips. Blood dribbles down their necks as the lines of their mouths creep across their cheeks, touching the edge of their jawbones and then...crack. Skulls break in half, teeth, tongues and bloody gums exposed.

"*Fipping pidge.*" I wish I could shut my eyes, but I can't. Bones and flesh mesh together, their skulls fusing into one. I throw myself backward, staggering when my hair is released, watching as they meld the rest of their bodies together. Their filthy rags seem to melt away as skin bleeds through the fabric, merging until they become a triple-armed, three-legged entity with a trio of eyes and one monstrous mouth.

Chimera.

"*Ayo, rapi.*" The deep voice rumbles in the giant chest.

My body goes rigid. I know that voice. My mind takes me back to Onkurus, after being fished out of the pond that would have been my coffin. Surrounded by red-eyed enemies with serpent slit pupils and sharp teeth, this man had wanted to take me as his pet. A spoil of war. He'd had the black diamond teeth denoting him as a Ruj general.

"You should have honored me with death after your victory," the general says.

What is it with Ruj and wanting to die? "You're one of Pandemonium's chosen Champions," I say. "I saw it. Are you also prophesized to end the war?" No one on my side of the war knew Pandemonium had Champions, not until I came back with the news. The Nazflit Coalition and Su Allegiance don't boast about prophecies and holy mandates for leaders and monarchs. The Prophetic Cycle texts only preach about Order's ten champions.

"Arrogant of you all to believe that Lord Pan does not have disciples who pass on their Gifts too," the general says.

"What do your Gifts do?" I ask. My eyes dart to the barrier. I toss an analytic rhythm at the boundary, studying the threads of magic piecing it together: thick, strong ropes of dark fiber with no room between the seams.

The general laughs, drawing my attention back to him as he grins. The conjoined teeth of the two prisoners grate together, white flecking off to reveal onyx veneers. A *fipping* possession token. Had the prisoners swallowed them before capture?

He ignores my earlier question. "Thank you for coming to visit. I was hoping you'd come alone. I've been waiting for you, Corin."

"Evan," I correct.

"I smell him in you. I'm sure I'd taste him too, if I drank your blood," the general purrs like a greater feline. "I'm sorry I let you get away."

"Did you mean to capture me in that last battle?" I play a ballad in my head, mimicking the weak whistles of the air trapped inside the ward with us. The air reacts, swirling around my body, then racing to the magical barrier, scanning for breaks.

"No," the general says. "I meant to talk. I like you, and I would like to extend an offer."

My skin crawls at the way the words 'I like you' drips from his tongue like slime. Three red eyes glaze as they travel over my face and body. "You wanted us to bring these pilots here."

"I wanted them to bring you to me," the general says. "This was a last resort. But no matter. You will join my side soon enough."

"Why is that? I hope you don't think your people are taking Sector 2. The Silver and Gold Allegiances won't lose any more ground, especially not this one."

The general chuckles and gives me a condescending smile. "I know something your Lady Order will not tell you, and neither will your Maidens, or your Remasian councilors."

Truth sings pure in his words.

I feel the memory of Corin Peredil's ghost pressing his lips to my ear, cool breath whispering, *"Trust no god."*

Lady Order has secrets. "I'm listening," I say.

"I do not know how your primitive Allegiance schools work." The general stands his horrible body up, posture regal, as he scans the cell for something. "But I know they teach all *politicos* to read the Old Texts." He disappears into a dark corner. Metal grates against stone as he drags a stool to the bars. "But do you read the original versions or translations?"

"Translations," I drawl. "No one can read those old tomes but The Maidens."

The general sits, back straight, and places his middle hand on his middle knee, letting his other two arms hang limp at his sides. I watch those long arms and stay out of grabbing distance.

"Let me guess, *you've* read the original texts," I say. "But your texts would be recorded by Su and Nazflit historians. They'd be different anyway. Is there a prophecy in yours?" Maybe if I keep asking, he'll slip up and tell me what their powers are.

The general taps fingers on the middle knee. "There is no prophecy." His tone is flat with a ring of finality. "Only the truth. I wonder what you might find if you were to read what your Maidens store in their treasuries."

I narrow my eyes. He's stalling.

"How much do you trust those around you?" the general asks.

"Depends on who you're asking about."

"Do you trust your council or even your fellow Champions?"

"To an extent." I keep probing the barrier for an opening. "Are you suggesting I should trust you?"

He barks out a laugh, then leans forward in his chair, his side arms swing up, rough hands clamping around the bars. The filthy skin across the knuckles stretches as he tightens his grip. "That decision is up to you. However, I have for you a clear message: Your council and those Maidens do not have your best interests in mind, and neither does that goddess."

I snort. "Everyone's in it for themselves. When the war is over, they'll get to redraw Sector lines and claim new territories. There will probably be other wars, but maybe I won't have to be a leader anymore."

The general rubs a bar with an index finger. Silt flakes off and drops into a murky puddle. "Maybe you won't have to be anything anymore. Do you know what happens if Order wins?"

I shrug. "The Allegiances inherit a lot of new territory."

His eyes twinkle with condescension. I bristle as he licks his elongated lower lip with a pointed red tongue. "You know nothing of standard theology. Nothing about celestial hierarchies."

"I have better things to study." I glance at the ward again, willing the air to work faster. Find a break and get me out of here.

The general tuts. "I bet you don't even know your true goddess's name, other than the fact that She is not Order. Do you never wonder why a foreign goddess would favor beings She did not create?"

"Because She hates Pandemonium, and it was the only way She could go after Him. The beings She created are useless for war." Magic Breeds. Order created the fae, powerful as *fip*, but dumb as *sludge*, and perfect temptations for my Lauduethe ancestors.

The general chuckles. "Do you truly believe a goddess would wage war simply for hate of a son? There's a grander game being played here, leader."

"I'm sure there is," I say. "Look, I don't care about who's fighting for what. The only thing I'm worried about is the welfare of the people who'd pitch themselves into a hell for me."

Air trembles around my ears, a victory whistle, as it leaks though a small cavity in the ward. A break, finally. "Sorry to disappoint, but I'm not interested in the laws of godly games. Now, if you want to come right out and state why I should care, then…" I send out another trill and more air swells around the fissure, forcing it wider, but it moves so slowly. I still can't hear anything from the outside.

"You're a good strategist." The general nods. "You don't sacrifice what you don't have to. But your 'betters' are not this way."

"And you are?" I meet his red eyes, letting my gaze travel over his stolen and distorted body that had cost the lives of two of his own. "Is Pan?"

"No." He grinds his teeth. "But Pan does not lie to those He makes deals with, so He has not lied to me. I know my scriptures. If there was time, I'd urge you to know yours as well, but there isn't. Your choice now can save you. Pan wishes to offer you a deal."

His words ring true again. He believes he's spoken to Pandemonium. I flashback to the battlefield, the vision of a man sitting on top of an altar with four black holes for eyes, and lips stained by blue blood. *"Our Lord Pan."*

"He wants your Stone," the general says. "Stand down and give it to Him, and He will spare you."

"And the rest of the Silver and Gold Allegiances go to *pidge*? How is that better than keeping my Stone and helping the Allegiances win the war, which in turn saves everyone I care about?" Why would he want to talk to me about something as empty as this?

"You need to know what happens when gods win," the general spits, eyes flaring like a fanatic. "Everything begins and ends with blood."

I won't go closer to him, but somehow the monster looks sympathetic, like a teacher trying to get through to an awful student burdened with potential. And something sings to me, an undercurrent, telling me: listen.

"I am protected," the general says. "All of my companions are, but Order would only save some of you." He slaps the bars with his palms, countenance shifting from teacher to war lord. I gulp, skin prickling as the room goes cold. "The Nazflit come now. We have taken the Cold Zone around Sector 2 and have lurked in the outer planets of the Lenoran System since before you set course. We've been waiting for you."

Shadows emit from the general, wrapping him in

darkness. He stands, kicking back the stool with a crash. "What is your decision, leader? Your council will betray you, your Maidens seek to save only themselves, and your borrowed Goddess will devour you. But Pan, He is honorable."

"What..." The air freezes in my lungs, heavy and sharp, like ice in my chest. I wheeze and cough, frost crusting my lips. My core flame sputters, dying down to an ember. I fall to my knees.

"You will not be allowed to make choices that threaten the survival and livelihood of my people. You will not strike against the great Pan. Give me your answer, child, and I will end this one way or another."

All planned. The prisoners were a plant. They manipulated the entire battle. All for this. If I choose to side with this general, Pan gets my Stone. If I die here, my Stone is useless. Either way, there'll be no Four of Rema. How much would my brothers' choices matter without me? The Peredil brothers weren't able to win without Corin.

"Everything begins and ends with blood."

I whistle, the sound faint, the song sloppy, feeding the last of my strength to the air. I feel it tremble and burst through the ward like breaking a dam. Sound surges in. Warrior cries from Desiri and Xijure who are probably physically striking the ward, furious chanting from Jalee, the sloshing of water spells from Adonis.

Booted footsteps charge into the area. Arms grab me from behind, lifting me up and dragging me back. Desiri leaps, landing in a crouch in front of the bars. In a blur of motion, she kicks out. Her boot blazes with fire magic amplifying her strength. The bars shatter. Using her momentum, she grabs the general by the neck. Her hand smokes and sizzles where she touches his skin but she doesn't flinch as she yanks out a blue barrette and stabs it into his throat.

The general roars and flails as Desiri jumps back. His three hands scrabble for the poison needle in his flesh but can't grip it. He crashes to the ground, face first, seizing until he's still.

"*Avrashti fip o mae raigo,*" Desiri growls, kicking the body.

"Evan, look at me!" Jalee kneels in front of me. "Hold his head, Adonis."

A hand takes my chin, holding it upright. My body rests against another's. I feel the pulse of Adonis's life song and relax as Jalee pushes a thumbnail-sized poultice under my tongue. It's salty and sour. I flinch and retch, but she holds a hand over my mouth.

"Keep it under your tongue." Her voice is soothing. "Just breathe. You're okay now." She gazes over my head. "What's taking Devon so long to get somebody down here?"

I wheeze, the ice in my lungs melting as the vapor in the poultice flows down my throat.

"What in *Nth Hell* happened?" Xijure booms, rolling the general's body onto its back. "What is this beast and where are the prisoners?"

"Possession tokens," I say.

Jalee touches my cheek and forehead. Her brown eyes simmer, her face hard. "What?"

"The prisoners," I rasp. "They must have swallowed them before they crashed. The Ruj general from Onkurus, the one I burned, he spoke through them. He said…" *Niobe-va.* "The councils."

"What about them? What'd he say?" Xijure kneels

down beside Jalee. Desiri stalks past us, peering down the corridor. The echoes of running feet head in our direction.

"The councils have to meet now," I say. "The Stone quest teams have to leave immediately, maps or no maps. The Nazflit are here and killing that chimera probably gave them the signal to close in."

I cough until my vision spots. Adonis pats my back.

"In here!" a voice yells.

"Help me up," I hiss.

Jalee stands. Adonis shifts behind me and tugs me to my feet. I lean back into him, dipping into my core and breathing poultice vapors into its hearth. The ember glows and a ripple of yellow flame springs from it, billowing upward. My body warms and I steady myself. I turn to greet Caea and Ramesis Harliel and their squadron of Zaran soldiers.

"What in the name of Krevai happened here?" Caea asks, her eyes wide but her mouth set in a warrior's grimace.

"Call the councils together," I say. "We need to prepare Lenore for attack."

6
LAWRENCE

ROUGH HANDS SHAKE ME AWAKE.

"Shizz, Chasyn!" I roll onto my back, glaring at the gangly red-haired guy with a wannabe goatee.

The final trial to pick my court roster finished hours ago, and this guy wasn't a part of it. He, instead, was hand-chosen by both Theorne and Viveen without being tested. They say I need him on my personal team because they claim he's good at creating tornadoes and thunderstorms. I haven't seen him do shizz but eat like a cow and make fart jokes. I can't deny that some of the jokes are kinda funny, but still. Bet Dev and Ly won't get a fart guy on their courts.

"What do you want?" I slur, rubbing the sleep from my eyes as my brain fully catches up to where I am.

Chasyn gives me an unimpressed look. His eyes are a deep, muddy brown that churn like molasses when he's thinking. "The quest ships are launching now. You have to get some pants on, *gikak*."

Gikak—the Remasian equivalent of 'brah' or

'dude.' Sounds lame when I say it, but I don't mind it so much when he does. Makes me feel like I can relate to somebody else besides my brothers since Devon, Lyle and I will be off on our own separate quests soon, while Evan stays here.

"Wait. What? We're launching?" I spring up, nearly knocking my head into Chasyn's chin, and the guy jumps back, cussing.

"What do you mean we're launching now?" I leap off the long-leaf hammock, my bare foot getting caught in the vines. I stagger then stumble, crashing to my knees, before scrambling up. Chasyn shakes his head and goes to the pile of laundry next to my suitcase. He starts flinging clothes my way.

I catch a shirt made of corded fabric and a pair of military cargos. Okay, soldier clothes. Locusts and 'gotta do something' shift around in my stomach like a newbie trying to balance on a long board.

"What happened?" I ask, pulling on my clothes. Hot shizz. We're leaving on the quests to find the Stones now. "Where are my brothers?"

"On route to the launch pad." He lobs a belt at my head.

I glare at Chasyn and, before he throws shoes at me, I hunt up my badass alien combat boots and stomp into them.

Chasyn nods and heads for the door. "Come on, *gikak!*"

"Yeah, yeah." I jog through the door and fall into a light run beside Chasyn. The palace halls are a ghost town, but there's a stinging pop of extra oxygen in the air that charges my body and helps me keep pace with Chasyn's longer legs. "You gonna fill me in now?"

Chasyn nods and rattles off a story about Evan cowboying up, interrogating the prisoners on his own, and finding out how screwed we are.

"Holy shiggity! And it all checks out?" I ask. 'Gotta do something' pulses under my skin like it's had a triple shot of espresso.

"The Allegiances had already ordered more assistance in this Sector just this morning, but half of it ran into Nazflit blockades. They've been fighting for hours and nobody knew. Communications from them are *dilch*. Leader Lauduethe's, uh, Leader One's discovery prompted the release of secondary units to check on the first wave that never made it through."

"So, why don't we just get ready for an attack on this place?" I ask. "We're not gonna get far if Nazflit's out there."

"Don't worry about that," Chasyn says.

We run up a flight of grass stairs. The roar of ship engines and the clamor of mechanics and soldiers hustling around just out of view flip a switch inside me. I outstrip Chasyn, sprint up the last flight of stairs and out into the open air of the launch site. My boots practically squeal as I skid to a stop. My heart pounds.

The sky's on fire, the atmosphere a blend of blood red and deep orange. Black and yellow ships swarm an invisible barrier of magic around the circular fifty-foot launch pad. A ring of Lenorans line the edges of the pad, hands joined, keeping the magical barrier up. Each time an enemy ship fires, the air seems to waver, making the barrier momentarily visible, like a plastic bubble bending under pressure.

"How long can they hold that?" I shout as Chasyn jogs up to me. He shakes his head, eyes wide as he watches the sky, then grabs my shoulder and turns me to face three spaceships the size of cruise liners: our quest vessels. They're parked in a sloppy row. The onyx lacquer of each gleams. In front of the first ship sits a sixty-foot portal hub, a wormhole born of magic and science. The portal looks like the Mecca of all vacuum hoses. It makes a perfect, free-standing 'L,' short-end fused to the ground, long-end extending into the clouds. Its looming entrance gapes like a maw, the wiring inside its transparent lips shimmers a honey yellow as engineers feed the machine coordinates from handheld compals.

"Lawrie!" Devon's voice steals my attention away from the magic and tech. I hear Chasyn behind me as I run to my brothers.

Devon and Lyle walk toward me, dressed in matching cargos. Hah! Mom would love a picture of them in twin clothes. They haven't dressed alike since third grade. Devon throws his arms around me and squeezes, before pushing me away. "Jesus, what took you so long to get up here?" His hands are shaking.

"He was taking a nap in his *roos*," Chasyn says, and I punch his shoulder.

"Another nap?" Lyle frowns at me. "You're pushing yourself too hard."

I roll my eyes. "You're one to talk. And now's not exactly the time to hold back in training." I wave my hand at the ships. "This is..." My stomach flops. This is the last time we'll see each other for who knows how long.

"We need gaps in the spell circle!" a deep voice shouts.

I turn around as the Zaran monarchs—Xijure, Caea and Ramesis Harliel—run out, big weapons, gifts from

Order, at the ready. A mass of soldiers in gray Zaran uniforms march behind them. I can't keep a grin from splitting my face as Ramesis whips out a battle axe better than anything I've seen from *World of Warcraft*. It glints silver, sparks flaring from its double blades. Caea and Xijure fan out on either side of him, Xijure with a four-foot sword and Caea with a pair of foot-long daggers. If I was into RPGs, these guys would so be my wrecking squad.

A few of the Lenorans holding up the barrier unlink their hands and the spell circle opens. The Harliels and their soldiers run out onto the grassy clearing that extends for miles around the palace before becoming a thick woodland area. Ships fire on the Zaran force as they break into various formations, dodging blasts. The Zaran soldiers retaliate with shoulder-cannons, blasting yellow lightning at the ships. Explosions make the sky ripple.

Enemy soldiers parachute down, hitting the ground running, fighting with lasers, guns, and magic. Fire and neon light blaze from weapons and hands. The Harliels lead a charge right down the middle of the enemy's ground troops, the three of them as good as any medium-sized army. They move at incredible speeds as they practically blur across the field, their weapons blazing with silver light.

I don't think they're enough, though. More enemies parachute from the sky as ships close in on us, hovering above the ward. The Lenoran spell circle chants louder, some members starting to sweat.

"*Vayal ta mi!*" Evan's voice rings out.

Devon's big hand grips my shoulder, yanking me backward with him, as about forty Remasian soldiers rumble up the stairs and spill onto the launch pad, charging our way.

"*Sakar te!*" The soldiers bolt toward the opening in the spell circle.

Evan, flanked by Desiri, Adonis and Jalee, runs to Devon, Lyle and me. Desiri continues past us, charging onto the battlefield with the troops. Evan's eyes are wide as they scan the premises, like he's taking the whole world in at once and cataloging it for future reference.

"What do we do?" Devon asks, the last word squeaks and I pretend to cough so I don't laugh.

Lyle's tense on the other side of me. I don't know what he expects. Does he think Evan's going to tell us to throw ourselves out there with the Harliels and the soldiers? No. That'd be dumb. We'd just get in the way. But if he did...well, maybe I wouldn't mind being on that field, testing what I've learned. I should be helping.

"Board your ships," Evan says. "The portal's hot and locked onto your coordinates and I was told your maps are complete."

Board. I glance over my shoulder. Chasyn's gone. I look toward the ships. Men and women, some I don't know and haven't seen before, are ascending the short ramps onto the vessels. I bet some of these guys are on our courts. Crap, which ship did Chasyn go into? I have to know which group is mine.

Evan scowls at the fight. The cacophony of clanging weapons, energy blasts, grunts and cries along with the wail of different engines isn't as loud as it should be. I think the magic barrier's protecting us from the worst of the noise. I study the Lenoran circle. One man's down on his knees, looking ready to pass out.

The magic won't hold.

"Come on." Evan grabs my arm, pulling me. I turn my head, seeing that he's got Lyle too. Devon follows. Evan nods over his shoulder at Jalee and Adonis who reciprocate and head for the spell circle. Jalee hurries to the man on his knees, rubbing his shoulders and taking his place in the circle. Adonis stays at her side, peering back at us. Well, probably at Evan. The guy's like a Rottweiler in that regard.

We reach the first ship. Devon staggers to its oval entrance, his feet moving like they're made of cement. He faces us. His Adam's apple trembles, like he's choking something back and he blinks rapidly.

Oh shizz, is he gonna cry? He can't. If he does...

Fugnugget!

Devon throws his arms around Lyle, hugging him for all he's worth. I shake my head at the twins, watching them squeeze each other and say nothing—nothing out loud anyway. Evan clears his throat but makes no effort to break them up. If he had something as mundane as a watch, I bet he'd be tapping it, though.

My insides tremble. Time. We don't have any more time to prepare, to learn, to be together. It's all happening too fast. I knew we were gonna split up for the quests, but I put those thoughts aside. We still had time. But we never really did.

What if one of us doesn't come back? What if I don't come back?

Devon and Lyle pull away from each other, and Devon catches me in a hug next. He really is strong enough to crack me in half, and it almost feels like he's attempting to do it. I wheeze, struggling to breathe, but I don't complain. This could be the last time my big brother almost kills me. He lets me go, and I cough, patting him on the shoulder. Our eyes meet, his glisten, tears on his lashes.

Dammit, Dev. I wipe at my own eyes and turn away from him.

I hear the murmur of Evan's voice behind me as he talks to Devon, and then I hear him "oof." I chance a look, not quite smirking at Devon hugging the hell out of Evan too. Then Dev's running to his ship, going up the short ramp and disappearing inside. When I see him again, he'll have his red Stone. If I see him again.

Lyle's next. An arm drapes over my shoulder. Lyle's breath is heavy, and he doesn't look at me as we move together toward his ship. What's he thinking? I remember wishing that I was psychic instead of him, but that'd been before we'd left Earth. Before I'd seen how hard his powers hit him. Now, I'd rather him just tell me his thoughts. I'm okay with not knowing directly.

Ly, are you gonna be okay?

I bet Devon asked him that. But hell, Lyle's going out there without Dev to talk to and without Jalee to coach him. It'll just be him, his powers, and that psychic Tylenol. I recall Lyle weeks before we'd left Earth, how much he'd struggled. I see him now, still pale with dark circles under eyes that seem a little drug-glazed.

/I'll be fine./ The response is too soft. /My court's all psi. They can help me./

Right. But…

/Are *you* going to be okay?/

I put my arm around his back. *I'm about to get on a friggin' spaceship and go on a quest for a magic rock. I'm a friggin' space cowboy! I'm…*

We reach Lyle's ship and I can't finish what I'm thinking to him.

I hug my brother. It's not rib-crushing or long, but it's enough. I watch Lyle shake Evan's hand and give him a short hug. Evan levels Lyle with an intense look. Lyle's eyes widen slightly, and he nods.

Shouting and more stomping feet. The sour smell of blood and the musty stink of tech oil almost knock me over as Caea, Xijure and Ramesis, gross and drenched in battle fluid, run toward us. Xijure splits from the trio, detours toward Devon's ship and jogs up the ramp.

Wait, he's going with Dev?

Caea and Ramesis stand a few feet away from Evan, Lyle and me, their expressions solemn, almost respectful, their weapons holstered. It's amazing the way their OWs—Order's Weapons—shrink down so they can store them in regular-sized weapon loops in utility belts that put Batman's to shame. But then again, it'd be damn awkward lugging those big things around when you're not chopping off somebody's head. Pretty nice of Order to do that for them.

Lyle looks towards Devon's ship, then at Caea and Ramesis. "Is one of you coming with me too?"

"We thought it best for one of us to accompany each of you, to be your temporary seconds-in-command." Caea doesn't blink.

Temporary seconds-in-command? I almost laugh. They're undoubtedly going to lead our teams, because what do we know about leading. And learning that kills off some of the locusts I didn't know were hanging around, because I subconsciously feared I'd be leading a team all by myself.

"I'm with you," Caea says to Lyle, then nods toward their ship. "Let's go, Leader Three."

Lyle doesn't get a chance to agree, and just stares as

she jogs off. He turns to me with a half-shrug, and friggin' waves at me. I snort, waving back. Dork. He heads for his ship, joining Caea on the ramp. I don't miss the way Lyle wrinkles his nose and her glare, then they're gone too.

"I apologize for my odor," Ramesis says and I glance at him. In Common Years, he's twenty-two, but if I do all the crazy conversion math, he's my age, sixteen. He's also the youngest Harliel prince. Nope, wait, king! He was coronated the day before we left Earth.

"You've never apologized to me for smelling like *sanrat*," Evan grumbles as he squeezes Ramesis's shoulder. "You had better take care of my little brother, Ram."

"Of course." Ramesis's light brown eyes as serious as they are curious. The guy's like a cat. He's been slinking around Chasyn and me, only joining conversations when prompted, but I know he's got a lot more to say. Wonder if he's like that around his big bro and sis.

Devon's ship, Ship One, guns its engines and motors toward the portal. The Mecca vacuum hose lets out a wail, like an emergency broadcast signal from an old TV. The wind picks up, and I gasp as a black hole opens in my stomach.

Shizzshizzshizzshizz. I clutch my gut and double over. Arms wrap around me and hot breath touches my ear. "Get used to this feeling, little brother. They draw their energy from air and fire." Evan.

"Feels like…" Like it's killing the elements.

"Just count, sing, make up a rhyme," Evan says, rubbing my back. "Distractions help. It's almost over, for now."

My stomach bottoms out and I dry heave a few times, before the noise dies down and Ship One's sucked into the portal. Devon's gone.

"Come on, let's get you on your ship before you embarrass yourself," Evan says, helping me straighten up.

Gah. I sniffle and wipe my mouth with the back of my hand. I feel like a wrung snot-rag. "If that's what it feels like just standing around while it happens, what's it gonna be like when I actually go through it?"

Evan's smile doesn't quite ring innocent and he's quiet, which says a lot because the dude can't lie.

"Do you feel it too?" I massage my temples as my insides swish around like a washing machine on heavy duty. If he does, I'll bow down, because he can still walk a straight line. Another warm body presses against the other side of me, a hand patting my back. I cast a slow look at Ramesis. The guy doesn't return my gaze.

Evan hums lightly. "I'm more attuned to fire than air. My body temperature drops." He touches a hand, that feels like it's been clutching a Coke straight from an ice chest, to my cheek. I yelp.

"I used to pass out and wake up bundled in blankets and heating spells," he says.

The portal wails again and my guts twist. "Ah…" I bite my lip and try not to face-plant. Ramesis and Evan tighten their holds on me.

"Your ship should have gone first." Evan's words are bitter. I frown at him, trying to interpret the odd expression on his face, while keeping lunch in my stomach.

"We're rushing, Lauduethe. You can't control everything," Ramesis says.

Evan grouses under his breath, shoots Ramesis a dark look, then stops, eyes going wide as he tilts his head back. The world spins, goes dark, and my knees give as the portal shrieks and that black hole rips at my innards again. I want to ask Evan what he's looking at, but I can't. Glass pebbles prick my kneecaps through the cargos and cut at my palms. Who the hell thought glass rocks were a good idea? Shizz.

Lyle's ship, Ship Two, roars. Wind and exhaust whip over me, hot and ripe with the stink of burned rubber and friggin' basil of all things. I won't ever think of spaghetti in the same way again. I spit up a mouthful of bile, barely noticing the lack of helping hands patting my back and shoulders.

"*Fip!*" Evan shouts over the noise.

The ground quakes and the air around us thins.

And the sky explodes, showering the barrier with metal wreckage from ships, severed foliage and dirt. The launch pad goes dark, like night has fallen. The air above seems to shudder, a transparent film that has to be the magical barrier wavering. If it breaks, we'll be buried under all of that crap blacking out our view of the sky and field. Hands grip my shoulders and I'm hugged tight. My brother smells like sweat and soot. I barely get my arms up to return the embrace, before he pushes me away.

"Get to your ship!" His voice is sharp. I stagger back and cry out, dropping to my knees. A black hole rips my stomach apart as Ship Two vanishes through the portal.

Ramesis grabs my arm and pulls me up. I stumble behind him, heading for Ship Three, and slam into his back as he halts. The portal screams, the honey glow of its wires burn red.

"Unstable portal connection. Coordinate verification lost!" someone shouts.

"Shut the portal down! Evacuate Ship Three! If you're not a warrior, go to ground!"

Evan sounds like he's hollering through a megaphone. His voice echoes and people move. Technicians and mechanics scatter like cockroaches. Chasyn and a group of other people run off the last ship, Chasyn sprinting in my direction.

Ramesis pivots, yanking me after him so hard my feet leave the ground. I'm a zombie with no sense of direction for a few seconds before my legs steady. My stomach settles, and I no longer hear or feel the effects of the portal.

"Faster," Ramesis says.

Chasyn catches up, taking my other arm and keeping pace with Ramesis, as we aim for the stairs that brought us up here. The launch pad is suddenly huge. The staircase seems miles away, the distance increasing instead of shrinking with each clumsy step. The ground quakes again, and we fall. Ramesis rolling with it and ending in a crouch, and me landing on my knees with Chasyn patting me for injuries.

The Maidens appear from somewhere. I crane my neck, following their movements. Hellene, Imari and Nialiah waltz to the center of the launch pad, spreading their arms like they're warming up for yoga. They take each other's hands, making a new spell circle, and rotate like they're playing 'Ring Around the Rosie' in the middle of Armageddon. Their arms come up, long gauntlet sleeves falling back, pooling around their shoulders. Silver arm cuffs above the elbows of each arm gleam.

A wave of cool energy rushes from The Maidens. The air quivers. The crushing sounds of an avalanche over our heads make me look up. The debris covering the barrier shield crumbles away, revealing the blood red sky once more. Enemy ships set fire to the forest. More soldiers drop from the ships, touching ground and engaging our squads on the smoky battlefield.

The large spell circle collapses completely, the casters sprawl on the ground like corpses, but the barrier overhead holds. I gaze at The Maidens, watching them spin, feeling that weird power humming around them. Those arm cuffs...

"Their Gifts," Ramesis says, "from Order."

And I realize that we are just sitting here, like we're watching TV. Ramesis stares at The Maidens, awestruck. Chasyn squeezes my arm. "We need to get up!"

I let Chasyn help me, and Ramesis shakes his head, jumping to his feet. The staircase we aimed for is now crowded with technicians and mechanics shoving each other as they try to escape ground zero.

"That route is no longer an option." Ramesis's voice is grave. "The other way is..." He nods to the place where soldiers, Remasian and Zaran, pound up a second staircase, stomping across the launch pad and passing through the barrier as if it's not there. I stare at the empty spaces where Devon and Lyle's ships had been. My ship sits lonely, abandoned.

Evan joins Jalee and Adonis as they try to get the members of the outer spell circle to their feet. Evan gestures with one arm and the dazed casters stagger away from the edge of the launch pad, heading in a single direction.

"They must be going to another exit! Let's..." Chasyn trails off, staring at something. I follow his gaze, barely able to tear my eyes away from the battle scene, and almost fall over. The swarm of technicians and mechanics clogging the first stairwell parts as Councilor Theorne glides through the divide. He steps onto the glass-pebbled ground.

What's he doing out here? The councilors don't fight battles. They go where it's safe.

Theorne, dressed in a black jumpsuit, tall and lean, is a modern day, pale-skinned Jafar, penciled mustache, goatee and all. He walks across the battlefield like he's having an evening stroll, hands tucked inside his long gauntlet sleeves. He breezes past Ramesis, Chasyn, and me, ignoring the soldiers getting into formation around him.

We can and should go. Escape routes should be clearer. But I can't move my feet. Chasyn and Ramesis are still. Something is going to happen, and the few survival instincts I have are watching the show too.

Evan seems to turn in slow motion, head tilting as he catches sight of Theorne. The councilor pulls his hands from his sleeves, fanning his arms out as if he's about to start some kinda lame dance.

My heart pounds.

Something's in his right hand. He turns it over, opening the palm.

Ba-bump. My pulse is in my throat. I hear Ramesis's breath and sense Chasyn's body tensing.

A pale, gray rock sits in Theorne's hand. The Stone of Magic? Evan's Stone. But I feel its presence, its power, like an overheating battery.

Theorne's lips move and Evan shakes his head. Theorne says something else and Evan flinches.

He doesn't want the Stone. How can he not want it? An itching need, the feeling of something lost, missing, fills me. I scratch the lines of my palms and flinch at the dampness. What the hell? I shake my head, trying to get rid of the feeling. The residual ache left behind feels like a hunger pang.

"*Krevai-va.*" Ramesis stands beside me, the head of his axe on the ground.

Evan's shoulders slump as Theorne continues to talk. He gazes out onto the battlefield, and I look out to see what he does. Destruction, fallen soldiers on both sides, razed forests, scorched earth. All that beautiful land out there ruined, all those people dead, and it's not over yet.

Evan straightens, his face determined, and takes the Stone from Theorne. The councilor nods and jogs across the launch pad, passing us again and heading down the stairs. I swear he's smiling, maybe even laughing, but I'm not sure. My focus is on my brother.

Evan holds up the Stone of Magic as if inspecting it. The dull gray rock transforms, becoming an emerald the size of a fist. It throws a green light over Evan, casting strange shadows over the planes and angles of his face. He looks sick for a moment, then his face turns hard. He closes his eyes; his lips move and the translucent barrier The Maidens are holding steady glimmers a pale green. He tilts his head back, and, though his eyes are closed, I get the feeling he can see. My legs move before I know what they're doing.

"What are you doing?" Ramesis whispers.

Chasyn reaches for me but doesn't try to grab me. His fingers brush my arm as I go to my brother. Locusts buzz in my chest; 'gotta do something' pulses in my temples. I move in front of Evan, resting my hands on his shoulders. A flash flood of crackling energy shoots into my palms and races through my body, locking my joints in place and cementing my feet to the ground. Earth shifts beneath me, its solid power gripping my ankles. Shizz. Memories of four months ago on the Kemah Boardwalk flood my mind. Using earth as a weapon had almost killed me then. But I know how to use my powers now. I can handle this, right?

I must have trembled, because Evan, voice smooth as silk in my ear, says, "Relax, little brother. Nothing will hurt you."

I stare at him. His face is still serious, eyes flat. I don't recognize my brother. Energy swells and whirls around my body, slapping my skin, as still air becomes hella crazy wind. Pebbles shatter, debris goes airborne. Yelps and cries from whoever's still left on the launch pad. Glass cuts tiny diagonals on my exposed forearms and bites into my cheeks. I squint, hoping this crap doesn't get in my eyes.

The Stone of Magic flares, the light blazing like a bonfire hyped up on gasoline. I shut my eyes on another flashback: University of Houston, the fire started by a peaceful protest group turned violent by fed-up vulattos. A hand grabs my arm, strong fingers squeezing my bicep. I can't open my eyes. Glass nicks my forehead. Voices scream in other languages, the translation clear: Get down! Get under!

"*Tacivi*," Evan says.

A beat of dead silence. I open my eyes as a hurricane of white noise erupts into the sky, rupturing the magical barrier as it rampages out to desecrate the enemy ships above and beyond. The winds rip the baddies apart, eating up everything in their wake. There is no rain of metals or plastics, no screws or bolts, no blood or parts. The air is left clean and untainted as the storm surges on to take out the rest of the fleeing enemies in the skies.

Our troops on the field suddenly start fighting like they've been bombed with Red Bull. Enemy soldiers fall. I make out Desiri and Adonis. Desiri cleaves a guy in two with a sword that looks like a butcher knife on steroids while Adonis drowns three more in a six-foot tall geyser he must have summoned from the earth. The bodies float, lifeless limbs bobbing. I shiver as sound pours back into reality. My ears hum under the cacophony of multiple people shouting orders or demanding the status of other soldiers.

My hands cramp and my arms fall to my sides. Taking a deep breath, I turn my attention to my brother. Evan clutches the Stone in his left palm, staring at it like he's found God...or a goddess. He strokes it with his free hand.

"H-hey," I say, not wanting to touch him again just yet.

He jumps. Did he forget I'm here? "Hey." I chance poking him in the gut with an index finger and he catches my hand in a monster grip. Holy shizz, he can be Superman's sidekick. He lets go, and I snatch my hand away, staring at him as he drops the Stone and stumbles backward.

"*Fip*," he mutters. "*Fip. Fip.*" His green eyes are dark as he surveys the scene around us. Rubbing my hand, I take it in too. The skies are clear and the ground forces are winning. Extra soldiers trample across the broken launch pad to either help take out the leftovers or recover the injured or fallen.

A wave of stench rolls in—burned pork, sour milk, rotting veggies, and tech oil. I don't want to think about what the burned pork smell is from. I avert my eyes from the splashes of red and black blood on the ground and coating some of the soldiers.

Nerve endings fire and I fidget, muscles twitching. I need to move, to do something else. Standing here is wrong when people are hurt on the field. Medics charge out, rushing past us. Some openly stare at my brother like he's some kind of demon messiah. Some of them look at me that way too. Discomfort sits heavy in my chest. Evan takes a sharp breath, and I blink back at him.

"Ev? Are you...?"

Evan walks away from me, like I hadn't spoken, leaving the Stone on the broken ground. His footsteps seem loud to my ears as medics and fresh soldiers part to let him through.

I should follow him, but I kneel to pick up the Stone of Magic. I've never touched it, had only seen glimpses of it on the ship. Curiosity burns a hole in my brain. I wait for electricity, hell, magic, but I get nothing. It's a hunk of gray rock on my palm. What happened to the pull I'd felt earlier when Evan had held it? Is it because it's not mine? *My* Stone is waiting for me. A pang of emptiness in my gut makes me flinch. I should be blasting off on my quest right now, going to find it. I look back at the dark ship that had been mine; a sinking feeling tells me my ship isn't going anywhere today. "Leader Four?" Chasyn's voice near my ear.

I start, meeting his nervous brown eyes. "Are you all right?" he asks.

"I don't know." I take in the entire scene again.

The medics are stationed at the edges of the barrier now, treating injured people that are carried from the field back onto the launch pad. The Maidens still hold hands, but their circle no longer rotates. They're statues with their linked hands lifted to the sky. Everyone's busy, but me.

"We should go below," Chasyn says. "Ramesis already went down. Said he had to send word to the Zaran Parliament."

"Go below to do what?" I ask.

"Wind you down," Chasyn says.

"No." I shake my head. "I need to do something. Something useful."

"You can't go out on the field. Not even with the fighting just about over. You're not ready for it." Chasyn's expression is firm.

Frustrated, I growl. "Since when does it matter what I'm ready for?" But looking at that bloody field again makes my stomach churn. I-I won't go out there, not today. Chasyn's right, but I won't go 'wind down' either. Squeezing the cold Stone of Magic in my hand, I say, "I'm going after Evan."

I RUN DOWN THE STAIRS, jumping the bottom few steps, boots hitting the landing with a soft thud. A few soldiers—two guys and a lady—in gray and green Zaran jumpsuits, are stationed against a wall. They stand straighter as I approach, their eyes scanning me.

"Commands, sir?" the lady asks.

Commands? Geez. "Uh." I clear my throat. "My brother, Leader One. Did he go...?" I swing an arm out to the left and then to the right. The corridor splits two ways.

One of the male soldiers clears his throat, sounding nervous. The other pulls at his high collar.

"I'm not certain you want to follow him just yet, sir," the lady says. "Perhaps some cool down time is needed."

I tilt my head, studying these guys. They seem comfortable enough with me, not scared, and they'd gotten right to the point. "You've worked with my brother before?"

They chuckle, faces lighting up, and I notice they're probably near my age. Seems no matter the planet—Earth, Zare, Rema—all militaries love young soldiers. I mean, there are older people in uniform, but the ones I work closely with aren't much older than what would be considered early twenties on Earth.

The lady touches my arm. She's tall and slim with dark skin and close-cropped purple hair. She leans close to my ear and whispers, "You might not want to bring that with you."

That. She pulls away, her bright blue eyes dropping to the Stone clutched in my left hand.

"I…" can't just leave it somewhere. "Maybe…" I tense as the soldiers stiffen.

Approaching footsteps from the right side of the hall. The soldiers gaze at the newcomers and, from their nervous expressions, obviously want to be elsewhere.

Great. I turn, not really surprised to come face-to-face with Councilor Theorne and Councilor Viveen. Theorne dwarfs Viveen, but for some reason Viveen creeps me out more. Her facial features are sharp, her nose beaky, and her arms and legs are long and thin. She's like a wingless vulture ready to scavenge the bones of whatever's left behind.

Neither councilor smiles. Viveen folds her bony arms over her chest, black eyes drinking me in. I steel myself, refusing to look afraid of this woman. 'Gotta do something' bounces, ready to fight, or run. "Councilors."

"Leader Four," Viveen says, her voice rich and resonant. "Where is Leader One?"

"I don't know." If he's 'cooling down' I doubt he wants to deal with these guys. "But he left this. Here." I hold the Stone out to them. They've kept the thing up until now, so I have no qualms about handing them the Stone. They can't use it and if they refuse to give it back, I don't think Evan will mind.

Theorne takes the Stone from me, holding it out and then making it disappear in the folds of his gauntlet sleeves. Viveen looks to the soldiers and they stand at attention.

"Leader One retreated down this hallway, councilor," the lady soldier says. What is she, their elected spokesperson?

Viveen nods and she and Theorne proceed on down the hall, like they know where they are going. Yeah, Evan might have gone that way, but how do they know where he went after that? I frown, gazing at the soldiers who give me looks of concern.

"What?" I ask.

"You shouldn't follow," the lady says softly. "Stay with us."

I almost want to, but the way their eyes twitch in the direction Theorne and Viveen headed and the worried pitch to their tones makes me shake my head. Everything in me says I need to follow the councilors, because… locusts flutter in my stomach.

"Is he in trouble?" I ask. Theorne and Viveen are never fun to be around, but just now they seemed... "Can they hurt my brother?"

The soldiers stare at me.

Aw shizz.

'Gotta do something' says go. Locusts say stay. They duke it out in my gut. Earth shifts beneath my feet; the smell of mixed ore breathes heat into my blood. *Go*, 'gotta do something' hisses. *Go*.

I run after the councilors.

It's easy to figure out where Evan went. The air shimmers with heat. Sweat breaks across my forehead and dribbles into my eyes. The thick green and brown vines decorating the empty corridor shudder, veiny skins puckering. Those guys really weren't kidding when they said Evan needed to cool off.

My eyeballs dry in their sockets. I squeeze my eyes shut, trying to produce tears and feel individual atoms of hydrogen and oxygen tingling around my body. I take a breath, focusing on binding the atoms together. It's like making lemonade, two different substances combining to make something totally new. Cool, misty rain coats the hallway. The heat dissipates, and the vines seem to relax. I turn a corner, stop short, and backtrack a few steps, keeping myself out of sight.

Theorne and Viveen stand across from Evan who's casually slouched against a wall. His eyes track them in the way a fighter watches an opponent. A flicker of heat surges in the air, flaring in the mist. Evan puffs out a tendril of white smoke.

"Do you really want to do this now?" Evan asks.

"It's better here, where there is no one to see you fall," Viveen says, voice pleasant. "The common people do not like to see their heroes weak."

Evan snorts. "But we do have an audience."

Both councilors turn their heads. They can't see me, but Evan has to know I'm here. He probably smelled me coming, before he felt me use my powers. The misting rain becomes a drizzle as molecules dance over my skin. Wet curls flop into my eyes as my uniform sticks to my body. The water soaks through my clothes, its calm strength flooding my veins. I come out of hiding.

"Yo!" I give a two-finger salute and grin at the double glares I get from Theorne and Viveen. I strut forward. "Figured if there was gonna be a meeting, all leaders in residence should be present, right? We should call Ramesis and The Maidens too. I mean, things are wrapping up out on the field. Bet nobody would miss them too much."

Viveen's black eyes glitter. "Perhaps, it is best that you are here." A Grinchy smiles crosses her lips and makes her features seem pointier. This woman can probably cut glass with her face. "Leader One, remove your jacket and tunic."

Surprise flashes through me. I blink and look over at Evan whose face is set in a scowl.

"Or we could teach Leader Four a new fact," Theorne says, deep voice almost gleeful. "You are ever enthusiastic about your education, Lawrence. I'm sure you wonder how an aging council keeps such a firm reign over such powerful young leaders. There have been so many I find I lose count."

"And, of course, there were those who just were not interesting enough to remember," Viveen purrs. "There were a handful of leaders who looked like you or one of your brothers. Each time, we suspected they were a reincarnation of a Peredil. We were wrong, of course. Those leaders certainly were strong, but never strong enough."

Water slowly evaporates from my skin as I lose my focus. Theorne and Viveen try to circle me. I put my back against a wall to keep them in front of me. "I've seen the yearbook pictures." And there are a lot of images of people who bore the ol' family resemblance. But what had Viveen, Theorne and the rest of the Remasian Council done to them?

"Lawrie," Evan says, voice tight, "get out of here."

My feet are rooted to the floor. I'm not leaving him here.

"Remove your jacket and tunic, Leader One," Viveen says.

"Lawrie, go!"

I hear the soft thump of cloth hitting the floor. I glance over to see Evan naked from the waist up, his left shoulder whole and without scar. He shoots me a look, eyes bright with urgency. The air thickens, temperature rising, sweat rolls down my forehead again. I reach out, ready to make water, and pause.

He really wants me to go.

Something horrible is about to happen.

"We have neglected your education, Leader Four," Theorne says. "We've been too gentle by simply teaching you politics and manners and letting you train your infant powers. Now, it is time for you to learn the benefits of obedience and the detriments of insubordination."

"Turn," Viveen says and Evan exposes his back to her. The Mark is an awesome artistic blend of shapes and symbols spiraling down the ridges of Evan's spine. Viveen's long, bony fingers hover over the Mark. She runs a nail over Evan's skin, then her lips move in a whisper so soft I can't make out the word.

Evan screams and jerks, body crashing to the ground face first. He thrashes and convulses, fists beating the floor. But he doesn't beg for it to stop.

I do. "Leave him alone!" I rush at Viveen but get tossed back by Theorne.

Oh, hell no. I grab at the atoms for water. I want a wave. I want a geyser like Adonis's. I'm drowning these.... Ice burns down my back and through my legs, paralyzing me from the waist down.

I can't feel my legs.

I fall, arms locked at my sides. I can't catch myself. Pain clouds my brain and darkens my vision.

Am I blind?

I can't...move.

"Would you like for it to stop, Leader Four?" Theorne's voice.

"Y-y..." I sputter. Am I going to die? Are they going to kill me here?

All at once, the pain stops. Relief filters into my system. My legs itch and cramp, but I feel them again. My fingers clench and unclench. My throat is raw and my eyes sting as my vision clears. I stare at the black toe of Theorne's boot.

The skin over my spine prickles, the bundle of nerves beneath it aches in the shape of the Mark.

I turn my head to see Evan lying prone on his side, back facing me. I stare at his sizzling Mark, the flesh around it red and swollen.

The Marks, they caused this pain, and Theorne and Viveen have the power to make it happen. Why would Order brand us? Why would She give the council that kind of power over us? We're supposed to be Her Champions.

Champions.

Prize fighters. Attack dogs. Theorne and Viveen were around in the Prophetic Cycles, so were some of the other councilors. They're wranglers. They can control us. For Order? For themselves? I want to tap Evan. I need to talk to my brother, have him explain.

As I lay on the ground, Theorne and Viveen casually discuss what they should have for a late lunch. Minutes later, I hear them walking away. I push myself up on my hands as nausea wracks my body. I throw up so hard my head spins and I almost forget the pain in my back.

Almost.

Holy. Friggin. Shizz.

The Mark is a bridle, a noose.

Like in a friggin' fairy tale, I'm cursed.

We all are.

7

DEVON

I SPEND THE FIRST TWO days of the trip holed up in my cabin. I ignore all knocks on the door, barely eat the food that appears on my bedside table...or sac-side table. Whatever the hell it's called. I hate getting used to alien terms for regular crap like 'bed' and 'food.' The translators everybody wears around here speak for me just fine. But people get on me about trying to learn some Common Tongue. Why? It won't be long before I'm fitted with one of those translator devices too.

Rap, rap. Someone is at the door again.

I roll over, the leafy cushion beneath me molding to my new position. I love this thing. I don't need sheets or blankets; it adjusts to my body temperature and keeps me level.

"Devon. It's time to get up." Xijure's deep voice.

I frown. He has only knocked and called to me once since I came in here and sealed the entryway. Guess kings have better things to do than talk to wussies like me. I rub the heels of my palms over my closed eyes as a wash of self-loathing sinks in again. Xijure had warned me portal-travel affects people in strange ways. Some folks get tired, some get depressed.

Guess I'm depressed, but I can't just blame it all on the portal.

"Devon." Xijure again. He sounds calm, like he could stay out there all day if he wants.

Go away. I roll onto my face. I think about Lenore and all those people fighting. My ship left first, so I couldn't see what happened to Lyle, Lawrie, and Evan. There's been no contact with anybody. I listen to the people who talk at me through the door, and sometimes I ask questions. They say we're on a temporary communications blackout to keep our current coordinates secure from enemies. To me, it just means I can't talk to Lyle.

I bite my lip. Something's wrong with me. I mean, I feel—no, I don't feel. I don't feel Lyle. I didn't realize it, never realized it. But no matter how hard I pushed him away, and how distant we became with each other, his presence was always with me. I didn't know it before, because it's never been gone. I shudder.

"This is your final warning." Xijure.

I frown. Final warning?

The tooth-grinding screech of metal against metal. I jerk up, staring as his sword eats its way through the black oval that is my door. A Xijure-sized hole is cut, and the king enters, looking cool in all black gear and boots. He scowls at me, dark eyes glinting and my stomach twists.

Xijure is a great guy. He spent some time training with me. I want his respect, but I cover my face with my hands. "Look, man, I'm sorry. I just—"

"You're suffering from separation anxiety." Xijure

sounds matter of fact. "You have never been far apart from your siblings. I also…" He comes closer to the bed, towering over me. The dude's big when I'm *standing* next to him. He's a mountain from this angle. "…think that what you're experiencing may be worse, due to your twin brother being psi."

"What does Lyle being psychic have to do with anything?" Since when is this guy a parapsychologist? Not saying I don't think he's smart, but he usually likes to talk about weapon maintenance and, of all things, freakin' nutrition. He is a protein, veggie chugging beast.

"Before we left…" Xijure starts, then scowls again. "You know what, I can't talk to you when you look like this. Please bathe." He gestures toward my cleansing chamber. Ah, screw it, my broom closet-sized bathroom.

I groan and my limbs sag. Energy seeps out of my system like suds from a sponge. "I don't want to." I lie back down, staring up at the man. If he understands my 'separation anxiety' can't he leave me to be a loser in peace? I wish he hadn't seen me like this. My rep is damaged beyond repair at this point.

"Whoa!" Big hands grab me by the shoulders and yank me out of bed. I'm airborne for a few seconds before my chin eats metal floor. I roll onto my side, checking my teeth with my tongue for cracks.

"The only way to recover," Xijure comes down in a football kneel beside me, "is activity. You must exercise your mind and body. If you wallow, it will only get worse. In a *jewel*, we will exit Portal Space and four *jewels* after that we will arrive at our first stop. When we dock, I would like for us to present a strong Allegiance front. We cannot do this when you resemble a *dram rag*. Now, up! Or do you need my help again?"

I hold up both hands in defeat, before Xijure reaches for me again. Scrambling to my feet, I call over my shoulder, "Give me a few minutes."

My shower is quick. The system is the same as the one on the Ievisara. It's scary that I feel a flash of comfort at the familiar equipment, almost as if space travel is becoming normal for me. I don't want to adapt, because it seems like I'd be letting go of the old me entirely, but I have to get over this. I scrub my face over a bowl that fills with water when I run my fingers over the rim and run a wet hand through my hair. It's getting longer, falling over my forehead. Nobody around here talks about haircuts, so I never brought it up, but I'll wear skinny jeans before I ever put my hair in a man-bun.

Outside the bathroom door, suitcase zippers sing. Is Xijure going through my stuff? I burst out of the bathroom, staring at the king who's got a pile of my clothes spread out on the bed.

"Wear that," Xijure says. "It's decent enough to make appearances in and won't restrict movement."

"Okay." I pull the shirt over my head and tug the denim over my boxers. The pants fit like jeans, but breathe like sweatpants.

The heavy thunk of a pair of boots hitting the floor next to me makes me jump.

"Put them on. Let's go," Xijure says.

He steps back through the hole he made. I sigh, squeezing my feet and ankles into the combat boots. These things suck. They're heavy and the thick soles are clunky. I feel like a dancing donkey in them, but Xijure says they're leg-weights. I'll get used to them and, in the end, have better balance as well as better kicks.

I go out through the Xijure-hole too. "Who's going

to fix that?"

"I don't know," Xijure says. "Maybe we should leave it like that. You would spend less time in there."

I glare at him, and he smiles.

He strides through the silver and brown corridors of the ship like he owns the place, with me trying to fall in step beside him. We pass a few open doors to rooms with one or two people inside fiddling with hardware. A few of them shoot glances my way. Some of their faces I recognize from the Ievisara, some are strangers. I don't know if everyone's Remasian. Some might be Zaran. They all look human to me though, so no Lenorans.

Xijure presses his hand against a wall panel by a closed door and it slides up into the ceiling. He steps in, motioning for me to follow. I frown, hesitating for a minute. Am I about to walk into a room of people having a meeting? I'm not in the mood to talk or listen.

"Hurry up!" Xijure calls.

I scowl and go inside. Cool air brushes my skin as I gaze around the medium-sized, bronze-walled room. Near the back, two people, a man and woman, spar, hand-to-hand, on a wall-to-wall length mat. They wear denim pants and clunky boots like mine. In the center of the room are parallel bars and gymnastic rings.

A gym. Relief courses through me. I hadn't wanted to get out of bed, but now I can't wait to jump into a workout routine. Lyle would call me an idiot and remind me that working out is how I deal with tough shit. Thinking about Lyle is a punch in the gut.

I move in the direction of the rings, but Xijure catches my arm. Empathy flashes in his eyes as he says, "Later. I have to introduce you to your court and discuss mission plans with you first."

I trudge after him as he moves to a kitchenette-corner in the back of the room, past the fighters who stop to watch us. He gestures to a round metal table surrounded by stools and then opens the door to a mini-fridge-thing, pulling out a tray with four tall glasses of brown stuff. He sets it on the table, and I marvel at its thickness. It looks like a peanut butter, dirt and grass smoothie. Heavy footsteps and hard thumps across from me make me look up from the drink. The fighters from the mat grin at me.

"Greetings, Leader Two," the lady fighter says with a thick accent. She sounds like a Russian spy from an old-school movie. "I am Mineshka."

"I am Loniad," the guy says, bright blue eyes peering at me through a black beetle unibrow. He talks with the same accent as the woman. "Mineshka is my sister."

"Older sister," Mineshka says with a smile.

"Only by a *jewel*." Loniad rolls his eyes.

I blink, staring at them hard. Mineshka's tall and thin with reddish hair, olive-toned skin and angular features. Loniad's short and stocky with a face made for scaring babies. 'You don't look alike' perches on the tip of my tongue, but I hold it in. I don't look like all of my siblings. I force a smile at Mineshka and Loniad. "Twins?"

"Yah," they say in unison. Now they're both smiling with even white teeth. Their dimples are identical.

"These two," Xijure pushes a glass toward me, "were selected in the trials for your court. We'll pick your final member up when we dock."

"Oh." My body runs cold as the twins continue to smile at me. My court. The people who are supposed to fight by my side and protect me. Their powers should be similar to mine. I close my eyes, recalling the sparring match between the twins. They're damn good. What will these guys think when they see me try to fight?

I wrap a hand around the cold glass in front of me, peering down into my mulchy drink. "Nice to meet you." And I should probably say something else to them, but I got nothing. Except… "Wait, we're *picking up* the last member of my court? That means they weren't a part of the trials. How did they get chosen?"

"Ilea is a given," Xijure says.

I blink at him, making a face as he throws back his drink. A given? How can someone I've never met be a given? "Is that fair? Was anyone on Evan's court a given, or did they go through trials too?"

Loniad slurps his drink and pounds his chest, nodding to Xijure like 'thanks, man,' then turns to me. "Leader One's entire court is comprised of 'givens.' Your council handpicked Desiri Lilias and Jalee Orcharest. And Adonis Maeve is practically a relative of yours. His maternal aunt is married to one of your paternal uncles."

"Come again? Adonis, the ice statue, is related to me?" Of course, Adonis wouldn't say anything, he doesn't talk, but Evan never brought it up.

Loniad snorts. "Only through ceremony, but it was to Leader One's advantage to have such a strong magic-user on his court who was tied to him by more than just duty as a child."

I blink at the man, taking that in. I picture my brother as a lonely little kid on a foreign world where no one spoke his language. I'm seventeen cringing at everything being thrown at me. He'd been five. I think about how protective Adonis is, and remember that he and Evan live together on Rema. Huh. Maybe I'll try to get to know his creepy ass when I get back.

Mineshka clears her throat to get my attention. Hers eyes twinkle at me. "The way Leader One's court was selected was unusual, and not ideal for building a good court, *babila*. Traditionally, courts for Remasian leaders are built through trials. Warriors from all over the Allegiances are invited to audition. *Our* trials tested our strength and endurance as well as our combat abilities. I assure you, Devon, we are the best." She makes a fist and touches it to her chest.

I dip a finger in my drink, stirring the lumpy liquid as the twins' words hit me. The best. I don't measure up to the best. My stomach churns, and I hear Lawrie in my ear, telling me I'm going emo. I agree.

I glance up to catch Xijure's lingering gaze. He nods at me and clears his throat. "It's business time."

My heart jumps. "Yeah, okay. I-I guess I need to know what you all expect me to do."

"There's no 'me,' Devon," Xijure says. "We are a team. You will not be alone in anything you do." His tone's not exactly warm, but I feel a little better.

"We're going to dock with the Jintelier Spaceport a few *jewels* before Ilea arrives. There's a parlor onsite that can install your translator device. After that is taken care of and Ilea has joined us, we will re-board this ship and head to Disiez," Xijure says. "The planet's population lives on an archipelago. The cities are small, but the technology is impressive. The rest of the planet is ocean, and deep under those waters are where our map says your Stone is."

I blink at the flood of info. Translator installation, good. No more uttering insults in other languages around me. A scuba mission? Crap. Is now the time to mention that I don't like dark water?

Loniad puts a hand on my shoulder and leans in like he's gonna tell me a secret, but his voice booms. "Hundreds of years ago, the people of Disiez angered its god. A series of tidal waves flooded ninety-five percent of the planet. The current island chain is the only thing that stays above sea-level." He pulls his hand away.

Is this guy trying to scare me? I crack my knuckles, nerves popping. Scuba in an ocean made by an angry god. This just gets better.

"Don't believe him about the gods." Mineshka rolls her eyes. "*Mai-mai* told him too many stories when we were little! Gullible *dolte*."

Loniad bares his teeth at her as she dimples his way.

My head goes back and forth between them. "No angry god?"

"No, just global warming and a mass eruption of underwater volcanoes." Mineshka reaches out to squeeze my forearm. "The mainland was not an island chain before the disaster. They pump water from their cities daily. In exchange for allowing us into their territory, their chieftain has asked us to establish a magical barrier for them, like the one on Amphora that protects the planet's atmosphere from the heat of your sun."

"My sun?" I frown.

"The solar system you lived in. Your sister planet is too close to the sun." Mineshka presses her index finger to my forehead as if telling me to use my brain.

Amphora is Venus. I knew that.

"So, did we tell them we could give them a barrier? Can we give them a barrier?" I ask.

"Yes, we did agree to help erect one." Xijure's brow furrows. "However, Disiez is not an Allegiance planet. It's located in a Cold Zone. They've done some business with Nazflit."

Cold Zone. Neutral territory.

"But they want to join the Allegiance, right?"

"Only because we are providing them with the magical aid they need." Xijure puts his elbows on the table and rests his chin on kneaded fingers. "This is why Ilea was chosen for you. She is a mage who can build and cast protection wards. A small barrier shouldn't be too hard for her."

"A mage? Like Desiri?" I perk up. "But I thought my court wasn't supposed to have magic-users on it?"

Loniad snorts. "It should not, however, we need Ilea in order to collect what is yours. Ilea is also a highly skilled fighter. More warrior than mage, though her magic is strong."

"Desiri's more warrior than mage," I say, "and she's scary. I'm okay with having somebody like that on the team." I glance at the twins. "But, uh, you guys kick total ass too."

The twins glare at me, then laugh, full and boisterous, like a bunch of guys watching the Super Bowl in a basement man-cave. It makes me want to laugh with them.

"Lilias held back on you, if you believe she is more warrior than mage," Mineshka says. "She wanted to teach you technique."

Xijure grins, eyes gleaming.

"Your Majesty, that is not the technique I am talking about!" Mineshka punches Xijure's arm. He tosses his head back and laughs, rubbing his arm where she'd hit him.

I'm half amused, half terrified. "Desiri held back?" Hell, what else can she do?

They laugh at me, not answering. Xijure pushes the glass of yuck into my hand.

"Drink up. You'll need every ounce of your strength. You wanted to workout and I want to show Min and Lon what I've taught you. If you make me look bad, I promise to make you drink another beverage before dinner, and I'll make it extra thick."

He grins a crocodile smile that makes me scoot back. I suddenly know why he and Desiri are so into each other. They're both friggin' monsters.

8

DEVON

THE FRIGGIN' TRANSLATOR ITCHES LIKE a mosquito bite at the base of my skull. I keep scratching at the lump beneath my skin, glad my hair hides it.

"*May-iie-skimo?*" Are you all right?

I blink, jerking my head up to meet Chief Owelu's golden gaze. He's a few inches taller than me with goldfish orange skin and a long mouth that could probably fit a whole taco lengthwise.

I scratch the lump again. The butch lady who'd put the translator in a few hours ago said it'd take a while for everything to sync, but hell. I think this thing's busted. Whenever anyone not wearing a translator speaks, I hear their native language first. Then, a second later, I get an echo effect, but in English.

"*Ikii-da-tama?*" Is it too hot?

"Ah." I clear my throat, hoping the guy doesn't realize I'm staring at how weird he looks. He's not even that strange looking. He's as humanoid as most of the people I've been around so far. "Nothing I'm not already used to. Where I'm from, it's hot and humid like this most of the time."

Owelu raises a brow ridge at me, his lack of eyebrows making his square forehead seem broader. "Oh?"

I nod and take a deep breath, inhaling salty ocean air. The thick pang of homesickness in my throat is hard to get rid of. The capitol island, Maumo, with its skyscrapers and winding freeways, reminds me of downtown Houston. I bet when the sun sets, the tall glistening buildings light up like Christmas, creating a postcard worthy skyline: 'Wish you were here.'

Wish I was there.

Owelu shifts closer to me as I shut my eyes, listening to the ocean sloshing against the five-story, sand-colored sea wall ringing the island chain. Swells of sea foam spill over its top, turning the sand at its base into a muddy moat. My heavy boots sink in the sand as I move forward, opening my eyes and taking in the small beach. There are no families spread out on towels, no sunbathers. It's pretty much the edge of the world for these guys. Sand, then a concrete barrier protecting them from the ocean.

"*Motoi nea lae oha*?" My home is pretty, yes?

"Yeah," I say with a light nod. "It's pretty." And screwed. The seawall isn't enough to keep this place from becoming the next Atlantis.

Owelu smiles, his pale orange face open and honest. "Your tone suggests that you understand our immediate need." His deep voice reminds me of the guy who read the *Harry Potter* books without the British accent. It's soothing and makes me want to smile.

"Well, yeah," I say. Sweat beads my forehead and dribbles into my eyes. I wipe it away. "Bet those waves get a lot bigger when the sun sets."

"The pumps run at night," Owelu says.

I blink. "Say that again."

"The pumps run at night," Owelu says, and I fight back the urge to whoop.

The words he just said had come in real time. My fingers go to the translator lump. It's working. I laugh and catch a flash of what might be surprise in his round eyes. I shouldn't laugh. We're talking about his sinking city, after all.

"I'm sorry, chief." Crap. No, his spoken title isn't Chief, it's Highest Owelu. I hate honorifics. The thirty-minute refresher course on diplomatic etiquette while the ship had hovered above the skyscraper landing pad wasn't enough.

"Highest Owelu," I say, smiling at the last second. "Sorry, again."

Xijure said smiling and showing humility is good when dealing with Disi, but it makes me feel stupid and fake as hell.

"From you, 'chief' is fine, leader," Owelu says, tilting his head, gaze intense. "I do believe your rank is much higher than mine."

And there we go with that. I crack my knuckles and look away, not wanting Owelu to read anything off my face. I'm used to Xijure. Yeah, he's a king, but he's close to my age and likes to lift. Caea and Ramesis are cool too; none of them like being called 'majesty.' But this guy Owelu? He's got to be older than my parents and he looks like a president in his black-on-black business tux with gold-fringed jacket pockets.

"I don't..." consider myself to be more highly ranked than this man. I wish he wouldn't either. "Call me 'Devon,' please. The title 'leader' implies that I've accomplished something."

Owelu's eyes soften. He places a hand on my shoulder. "Very well, Devon. I do not like titles either. You may call me Owelu." He gestures toward the small cluster of people a few feet away from us, nearer to the wall but not quite standing in the mud moat. "I bet His Majesty does not care for his title either. I took this position from my father and do nothing but watch my cities drown and beg for help."

I fight the urge to groan. Is Owelu going to start poli-talking me? I don't speak politician, and I doubt my translator can fix that problem.

"I am grateful that the Silver and Gold Allegiances have finally decided to acknowledge our request for aid," he continues.

Because we need something. He doesn't have to say it, I hear it. I don't know how to respond. Hell, I don't even know what facial expression to wear. Apologetic? Disinterested? I could smile again, but don't. Instead, I fix my eyes on Xijure, Loniad, Mineshka and my new mage Ilea. When we met her, I'd expected another Amazon like Desiri, not a short, round-cheeked girl who looks like she sells Girl Scout cookies. Ilea digs a circle in the sand with a long stick, while the others plant blue candles around it.

I move toward them, but Owelu grabs my elbow. He lowers his head, lips near my ear. "Had your help come but a week later, we would have accepted the offer given to us by the Nazflit Coalition. However, we were hopeful that it would be your Allegiances to extend aid."

"Why?" I ask, stepping away and rubbing my ear. The only lips I like that close to me belong to my girlfriend.

Owelu shrugs as he side-eyes me. "Let us just say that when the time comes, my people would rather be in favor with those whose choices will decide who and what survives the grand war."

Ugh. "Oh."

"We look forward to joining your Allegiance, Devon," Owelu says.

"Thank you," I mumble. "I'm going to go see if those guys need anything." I gesture to my court and Xijure. I tread across the sand, leg muscles loving the workout. Jogging and running in sand is the best, but I can't run now. It might make Owelu think he scared me.

And he'd be right. People are jumping into allegiances and alliances, picking sides, all because of the choices I'm supposed to make. My head aches whenever I think about the prophecy. I know smarter people than me have thought this thing out and figured it's nothing to worry about, but nothing in those stories say that the choices of The Four actually save anything. If I was a regular person in all this, I'd probably jump on the Su or Nazflit side on account of The Four of Rema being a bunch of clueless high school dropouts.

But since I'm not a regular person, I hope that divine guidance intervenes whenever I need to make world-changing decisions. But hell, I might not even know that I am making a world-changing decision. Want a burrito or pizza for lunch? Pizza. Bam! World dead.

"Hey! Watch it!" Suddenly Xijure's in my face, shoving me backward.

I waver but don't fall. Something that might be pride flashes in Xijure's eyes, before he arches a brow at me and says, "You almost knocked over a candle. Ilea's ready."

I jump back. Crap. I'm a foot away from Ilea's circle. Mineshka and Loniad rise from crouches after sticking two more blue candles in the sand. Twelve candles in a perfect circle. Ilea sits cross-legged in the center of the ring. The twins join Xijure and me as we watch her. Her full lips move, but I don't hear anything.

A quick wind rustles my hair, and the candles light themselves.

Footsteps in the sand. I look over my shoulder to see Owelu and two other guys in black tuxes without golden fringes standing behind us, both as tall and orange as their chief.

"This is a great day for Disiez," Owelu murmurs. "An apology from Himmael."

Who the crap is Himmael?

"The god of Disiez," Xijure whispers in my ear. "They still pray to him."

The god who supposedly sank this place. Why still pray to that douchebag? If he's even real. I shake my head. Call me a skeptic and non-believer, but I'm someone who says: 'Oh my God,' and just mean: 'that's crazy!' I never thought there was a God out there to be offended by me, not before all of this.

Ilea chants in a language my translator doesn't fully get.

"*Batya* comes *aveque*
Anta water way *viust*
Mibatya spirit…"

She rocks to the rhythm of the waves striking the walls. I sway to it until my stomach complains. A cold wind plumes out from the circle, whipping across my skin and blowing up my pantlegs and sleeves. My clothes balloon around my body. In my peripheral vision, I catch Xijure, Loniad and Mineshka patting at their clothes, Loniad struggling to tuck his shirt back into his belt as it flies up over his abs.

The cool air feels great against my skin, a blast of air conditioning after being outside on a day that rivals mid-August in Texas. Ilea's golden red hair flutters around her freckled face as the air around her becomes a visible dark blue, like the candles, but transparent as a silk screen. The ground quakes, Owelu and his guys shout, but my court and Xijure are quiet. I bite my lip, holding back a yelp of my own. If my squad isn't screaming, I can't either. I stagger from side to side, glad to see Xijure, Loniad and Mineshka doing the same.

"*Manya* seal *forbatya*!" Ilea shouts, head falling back, eyes closed.

The earthquake stops.

I frown. "Uh…" I'm not the best at geology or anything, but don't quakes cause tsunamis? I stare at the wall, nerves ticking, waiting to see a monster wave rising up to drown us all. Nothing. If I hadn't been here to feel it, I wouldn't know that anything had happened.

"Did it work?" I ask.

"Of course it worked," Ilea snaps. She rises in one motion, dusting sand off her green cargos. She stomps over, her boots are steel-toed with cleat-like soles. She only comes up to my pecs, but I give ground as she nears. She glares and I try not to think of those creepy Cabbage Patch Kids Grandma saved from when Mom was a kid. Ugh, she's baby doll cute, like my little sister Nikki. It makes me feel a little protective, until she digs her index finger into my solar plexus; her blunt nail pressing until I "oof!"

"Don't doubt my abilities, baby leader," she hisses, "or I'll prove myself to you right here. You'll find that sparring with Xijure is nothing compared to sparring with me." Her light blue eyes gleam.

Geez. What'd I do? I open my mouth and a large hand clamps over it. I grab at the hand, glaring at Xijure, who grins at me.

"Let it alone, Devon," Xijure says. "Trust me on this."

The king pulls his hand away as I stare down at the smug little girl.

"I think I'm going to like you quite a bit," Ilea says. "But I'll warn you not to fall in
love with me. I'm married."

I choke on spit. "What?" Not only had that come from nowhere, "But you're..." a kid.

She laughs. "I'm older than you, *daftkin*."

D*aftkin*. Various words race through my brain, meaning there must not be an exact English translation for *daftkin*. Dough...sweet lump...stuffed roll...dumpling. Did she just call me a dumpling?

"The base spell is set," Ilea speaks to someone behind me.

I turn, facing Owelu and his entourage. "Excellent," Owelu says. "Now, we can escort you to the boat, so that you can complete the barrier."

Xijure clears his throat. "After we find the Stone."

I don't miss the way Owelu's eyes shift to Haribu, sheathed and belted across Xijure's back. Unease slithers into my chest. What's he worried about? I glance at Xijure, then over at Loniad, Mineshka, and Ilea. Did they see that? If Lyle was here, I would be abusing the hell out of the link between us. I miss it.

Lyle, where are you? Are you okay?

And of course, there's nothing. Dead air. Dead space. Loneliness presses down on my chest like a dropped barbell. I struggle to breathe normally.

Lyle's okay. He's just really far away right now. He's fine. I'll see him later.

The mantra eases the ache but doesn't take it away. A sharp poke in the ribs. I side-eye Xijure who gives me a slight frown and a barely perceptible shake of the head. I do my best to suck it the hell up. I have a foreign leader to impress and a clear goal to achieve. I feel my spine straightening, my shoulders rolling back, and my chest puffing out. Ah crap, had I been hunched over?

"Let's go then," I say, my voice deep and steady. Good. I glance at Owelu and company to find them assessing me, mouths straight lines. I hope I didn't just mess this up by having a punk moment. I hold the chieftain's eyes until he blinks.

"Yes," Owelu finally says, a soft smile curving his long mouth. His eyes roam over me again, as if he sees something he likes. Good or bad, I don't know, but he inclines his head to the north, toward a sidewalk in the sand that leads up a dune. "This way."

The concrete trail up the mile-high hill of sand leads us to a red, metal lift grafted into the seawall. I kick wet sand off my boots as I follow Owelu, his guys, and Xijure onto the square platform that might fit about fifteen people at a time. Mineshka, Loniad and Ilea get on last, positioning themselves in a protective triangle around me. I've seen Adonis, Jalee and Desiri stand in similar formations around Evan. It makes me feel weird, like I've got bodyguards. I shift away from them, closer to the lift walls, touching the gritty red metal. It reminds me of a waist-high picket fence. If somebody pushed me, I'd flip headfirst over the side, but the sand's slushy enough to keep a person from dying when they hit the ground.

Owelu pulls what looks like a garage door opener out of his pocket; it's black with three square gray buttons in the center. He presses one and the lift shudders, then rises with a deep moan. I gaze out at the capitol of Disiez, admiring the horizon. The yellow sun casts a warm pink tint across the pale blue sky. It's nice seeing a blue sky again, not green or purple. I even like that the air smells like salt with a tinge of stinky fish, rather than cupcakes and cinnamon like Lenore. At this point, I'd even appreciate a whiff of diesel or road tar.

The lift continues to climb upward and I feel like I'm on one of those rides that takes me up so high I expect to blow clouds out of my eyes, and then, click, click, drop. I tighten my grip on the metal fence. I hate amusement parks. I hold my breath until we reach the top of the seawall and the lift jerks to a stop.

A long pier made of yellow wood and red metal stretches out in front of us, extending a few miles out over the dark blue ocean. The waves glitter, and I blink as a spray of salt water spits in my eyes. The water is high, maybe a few feet short of reaching the deck. Three boats bob around the pier: a yellow and white skimmer, a simple rowboat, and a medium-sized fishing boat with a cabin.

"Devon." Xijure nudges me with his elbow. "Come with me to inspect our ship while Ilea gives Owelu more information about the spell." He gestures to the fishing boat.

I nod. As Xijure and I move forward, Mineshka and Loniad make a people-wall behind us. Xijure stops at the edge of the pier, studying the chains holding the fishing boat in place. I step over the short white railing onto the boat's wooden deck. Bet it'd fit about four to six people standing up. The cabin's toward the back. I head for it, hearing Xijure's heavy footsteps behind me. The structure is made of wood as well and recently painted from the smell of it. I open the side door and have to duck to enter.

"With Owelu and those guys being so tall, you'd think they'd have bigger doors." At least the ceiling is higher; I can stand up with room to spare. Lights from each corner of the square room flick on, and I make my way to the captain's pod, lowering my head as I step inside. Running my hands over the cool silver of the steering wheel, I stare out of the tinted bay window that serves as a windshield. The ocean spreads out into infinity.

"Owelu is hiding something," Xijure's voice drifts through the open portal.

"Huh?" I back out of the pod and face Xijure, watching him close the main cabin door. "How can you tell?" It's Lyle's job to read people, not mine.

"Just an inkling," Xijure says. "He does not seem like a ruler on edge, even though these islands will not last another six months. He's grateful to us, yes, but to be that calm? He has to have a failsafe."

That doesn't sound so bad. "I'd have a back-up plan too."

The Remasian Council was willing to screw Evan on Onkurus and the Allegiances had been okay with it. Evan's on their team. People who'd sell out their own aren't trustworthy. And here I am, working for them.

"Are you worried?" I ask.

Xijure sits down on a bench, stretching his long legs

out over it. "That Owelu is a fool? Yes."

"Then, what are we doing here?" I ask. "We should leave. We could—"

"We could," Xijure drawls, gazing back at me, "lose the opportunity to retrieve your weapon. We're too close to go back now. Do you feel your Stone's presence?"

I frown, shaking my head, and squashing down the urge to mentally reach out to the thing. I don't want to end up Stone-Zoning like Evan. But it never seemed like he had to reach out for it. It called him. If mine's nearby, shouldn't it call me?

"Is that bad? Maybe somebody took it already," I say.

"Or maybe we have to unearth it," Xijure says. "Or there could be too much interference from the water, who knows? We'll find out when we get to the exact co-ordinates. And if Owelu chooses to betray us then, well, you'll have your Stone, I have Haribu, and Ilea will re-purpose the barrier."

"Repurpose?" I hate when he talks to me like I know stuff.

Xijure gives a half smile. "She cast the base spell as an anchor for the true barrier to secure itself to. However, the true ward needs to be built from the sea. Its original purpose is to hold the ocean at bay. If we are deceived…"

"She'll flood the place," I breathe. "But what about the people who live here?"

"They will suffer for the dishonor of their leader," Xijure says, sounding almost bored, like he just said, 'Let's go home and watch a movie instead of going to the theater.' Does he really not care? Did this job do that to him?

"And how do we avoid getting flooded out too?" My voice is soft.

Xijure hums. "Do you really think Ilea couldn't protect herself from her own magic? We'll be fine." He gets up and walks past me to jiggle the handle on a locker that looks like the ones in high school, but without slats and combination locks. Metal rattles and the door pops open with a hydraulic hiss. I cover my nose at the musty, dirty sneaker stench.

"But…" Xijure says, reaching into the locker and dragging out a dark green bodysuit with footies, "maybe we'll keep these on, just in case."

"That's diving gear?" Oh hell no. I move to his side, grabbing the suit in one hand, eyes widening at the feel of the material. It's rubbery but soft with a gritty after-touch. I examine my fingers, frowning at the green powder on my thumb.

"It'll keep you warm and protect us from the water's pressure," Xijure says. "It's a good thing the Disi are a tall people, or you and I would be out of luck in finding suits that fit. Ilea may have a problem."

He stuffs the suit back in the locker and moves so I can look inside. Gah. They really need to keep the locker doors open to air this stuff out. A second green suit is draped over a hanger. A shelf above the rack holds two helmets with glass face plates and green cloth coating the back. I reach up to touch one. It feels like the suit; even the face plate is soft and rubbery. It's not glass at all, just clear. Okay, that's weird. I'm no scuba expert but I don't think Earth equipment is like this.

"Where do the air tanks connect?" I ask, shutting the locker door. The disgusting odor lingers.

"Air tanks?" Xijure asks.

"Um, yeah, the things that provide oxygen, so we can breathe while we're under there." I talk slow, trying to remember if this was something he'd told me about and I'm just blanking on it.

"The suits have gills in the neck," Xijure says. "Water passes over them and the suits convert it to oxygen and pass it into the headpiece. You'll feel claustrophobic." After a short pause, he adds, "It's not my favorite thing either. I've only been diving twice before this."

He sits on another bench, closing his eyes. "I prefer land travel to anything else. Space travel can't be avoided, but I hate long voyages. I love being planet-side."

"Yeah?" Feelings of camaraderie persuade me to forget what Xijure had said earlier. It had been easy to change the subject, to talk about another part of the job, but, "Hey man, are you really okay with flooding this place out, if things go bad?"

His eyes open, focusing on the wall before finding me. "You can't always put things on a personal level, Devon. This is business. You can't look at them and see people, until it's clear they are on our side."

Not see the Disi as people?

"And trust me," Xijure says, "they don't look at you as a person either. We're all just pawns in a big game."

I shudder. "And you're okay with that?"

"I have to be. You're the one who has 'choices,'" Xijure says, not quite looking at me.

I blink. No other Champion—not that we've all sat together and talked—has brought up how they feel about The Four seeming to be more powerful than all the others. Order made us OP characters. Well, Evan, Lawrie, and Lyle are OP. Their powers are scary. But why unbalance a team like that?

"Blana koweiku," Xijure mutters with a chuckle.

Blana koweiku: You are cursed with terrible circumstance. Bad time to be you. Unlucky guy. More phrases cycle through my head until the translator settles on one: Sucks to be you.

"Dude!" I shout. "Really?"

Xijure shakes his head. "I'm glad I don't have your job. I just need to fight my best. Your part…well, your part doesn't make sense. To anybody. Except maybe your council and my parliament, and perhaps The Maidens, because they were actually at Order's Table." His eyes narrow. "What do you think of them, The Maidens, I mean?"

The Maidens? I shrug. "I don't know. It's not like I hung out with them or anything. They read our Marks. That's it."

I frown at Xijure, trying to analyze him the way Lyle would. He'd note the serious set of Xijure's mouth and tension in his posture. He wants me to say something.

"They make me nervous," I say.

"Do you trust them?" Xijure asks. "To fight with you, with us?"

I blink. "I guess." They're Champions. "I mean, we don't have a choice in that one, right? We're, like, destined to fight together."

Xijure snorts, but there's no humor in it. *"You* don't have a choice?"

Shit. "What are you getting at, man?" I hate prophecy riddles. I hate subtle hints. "You think The Maidens are shady?"

Xijure sighs. "I think a lot is 'shady' as you say, and that it involves more than just The Maidens. Do you like your Remasian councilors?"

I blink. "Not particularly. But I've only met two. The rest could be cool." Or not. Evan never mentioned any that he liked.

"I hate my government," Xijure says. His face is grave. "Hate having to pay my familial dues. As a Champion, now, I should be able to fix that, right? Change the government because I'm chosen?" He shakes his head. "Instead, I feel more trapped than before."

I blink, not knowing what to say to that. "I'm sorry, man."

"Don't be sorry," he says, studying his large knuckles. "I'm glad I'm with you, another Champion, one who might be able to do things I can't."

Like what? He said it himself, 'it sucks to be [me].' And now I feel like he's looking at me as Mineshka and Loniad did on the ship, like I'm something special. He should know better. "I don't know what you want from me."

The big king glances up from his knuckles, eyes wide, the expression making him look years younger than me instead of my age. The smile he offers is almost shy, which seems weird from him. "I'm probably one of the few people you'll meet, who doesn't want anything from you. I just wanted to talk a bit, alone, Champion to a Champion who's not my sister or brother. Who knows when I'll get a chance like this again?"

"Are you saying you want to be friends?" I'd like that. I need friends; people I can trust to be in my corner, to back me up, even if when it's not their job to. But I don't know Xijure like that yet. His look is as uncertain as I feel. Maybe he's thinking the same thing.

Voices and footsteps sound on the dock, heading to

the cabin. Xijure breaks eye contact with me, as the cabin door opens and Loniad, Mineshka and Ilea troop in, Loniad belly-laughing at something Mineshka's saying. Ilea scowls at the twins, then at me.

"You two look cozy," Ilea says. "Did you check out the equipment? Is any of it going to fit me, or is it all for freakishly large people like you?"

My court parades around, opening lockers and discussing equipment. One of the men who had been with Owelu enters the cabin, bowing to me first, then Xijure, before proceeding to the captain's pod. Xijure lounges on his bench, eyes closed, like he's taking a nap, but I know he's alert.

"Devon!" Loniad shouts. "Come and see the tiny suit for Ilea!"

"It's not tiny!" Ilea snaps. "It's normal size!"

I glance at Loniad standing in front of a locker next to Ilea. He looks over his shoulder, wide smile in place, eyes twinkling. Ilea glares back, but there's no heat in her gaze. Mineshka takes a seat on a bench, looking amused. She winks at me.

I like Loniad and Mineshka. They seem so open. I wish I could think of them as future friends, but they can't be. Maybe I'll like Ilea. She's interesting, but she's here to protect me too. They all have an ulterior motive for supporting me.

Maybe it can change. Evan's court is full of friends, though they've had years to become so. I don't want to be a leader for years without anyone I can call a real friend outside of my brothers. A surge of loneliness almost has me choking on my own spit.

Xijure's eyes stay closed as I take a breath and make a choice. Please don't let it be one that spells doom for mankind and everything else. I just need someone to be close to.

"Yo, Xijure. Come look at this munchkin suit with me." I kick the king's leg and laugh as he jerks up, scowling at me. I smile and extend a hand down to him, waiting for him to take it.

Friends? I don't ask it aloud, hoping he reads it in my posture.

After a brief stare-down, the king of Zare grips my hand.

MY LEGS FEEL WATERY AS I peer down into the abyss, fear of falling temporarily gripping me. The constant roar and screeching metallic groans of monster drills eating through layers of permafrost and digging into the harder stuff underneath, set my teeth on edge. The earplugs the Matriarch had given to us before we'd come onsite drowns out the worst of the noise, or so she claims. I think she's full of shit.

...handsome, like his father, but not as dimwitted.

I hear her, but keep my face smooth, calm, as I gaze at the Matriarch, Shreti-Hak. She's a thin woman, who seems about forty, but I know she's old as dirt, with bright red paint on lips so thin they look like bloody earthworms.

"Do you really think this tunnel will be stable enough for us to travel down in the morning?" I ask.

A flash of irritation from her, though she smiles. "But of course, my young leader. My terra-technicians are extremely competent." *...brat...should be grateful.*

I nod and glance at Caea Harliel on my left. She's an ice queen as she stares Shreti-Hak down. "If you trust in the competency of the people who will be coming down with us to lead the way, then I am confident all is well."

Shreti-Hak's paper white skin flushes, black eyes glinting, before her cool returns. She smiles again. I suppress a shudder at her rounded, yellow teeth and purple gums. It's the funkiest thing. The other Kupi look completely human—copper-skinned, brown, or even pink—but their queen is whiter than milk with Simpson teeth and grape jelly gums. Maybe that's how she got elected. I was chosen by an after-birthmark, she was chosen for being a mutant.

Shreti-Hak glances at Caea. "From one queen to another." *Uppity child ruler. Ludicrous. If the Allegiance wasn't our only choice....*

My head throbs, the pain a permanent companion today. I rub my temples and try to play it off by running a hand through my hair. The move is awkward in thick gloves. The woolly hood of the heavy fur coat flops back and I fight back a groan at the immediate drop in temperature. Damn. I snatch the hood back up, but the damage is done. Cold floods through my system. My teeth chatter.

Stupid jacket. Once part of it comes off, it forgets my normal body temperature and resets to standard room temperature, which is about forty degrees on Kupiku. My head pounds harder, amplifying the noise of the drills. The rusty smell of burning ore and stale ice is enough to make me sick. /Caea, I need to go. Now./

"Well," Caea says, sounding casual, "since things seem to be proceeding without cause for concern, we will take our leave."

"Of course, Your Majesty," Shreti-Hak says, bowing her head slightly. "Young leader." Her black eyes flicker over me. Interest swells inside her. *...looks ill. A weakness. Poor representative...but handsome, still. Is he fresh...?*

I throw up a heavier mental shield to block her out as her thoughts turn dirty. Ugh, images of her putting those nasty lips on me come through anyway. I turn and start walking away, body half frozen, boots crunching across ice and snow, heading for the rover that'd brought us here. I hate this place, hate Shreti-Hak, hate this damn headache. It's like knitting needles boring through my temples trying to make quilts out of my brain, and Aderyn's medicine isn't working.

I pull open the round door to the rover and climb into the warm vehicle. Hell, it's a hummer limo with heavy duty snow tires big enough to fit on a school bus. Kind of reminds me of the pick-up trucks back home, with monster wheels so tall it takes a foldout ladder to get in and out. The long bench seats in the passenger compartment smell and feel like cowhide leather, soft under my aching muscles. I sprawl out, face down, digging my fists into my eyes. The mental voices of the terra-technicians and Shreti-Hak's bodyguards are white and gray noise, muffled, but present. I try to shut them out too, but the knitting needles drive deeper into my skull. Crap. Crap. My cheeks are wet, nose runny. Just pass out already. I wait for the black out. I'd passed out for two full days after the portal jump from Lenore and have blacked out for hours at random since.

I think this is going to kill me. And, at this point, I don't care.

Someone's coming. Their thoughts are a blank spot

on my radar, their feelings clean cotton, soft and empty, as they float over my shields. I mainly sense a presence, an aura—meaning it's either Caea or somebody from my court, another psychic. My consciousness slides behind their eyes, scanning the frozen terrain of Kupiku, a planet stuck in a nuclear winter that's gone on for more than ten Kupi years. Mountain peaks and ridges line the horizon, the setting sun turning the snow-covered giants into prisms glinting pink, gold and blue. Beautiful enough to sketch, but my fingers are too clumsy to hold a pencil.

The rover door opens and cold air whips in for a moment, before a body pulls itself in and slams the door shut. "*Ayo.*" Deep voice, heavy footsteps, thwump on the seat across from mine: Orion. "How bad is your pain, Lyle?"

I told them to call me by my name. I don't like 'leader.' /Bad./

"Can you wait until we get back to the suite for treatment?"

/Before I pass out?/ No, I hope not.

"Okay. Hold still, then."

Like I can move.

Something pulls at my fur jacket. I flop upward as Orion peels the jacket off and lays me back on the seat. I bite my lip until I taste blood, my eyes clench shut so tight it hurts. My stomach churns as I inhale the scent of leather and ice that'd flaked from my jacket onto the seat. The tiny bits of cold bite into my cheeks.

Warm hands push hair off my neck. "This is going to feel frigid, boss, but I promise you'll feel a lot better after."

I don't care enough to ask what he's doing.

A gooey mound the size of a quarter touches the

side of my neck, latching on like a leech. A bolt of cold shoots down into my shoulders, then rebounds up my neck, hitting my brain like a thick gulp of a McDonald's milkshake. I choke, back arching, once, twice, till I feel like my spine's going to break in two. What the hell did he do to me?

Oh. God. Stop. The. Pa—

....

It stops.

The seizures. The cold. The mind melt. The knitting needles. Gone.

I lie still, afraid to breathe, not wanting to jumpstart the pain. Is it really gone? My ears ring with leftover achiness, but…I take in a shallow breath, then a deeper one. It's gone.

Better? Orion asks.

His voice in my mind doesn't hurt, but then again, his voice never hurts. Psychics know how to get in and out of heads without ringing any doorbells or breaking windows. I never thought about how my presence feels when I send my messages to other people, but Orion says I don't hurt his head either.

/Yeah. Better./

I don't feel a swirl of emotion from him. Don't even feel him receding from my mind. His shields are friggin' amazing.

"Good," he says. "Sit up slowly and don't open your eyes until you're all the way up. You're going to be a bit dizzy for a *jewel* or so. Careful now."

I push myself up into a kneel and swing my legs off the seat, sitting up at a leisurely pace. My head swims for a second, but it fades as I open my eyes. Orion sits across from me on the other bench seat, pale gray eyes watching my every move. The guy is tall and skinny with a beaky nose and cat-slanted eyes. He sort of looks like a bird, but it works for him. Lots of Kupi girls and guys send glances his way while they shrink from me. I scare them.

"What'd you give me?" I rasp, hand going to my neck, fingers searching for the glob he'd stuck there. Lukewarm syrupy goo meets my fingers and I snatch them back. "Gross."

"Murflad essence. It passes through the skin barrier pretty fast," Orion says. "It does feel rather disgusting, but it is great in emergencies."

"How long does it last?" I ask. I took Aderyn's cocktail a few hours ago, not that it'd done much, but I'm not trying to overdose.

"Not long," Orion says. "As I said, it's an emergency treatment, field medicine. It shouldn't interact with the drug already in your system." His lips twitch and he looks at the ceiling. I don't need to use my powers to know he's got an opinion on the 'drug,' they all do, but he keeps his mouth shut. His eyes shift from brown to blue. At first, I thought they shifted with his moods. Nope, they change when he wants them to.

"Where's everybody else?" I mumble, rubbing syrup on my pants. I don't want to extend past my shields to find them.

"Her Majesty Harliel is explaining your hasty retreat to Shreti-Hak," Orion says. "And Falun is with the terra-technicians' foreman. Their equipment is picking up an energy source as they get closer to your coordinates. They think it may be your Stone." He studies me, eyes turning purple. "You do not seem excited." His tone is flat.

"Do I ever seem excited?" I ask.

He snorts. "All right. That is fair, but I cannot help but be concerned about your lack of enthusiasm. You are my leader. My life is yours, but you do not seem to care much." His tone is light, but there is an undercurrent of distaste.

I shrug it off. I've only known this guy for a few days, and don't owe him anything. If he wants to throw his life away for a stranger he didn't vote for, well...I don't know. I can't hate him for thinking I'm worth all that, but it's not like he's on my team out of the goodness of his heart. He honestly believes in the goodness of Goddess Order and thinks he's going to be part of the squad that saves the world.

Orion gives a heavy sigh and tilts his head to look at the ceiling again. Good. I hate socializing. The only person I want to talk to is Devon. I flinch, reliving the blinding pain of having my soul ripped in half when our ship had jumped through the Lenoran portal and slid on course for Kupiku. I had expected to miss him, but no one had prepared me for that knife in the heart. I swallow hard, glad I don't eat much these days.

"You should come out with us tonight," Orion says.

I blink at him. Huh?

"You need to spend time with other psychics," he says, "see how we cope. It will help you."

I frown at him. We've only been here a day. He and Falun had gone out last night and come back early this morning all smiles and anxious to get to work. I didn't care what they had done so long as they kept their annoying, bubbly buzz away from me.

The door opens and Caea climbs into the compartment. She closes the door and pushes the wooly hood off her head. Her black hair sparkles with bits of snow. She rolls her brown eyes in my direction, giving me an unimpressed once over. "Shreti-Hak thinks you're an invalid. She offered to send a doctor to your room after we get back to the guest compound."

"Did you decline?" I ask.

"I told her a mind-healer was selected for your court for that very reason. But…" Caea removes a thick, white glove and presses her cool hand to my forehead, "she might have a point. You're not doing well. We shouldn't have left Sensuen behind."

Sensuen, the mind-healer, the oldest member of my court, had stayed at the compound.

I close my eyes. "Are we leaving now?"

"The driver was just behind me," Caea says. "Falun's staying. She'll come back when the tunnel is complete and up to satisfactory standards. Only the best for you, Leader Three."

I lean back on the chair, not rising to the bait. Caea doesn't like me and has made it clear since we landed that we won't be friends. It's fine. The most important thing to me is that she has good shields for a non-psi. Her thoughts don't pound my head.

The car shudders to life and glides across the ice. The dig site is almost an hour away from our 'hotel' and I intend to sleep through the trip.

"You're not trying hard enough to get your head together," Caea says suddenly. "You're still a mess."

"What do you know?" I tune out whatever she says next. If it's important, she can tell me again when I wake up.

Right before I fall asleep, a few words become clear: "…terrible leader."

My lips twitch. She may not like me, but I do like

her. She's honest. Makes me feel better.

Consciousness drifts, then fades. Silence complete.

SENSUEN IS THE BEST MIND-HEALER in the Silver Allegiance army, top of her class, trained by the best, or so everyone says. Her large, rough hands, callused from years of weapons training, have healing qualities. When she touches my temples, soothing warmth trickles in like hot tea against a sore throat. I moan into the pillow as she works like a masseuse, rubbing her hands over my neck, back, shoulders, cheeks, ears and temples. She says she pushes her clean aura through her hands, using it to cleanse away negative feedback left behind by outside interference. Whatever she does, it feels good and the effects last for an hour or so afterward. Wish it was a permanent deal.

"You need more than me," Sensuen murmurs softly. Her alto voice is nice for talking, but horrible when she sings, and she sings a lot. "You need an isolation ward for training and a month of solitude afterward to even begin repairing your psi damage."

"Mmm." I keep my muscles loose. She'd said that last night too.

"I've never worked on someone with powers like yours. The magnitude of your abilities…" she trails off. "Normal shields couldn't hold this in."

I was never able to build proper core shields on Earth. So, my mind didn't learn the right way to brace for impact. Now, I might be too old and wrecked to learn.

Those thoughts leaked from the green ladies of Lenore who'd tried to help me.

If I'm too broken, why am I here?

"Because you were Chosen by Kahanna," Sensuen says, tone reverent.

Had I said that out loud?

"No," Sensuen says, "but don't worry. You are shielding your thoughts quite well. It's just hard to hide them from your mind-healer while she's touching you."

I sigh. No privacy then.

"Your apathy grows," Sensuen says. "I understand it. You've been whittled to almost nothing and you carry a heavy weight of guilt. I cannot tell what it's for, but I assume it has something to do with your addiction to psimitrol?"

/What's that? My medicine?/

"Yes," Sensuen says. "I will be taking it from you after the Stone is retrieved. You should no longer need it, once you are touched by the goddess. She will heal you, I'm sure."

I roll my eyes into the pillow. Sensuen isn't a fanatic, but she'd studied theology along with healing within the Remasian military and loves her some Order. She believes every prophecy written, chants sutras, and can even read a few of the old scrolls only people old as dirt recognize.

/What would you think of me if I told you I don't want the Stone?/

She massages the base of my skull. Endorphins release, and I can't help another groan. I don't care that this woman's nearly a foot taller than me and could carry me over the threshold. I want to marry her.

"Don't be silly, Lyle," she says, voice dropping to a

whisper. "You want the Stone."

A slow burn of annoyance ruins my pleasure buzz. /No, I.../

"You can't hide from me when you're like this," Sensuen says. "You've felt the Stone's power, its healing properties."

I grit my teeth, blocking out the flashbacks of how good it'd felt to accept the Stone's power. /It felt good, but it isn't right. If you know what I felt, tell me how it's different from the medicine I got from Dr. Aderyn?/

Sensuen laughs. It's a beautiful noise, but the wrong reaction to my question. My jaw stays clenched. "Because it's from Her, Lyle. You are Her Champion and She needs you healthy and strong."

I need to get up now. I don't want to talk to Sensuen anymore. She rests her hands on my shoulders, and another wave of calming heat pours through me. I relax my jaw.

"You have to know that your mind can never be fully repaired," she says. "Not without it being completely broken and rebuilt from the inside. Not many people survive that without going completely mad. An outside source of strength and protection is your only choice. Pumping daily dosages of drugs into your system will eventually kill you. The Stone offers you more than the drugs without poisoning your body."

Just my mind. *"Don't let her take your mind."* Corin Peredil had told me that.

"Haven't you read any history?" Sensuen asks. "I spent nine *sessions* studying the Prophetic Cycles. Padain Peredil often used the Stone as a psychic analgesic. His powers were like yours, immense, and he had the added advantage of being raised with training. Order takes care of Her own."

"Then why did they die before they finished any-thing?" I sound like an asshole, but I want to know her opinion.

"They all veered from the path," Sensuen says. She squeezes my shoulders and puts her mouth near my ear. "It started with Corin Peredil. His mistakes swayed Aman and Padain. Jain was the one who tried to hold them on course, but in the end, he was weak too. But the First Four didn't have courts to help them find their way."

I frown. "Who decided leaders needed courts?"

"Viveen actually," Sensuen says. "One account says she blamed herself for the failings of the Peredils. She used to be the highest-ranking councilor but gave her position to Theorne because she felt he could take his personal feelings out of the equation better than she could. Viveen was a friend of the Peredils' parents."

I curl my lip. The vulture lady had friends? Bullshit. I really think the Old Texts that people quote prophecy stories from are the same as holy texts from Earth: mul-tiple translations with meanings lost or changed over the years to suit whoever's in power at the time.

"You won't have any more doubts after tomorrow," Sensuen says, a smile in her voice. "You'll be so much better you'll wonder why you ever had these questions."

Her words make my skin crawl. She sounds like a brainwashed recruiter from a cult. I want her hands off me, now. I concentrate on the healing energy running through my body. My mind's cool, barriers intact, power under control. I reach for my telekinesis, finding its in-visible hands and pushing them toward Sensuen.

She squeaks and her power breaks away from mine.

I roll onto my back and turn my head, studying her sprawled form on the floor. She gets up, gray-blue eyes on my face. "That was good, Lyle. Very controlled." She dusts herself off and gives me a business-like nod. "That session should last you through the night, but if it doesn't, please summon me before you take anything else."

She leaves the room, and I sigh. Glad she's gone. The ceiling of my guest quarters glows a dim blue, making the whole room look like a scene from *Ghostbusters*. I keep expecting for the furniture to float, the walls to bleed and something with claws to grab my ankles and drag me under the bed. Lawrie would probably love this place for its weirdness factor alone. Devon would probably make some excuse to need to bunk with me. I rub the ache in my chest.

I found the limit to my powers. I can't reach Devon across galaxies. I tried. A void sits where his presence used to be. I let out a shaky breath. Who would have thought I'd miss having constant company?

I sit up, loving the fact that the world doesn't spin. The bed's feather soft, the kind that tries to drown a person as it sags under their weight, and warm, made to seal out Kupiku cold. The compound is insulated, and heat pumps from the floor vents to ceilings that regulate the temperature, but it's still too cold for comfort. I'm glad for the Dallas Cowboys sweatshirt I stole from Dev before we left Earth.

I push off the bed, padding across plush carpet to the cabinet my stuff's in. A duffle of clothes and a backpack full of sketch pads, coals and colored pencils had been stowed aboard the ship for me. I don't know who'd thought to include my bag of art supplies, but I'd thank them if I could. I slide one strap of the pack over my shoulder and step into the tan leather boots Shreti-Hak had gifted me with when we'd first arrived. I don't like her jelly-gum ass, but the boots are nice.

I walk to the entrance. "Open up." All of the doors to private rooms are voice activated. Mine only opens for me, my court, and, of course, Shreti-Hak. A chill flows down my spine as I think of that woman being able to creep in and watch me sleep.

The halls are pretty quiet except for the faint sounds of Orion playing his skinny violin, or mansoki, in his room a few doors down. He says it soothes him. I learned every psi needs a 'thing' that can take them away from the physical present. I pull the strap of my backpack higher on my shoulder. The pencils rattle inside. My hand itches with the need to draw. My mind wants to create, and I finally feel well enough to let it happen.

The atrium is in the center of the compound. Nothing special or elaborate. Like the rest of the house, it's a simple space. I slide open the wooden door and step onto green carpet made to resemble the grass Kupiku had before it'd frozen solid. The walls are murals of forests with streams and animals long gone. The ceiling is treated glass, letting in the blues, greens, and pinks of never-ending daylight.

"You look lost." I jump at the sound of Caea's voice.

Holy shit. My powers are pretty much 'off' right now, because my shields are so thick.

Caea sits cross-legged on the grassy carpet in a corner of the room. A manila colored canvas is propped on a small stand in front of her as she mixes paint. I find myself drifting toward her, gazing down at her canvas and falling into her wash of Kupiku's sky.

"This is what I take away from jobs," Caea says, as

she uses a slim brush to twirl silvery white paint. "New landscapes. Some I keep, some I donate to the palace walks, some I sell under a pseudonym."

"You make much?" I ask.

She focuses on blending the right color. "Enough to sneak and purchase my own cottage in the hills where no one recognizes me. Not that I get to stay there much."

I sit a few paces beside her, unzipping my bag and pulling out a medium-sized sketch book and a Number Three pencil.

"I've known Orion and Sensuen for a while," Caea says, after a beat of silence. "They're good people and will teach you what they know."

I nod, waiting for it.

"They truly believe in this cause, this war," Caea says. "That's why they were chosen for your court. Too bad you're too much like me to be excited about them joining you."

"How am I like you?" I ask. Lead meets paper, but instead of a soft line, I shade, turning the page gray.

"Being a leader is a job neither of us applied for. We may be qualified, but we're a poor fit."

I blink, looking over at her. Her large almond-shaped eyes are on me, lashes thick and dark, cheekbones high and framed by tight black curls. This queen is beautiful and wears no make-up to enhance it. My hand moves on its own, fingers smudging the pencil marks, then using the lead to create an oval-shaped face.

"We don't want to fight. I'd rather be doing this, while cheering from the sidelines." She gestures to her canvas, her dark, slender hands stained with silver and pink oil. I admire her work, and minutes pass, before she speaks again. "What do you think about Order and

Pandemonium?"

I sigh. "The good and evil stuff the prophecy goes on about?"

One side of her mouth quirks. "Good and evil, Lyle? Really?"

I chuckle, can't help it. "No one's told me what really happens if either of Them wins. Who's to say Pan is any worse than Order or if things will really change? What's to stop another war to challenge the outcome of this one? I mean, unless our choices end up destroying everyone who could oppose the Allegiances, then...I don't know."

"Well," Caea says. "I can tell you that neither side will favor the enemy's champions, so if Order loses, that's it for us. However, I wonder if that might be for the best. Without super-powered people scaring ordinaries half to death, maybe others will be able to get along. Maybe the choice should be to let the Champions—Pan's and Order's—do away with each other and the government leaders too, and let the world reshape itself."

I shake my head. "Why do we have to play a part in that? We could just say 'to hell with it' and not fight."

"Everybody would have to agree not to fight," Caea says. "We don't know Pan's Champions. Didn't even know He had Champions. Unlike us, they don't broadcast their identities. The enemies have been waiting centuries for us, knowing just about everything we'll bring to the fight. But them? Nothing. That doesn't seem strange to you, how the councils didn't panic, how we're still out here trusting we won't be ambushed?"

I laugh, it's not funny, but it is. "Of course it's strange, but nothing about anything makes sense to me anymore, so..."

"You don't care." Caea sighs and dabs her paint brush on the canvas. "Which is why you're a terrible leader."

"I heard you say that."

"I'm surprised," Caea snorts. "Thought you had gone to sleep before I got to that part."

Leaning closer to her, I say, "I will admit I didn't hear much before or after that. Will you tell me why I'm terrible?"

"Of course! I love pointing out other people's flaws." Caea dimples.

"I figured that. You're royalty. A little bit of pompous brat attitude is to be expected, right?" I switch from using the pencil to smudging again. For some reason, I'm comfortable here, talking to her. I don't need powers to tell me that everything she's about is staring right back at me.

She blinks and lets out a sharp laugh. "You're really something else, you know that?" She shakes her head. "Okay. You're a terrible leader...because you don't care about people."

I roll my eyes. "I don't have to—"

She swats the air in front of my mouth with her paintbrush, and glares. "Not caring about power, land and politics is fine, but you have to care about the people on your team, and the public who believes you are in this to save them. They can't fight, but you can. You have to care that winning means they're safe. I don't like fighting, but I love my people. If I defeat Pan's Champions and that helps you make the right choices for Order to win, which, in turn, protects my relatives and subjects, I'd be happy. Knowing this inspires me to strive to be a good leader." She pauses, eyes distant, as if she's pondering something. "Is there anyone you'd rather not see hurt in all of this?"

I wipe at my mouth, making sure no paint got on it. Crap. "My family."

"That's a start," Caea says. "Once you get to know Orion, Sensuen and Falun, maybe you won't want them to get hurt either, because your court should eventually feel like family to you. That family could continue to expand to include your army and, eventually, the Remasian people." She tilts her head, frowning at me. "One day, you'll want to fight to protect all of them."

I don't feel like she was talking about me in that last sentence, and I don't know what to say to any of it. Will I always end up wishing I was a better person for someone else?

Caea seems to read something off my face. "Or maybe you won't." She adds more color to her sky. "Okay, moving on. Another reason you are a terrible leader is because you don't have tangible goals."

I shade a little more.

"I've known my fair share of psychics," Caea says. "Most aren't social, so I guess I can understand people not being big motivators for you to do your job properly. However, the psychics I know have goals they wish to achieve. You need drive. If helping other people doesn't drive you far enough, how about helping yourself?"

"You're telling me to be selfish now?" I ask. Didn't she just berate me for not caring about strangers? I almost want to tap into her head to see what she's getting at.

"I want to own art galleries and fill them with my work," Caea says. "I want to use my real name and travel around doing art exhibitions and have people call me '*maistre*' instead of 'Your Majesty.' I want to live off my own earnings and invite family and friends to visit my cottage. I want to help my brothers embrace their other talents and live on their own too. Winning the war could mean that. If I don't die, maybe there won't be a need for warrior kings and queens, and I can retire and pass my crown to someone else. Or give it back to my mother."

"Why did you take it from your mother in the first place?" I ask, totally distracted. She wants to travel and do art for a living?

"I didn't take it. It is Zaran law. Once a monarch reaches a certain age, they aren't considered prime anymore and their crown goes to the next worthy descendent. I was the right age and the best fighter in my class."

"You're all trained to be warriors?"

"We learn to read, write, and fight." Caea nods. "Activities like this," she gestures to her canvas, "are highly frowned upon, but we're allowed to have hobbies." Her voice is matter of fact instead of bitter.

"So…" I drawl.

"So, if we win the war, what does Lyle Lauduethe want to do with his life?"

My pencil stops as I look at her. "Huh?"

"What are your goals? Your future plans?"

"I'm seventeen," I say. "I…" Hell, I was going to go to college, because that's what people do. I had planned to major in architecture and only minor in art so Mom and Dad wouldn't complain too much. I'd probably have rented an apartment off campus, avoided social events, graduated, got a job and lived…alone. I shudder at the thought of getting married and having kids.

Those probably aren't nice, shiny goals like Caea's, but it'd been my plan. Nothing exciting, just something

I could possibly do. Doubt I'd do any of that now. No college on Earth would take me after helping burn down a university, and I don't think I qualify for any higher educational institutions outside of Earth. But do I really want higher education anyway? It's not exactly a societal expectation anymore, not here. And a job? Would I ever need one of those? I don't know much about leadership perks, but I never heard Evan talk about paying bills.

If we win the war, would I still be a leader?

I bite the end of my pencil. "I don't know what I want."

Caea tilts her head, nothing judgmental in her expression. "Well, what do you like?" She nods at my sketchpad. "I've seen you a few times with one of those, moping about Lenore. You seem to know what you're doing."

"I'm okay." I chew on the pink eraser and gaze down at my sketch pad. The smooth curve of Caea's small chin is done, but I'm not in the mood to do more. I start to close the book. Caea catches my hand.

"May I?" she asks.

A flash of fear and nerves makes me snatch my hand back and clutch my drawings. Other people have seen my stuff, I don't care, whatever, but her looking at it seems strange.

"It's not very good, okay?" I pass the book to her and plant my hands behind me on the shag green carpet, sprawling my legs and lifting my head toward the sky-light. I don't want to watch her face.

Unlike Devon and a lot of the girls I dated, Caea takes her time. I listen to her hum and the slow shuffle of pages being turned. What feels like twenty minutes passes, before she speaks to me again. "You're good."

I shrug a shoulder. "I've been told that." But it does feel good coming from her.

"Do you like doing this?" Caea asks. "Or is it just what calms you when your head hurts?"

I frown, blinking away from the sky. Traces of brightness stain my vision as I try to look at her. Her face glows, a golden halo glimmering around it. "I…" Drawing takes my mind off things. I can lose myself and the real world in it. I'm in control, creating what I want. Sometimes, other people's thoughts shape what goes on the page, but I choose how. Makes me feel powerful in a way I'm not when I don't have a pencil.

I rub my eyes, trying to get rid of spots, mind churning. Powerful? I feel power with a damn pencil, when I can melt people's brains with a thought? Change people's minds because they're thinking about things I don't like? I swallow sour spit, silver eyes invading my mind space again.

"Maybe you want to take classes, to study this," Caea says. "There are many academies that can teach you how to use tools and mediums you've never dreamed of. You could travel from world to world, taking in sights, seeing new colors." Her tone is wistful, almost dreamy. A soft hand touches my arm. "Hey."

I open my eyes, gazing at her. The spots are gone, halo faded, but her eyes seem to glisten with a warmth I haven't seen there before. "Just think about it. Like you said, you're seventeen. Now," she grins, "when I was your age, I was queen and had a life of fighting and attending galas ahead of me. I liked to dream about my escape. Maybe having an art gallery sounds frivolous, but it's what I'd do if I had a choice."

"You're technically only a year older than me," I

say.

"Hm." Caea nods. "Do you think I'm too young for goals?"

I shake my head. "Just think it's cool that you have them. And…" I don't think they're stupid. I can't say it, though. It's not…I don't say things like that to people. It makes them open up, like they know me or something. They start wanting to be friends, wanting to be close. "I have to go."

Her hand clamps on my wrist. "How often do you actually talk to people, for real, not just reading minds or listening to stray thoughts?"

Never. I mean, maybe Devon, but—

"You're not speaking your thoughts," Caea says. "Do you even realize it?"

"I don't want to speak my thoughts," I say.

"But you should." She releases my wrist and waits, like she expects me to run away now that I'm free. But I can't. Curiosity keeps me in place. Why does she think I should be open with her?

She frowns, her gaze seeming to turn inward before focusing on me again. "You don't know me very well, but you and I are leaders, selected by a higher power, to complete a mission we don't fully understand. If you ever need to speak privately to anyone, to share your concerns about what we're doing, I'm the most likely person here to understand your plight."

My hands shake. I put them in my lap, trying to hold them still. I don't like this. I don't like her being so close to me, and saying things that make me want to… "You wouldn't like me at all if you got to know me, if I talked to you about what I feel and the things I've done."

"I don't have to like you," Caea says firmly. "I just

have to work with you, and to work with you, I need you functional and rational. For that to happen, you need a focus, cares, wants. That is your task."

"I thought my task was getting the Stone."

"That too," Caea says, "but what does it matter if you don't know why you're getting it."

"To complete a stupid prophecy."

"That is open-ended," Caea says. "Your choices decide the outcome of the endgame, but we don't know what that game is or what it means. If you had a focus, maybe you could guide it. But I don't know, I'm just talking." She sighs through her nose and goes back to her painting. "You're lost, Lyle. You won't survive this war in the mental state you're in. You need to think about what you might want after all this. Figure out what personal goal you want to accomplish and why. Every warrior needs something to fight for or it's over before it starts."

"I'm not a warrior."

"You didn't choose to be," Caea says. "Ironic, hm? A man whose choices will predict the end, had no choice in what he had to become."

Poetic.

I jump at the feeling of something flat dropping into my lap and look down. My sketchpad. I frown over at Caea who's leaning over her canvas and pick up my pencil.

"You really want to do that art gallery thing?" I ask.

"You're not just going to read my mind and find out?"

I shake my head. "I...actually don't like doing that."

Caea chuckles. "I'll remember that, and yes, I do. If you wanted to join me for a little while, you know, until you found yourself, you could. I'd like to see more of your artwork."

Something shifts in my chest, like a window being opened to let out a bad smell. I've never just talked to anyone this way before, not even Devon back when we used to be closer. It's…I thumb to the half-finished drawing in my book…nice. Observing her from the corner of my eye, I start on her cheekbones.

TIME PASSES, HOURS MAYBE. I don't wear Allegiance time-keepers and the sun never seems to move, so I have to guesstimate by how numb my butt is. I groan, drawing-trance broken at the sound of feet on the carpet. Shifting onto my knees to get the blood moving again, I stretch. Orion and Falun walk toward Caea and me, Orion in a fur-lined tunic and thick leather-like pants and Falun in a fuzzy brown jumpsuit that zips up to her chin, the equivalent of clubbing clothes in sub-zero weather.

"You guys are going out?" I ask. A wooden snap. In my periphery, Caea's packing away her art supplies.

"The tunnel's finished?" she asks.

"Almost," Falun says as she and Orion stop in front of us. "The Kupi claim there are a few things that can only be done in daylight, but it won't take long. We'll have full access by mid-morning, so we should celebrate."

Falun smiles, her ruddy skin and green-streaked orange hair make her look like a strawberry, brown freckles and all. She's not actually pretty, but something about the way she carries herself makes her seem that way: head high, shoulders back, narrow hips swaying. She crouches to be at eye-level with Caea and me. "You're both coming this time, right? The queen promised."

"It'll be fun," Caea says, nudging my shoulder. "You should get to know the people you work with."

I frown, feeling her nudge my mind as well. /Yes?/ It's not hard to send my thoughts out, but thinning the wall to let her in is like peeling a Band-Aid off a fresh scab.

You at least owe them that. Who knows, you might like them if you give them half a chance.

I stare at her so long Falun blinks between us. "Are we interrupting something?"

"No," Caea says, standing up in one motion, supply bag slung over one shoulder, canvas tucked under the other. "Let us put our things away and we'll meet you in the front foyer." She glances back at me, eyes brooking no question. Now it's not just a suggestion, it's a command. *You're not the only one who has to work with a new team. Give them a chance to know you too.*

I sigh, long and deep, leaning my head back, eyes closed. I thin my barrier a bit more, reaching out to brush the exterior of Falun's mind. Her frenetic energy stings, but her intentions are clear: fun before work starts. She needs to release the fizz she's built up since we landed and started talking tunnels. A cool, professional shell lies under the bubbles, but I don't penetrate. Though she's a pyrokinetic with no mind-touching gifts, she's got solid shields like Orion. It'd be an invasion to break her walls.

I don't do that, not anymore.

Guilt makes my chest tight. I take a shallow breath, before opening my eyes. Skylight nearly blinds me. I shield my eyes and look back to Caea, then Falun. Both women watch me, curious, maybe even amused. Falun's mouth is slightly curved, not quite a smile but getting there.

Orion clears his throat from the doorway. "The rover will be here soon."

"Well?" Caea asks.

I put away my pencil and close my sketchbook. I can't make myself excited about the idea of going out into a crowd, but, "Can I wear this?" I tug at my sweatshirt and gaze at the three waiting for me.

Falun laughs, loud and hard. "With that face, you can wear whatever you want. But you'll still need your coat."

I get up, walking past Falun and Caea, and try to ignore Orion's look of pleasant surprise as I join him at the door. It makes me feel odd, having these strangers seem happy about me hanging out with them. The only people who'd wanted my company before all of this were girls interested in proving my reputation true. Shallow people that didn't suffer from conscience or higher thought processes.

I don't flinch when Orion puts a hand on my shoulder. "Take your time. We'll wait the rover for you, Lyle."

I nod and head for my room, ears burning as the group behind me plans the evening.

10
LYLE

THE PARTY IS TWO-STORIES UNDERGROUND, accessible by slanted tunnels lit by glass torches. Bodies pack into several, dimly lit medium-sized rooms with white-frost coated floors that crunch under dancing leather shoes. Though, I don't know if I can call what the Kupi do dancing. They kind of shake and hop around like they're putting cowboy boots on one at a time and trying to keep their balance. It's not sexy or cool. I slouch against an icy wall, wishing I had my phone. I'd record this for Dev and Lawrie.

I bite my lip, pushing them out of mind. It's easier to do here.

Falun and Orion work their way through the three rooms, brushing their bodies against Kupi men and women, bouncing with their rhythms but in their own style. I like watching Falun and Orion move together. Their motions are a mix of grinding and acrobatic contortions that complement each other in a weird modern ballet sort of way. Caea wiggles through the crowd, using her hips and upper body more than her feet for dancing.

The music pours through the rocky ceiling and floor, pulsing and loud, the drumbeats echoing through my chest. My head's fuzzy and light, but in a good way. I'm relaxed, my body loose, as I study people having a good time. I let their aroused emotions rub my barrier, tendrils of them slipping through, caressing my mind. Feels as good as a massage. A smooth current of unintelligible thought runs through me like tepid bathwater filling a tub. I can fall asleep to the sound of running water.

I'm glad I came.

A hand grabs my wrist, pulling me forward. I yelp, and gaze down...

My heart pounds.

A girl, silvery pale and slender, with silver eyes and a heart-shaped face looks up at me. She smiles, tugging me until our bodies touch. She moves against me, torso and hips in time with the drums, hands traveling up my arms and down my back. Her short, purple hair tickles my chin; I inhale and cringe at the sharp scent of smoke and gasoline. My mind whirs, flying into memories of a mom-and-pop gas station convenience store, a smooth hand on my cheek, a pretty face gazing into mine and telling me my pupils were blown to Hades.

"Nisse?" I breathe.

She arches her brows, gloved hand touching my face. I jerk back, trying to get away but bump into the dancer behind me. I'm trapped in a cage of tranced people who don't even notice that I need to get out of here. Pushing doesn't work. They press against me, dancing, sending me back in her direction. Hands travel down my shoulders. I turn, opening my mouth to yell, "Stop it!" and come face to face with a concerned Caea instead of gyrating Kupi.

Where did she come from? Where's…?

Caea knocks on my mind. *Are you all right? You look sick again.*

/I…/ I look around. Where did Nisse go? There's no way she could have slipped out of the cave. /I need water./

Caea points to a back corner. *There's a spigot over there. Don't forget to take a capsule first.*

/Capsule?/ I frown at her.

So the minerals in the water don't make you sick. She takes my hand. *Come on.*

She squeezes through the crowd, leading me like a two-year-old who needs the bathroom. I scan the crowd, ignoring the writhing limbs rubbing against my clothes and the interested looks, searching for glimpses of silver.

"Ah!" A sharp jerk to the left and my hip bone smacks into stone. Catching my balance, I shoot a glare at Caea and rest my hands on the edge of a rocky fountain shaped like a gourd with blue water dribbling from a spigot in the ceiling.

"Comes from the ice between the layers," Caea says. "It's a little gritty."

The music is quieter in this corner. I can hear her without straining. "Yum," I say. Cups hang from hooks around the wide lips of the gourd. "How clean are these?"

Caea chuckles. "When you take one, you don't put it back. A guy comes every now and then to replace them and take the used ones."

I grab a clay cup and fill it with water. Caea puts her hand over the top before I can take a drink. "Capsule, Lyle."

Right. I fumble in the pockets of the fur coat, finding

the smooth box of purifying pills and pop one. "There."

She leans on the wall, nods her approval, and asks, "What happened over there?"

I toss the icy water back, cough up the crunchy dirt particles caught in my throat, and spit back into the cup. "That's disgusting."

"Stop stalling."

"I thought I saw someone. Someone I knew from Earth. A girl. She..." But why would she willingly touch me? Dance with me? I massage my temples, a mild headache forming. Crap, it's too soon for Sensuen's work to be wearing off.

"An Earth girl here?" Caea asks, tone dubious.

"No, she was Visiting from another place. It wasn't her. It can't be. I'm just..."

"Your head hurts? I thought Sensuen helped you."

"She did." A flash of silver. I jerk my head in its direction. The girl dances with another guy but turns her head to leer at me. She slides through the crowd.

A deep chill creeps down my spine, and the cup slips out of my hand. It bounces off my foot, spilling dirty water on the frosty floor.

"Lyle?" Caea reaches for me, but I jump back, shaking my head.

"I'll be back." I dart into the throng of people. I dance with some. Moving with the masses helps me get through them faster. I harden my barrier, letting nothing in, no distractions, as a slow throb works its way behind my eyes. A ripple of fear tremors in my stomach. If I lose it here with all of these people surrounding me.... I push harder, throwing myself into a threesome of guys convulsing like they're being electrocuted. They grin at me with white teeth, glowing bands around their throats.

They spin me and I use the momentum to surge through several more couples and quartets until I see her again, slipping into another room.

I follow blindly, no longer seeing the people who touch me, only her. Why do I want to talk to her? What more can I say to make it enough? Maybe...maybe I hope she's leading me into some ambush. A bunch of dudes with steel-toed boots will jump out of the shadows, knock me down, and kick me until I bleed. She needs to hurt me. I want her to. It'll make us even.

I emerge from the last room, entering one of the tunnels that leads up to the surface. Torchlight from up ahead catches on the white fur of her coat. I pull up the hood of my jacket, not wanting to be attacked by the cold when we exit the tunnel. Nisse doesn't seem to care about it. She reaches the end and forces the vaulted door open just wide enough for her to squeeze through.

I run to catch up, pushing with my hands then adding an extra mental shove to get the door open. It's heavy. I don't remember Nisse being particularly strong before. This doesn't feel right.

I flinch as a thin crack spreads across my mental barrier. Party-goer emotions seep in, bulging against my thinning wall. The pain behind my eyes multiplies, my ears ring. What's happening?

/..../

/..../

I can't send a message? Fear is wild inside me. It's the ambush. It's what I want, right?

I'll take it. I need to take it. The vault door creaks, about to shut again, howling wind beating against it. I catch it with one hand, and wriggle through the opening.

"Nisse?" I call.

And she's there, alone, back to the wind, waiting for me. Her hood's still down, hair blowing free around her face. She holds out a gloved hand. "Hello, Lyle."

Her tone is neutral, not furious as it'd been when I'd last talked to her. I flashback to being on Earth. To her face contorted with rage as she realized what I'd done to her mind and that we had made-out for nearly ten minutes without her being 'present' for it.

"What are you doing here?" I ask. Kupiku isn't a tourist trap. Outsiders usually come for business purposes.

Her smile is slow, her left cheek dimples. "I'm here to help you."

The crack in my wall spreads, fissuring out, a webbed windshield. Wetness on my upper lip. I touch it with my tongue. Salty copper. Blood. "What's happening to me?" because she has to know. I was fine before.

"It's all unraveling," she says slowly. "Your power. You can't fix yourself with temporary solutions. You know what happens when you do. Let me take you somewhere. I know what you need. We'll get it tonight."

She removes a glove. Her smooth hand touches my chilled face.

I jerk, a current of cold fire running through me. Freezing air burns my lungs.

Nisse wavers in front of me, suddenly taller, voice echoing. "Come with me. Let me show you how good it'll feel. You'll know you can't live without it; without Her. She's Gifted you. You are Her favored one now."

"Lyle!"

My consciousness splits as Nisse fades, replaced by a monster. Black empty eyes, sharp, shark teeth, long black hair, mental voice like a searing brand on the brain.

She stretches a shadowed hand to me. Feelings of desire, need...and surrender flood me. A cool blanket lays itself over my barrier, healing the fissures, stopping the shrill scream in my ears.

No more arguments, no more resistance. I need your help and you need Mine.

"Lyle!" Familiar voices call my name—Caea, Orion and Falun. The other side of me, the side that's terrified, stirs.

I'm bodiless, loose. The world slips as the ground comes closer to my face. Wind whooshes around my head. Impact is heavy, the thud hard. Pain rebounds through my skull. I bite my tongue, closing my eyes tight.

"I have him!"

"Why did he come outside?"

"Lyle, can you hear me?"

"Is he conscious?"

They all fade away on tendrils of silver smoke that remind me of the way Nisse's hair had blown around a face that had changed into something else.

Order was here.

My awareness dissolves.

SENSUEN STAYED WITH ME ALL night, keeping nightmares away. I wake up in a haze, auto-piloting through a morning routine and eating whatever's put in front of me. I ignore the concerned looks from Orion, Falun and Caea, and cut Sensuen off when she wants to talk about the Stone. I don't want to talk about it, or Her, or what happened last night, because I think I'm crazy.

I shudder. Can't get warm. Devon's sweatshirt is rank with sweat, but I won't wear anything else.

"We shouldn't have taken him out," Orion is saying as I approach the front foyer where they're waiting for the rover that'll take us to the dig site.

"It *was* good for him," Falun says, shaking her head. "He was unwinding. I saw him smile. I wish I knew what happened, why he went outside."

I clear my throat and they stop talking, staring at me. "No, no, keep talking about me. I'm not really here."

"All right then," Falun says, clapping her hands together. The sound's muted because of her gloves. Orion and Caea shoot her warning looks, and Sensuen frowns, but Falun waves them back. "You should stay here. We'll retrieve the Stone. I think the council should keep it, while you go to an isolation ward. I recommend the one on Bruhje. You shouldn't be out in the field. You're too…"

"Cracked?" I ask. "I know."

The foyer's skylight gives the room a warm tint, throwing dusty sunlight on the beanbag couches slouching in corners and the brown rug hugging the floor. It fails to brighten us up, though. Falun and Orion look shadowed, Caea uncomfortable, and Sensuen troubled.

"We can't change fate," Sensuen says. "The Stone will heal him."

"The Stone's nothing but a power amplifier," Caea says. "If he's shattered inside, then it'll wreak havoc."

"You don't understand," Sensuen says. "The Gift is touched by the goddess."

"A goddess not known for her healing hands," Caea

snorts. "I'm with Falun. Orion?"

Orion sighs, looking torn. "I..." He gazes at me. "Whatever you say you want to do is what I'll follow."

Running a hand through my hair, I plop down on a beanbag couch, sinking into the dark leather. My head's full of cotton balls, but it doesn't hurt; my shields are solid, but permeable. Day-mares taunt me. I feel them trying to sneak in and make me see Her. I bite my lip. Should I tell them Order spoke to me last night, that She was the reason I'd gone out?

Sensuen and Orion would probably believe me, and maybe Falun too. Caea had said they all believe in this cause. But did they all believe because of the goddess, or for love of the Allegiance? Orion and Falun might change their minds and pressure me to go down into the tunnel after all.

And I don't want to meet Order again, if She's down there. Her power, the way She makes me feel is amazing. But it's wrong. It's just another drug with another stupid catch. I need to be stronger before I touch anything made by Her. I can't need it.

"I'll stay here. You guys get it. I don't want to see it."

Falun's shoulders slump, relief on her face. Caea nods.

"You heard him, Sensuen," Orion says. "We'll retrieve the Stone and put it in a ward-case."

Sensuen is silent. I gaze at her. She stands by the door, mouth pressed into a straight line, posture at attention. "This isn't right. We're going against the instructions of the council, of Order Herself. This will bring about our destruction. This can't be a choice you make, Lyle!"

"I can't." I shake my head.

"And so, you won't," Falun says. "That is what we're here for. Don't worry."

The whirring of a rover comes from outside, an engine cuts.

"They're here." Caea frowns at me. "But you shouldn't be alone."

I should protest, complain that I'm not a baby, but I can't. I rub my thumbs on the fold of the sweatshirt. I wish Devon could hear me. He wanted to talk a lot, and now I finally want to talk, to not be alone. "Yeah, okay."

Caea pulls off her gloves. "Do you all need me to lead you, or can you go on your own?"

Orion actually laughs. "Majesty, you know I was a captain before this. With your permission, Lyle, I'll lead the team."

He and Falun are looking at me like they're about to get down on one knee. I almost want a picture of this. Knights in long fur pimp coats kneeling down in front of a king in a dirty sweatshirt. I can't hold in my laugh.

"Yeah, sure, man. Do what you do," I say. He'd do it better than me anyway.

"I should stay with you," Sensuen says in a low voice. "I can help you sleep." Her eyes glimmer. It takes me a minute to realize they're wet. Is she crying? Seriously?

I shake my head. "No, you should go." I don't want to deal with someone crying over me. I wince, seeing Nisse from last night with Order's black eyes, then remembering her real face, and her feelings under all that rage. She'd been devastated, because she had liked me before. I drop my face into my hands. "And when you guys find the Stone, maybe *you* should hold it and give it to the council, Sensuen."

"If that's really what you want," Sensuen says slow-ly.

"Yeah." I lift my head, taking them all in. Orion and Falun look ready for anything, Sensuen clasps her hands in front of her, head down. Caea's already stripping out of the coat and tossing it over on a couch. Underneath it, she's got on a pair of loose leather pants and a long-sleeved tunic. She could hang out at any mall in that, but something about her stance keeps her regal.

Falun opens the door before the driver can knock, letting in a gust of cold air that's devoured by one of the floor vents before it gets to me.

"There's been a slight change in plans," Orion says swiftly. "Only the three of us will be going, so we'll need extra technicians underground. Can you send the message ahead, so they'll be ready before we arrive?"

I admire Orion's confidence. His chin's high, and his words are smooth. That guy should be leader, not me. Order's one dumb goddess. Go torture someone else. I watch Orion, Falun and Sensuen pass through the door. It closes on its own.

A soft thump and a depression on the cushion next to mine makes me look over. Caea sits with one leg crossed over the other. "That was good," she says.

"What was?"

"Your decision." She palms my forehead. "You're clammy and pale, and..." she wrinkles her nose, "that shirt smells terrible. You are a mess, and a leader needs to know when they are a detriment to their own team. They would have been babysitting you down there."

I shrug. "You act like you think there are going to be monsters in the tunnel."

She hums. "I never trust untested places underground. The worst of the worst like to hide in the dirt."

Guilt and worry almost get me to my feet, to call my court back. It'd be my fault if something ate them.

Caea smiles. "They know how to fight, and Shreti-Hak is sending soldiers with them. They'll be fine, especially since they won't have to worry about carrying you around when you freeze up. New soldiers always freeze."

"You were just going to let me go down there and be surprised by tunnel monsters?" I ask, letting my mouth fall open at her grin.

"Not monsters," Caea says. "Animals. Creatures. They can get really big. I didn't want to scare you; I would have protected you with my Ansilse."

I scowl. Her Ansilse, her stupid daggers. The blades are longer than her forearms and gleam like polished glass, refracting the light like diamonds. But daggers against 'creatures'?

"I wish you were the brother who fights with his hands," Caea says with a sigh. "Xijure gets all the fun."

I roll my eyes. "You wanted to go with Devon instead?" I don't know why that thought makes me feel strange.

"Truth?" she asks, and I nod. "I didn't really care which one of you I got, so long as I didn't end up with the one who talks a lot."

Another laugh escapes me. "Lawrie? Yeah, he doesn't shut up, ever." Unless something's wrong. I hope he's okay.

"He'll be fine," Caea says.

"Did I—"

"No," Caea says. "I saw it on your face. My little

brother is with him. Ramesis is very responsible." She blows a raspberry. "Xijure is too. Your brothers are in good hands, and I'm sure Xijure and Ramesis are telling them the same things I'm telling you."

We don't talk much after that. Caea suggests I take a nap, but I don't want to sleep without Sensuen here to keep bad dreams away. She tells me to change my shirt, but I need to keep it on. It's become a security blanket. We end up back in the atrium, Caea teaching me how to mix colors. Her paints are water-based but they spread like oil on her heavy canvas paper.

"I want a set of paints like this." I look over at her cleaning her brushes.

She has the best profile I've ever seen. I want her to model for me, and I'm excited by the thought of turning to a blank page and starting a new project.

"Great good gods!" Caea shouts, her smile is full, eyes bright. "Is that a real smile, Lyle Lauduethe? Well, look at you! I knew there was a good-looking guy in there somewhere, even in that horrible shirt!"

I let out a breath, half-laughing at her. "You wish you had a shirt like this."

"Yes, so I could get paint on it and not care, be-cause I'd throw it away after." She chuckles and sets down her brushes, leaning forward and resting her chin in her hands, just watching me. "You aren't a very happy person, are you?"

I look away from her. "No."

"I'm sorry." Without reading her thoughts or emo-tions, I know she means that.

"Yeah." I put the stick down and snort at the dark brown fingerprints on Devon's shirt. "Oops."

Caea tosses back her head, a true cackle coming out

of her. "You'll have to throw it away."

"Never. I'm going to wear it the whole time we're here, just for you," I tease.

She blinks and gives me another full smile. "Hah! You're almost like a real person now. Is this who you've been hiding?"

A weird sensation flickers through me. It's not bad. It's just new and I don't understand it. She runs one of her fingers across a stain and stares at the color on her hand, showing me that awesome profile again. I like it. I...

"I like you, Caea," I say. "You don't bullshit."

She seems startled as she meets my eyes, long lashes flutter. "My translator is only so good. I don't what?"

"Bullshit," I say. "I can trust you to tell me the truth. And..."

"And?"

"Thank you for sharing this with me," I say, slow, nervous. I don't do things like this. "You didn't have to. I know I'm an asshole, but before, you overlooked that for business reasons. Now..."

"...I actually like you as a friend," Caea finishes for me. "Yes. You're right, you are an asshole, but that's not all you are."

The door to the atrium flies open. I spin around as several Kupi men in green and white leather onesies storm into the room. The guy in front rushes up to us, his boots stamping on the brown and gold color sticks I had laying out.

One look at his flushed face and wild eyes makes my stomach drop.

"What is it?" Caea asks, her tone commanding. She's on her feet, looking every inch a queen despite the paint staining her fingers red, brown and purple.

"There is a problem in the tunnel," the man states. "An energy ward has trapped the court inside. We cannot get to them and cannot see what is going on. We can hear them though. Captain Orion told us to get you. He said…" the man trails off and shuffles his feet.

"He said what?" I ask, standing up.

The man stares directly into my eyes. "He said the goddess wants you. She won't let them out, unless you come."

I step back, feeling a color stick break under my boot. Oh crap, oh crap.

Caea's strong hand grips my wrist.

Black eyes and sharp teeth invade my head. I rumple my hair with the hand Caea's not holding. I don't want to go. I can't go. I'm going to freeze. I'm going to panic. I'm going to throw up.

"I'm a terrible leader," I mutter.

But I can't leave them down there. They went because I told them to. Because I couldn't.

I make my legs move through the atrium door, Caea at my side. The men follow us, then branch off toward the foyer area as Caea and I head for our rooms to suit up.

I don't want to go.

I don't…

I throw up twice after getting dressed and set out to meet fate, or something equally awful.

CHAPTER 11

EVAN

MY HANDS SHAKE FROM DRINKING too much *kava*, but it's the only thing that keeps me awake after the *rax*. A deep itch runs along my spine, the endorphins in my blood telling my brain to shut down, to sleep, while they combat the pain. I hold out my cup for a refill.

Red liquid flows into it and I scowl at Jalee.

"I'm cutting you off," she says simply. "You won't sleep for a week, if you have any more."

"Good," I say. "I'll get more work done. What's going on out there?"

Jalee sighs and sits on the bed I refuse to lie in. "This planet's airspace is clear for now, but the rest of Sector 2 is in conflict. No ships can launch from here, and the communication silence with Leaders Two and Three is still in effect."

I sigh, pacing the healing chamber, the one I thought I'd escaped. I'd been carried right back here to recover from the *rax*. I growl through my teeth. *Fipping* Viveen. Great idea, disable your weapons during a war, because nobody needs us right now.

"What else?" Because I know she's holding back. Whatever's last is the worst.

Her brown eyes are steady. "Sector 4 is also in conflict. Rema and Zare are under direct attack."

F*ip*. My insides lurch. "My dad?" I'm the only one in my court with a parent still on Rema. I close my eyes to flashes of being twelve and coming home injured or soul-weary from training or battle simulations, hoping Devrik would be there to console and talk to me. And not being surprised that he wasn't. It took him months to notice when I moved out later that year, and longer than that for him to ask why. He doesn't like conflict and complications. Guess having a kid is both. He didn't comm when I almost died, never sent word when my brothers were named leaders. Hasn't tried to support me in any way, but the man is still my father. I can't say I don't care.

"Devrik was evacuated."

I sigh.

Jalee continues. "The rest of the Remasian Council and Zare's Parliament are safe as well."

"The people?"

"In shelters, still on planet. Our Home Guard is holding its ground. It is predicted that Remasian and Zaran Airspace will be clear in a few more *jewels* with only minor damages incurred."

A distraction then, but for what?

I need to get out of here. I growl and take a breath as the temperature in the room rises. Calm down. The Councils sound like they're handling things. But...but... but...

Another breath. "Any word on when I can see my

brother?"

Jalee shakes her head. "He's resting. You remember the first time you…" she trails off, brown eyes darkening. She falls in step with my pacing and halts me with one hand, while using the other to push the cup of red liquid to my lips. "Drink it all. You need it."

I sip at the cloyingly sweet berry juice, the extra sugar almost hiding the bitter bite of a revitalizing elixir. Jalee tries to camouflage terrible tasting potions in sweets, and never quite pulls it off. I shoot her a cross-eyed look of disgust as I chew on an ice chip. After a *wisp*, the tremors in my hands calm, but the pacing starts anew. "*Niobe-va.*"

I was unconscious for two *jewels* and can't go back on active duty for at least two more. Viveen must have been livid this afternoon. She only holds the curse for a few *wisps*, causing enough pain for me to get the point, but still be able to function. What possessed her to keep me under for more than a minute?

"*…remember the first time…*"

I was thirteen and I didn't want to practice anymore. Viveen held the curse for a minute and a half to truly let me know how terrible it was.

"Did Lawrie scab?" I ask Jalee. After my first *rax,* my skin had been burned to the point of peeling. I'd had to wear a flat membrane on my back for a week before it fully healed.

"No," Jalee says. "I was told it isn't that bad. He's just working through the shock."

The deep itch in my spine persists and my muscles twitch in response. Think of something else, something else, something else.

"Do you want to tell me what happened with the

Ruj prisoners?" Jalee asks gently.

Everyone's been skirting the topic with me. The vibe in the air is: Fix the weapon; don't set it off. Which means: Don't upset Leader One.

"Oh, now it's okay to talk about that?" I ask.

Jalee glares at me, then pinches my thigh. Others would take offense and call me a *cratch*, but not her.

"What did the monster tell you, Ev? You look haunted."

"Haunted?" I shiver, hating that word. "I'm not..." I finish the elixir and clutch the cup in both hands. "The invasion was the last thing it—the Ruj general—spoke about. The whole conversation he *wanted* to have was about Pandemonium and Order."

"On Onkurus, he claimed he was going to bring you to Pandemonium," Jalee says, "among other things." Her lip curls as my stomach churns at 'other things.' She leans against me. "You need to stop looking so pretty."

I snort, tension in my gut loosening as I kiss the top of her head. I love Jalee. My brothers tell me I have a sister on Earth, and I tell them they have one here. Jalee and I don't do this comfort stuff as much as we used to when we were little, mainly because others perceive it as weakness, but every now and again, we both still need it. Even Adonis and Desiri need it. Too many bodies, too much time on a cold ship, too many strangers in uniform not to be trusted.

I swallow a lump in my throat and tell Jalee what the Ruj general told me about Pandemonium's offer, his barbs about me not knowing much about godly hierarchies, and his warnings about The Maidens and Remasian Council. She listens quietly, then scoots away from me, head tilted, a signal that she's deep in thought.

"What are you thinking?" I ask. She's probably about to point out something I should have caught onto right away.

"That the others need to hear what you told me," she says. "I'll get them in."

I don't ask how she's going to do that or who she'll bring. Adonis and Desiri are givens. She leaves the room and I stare into the empty cup, depression seeping in. I'm always depressed after a *rax*.

How many times have I been burned now? Over the years, I forget. Viveen calls me her most stubborn. All her other leaders listened after the first or second time. Her words ring true. No one else fought her much. But how many people were hurt that didn't have to be, because no one said 'enough' or 'no' to her or Theorne?

Exhaustion fogs my mind, making everything less important than the need to sleep. Revitalizing potions pale in comparison to *kava*, the drink Lawrie dubbed the equivalent to an Earth beverage called espresso, only nastier. I sniff around the room, in search of more kava leaves to grind and boil. The door opens before I finish rummaging through a healer's drawer and I turn, heart lifting at the sight of Lawrie with Jalee and Desiri.

Lawrie, pale and drawn, looking so much like Dad after he'd had a long night out and trudged back home only to re-discover he had a kid, walks directly to me. He grabs me in a loose hug and pulls back, pupils huge.

"Are you okay?" His voice squeaks like Devon's when he's nervous. I don't think I've ever seen Lawrie really anxious, and it makes me feel good to know that some of it's for me.

I nod, because I can't voice that I'm all right. It's not completely true. "How are you?"

Lawrie rubs his eyes with the heels of his palms. "My back's all weird now. The Marks are a curse, aren't they? It's how the Remasian Council keeps leaders under control."

He looks like he might be sick and closes his eyes. I watch his shoulders straighten, and he stands taller, an *iut* taller than me, as his facial expression morphs from horrible realization into something more neutral. "Did the Peredils have Marks?"

His complete change is borderline scary. A defense mechanism, maybe. I tuck that observation away for future reference. "I don't believe they were Marked. They didn't have to find their Stones or be branded as leaders."

"How were they controlled, then?" Lawrie asks.

"They spoke directly to Order," Desiri says. "Guess when a goddess tells you to do something, you just do." She shrugs and comes to me, peering into my eyes. "How's your back?"

"Itchy," I grumble.

Jalee sits on the bed again and snaps her fingers to get our attention. "Tell them what that Ruj general told you, Ev. Lawrence, sit down next to me."

Lawrie blushes and I chuckle under my breath. I think he likes her.

Desiri flops down on the grassy floor and stares up at me. I tell the story again. By the end of it, Desiri's twining her long copper hair around her wrist, a tick that tells me she's in deep contemplation.

"Do you believe what he said?" Lawrie asks, hands on his knees, green gaze intense.

"I think it's important to note that the general believed everything he said," I say. "He really thought he was offering me a chance at salvation. He kept stressing that I don't really know what happens when gods win wars, but he and Pan's people do. And maybe the Allegiance Councils and The Maidens do as well and aren't telling us."

"Which leads to the question '*why* aren't they telling us?'" Jalee says. "Everyone knows things are *adjusted* in the Prophecy-stories. No religion recounts the story the same way. I suppose it would be interesting to read them all and try to piece together our own truth, but that could take *revs*."

"And we don't have *revs*," I say. "I listened to the general more than I would have, because I had a dream about Corin Peredil and Lady Imari."

Jalee, Desiri and Lawrie stare me.

"I'm sure it was one of Corin's memories. We all know he figured something out about Order and was punished. But in this new memory, I, he, was with Maiden Imari, and she seemed afraid for him." I try to grasp the memory, but the only thing my mind wants to remember is how pretty Corin thought Imari was in that lighting. "I think she knows what Corin found out."

I don't mention the kissing part or that I suspect they'd been in love. It's not important. "And when the general was talking, it made me think that Order's deal isn't what we think it is. And if we knew what the plan actually was, we wouldn't like it."

The more I talk, the more uneasy I feel. "Should we really believe Order, a powerful goddess, would start a long dragged-out war, just because She hates Pandemonium, or thinks He's evil?"

"You don't." Lawrie's voice is firm. He rubs his back and grimaces. "Because it's stupid. Of course not. But does Her real reason matter? We're here, we're Marked, and the people we like are on our side of the war. For us to win is a good thing for them. But why would that guy make you question it?" He touches his back again, gritting his teeth, as if the pain helps him think…or reminds him of Viveen's control. Order's control.

Foreboding crawls beneath my skin and I repress a full-body shudder.

Jalee frowns at me and fingers a carnelian pendant she wears under her uniform tunic. Her lips move soundlessly, probably reciting her personal mantra: *Courage, confidence, drive.*

"May I theorize?" she asks, voice mellifluous. The priestess she would have been, if she hadn't been chosen for my court, seems ready to give a sermon. I shut my eyes, remembering the little girl who was laughed at for saying prayers out loud. She blessed our meals and cried for a family that still lives on Faran, two stellar systems away from Rema. After a few *revs*, she stopped crying and kept her religion to herself, though I told her she didn't have to.

"Say what you want." I glare at Desiri's rolling eyes and nod at Jalee to go on.

Jalee lifts her chin and begins. "There were once two goddesses, Niobe and Dane, who jointly Created several stellar systems to join the greater pantheon of higher gods. They grew in power as the worlds they Created thrived. They grew in influence as they built more worlds."

Desiri groans, and I shoot her another warning look. If Jalee is telling parables, there is a point. Jalee continues.

"Lesser gods appealed to them, asking to borrow space in their territories, so that they could Create their own worlds and grow in power themselves. Dane allowed it, because other higher gods often lent space to lessors, but charged a tithe. It was another way to gain power.

Galaxies bustled with life, until several of the higher gods became bored. They left to Create new worlds in other universes. Some didn't like to share. As higher gods left, more space was lent to lesser gods who were slowly becoming more powerful as they claimed more territory. However, they soon realized they could not gain power from places Created by higher gods. They could not collect tithe from beings who did not sacrifice to them. And so, it became a game of conversion or destruction. A planet that a god could not draw power from was a waste of territory. They could use the space to build new worlds.

But soon the question became: was it easier to convert a people or to build a new world? As new worlds were Created and Converted, lesser gods gained so much power that they felt they could challenge the higher gods. Wars were fought, god-blood was spilled.

Dane fell, and Niobe mourned Her sister goddess. Her tears Created the Ystalli lakes on Faran. The beings who mourned Dane became known as Danecian Priestesses. Niobe accepted blood tithes for Dane, taking in Her sister's strength, but chose not to stay.

The New Danecian Faith preaches that all of the gods are gone now. Only their traditions remain. And we keep them, in hopes that our devotion may bring Niobe back to us." Jalee bows her head, a signal that she's finished talking.

There's a beat of silence, before Desiri grumbles, "That whole story is *pidge*. Obviously, the gods aren't all gone. And what does it have to do with Order and Pandemonium?"

Jalee's eyes glitter. "It's just a story…" and I know it hurts her to say that, "but think about it. Many faiths acknowledge the existence of higher and lesser gods. I don't know all of their names, but the descriptions of what they do are the same. Apply that to Order and Pandemonium and tell me which type of god you think they are."

"Lessers," I say.

"Lessers that want more power by taking stuff from each other," Lawrie says. "So, they're fighting each other…using us. And the losing side has to give in to being conquered or bad things happen?"

"What happens when gods win," I murmur. Jalee's words rang true. She believes that story as much as the general believed what he said. This time, I don't repress the shudder. I feel like I'm being warned. A voice whispers in my ear, one I know, but strain to hear. *"Trust no god."* The lights in the room flicker, once, twice, then flare to full brightness. And I'm on my feet, ready to fight, pushing the voice away.

"That's a wake-up call," Jalee says, wary eyes on me. Not a moment later, both she and Desiri touch the base of an ear, the universal signal of accepting a compal network message. They nod.

"The Allegiance Councils demand your presence," Jalee says. "Adonis has been standing in for you, but they want you in the meeting now."

Which means nothing good.

I get to my feet, but let Desiri and Jalee lead the way because they actually know it. Lawrie falls into step beside me, marching like he's headed for an execution. I pat his shoulder once, and he grins at me with a second of warmth and reckless spirit. It vanishes as soon as we enter the meeting hall. I shield my eyes; a fake skylight throws bright artificial sunshine into the room, powering the digital long-table at its center. It takes a moment for me to adjust. The hallways are relatively dark compared to this. Desiri and Jalee shift, putting themselves behind Lawrie and me.

"Nice to have you functional again, Leader One." Theorne's tone is frosty.

I raise a brow. Someone is annoyed. "Stay close to me," I whisper in Lawrie's ear and make my way to the 'soldier-side' of the display table. Fighters and strategist always sit on the opposite side of the table from councils and presidents. I clasp hands with seven generals from Kregat and Ylaon: red robes for Kregat, baggy green jumpsuits for Ylaon.

I stop beside Adonis and Ramesis, and they move over to make room for Lawrie, Desiri, Jalee and me. Adonis gives me a once over, grey eyes sharp.

"I'm better," I tell him. His eyes close for a moment before he nods. I touch two fingers to my shoulder. "Hi, Ram."

Ramesis's lips twitch into a smile at my salute, then his eyes dart to the other side of the table, where Theorne, Viveen and seven other councilors stand with The Maidens, two of whom I've never met. They all look sour, aside from Imari who keeps her head down, long hair in a single plait over one shoulder. She glances up so quickly I almost miss it, her dark eyes flashing as they meet mine. I don't understand her expression. It's not afraid, not sad, just somber, resigned to whatever is happening.

"Someone leaked the location of the fourth Stone," a councilor with dark yellow skin and pupil-less fuchsia eyes—a Parfekan, Gold Allegiance—speaks in a tone-less voice. "There are Su flag ships portaling into the Sretha territories as we speak. Allegiance portal signals are still jammed. Without access to the network, all ships sent to protect the area will arrive *cycles* too late."

"What about Lyle and Devon?" Lawrie blurts. "Are there bad guys jumping to where they are right now?"

My chest tightens. Devon and Lyle aren't with large entourages, just their courts and one Harliel a piece. If Su or Nazflit are going after them in full, that won't be enough.

"We are still on communication silence from both parties to avoid any more leakage," says a male general, tall with bulky muscles stretching his red robes tight. "But no portal energy has rippled near their locations since their emergences. We believe those operations are running smoothly."

A small flicker of relief loosens my muscles.

"Our dilemma remains with Leader Four's Stone. We have our best working on the portal technologies. Perhaps, we can—" a general begins, but is cut off by an "Excuse me," from one of The Maidens.

"Why are portals the only means of transportation being discussed?" The pink-haired Maiden has the voice of a siren, unnerving yet alluring. Her dark eyes are dreamy and faraway. A smile touches her full lips.

"Portals are creations born of magic and science. Science fails, but magic does not falter." She raises her hand, blue and purple light, a congealing sphere of magical energy pulled from the surrounding elements, grows in her palm. "There are spells."

"That you are only mentioning now?" A general in a green jumpsuit snarls, then lightens his tone, pale yellow features turning apologetic. "I apologize, Fair Maiden Nialiah. But why withhold another means of travel from us?"

Lawrie shifts closer to me, his unique smell of salt and some Earth chemical tickling my nose.

"Because," the red-haired Maiden, who has to be Hellene if the pink-haired one is Nialiah, speaks up, "using Old Magic for travel comes at a price for bodies not in tune with that mode of transportation. Kahanna invented these spells for my sisters and me to record, but we have never used them."

I stiffen. *"For bodies not in tune... Kahanna invented these spells."*

"Are you talking about fae travel?" I ask. Magic Breeds can teleport, jumping between planets, planes of existence, or short distances, depending on their strength and type. But, so far as anyone knows, only full-bloods can do it. My brothers and I are one-eighth. The more diluted the blood, the less likely it is for offspring to have fae magic, much less display active traits. I'm an anomaly for having them, as is Adonis. But neither of us can teleport.

"Yes." Nialiah grins. "The magic that vibrates within them allows them to phase. The recorded spell alters living rhythms, temporarily making them echoes of the fae. During this time, the being in question should be allowed to slide between the fabrics and a guidance spell can direct the soul to its intended destination. In theory, of course."

"In theory?" A male councilor with a reedy voice speaks up. "Fair Maiden, this spell seems like it is complicated and perhaps even limited in the number of times you can perform it. Can it even be done on multiple bodies, on armies, with weapons and ships?"

"No." Nialiah's dreamy look fades, irritation shading her expression. "It is to be worked on a select few, and those few must be suitable subjects. And you are right in that we can only perform it so many times."

"Then, how——" the same councilor begins.

"We," Nialiah cuts him off, "will use the spell on our resident Leaders of Rema, King Ramesis and their chosen companions to send them as close to the coordinates of the fourth Stone as the magic can take them."

"And if our Champions are trapped on Nakshera after that, or captured, what are we to do then, my Lady Nialiah?" a fair-haired, brown-skinned female councilor asks.

Hellene answers the question in a superior voice. "You were all near enough to witness Leader One use his gift. Do you honestly think two leaders imbued with Kahanna's power along with a Harliel King could be captured or trapped so easily? One Peredil was more than enough to take down an army of fighters."

"But did those fighters include any of Pan's Champions?" I ask, honestly curious. If anyone would know, it would be The Maidens. "You knew Pan had Champions. Did the Peredils? Did the former monarchs of Zare?" I glance at Theorne and Viveen. "Did you?"

The generals and other councilors stare at Viveen and Theorne. Silence in the room.

"We have never seen them," Viveen says, her sharp face long and shadowed. "Only heard rumors."

"Kahine, or Pan, as you call Him, had no Champions, until after Kahanna's first mortal Champions were dead," Imari says. She raises her head, looking directly at me. "He adopted Kahanna's idea after He saw what bonded warriors could do for gods. He was not as successful. His first Champions were not impressive. We lost touch with that warrior line as we heard nothing more of them."

"Do you have any idea how many Champions Pan has?" I press. "In a fever dream I had on Onkurus, I saw about twelve of them."

"He never had that many," Nialiah says. "And He cannot have made more. He would have cast the same spell Kahanna wove. It cannot be adjusted."

"She cast a spell?" A councilor asks. "A spell for Champions?"

"How else do you think we were summoned to Her?" Hellene asks. "How the Gifts were created? Kahanna is a Goddess of Magic, as is Her son."

"Spells have rules," I murmur, thinking of Corin and Order. Did he learn the rules? Did he find a loophole or caveat in Order's plan for us? I toss a look at Jalee and Desiri, wondering if they're trying to piece together what I am.

"Are we proposing a travel-magic attempt to Nakshera to look for the fourth Stone?"

Hearing Ramesis's voice in a meeting is strange. He rarely speaks up in large groups. People called him the 'shy prince.' Now, he's the shy king. I shoot him a smile that he shakily reciprocates and turn my attention to the councilors who have final say on such a decision.

The councilors gaze at each other. I'm sure one is a telepath mentally connecting them all, because they seem to be communicating. Heads bob and shake, nostrils flare, ears wiggle, and scowls and sneers are exchanged.

I crack my knuckles and look to my own peers, meeting pensive gazes. The generals stand, jaws clenched, shoulders high. Imari stares at her small hands on the display table as her sisters trade long sighs.

Finally, a councilor clears his throat. "We will attempt the transportation spell. The fourth Stone must be retrieved as soon as possible."

I tap my index and middle fingers to my left shoulder, my signal of acceptance. The generals around the table mimic me.

Ramesis's lips thin and then he speaks again, this time directly to The Maidens. "The spell doesn't sound reliable. Have you performed it, or seen Order work it on someone not fae?"

Hellene's smile is flat. "No, but I have faith in the goddess. Do you?"

Ramesis is quiet.

An uncomfortable beat passes. Talk of religion hardly ever finds its way into our meetings halls, but it's a different game with The Maidens in play.

"Will one of you be coming with us?" Lawrie asks. "It'd be a good idea, since you know the most about the spell."

Hellene narrows her eyes, but before she opens her mouth Imari jumps in. "I will join my fellow Champions." She splays her fingers wide and lifts her head, gazing at Hellene until her sister looks her way.

"You are not the best—"

"I *am* the best," Imari says. "My talents would better serve the leaders and King Ramesis. They will need stronger protection circles and bindings than the ones their priestess witch and mage can cast. Also, you will need a destination anchor, a familiar aura that meshes well with your magic: me."

The councilors babble about proper procedures. Generals grumble about timetables and ask about transportable supplies. I let it all roll through me as I follow Imari's actions and reactions. She's cool and collected, seeming to take in the conversation, and avoiding eye-contact with me.

The meeting is dismissed moments later. The councilors and generals clear the room, and only the Champions remain.

"Stay here until we call for you," Hellene says, stern and proper. "Preparations for your travel must be made. We will have all of your needed items, such as weaponry and provisions, delivered. I suggest you use the networks to familiarize yourselves with Naksheran terrain."

She turns on her heel, breezing out of the room, her sisters following. I try to catch Imari's eye, but she keeps ignoring me.

When it's just me, my brother, my court, and Ramesis left, I turn to the display table, bringing up maps, information, and images of Nakshera. The small planet is half-wild, mostly jungle, with some villages and townships tossed in for variety.

"Do you guys know what to do in a jungle?" Lawrie asks, peering at the display of information. "I mean, I don't know all of your individual skill-sets and this place looks pretty rough. If the spell The Maidens are gonna work doesn't take us to the place we were supposed to land in, then we have to hike through these jungles. We can't even let the envoy who was originally going to meet us know we're still coming, so they won't know to look for us."

He sounds agitated. His fingers tap the screen. I understand if he's scared. I poke his forearm, offering him a smile I hope is reassuring. "We've all handled worse. You'll be all right with us."

His eyes glitter with something, curiosity, and maybe sympathy. Is he sorry for me, because I said I've handled worse? I poke him again and look to the group. Everyone is gathered around the display, prodding at information and enlarging images.

No one speaks, faces are tense. I smell salt on more than just my brother's skin now, but I won't ask how confident anyone feels about letting The Maidens attempt to cast our bits across the universe or if they think this plan will work.

Feelings and thoughts don't matter now. We have our mission. And once I accept a mission, I can't go back. Too much depends on its success.

Lawrie returns my poke and I gaze at him.

"Will you teach me how to skin a snake when we get there?" His grin is shaky, but he's trying to get back to being the crazy kid who helped me flood a ship's cargo bay. That had been practice.

I chuckle. "If we catch one, I'll show you how to make a belt."

This will be real.

He nods, eyes serious despite his joking smile, as if he knows what else I'm thinking about.

Barely a *jewel* passes before The Maidens re-enter the hall followed by the members selected for Lawrie's court carrying satchels or supplies. Hellene glares at us all.

"Let us begin."

12

LAWRENCE

THE GREEN LADIES OPEN A wall to a hidden room. The space is egg-shaped with a curved ceiling and floor. Feels like being cocooned, but the room isn't tight. We can spread out with gear on our backs, though Adonis and Ramesis have to duck their heads at times.

The Maidens go to a refrigerator-sized pantry built into a back wall. Bottles, jars, boxes, vases, and cups line the shelves. Everything's labeled. Wish I could read the language. I so want to grab a jar of eye of newt or powdered horn. Nialiah pulls a long drawer out of the bottom of the cabinet and removes a large black bowl while her sisters grab at jars and corked vases.

Beside me, Chasyn shivers. I glance at the redhead. Out of all my court members, he's the only one The Maidens deemed able to travel. The others, a guy named Tian and a girl named Bhela, failed the test. Only those of us who made Nialiah's rod light up, indicating a favorable response to magical energies, made the cut. She ran it over each of our bodies, and laughed when the wand spat sparks over Adonis and practically caught fire as it neared Evan.

Nialiah brings the black bowl to the center of the room and kneels in front of it, her funky harem pants pooling like a skirt around her. The stuff in the base of the bowl is crumbly until she pours in a liter of blessed water. Using a fat, marble-textured pestle, she grinds the materials and fills vials with the concoction, lining them up next to her.

She gestures to the vials. "The priestess and mage will drink first to gauge any reactions."

Desiri scowls. "Yeah, sure. I'll be a taste tester. I drink before Priestess here, though. I'm less likely to die of poison."

Nobody looks surprised. Evan told me Desiri ingests traces of different toxins daily to build up tolerances. It's a hardcore mage thing that I respect but think is crazy. Desiri takes a vial from the line-up, sniffing it once then throwing it back like a shot. If I had a lime, I'd toss it to her.

She hands the empty vial to Nialiah and thumps her chest with a fist. "Spicy." She sits down, crossing her legs. "My body's tingling. Vision's turning geometric. Everything's circles and rectangles."

"No pain?" Evan asks.

"No, just…" she stares off into space. "Is this what you and Adonis see when you analyze things? Particles, threads that move when you concentrate." She reaches out, wiggling her fingers in the air. "Feels cold, wet."

Adonis and Evan make brief eye contact.

"It's working," Evan says. "Tell us if you feel sick, Des. Jalee?"

Jalee takes her potion, sipping instead of downing it

in one gulp. She sits beside Desiri, waiting. Like Desiri, she describes what she feels—no pain, no dizziness, just tingling limbs and altered vision. Ramesis goes next.

"And now you," Hellene says to Chasyn, who presses his lips together before stepping forward to take his vile.

"Oh, hey." I put out an arm to stop him. "I think I should go before he does."

"And I think I should go before my brother," Evan says. He and Adonis move as a unit, coming to my side.

Nialiah chuckles. "Evan Lauduethe, you do not need to drink the potion and neither does your Naiad partner. You need no alteration, just the power. And…" She reaches into a deep pocket of her fluttery pantsuit and extracts a palm-sized cloth bag. She throws it to Evan, who catches it in one hand. He flinches, blinking at the bag and shoving it in one of his pockets.

His Stone?

"Its call is dampened by the wards on the new cloth I spelled for you," Nialiah says, "but you will need to remove it from those confines eventually."

Evan glares at her and turns his eyes to the circle of potion-infected people. "Ramesis, how are you feeling?"

"Bubbly," the king says, voice even. "How long does this sensation last?"

"Not long, which means we need to hurry," Hellene says. "We need to begin the recitation. Drink the potion, Leader Four."

"No." Chasyn places his hand on my arm, pushing it back to my side. "I need to drink it first, to make sure it won't hurt you. We're both elementals. None of them are, so we don't know how it'll affect us."

"But—"

He's drinking before I can get another word out. I watch as his face reddens, and he huffs. "My tongue's burning!"

"Ah shizz! Get him water!"

"He's fine," Desiri says. "The stuff is spicy. I told you all that."

"Spicy?" Chasyn shouts. "It's *nova*! *Oi Makla*!" Chasyn plops down next to Ramesis, breathing through his mouth now, and staring around in wonder.

I take the vial extended to me, observing the group on the floor reaching out to touch empty air and staring off into space like they're completely lit. 'Gotta do something' has me sniffing the liquid—smells like tropical punch—and slurping it up. It runs down my throat like thick cough syrup and burns like siracha. I sputter for a second, eyes watering, heart fluttering, as the world teeters, turning 2-D, people around me springing off the flat plane like figures from a pop-up book. The air shimmers, the wooden walls ripple, breaking apart into green and brown M&M-sized spheres that spin like planets. Curly strings sprout from the ceiling, tensing like cobras ready to strike. I reach up and a string-cobra rears, sniffing my fingers. They're cold, the fibers like mist coiling around my wrist.

I stare at the strings and particles hovering around me, body tingling, insides rumbling. Power. These are elements: hydrogen, oxygen, carbon. Instead of just sensing them, I can see them. Vibrant colors flare as I gaze at my brother and his court, at Chasyn and The Maidens. Their bodies are molecules that I can touch.

"Awesome." I stumble over my own feet. Something soft on my arm guides me to the ground. I sit, running my fingers over the grassy floor, counting the grains and threads.

"I think he's fine." Evan's voice hangs in the air, disturbing the water molecules, but blending with the air currents that swirl above my head. He and Adonis, flat like paper dolls, fold to sit with the group.

The Maidens chant, but it seems like they're each saying different things. The words clash with no harmony, the phrases crashing over each other, but at the same cadence. It sounds awful. Paper doll Evan grimaces, rubbing at his ears.

My stomach lurches. The air in the middle of the circle sparks a bright purple, then splits open like a piñata going one-on-one with a crowbar. A black ball of nothingness forms in the center of the room. My guts roll, I breathe through my nose, swallowing against the bile wanting to jump into my throat. The black hole pulls at my insides.

"It hurts," Ramesis says.

"Hold fast, king. It will only last a moment longer. I am going now." Imari leaps through the hole, body vanishing out of existence.

"I sense her," Nialiah says. "She has arrived. Mage, go!"

Desiri staggers to her feet, stumbling to the hole. She may have tried to leap like Imari, but she seems to topple in, disappearing with a short yelp.

"Contact," Nialiah says. "Priestess!"

One by one, Ramesis, then Chasyn, then Adonis disappear. Evan stands and reaches down to take my hand. "Do you want me to go first?"

"I..." I shake my head. If everyone else can jump, so can I. Just hope there's a barf bag on the other side. I let Evan pull me up, then practically fall through the hole, legs giving way.

Holy friggin' shizz... My head implodes, brains squishing, eyes popping, internal organs going to mush. Can't breathe, can't see.

And then nothing. I'm flying, but not. I don't have a body. There's no light, no sound. Free. Empty. Alone. Hot, wet earth. Sharp edges. Something pricks my skin. Skin. I snap up into a sitting position, hands and knees planted in thick jungle dirt, surrounded by tall blades of green grass. I gaze up at a deep blue sky almost hidden by green foliage. The trees sport fat, black trunks that erupt into skinny branches with tent-like leaves that cast shade on the jungle floor. They shield me from the worst of the sun's heat, but the humidity's like being in a rice cooker, condensation clinging to the glass lid as steam pours through its spout.

Sounds of retching to my left. I turn my head to see Chasyn in a crouch, shoulders heaving as he hacks and spits onto the ground. I crawl to him, my limbs heavy with exhaustion. I feel like I pulled two all-nighters in a row with no caffeine to stave off the shakes. I make it to Chasyn, barely able to stay up on my hands and knees. "You okay, man?"

He gives a couple of dry heaves, before he answers. "Not dead. So, I'm okay. Tired, though. Head's spinning. You?"

"Wiped out." I push myself fully onto my knees, my vision swims for a second and clears. "You still seeing molecules and shapes?"

"No." Chasyn wipes his mouth.

Around us, there are moans and groans. Desiri staggers to her feet and pulls Jalee to hers. The girls wobble together for a moment and stop. Ramesis is on his knees, rubbing his face with both hands. Imari touches Desiri and Jalee's shoulders and moves to touch Ramesis as well. They seem to steady.

But wait. People are missing from our group. Imari walks by Chasyn and me, her fingers brushing us as she lets her arms sway by her sides. A wave of cool energy shimmers though my body, not quite a Starbucks mochaccino, but good enough to knock the grogginess out of my system. I stand up, feeling Chasyn rising next to me as I look in the direction Imari is heading, wanting to find my brother, Adonis and Nialiah.

A crescent of black space the size of a long board spins like a pinwheel behind the outlines of three shapes. The shapes slowly fill in with color and mass. Evan, Adonis and Nialiah stand in a cluster, clutching each other for a minute, then jumping apart as if electrocuted. The crescent disappears. Nialiah wavers on her feet, green skin pale. Evan holds up his hands, staring at them, whirls around to look at the group, then back to Adonis and Nialiah.

He says something, but it's garbled. No, it's in another language. Imari speaks it back and Evan stares at her, like she's a new person. He cocks his head at an angle, and I frown. He doesn't seem all there. His eyes are open a little too wide. Maybe he's messed up from the trip. He says something else, sounds like a question. Imari answers, and his smile sends warning signals down my spine.

"Uh…" I step back, crunching down on Chasyn's toe. I hear hushed voices from the group behind me. Imari rushes back to us, yelling, "*Naxhis!*"

We're encased in a bubblegum white barrier so tight the bodies of the others behind me press into mine.

Somebody needs a mint. Bad.

"Nialiah! Cast a *restai*!" Imari shouts.

Nialiah sways, a drunk woman asked to walk the line. Adonis moves behind her, hands on her shoulders, resting his nose in her hair. From this distance, his eyes are completely gray, no whites.

"What's wrong with them?" Jalee asks. Her voice is loud in the bubble, rebounding and hurting my ears.

"The traveling, it seems to have affected them," Imari says. "It could have awoken dormant Magic Breed genes."

"*Fip-sha*!" Desiri spits. "Let me out. I can smack sense into them."

"No." Imari focuses on Evan and Adonis around her sister. Evan studies Nialiah, touching her hair and clothing, like he's never seen any of it before. Adonis snarls at him and Evan glares as Adonis pulls Nialiah to his chest. The Maiden sighs but doesn't fight the move.

"Her power is too depleted," Imari says.

"They're not going to eat her, are they?" Chasyn asks. "I heard that Breeds eat…" He trails off at the dagger-eyes he gets from Desiri and Jalee.

My stomach twists, watching my brother act like a great big cat inspecting a trapped bird. Maybe he *will* eat Nialiah, if Adonis doesn't first. But Adonis doesn't seem interested in her as food. He pushes her long hair aside, kissing her neck.

"What the—" Ramesis breaks off.

"*Niobe-va*," Jalee says. "Imari, *you* cast the *restai*! Or show me how to do it, before he rips her clothes off, and we all have to watch!"

I almost laugh. She sounds so scandalized. But I don't want to watch it either. We gotta do something.

"I cannot cast spells on *people*! I only lend power in those situations. And you cannot handle—" Adonis's hand slides under Nialiah's collar. "—by the *Bales*, Nia! Wake up!"

One of Nialiah's hands comes up to grip the back of Adonis's neck, something silver, probably Order's armband, glints under her long sleeve. Adonis falls back, stumbling and wiping at his lips, eyes huge…and normal. Well, as normal as they get. Nialiah turns on Evan, lips moving, hand out. Silver light glimmers as Evan looks ready to leap out of the way, up into a tree branch maybe. He can jump hella high. The spark hits him dead in the face and…he sneezes? Twice. Really? He shakes his head, gazing around the jungle, eyes fixing on us in our bubble.

Imari claps her hands and the bubble pops with a light snap. "Catch her!" She points.

Nialiah's black eyes slam shut as she pitches to the ground. Adonis grabs her, swinging her into his arms bridal style. He looks lost.

"Did…something happen?" Evan sounds so confused.

Desiri opens her mouth, but Imari talks, "Yes. And now it is over."

"What's over?" Evan scowls at us. "What are you all looking at?"

I don't know how to answer it. Should somebody tell him that he went kinda crazy for a few minutes? Would it scare him? He gets his magic from fae genes that are dormant inside me, but fully awake in him. With that magic comes drawbacks. Has he ever been like that before? I want to ask, but I glance around at faces that look uncomfortable and ready to move on with the mission. It feels strange to let it go, though.

"Come," Imari says, "we have ground to cover. We were not able to get as close to the Stone's coordinates as we hoped." She looks at the sky. "I think we are a half a day's trek from its location. Lawrence, do you feel anything?"

Huh? "Oh." I shake my head, still staring at my brother. He and Adonis come toward the group, Adonis carrying Nialiah. Chasyn moves closer to me, and yeah, he's the one who needs the mint.

I close my eyes, thinking about the Stone and wanting to sense it. "Am I supposed to do anything special?" I ask. I'm not some psychic trained to fall into trances.

"I don't think so," Evan says. "I feel this thing when it is rooms away, but not so much when it is warded, like now."

"So, it could be warded off," I say.

"But from what?" Evan asks. "I don't think anyone would sense it, but you. Do you sense my Stone when I'm not using it?"

I shake my head. No. The Stone of Magic has no pull for me right now. "Did you sense your Stone on Onkurus at all?"

Evan blinks and looks thoughtful. "No. I only ever felt it when I was dying." He fingers the end of his braid as he hums. "Not just hurt, but actually dying. If I'd been close to it before then, I didn't sense it. And, granted I was delirious, I don't remember traveling very far. Don't think I could have."

"Well, you did not know you had a map to the co-ordinates of your Stone on your back," Imari says, but her eyes are on Evan. "I memorized the course to Law-rence's Stone. Maybe he will feel it as we move closer, and we can figure out the distances you can be from your Gifts before you lose contact."

Ramesis clears his throat. "Let's pick positions and go then."

"Right." Evan tucks his braid inside his jacket collar. "Desiri, you scout ahead, Adonis, you stay in the middle with Nialiah, Imari and Lawrie. Jaleel, rear protections. Ramesis, you want a flank?"

Ramesis nodded. "I'll take the left."

Evan looks at Chasyn. "You're not mine. Follow your leader."

I stare. "You want me to give him orders?"

Evan rolls his eyes at me. "You do what you want. His job today is to protect you, though. I'll lead."

Just like that. Maybe Ramesis wants to lead, but the king doesn't say anything. He seems fine taking orders. The group begins to move, our pace steady but not grueling. Sweat beads under my collar and rolls down my back. I'm gonna have pit stains in an hour. Chasyn walks beside me, eyes darting left and right. I probably need to be as hyper alert as he is. This planet's writhing with things similar to black mambos, pythons, tigers and wild dogs with sabretooth canines. The *digi-reels* I saw in the display table in the meeting hall were not kid-friendly. Most of them featured after-dinner carnage and local survivors sporting stumps. I suppress a shudder as my anxiety locusts eat their young, then divide and make new babies in my chest.

A big black bug latches onto my cheek. I swat it off, feeling it burst under my palm. Itchy liquid coats my skin. "Ah shizz!" I use my sleeve to try to sop it up.

"Don't touch it." Chasyn shrugs out of his uniform jacket, leaving himself in a short-sleeved white shirt. He pours canteen water on the jacket fabric and dabs at the splotch on my face as my eyes water. Crap, this is worse than the poison oak I fell in when I was ten.

The group doesn't slow down as Chasyn tends to my face. I struggle to keep up. I feel the last of the gunk come off. My skin prickles where it was, but the crazy itch is gone. A circlet of cold air revolves over my cheek, cooling the surface—Chasyn's power.

"Better?"

"Yeah. Thanks." I watch him out of the corner of my eye. He nods and goes back to checking out the terrain. His fingers twitch like he wants to pull a weapon, though I know he doesn't need one. He's the weapon.

"There's a city ahead with red clouds over it."

Evan's voice comes from above me. I tilt my head back, gazing at my brother standing on a slim tree branch, knees bent like he's about to spring straight up. And he does. He disappears into the thick foliage for a second, then jumps down, landing in front of the group with a thud.

Evan rubs his hands together. "The red clouds look like the dust plumes thrown up by Su ground-rovers. We need to consider this planet occupied. Mission compromised at a red level."

"Meaning our end coordinates are probably being patrolled," Ramesis says.

Desiri seems to appear out of nowhere. "Enemy seventeen *ka* over. We need to redirect our course."

"How many?" Evan asks.

"Squads of six and eight, but there're more behind them," Desiri says. "I could take them out, but..."

"Everyone will know we are here." Imari looks up at the sky again. "We may need to go through the coves.

But it will add *jewels* to our journey, and I am sure the Su are already searching for the Stone. They could beat us to it."

"So, speed is priority." Evan tilts his head back, eyeing tree branches. "What say we go over them?"

"Over?" I ask.

"We'll climb the trees," Evan says. "Up past the layer of thin branches are thicker branches with leaves wide and strong enough to hold our combined body weight. I didn't see anything up top that could hinder our path."

"Except for the serpents and predatory felines!" Imari says.

"You have a better idea?" Evan arches a brow and Imari's cheeks puff out.

I chuckle again. She looks like an angry fourth grader. Wonder if she'll stick out her tongue next. This lady is no dignified Maiden. She's like a kid, like one of us, most of the time anyway.

"No." She sucks her cheeks back in.

"Ramesis?" Evan asks.

"If we're attacked in the air, will the branches and leaves support a battle, or will we be easy targets?"

Evan smiles. "Oh, we won't climb to the very top, we'll stay under leaf-cover."

"For the serpents to attack," Imari huffs.

"I'm not afraid of snakes." Desiri twirls a dagger between her fingers. "And I'm sure our priestess here can cast some protection circles. And maybe you too. I mean, that's why you said you needed to come with us. Funny how you only now let us know that you can't cast on people. You just make barriers and provide a power source for other people to work big spells with. Right, Maiden Girl?"

Imari doesn't flinch. "Sums it up. I am the most expendable Maiden."

"Yet, Big Red didn't want you coming with us." A feral smile stretches Desiri's mouth. "Doesn't seem like she trusts you much."

"Enough." Evan glares at them, then turns to Ramesis. "Matter resolved? Shall we climb?"

Ramesis blinks, as if surprised to be asked, before he nods and moves to the wide, black base of a tree, his small gray knapsack of supplies secure on his back. Ramesis climbs the craggy bark like a pro, followed by Desiri, then Jalee. I'm shocked she can climb. She seems too refined for scaling trees, but she's just as good as Ramesis and Desiri. They disappear into the foliage.

"Lawrie, you good at climbing or you need help?" Evan asks. "We can go up together. You're not that much bigger than me."

I blink at him. Go up together? "Dude, you are *not* giving me a piggyback ride like some baby monkey." I climb trees all the time, even skinny slick ones with no branches to grip. It's like going up a P.E. rope, wrap and pull. I march to the tree, running my hands over the hard, flaky bark. Up close, I smell its musky, dark chocolate odor and notice the shingled nature of the tree's coat. Easy for hands and feet to take hold.

I grab hold of a rough shingle, then another, and wedge my foot onto a lower grip. I jump to give myself a boost and up I go. The bark scrapes my palms and bites at my skin through my uniform, but I don't hear or feel any tears. The boots make me clumsier when trying to catch footholds, but it isn't that hard. Just wish I had a ski mask or something for my face. I taste blood from various nicks as it dribbles down my forehead and cheeks. I hear Chasyn beneath me, huffing and cussing. Guess tree climbing isn't something he does all the time.

Adonis, with Maiden Nialiah on his back, sails past me, straight up through the foliage. Evan follows after a beat. They both jump like anime ninjas. I don't know that I would have been mad had Evan told me he was going to *jump* up the tree with me on his back. That would have been fun.

Ouch! I scrape my face against the bark, skinning the bug-burned cheek. It stings all over again. I tilt my head back to see the thick leaves above, the ones that should be sturdy enough to stand on. Just a minute more.

My head breaks into the leafy clearing. Warm moisture coats my face, like I'm in a car wash getting a layer of wax spritzed on. The heat here is damper, muggier, than on the ground, probably trapped here by the leaf cage we're in. The darkness is broken by a glowing orb hovering over Jalee's open palm. I pull myself all the way up onto a thick branch. Like standing on a fat diving board, it dips a bit, but doesn't give way. Leaves thick and wide as tarps fan out from it. The others stand on the green leaf blanket as if it's carpet over a concrete floor, no worries of weak spots and falling through. I jump off the branch to join them, bouncing. It's like a trampoline reinforced with steel. I do a low back flip, almost landing on my feet. I sprawl on my butt. The leaf's skin is sticky and pungent with sap, like skunky maple syrup.

Imari comes up last, looking no worse for wear. She dusts off her palms, eyes scanning us, lingering on me still sprawled, and then she moves past us, going forward. "I should be in front." She holds up a hand to stop Evan from disagreeing. "I am the one who knows the way. It will be faster."

Evan nods. "Desiri, take the rear this time. Adonis in the middle. Ramesis and Jalee, flanks."

The group falls into their places around me, and I spring to my feet, following Evan as he moves to walk slightly in front of Imari. I feel Chasyn behind me. Walking on the leaves is as tiring as running on the beach. My leg muscles cramp and burn and sweat clings to my body making my fatigues feel like crusty bath towels after a while. Creepy cawing bird sounds and the purring of big cats in the trees with us have me whipping around in different directions. They sound too close. Every now and then, I catch a glimpse of glowing eyes, yellow and slitted, in the gloom beyond Jalee's orbs of light. She adds several more to the first she created, letting them revolve around her body before the tiny spheres flutter away, positioning themselves at the front, back, flanks and rear of our group.

Imari puts a finger to her lips and halts us. She gives Evan a sideways look before grabbing his hand and whispering something unintelligible. He balks, looking ready to snatch his hand back, then jerks, eyes going wide. A gust of muggy air nearly bowls me over.

"What?" I snap my mouth shut at the serious expressions I get from everyone else.

There are voices below, deep and urgent, talking in a garbled, throaty language. The sound is amplified, as if they're speaking into a mic. I wonder now about Imari's murmuring and the blast of air. Had she cast a spell?

"*Fip fa*," Ramesis says.

"I'll find that spy and eviscerate him." Desiri grits her teeth.

"What?" I ask again.

"They know we're here already," Jalee says. "Even

seem to know where our portal may have dropped us. They're going to raze the wood."

A shrill note of fear rings in my ears as my body goes stiff, then fear evolves as my heart thumps and adrenaline kicks in. My legs don't hurt anymore. I breathe in energy. The air is charged with oxygen, carbon and an unknown element that makes 'gotta do something' sing my high school's spirit song. I'm ready to fight.

"What do we do?" Chasyn asks, sounding breathless. I glance at him, noting his rigid posture. He scared? Maybe. He's a soldier, yeah, but he's not like Evan and his squad, or even Ramesis and Imari. Hell, he's not even like me when it comes to being crazy. But he places a hand on my shoulder, as if to say, 'I got your back, man.'

All eyes go to Evan. Even Imari is waiting.

Rumbling engines below. Sounds like tanks and eighteen wheelers. The leafy canvas under my feet vibrates, the air growing warmer, thicker. The musty smell of sap intensifies, sharpened by the tang of singed chocolate and rusting iron.

Fire.

"Run. Imari, guide me!" Evan hauls Imari to him, turning for her to climb onto his back.

"Left, go left!" Imari shouts and Evan veers into the darkness beside us.

"Keep up!" he yells.

Bright orbs encircle him as we follow, the green carpet under my boots starting to go gummy with heat. Shizz. The ringing in my ears increases as my blood bubbles, and soon I'm running fast enough to be a few paces behind Evan. There's no way he's going as fast as he would if he was by himself, but I still feel like an Olympian doing a 100-yard dash that won't quit.

The burning in my lungs and muscles, the ache in the arches of my feet, the cloying smell of smoke, the fumes stinging my eyes, all make me wanna howl and cackle. We can beat them. We can outrun the flames. We can do anything.

"Left! Straight!" Imari keeps hollering directions. An orb struggles to stay on Evan's tail, throwing light on his boots. The brief flashes letting me see which way he's going next.

"Here! We need to drop down here!" Imari says. "If we stay high, we will lose our path!"

"Is the ground clear?" Desiri asks.

"No." Adonis's cool voice is ice in a pitcher of black tea.

Evan halts. I nearly ram into him. The group crowds around, hot, heaving, sweaty, hands on knees, but seeming alert on a level I hope I'll reach one day.

"How many below? Desiri asks, extracting a long, thin sword from a sheath on her back.

Evan shuts his eyes. "I hear ten heartbeats. The rest are farther. Could be a basepoint."

"Do you think we can take them? Should we take them?" My voice comes out high, eager. "I mean, we have to go down, right?"

Evan's eyes open, the clear green ovals fix on me. "I'll go down. Wait for my signal to join me."

"*Ayo…*" Desiri trails off, staring at Evan. She shakes her head and bites her lip. Stalking toward him, she shoves the pommel of her blade in his hand. "Clean it off before you give it back."

Evan flashes a grin, leaps to a branch and steps off, disappearing through the green. There's no sound to indicate he ever hits the ground, but other sounds are unmistakable: a strangled scream and a loud curse cut short, followed by several solid cracks, like nervous knuckles, but magnified. Bones breaking?

Someone wails words, like they're praying, that turn into wet, throaty gurgles, then nothing. I hold my breath and smear wet curls across my face. I want to strip off my jacket. My hands shake. I want to see what's going on. Those noises... Are they enemies going down, my brother getting hurt, or both? He's all by himself. I whip my head around, trying to make eye contact with Desiri, Adonis or Jalee. One of them needs to go down. Hell, I'll go down.

The group stands in a huddle. Desiri and Jalee seem calm. Adonis, however, looks ready to drop Nialiah on her ass and jump down this tree. I open my mouth. "Adonis, we should—"

"Shh!" Ramesis hisses.

It's quiet below.

Then a soft *tap, tap, tap*, travels up the bark. Such a tiny noise, but I hear it loud and clear. "Is that…?"

"Our cue," Desiri says. "See you on the ground."

She bounds to the trunk of the tree, using her boot to push at one of the leaves, making an opening for her to pass through and climb down. Ramesis follows, then Jalee. Chasyn pats my shoulder. "You go before me, so I can watch your back."

I scowl, but do what he says. Whatever. I bounce to the trunk, doing as the others had, using my boot to push back a leaf. Holy shizz. They made this seem easy. Pushing this leaf is like using a leg-press. It takes me a few seconds longer to make a gap big enough for me to slip through. I grab the bark, groaning as it scratches at me again. Climbing down is harder than climbing up, because it's a blind descent. I stretch out a foot and kick in the bark for another hold. Above me, I see the top of Chasyn's boots as he starts down.

I can't look toward the ground until I'm closer to it. I study leafless branches of other trees, some bearing fruit that looks like purple apricots. Gray worms with heads the size of my fist inch around the food, nasty mouths full of feelers stretching out like tongues puncturing the bulbs.

"Don't stop climbing down, Lawrie," Chasyn says.

Had I stopped? I blink, turning my attention away from the worms and picking up the pace. Buzzing insects nip at my hands. I blow at the black bugs and chance a look at the ground to see how far I am from it. I make out the tops of several heads. Good.

A few feet closer and I hear bits of conversation.

"...in a crypt, deep."

"...catacomb."

I'm just above their heads. I push off the tree and fall the rest of the way. My knees buckle but hold. I straighten, eyes seeking Evan first. He's splattered in brownish-red goop. Free curls dangling around his face drip with the stuff. A rank, rusty smell wafts from him. I scan for the bodies of the soldiers he'd finished off.

"Buried in vines," Evan says. "Can't leave bodies lying around."

"Are you okay?" I ask.

Evan nods. He wipes Desiri's sword with a black towel and returns it to her. For effect, I guess, he tosses the bloody towel into the air, blows a small jet of fire at it and turns away, as the cloth erupts into flames, leaving nothing but a cloud of ash behind.

Chasyn thumps to the ground a foot away from me.

Chips of bark sprinkle on our heads from above.

"Move away from the base," Jalee says, and we all stand back as Adonis jumps down, landing right where I'd been, with Imari on his back and Nialiah in his arms.

The sleeping Maiden mumbles, her narrow features scrunching up, eyelids fluttering and black eyes cloudy. Imari slides off Adonis's back and touches her sister's cheek before moving to Evan's side.

"We should continue this way." She nods south.

Evan follows her gaze and frowns. I feel the wind blow unnaturally, like its being willed the wrong way. I want to pull it back. My guts grind. Someone's tampering with my elements. Wait…

"I don't sense anything that way. Move," Evan says to no one in particular.

Was Evan manipulating the wind so he could hear and smell farther out? I grin for a split second until a weird discomfort takes over me. Evan using his magic has never felt like a violation to me before. What does that mean?

My feet stumble forward as Chasyn pushes me from behind.

Desiri and Ramesis, blades out, cut through underbrush, thwacking vines and thick leaves out of the way as they travel up front, with Imari telling them where to go.

Evan walks next to me, but addresses Imari. "I picked up a little information from one of the soldiers. Right before I slit his throat, he was praying to Pandemonium, wishing him success in taking the Stone. It's in a crypt, through a catacomb in an old graveyard. Sacred site with a temple. It's undoubtedly surrounded. We can only get so close now."

Imari looks confused. "The only sacred sites on this planet are on the Makanac lands."

"Mmm…" a moan from Nialiah. I look back to see she's now riding Adonis piggyback. Her large black eyes are open, her hair a long rat's nest. "Makanac. The co-ordinates do not place the Stone in that holy territory. It should be in the eastern marshlands. There are no temples there."

"I don't like this. It sounds like someone's moving things around," Ramesis says. "We're walking into a trap."

But we don't stop moving south. The smell of the fires in the woods diminishes the deeper we go. What are we gonna do? I scour my brain for any tidbit of random genius and get Disney lyrics instead. Brain's got nothing.

"There is a village about twenty *ka* from here," Nialiah suddenly says. "By then I will be strong enough to cast identity illusions. We need a safe space to think and maybe a room for the night."

"Trohyaern?" Imari asks. "That is where—"

"Which is why we are going, Sister," Nialiah says, voice chiding.

Imari says nothing, and I don't miss the look Evan shoots her. She pointedly turns her head away from him, craning her neck as if searching for people hiding in the tall grass and bushes.

Evan snorts. "Twenty *ka*, huh? We can make that by evening, but we need to detour to a water source." He scratches at his blood-crusted clothes. He's pulled all his hair off his face, making a massive man-bun out of his braid. "I can't turn up in any village looking like this. Also, anything with a nose will smell me a *ka* off."

"There's a water source a short distance to the

west," Adonis says. "I sense it."

I hate to admit it, but I'm jealous. I reach out, letting my heart beat with the rhythm of the earth beneath my boots, wanting to sense the water too. There, a cold presence, hydrogen, oxygen, and minerals that feel gritty but pure. The molecules swirl. A moving body of water, a stream maybe.

Chasyn bumps my arm. I raise a brow at his smile.

"You're looking for the water with your power? You find it?"

"Yeah."

He looks like a proud parent. "It'll become second nature to you one day. You just have to be more receptive to what's around you. You won't even have to reach."

"Good advice," Adonis says.

Chasyn and I both jump. Of course Adonis can hear us. "You gave me great tips too, man."

A sniff, and Adonis goes quiet again. Nialiah rests her cheek against his shoulder. "Water would be nice. A good splash might clear my head."

"Adonis, take lead," Evan says, but 'gotta do something' wiggles in my chest.

"Uh…" I smile tentatively and Evan glances at me, a light frown on his face. Bet he hates that I interrupted him.

"What?"

"Actually," I stand up straighter, "let me guide us. I feel where it is, and I want to."

Evan sizes me up. "Fine." He turns to the group, walking backwards and gesturing at me. "*Ayo*, all, follow the leader."

He laughs and I feel good. I bet he knows the significance of that phrase from Earth. Fun game, but I don't remember ever playing it with him. Time to catch up, bro.

"This way."

I lead the team.

13
DEVON

I DIDN'T KNOW THERE WAS a balance between freak-out and geek-out, until I found it. Walking on the floor of an ocean is incredible. It's like walking upside down. Devices in the shoes of my wetsuit keep me weighed to the white, sandy bottom, but if I release them, I'll float over a hundred feet back up to the surface.

Coral-like structures, some as tall as me, some only to my waist, create rows and winding mazes for us to navigate. Ilea walks in front, holding a device with my Stone's coordinates plugged into it. A yellow light flashes, meaning we're still on course. The thing goes black at wrong turns. I thought following a map would be easy, but the display's not 3D, so bends on the map look like turns, when, in reality, they're just dips in the ground and we should have kept straight.

Every now and again, Xijure moves forward to take the device from Ilea and shake it. He reminds me of Dad battling the GPS on his phone. On a road trip, he snatched the thing from its mount and threatened to throw it out the window at least twice for telling him about an exit after he passed it. I bite back a laugh.

"How are you doing, *babila*?" Mineshka asks, her soft voice tickles through my earpiece. She and Loniad walk on either side of me, both on alert for danger. I learned that the twins' main task is keeping me in one piece through this mission. I thought I'd hate it, but Mineshka's coaching as we sank to the ocean bottom kept a real panic attack at bay.

"I'm okay," I say. She tried to coax me to forget I was under thousands of pounds of crushing water only protected by a skimpy alien wet suit. Nope. I can't forget those facts, but I can watch her and everyone else carry on the mission in spite of it and get inspired. If they can do it, so can I. At least that's what I keep telling myself.

"Stop." Ilea's voice is strong. She comes to a dramatic halt and we all gather around her as she stares at the map and then at her feet. "We need to go down."

"Huh?" I ask. "We're already down."

"We need to dig?" Xijure asks.

Ilea nods. "There's something under here."

A treasure chest? I want to ask, but I probably shouldn't spit out anymore stupid statements. Doubt they'd get the joke anyway.

Ilea passes the map to Xijure, then kneels, closing her eyes and scrubbing her hands over the sand. She murmurs a string of words, something about honor and permission. My translator catches every fifth or sixth word. Writing it off as another magic spell, I rock on my heels, waiting.

Ilea's head snaps up. "There's more water beneath the ground floor here, flooding some type of structure. I think it's a crypt."

My heart stops. A crypt. That's where they put dead people. "So, we're in the wrong place."

"We're not in the wrong place, little leader." Ilea sounds like she's grinding her teeth. "What we want must be in the crypt. There will probably be an opening here, since this spot is the exact coordinate on your back."

I gulp and watch as Ilea moves out of the way and Loniad, Mineshka and Xijure start plowing with their hands and shoving sand aside. Whoa. They put my moat-carving days on the beach to shame. I expect the ocean to wash all the sand back in place, but it doesn't. There's no current. I kneel, putting my hands in the sand and copy their movements. My fingers are rakes as I smooth away handfuls of grains. The hole we dig goes down about a foot, before I feel something solid under my fingertips. "I hit something."

"I feel it," Xijure says.

We work faster, scraping sand off the face of a trap-door made of metal. It looks like an entrance to an under-ground bomb shelter. Two metal rungs covered in green gunk sport finger grips. Xijure grabs them and pulls, muscles straining.

"*Fipping pidge, trefi ba ku…*" a steady stream of cuss words my translator won't touch pours through my earpiece as Xijure keeps tugging. "That's not opening. It must need a key," Xijure huffs, letting go of the rungs and rubbing his hands.

"Or," Ilea comes to kneel beside me, "it needs someone stronger to pull it open." She looks at me, and I blink.

"Me?" Of course me. But if Xijure couldn't…but then again, strength isn't his power. "Okay." I reach down, taking the rungs and giving a test pull. There's resistance. I tug harder. Nothing. I'm ready to let go, but, on my other side, Loniad nudges me.

"You're not trying," he says. "Pull it like you mean it." He mimics grabbing the rungs and flexes his muscles. "Pull."

I can't help but laugh. I love this guy. He's hilarious, but his words make me want to do as he says. "Okay, coach," I say. Pull like I mean it. I tighten my hold on the crusty rungs and breathe in, thinking about what I need to do. I remember fighting Xijure and just letting go, letting my body handle things. It seems to know its own power, and if I get out of my headspace and just go with it, maybe I'll know that power too.

I stop thinking, and feel my muscles begging for action, my heart pumping from…excitement? Realization hits. This is how I felt before games or meets, when I bounced and stretched, ready to play. But the feeling died down when the games actually started because I knew I needed to reign in my abilities or people would figure out what I was, and freak out.

Now, I grin, because this excitement doesn't have to die. Everyone knows what I am here and thinks it's the best thing since double cheeseburger pizzas.

I pull and there is no resistance. It's like yanking open double doors to a deep freezer. There's hesitation due to suction, but the trapdoors open without hitch. I push the doors down on either side of the opening, and stare into the darker water inside.

"I'll inspect." Ilea pushes me and swims through the entrance headfirst.

I stare at her, then at my hands.

Loniad claps me on the back. "Good!"

Mineshka squeezes my shoulder. "Excellent job."

I grin again, alive with energy. "That felt amazing!"

Xijure shakes his head. "I'm impressed. I really gave it all I had, and those things didn't budge. You didn't even look like you were trying."

Because I don't think I was. But I don't know how Xijure will take me saying something like that. The man's got to have some pride, and I don't want to embarrass him. I shrug at Xijure and rub my hands as he did earlier, though they don't hurt.

"I found a lever." Ilea's voice. I look down into the crypt and can't see her.

"Hold on, we're coming down." Xijure grabs the sides of the entrance and pushes himself through, swimming down as Ilea had done.

"You next, Devon," Mineshka says. "We will follow you."

Bracing my hands on either side of the opening, I heave myself through, pushing my arms down and kicking my feet as I go. A thin light shimmers through the darkness, Ilea and Xijure huddle in a corner of the empty square room. I maneuver myself onto its rocky floor, feeling the shoes of my wetsuit connect with the ground and clamp on. I shine the light in my headgear on the walls; they're bone-white and bare, no cracks, no wear and tear.

"Devon," Xijure calls.

I turn back to Xijure and Ilea just as Mineshka's body comes through the entrance. I trek over to the king and the mage and they part to let me see the metal joystick stuck in the wall. I look around for the old-school Atari it has to belong to. There are no buttons but, like the rungs, there are finger-grooves where a hand should grip it.

"Do you want me to push it up?" It's set in the down position.

"Wait until everyone's inside," Xijure says. "I think we have a good idea of what it probably does."

"And what's that?" I ask.

"It'll probably pump all of the water out of here," Ilea says, "or start the equipment that does."

"What about the open door?" I ask. "Won't that suck all the water out there in here?"

"It could." Xijure rubs something off the faceplate of his helmet. "But I doubt it. That trapdoor isn't made to be closed from the inside, so there must be some failsafe in place for when the water in here drains."

"If that's what it does," I say. "What if it lets in a bunch of sharks? Or releases a wall of spikes?" It is a joystick after all. This could be just like a video game.

"What is a shark?" Loniad asks.

Oh man. "It's…uh, just think huge, killer fish. Lots of teeth, attracted by blood in the water." Loniad's thick brows burrow together.

"I can handle traps," Ilea says. "Don't forget who you've got on your team, little leader."

I roll my eyes at her. "If you're god's gift, maybe you need to be pushing this lever, not me."

She puts a hand on her hip, mouth opening, but then she closes it and clears her throat. When she looks at me again, her mouth is a straight line. "I've completed many missions where I was the point person for setting off and diffusing traps on foreign terrain. Trust me."

I bite the inside of my cheek, not wanting to say anything that'll piss her off while she's being semi-civil to me. So, I nod. "Fine."

"Everybody, move in close," says Xijure. "Just in

case."

Mineshka and Loniad crowd against my back, and I grip the joystick, pushing it up. Something clicks and a whirring sound, like a large propeller or fan blade on high, erupts through the floor. The whole place shudders and the trap door slams shut. The room goes completely dark, except for the skinny beams of light from our head-gear. The sound of water draining from a Titanic-sized bathtub echoes around us. The sudden change in pressure hurts. My blood is on fire and my head throbs. I can't hear anyone else over the roaring in my ears. My eyes squeeze shut in an effort to keep them inside my head.

Stop. Stop. Stopstopstopstop!

Pop.

My ears unclog and I suck in air. My lungs ache from lack of oxygen. Was I holding my breath? Not a shocker. I thought I was going to explode. Who remembers to breathe when they're in the middle of blowing up?

"Whew." Loniad wobbles and falls to one knee on dry ground. Mineshka drops a hand on his shoulder and yanks him up, calling him the equivalent of a crème puff. Loniad grumbles at her, but he looks green through his faceplate.

It's awful, but seeing this tough guy turn green makes me feel better. Now I'm not the only 'crème puff' down here. Xijure and Ilea move along the wall, pushing on a particular section.

I pat Loniad on the back as I walk past him and his sister to join Xijure and Ilea. "Find somethi…" I trail off, staring at the long crack in the wall. "Is this a door?"

"Think so." Xijure stands back and gestures to me.

"Push it and see."

I don't think 'push it and see' is a good plan, but, like the joystick, it's probably what we need to do to go forward. I press my shoulder against the wall and put my weight behind the push. It doesn't take much for the wall to give way, opening into a hall with bright yellow stones peppering its sides. It's a glow-in-the-dark maze.

"Wow." I step inside and move so the others can follow. "We don't really need our lights anymore. Do we just follow this?" This could be it. At the end of this hall could be the Stone.

I close my eyes, remembering the hag goddess with four boobs, screeching and breaking a table that turned into weapons, jewelry and gemstones. My past-self, Padain Peredil, had held that thing for real, but I'd been him in that dream. Felt the Stone's power shoot through my hand, making me feel stronger. There was a need for it. A need I'm starting to feel now. I scratch my itchy palm, the one that'd held the Stone.

"Devon?" Xijure's beside me.

I glance at him.

"Are you all right?"

I bite my lip. I don't know. An anxious feeling stirs in my gut. I want to move forward. Something inside me whispers that I should go deeper into the maze. Is this Stone-Zoning? Do I look like Evan does when he thinks about his Stone?

"Devon?" Xijure's voice is louder. He waves a hand in front of my face.

"What's going on?" I hear Ilea ask. She appears in my periphery.

I need to answer them. "I-I'm fine." Or maybe I'm not. "I feel the Stone."

Xijure's eyes widen. "Straight ahead?"

"I don't know. I need to move forward. It's…" I struggle. "It's like a magnet pulling me." My chest tightens as I resist the call and keep my feet planted. But when I ease up, and allow my legs to move, the pain lessens. I have to go.

"Follow me," I say, relaxing, just like I did when I stopped thinking about holding back my power. My body knows what needs to be done. I walk forward, not looking back to see who's behind me.

ILEA HATES LETTING ME WALK in front, but I know where we need to go. Turn left, veer right. Bits of the yellow maze walls crumble as the halls narrow and I shove my way through, shoulders scraping rock. I hear groans.

"Devon, slow down," Xijure calls.

I don't want to. I'm too close to stop. My heart beats louder with every step. My hands tremble in anticipation. I'm almost there. "Catch up with me later." A small hand grips my shoulder. "Ah!"

I want to whirl around, but the space is too tight. Small, careful movements bring me face to uptilted face with Ilea. I feel like a giant confronting a kid. "What?" I ask, voice sharp.

"Half your team is stuck!" Ilea snarls. "Look at us!"

I blink and peer over her head. In the golden glow from the stones on the walls and the light from my helmet, I see Xijure, turned sideways, crab-stepping out of Mineshka's way as she tries to pull Loniad forward. He's too thick.

"If this hall shrinks anymore, they won't fit at all," Ilea says. "Do you notice how tight it's getting? Do you care?"

I duck my head. If I can barely fit through here, of course the guys behind me would have trouble. I hadn't thought of them.

I need to keep going.

"I…" A deep pain throbs through my stomach, like something pulling at my intestines.

"Are you okay?" Ilea asks. "You're flushed, and your eyes are glassy." She grabs my hand, holding me in place, so I can't move.

"Y-yeah. But the Stone's really close. How about I just run and get it, and all of you hang back?"

"You can't go on by yourself." Xijure huffs as he crab-marches to us. "But you're right that we aren't all going to make it. Ilea and Mineshka should go on with you. Loniad and I will go back to the start. You can contact us, if anything happens."

Ilea snorts. "And what will you do?"

Xijure levels her with a look. "What we can. None of us came down here expecting anything to be easy, but we'll figure it out. Order wants him to get his Stone, so this task obviously isn't impossible."

"Not for him," Ilea counters. "But for the rest of us?"

Guilt eases the tugging in my gut a bit. I don't want anyone getting hurt because I can't stop myself from running through this maze like I'm the only person that matters. "I really should just do this alone, and you guys should be finding a way to get out of here when I come back."

"The way to get out is probably on the side with your Stone," Ilea says.

"So, it's a deathtrap for anyone who's not me or too big to fit?"

"Who knows?" The snark is gone from Ilea's tone. Her eyes are grave. "But we all know what we pledged to do, and that's to work with and for you. Your success is ours. If this is it for me..."

"I know. Your friggin' husband kicks my ass!" The otherworldly tug to move forward is completely gone now. "Let's go back. We'll get that door open again and you guys will go out and I'll come back in."

"No," Mineshka barks and I jerk, elbow scraping against a wall. I stare at her, scared at the anger on her face.

"His Majesty can go back. But *we* are your court. You do *not* order all of us away. Our job is with you. Loni doesn't fit, I do, so I go. Ilea goes."

I don't know what to do, what to say, how to feel. They're not listening to me. I'm supposed to be the boss. If they get hurt, it's still my fault. My chest constricts, my breath shallow as my heart forgets its job. It pumps liquid fear instead of blood. I try to back away, but the walls hug close, making my retreat a struggle. I fit, but just barely. Claustrophobia sets in. I wasn't scared before. How was I not scared? How could I just... Spots swim before my eyes.

Something grabs my headgear, metal clicks, and fresh air rushes in. The faceplate is gone, pushed aside. I'm going to puke.

"Calm down." A small hand rubs my back. "You're all right."

No.

"Take a deep breath, or you're going to pass out."

No. I have to get this suit off. I have to get out of this tunnel. I have to—oh God. I'm underwater. If I get out of here, I'm still underwater. How did I even let myself go down—a blast of icy cold hair hits my face.

I feel ice at the tip of my nose. My eyes clear as I gulp a deep breath, then another, and look straight ahead, at Ilea. Her light blue gaze is steady. "You're panicking. It's all right. You have every reason to be afraid, but you don't have to be. Nothing will happen to you while I'm here. Nothing is getting past me, or Mineshka, or Loniad."

I breathe, still staring at her, locking into her calm confidence, wanting to make it mine. Where was that cool Devon who sank to the ocean floor like a boss? The Devon who forced open trap doors to get here and who surged ahead like a...

The pull. The need to move. The Stone.

It tingles in my stomach again. My breathing settles and dizziness fades, panic draining away, because the Stone can fix this, right? It'll get us out of here safely. I just need to find it, hold it.

"Your eyes are going glassy again, little leader," Ilea says. "Stay still for a moment." She removes her headgear and attaches it to the belt of her wetsuit. Then, she removes mine, setting it on the ground and taking my face in her hands. "You're very warm and your skin is slick. Is your suit running hot?"

"No. I don't think so." I don't know. I don't feel hot or cold, just the need to keep going. It's close. So close.

"What's wrong with you then? Are you sick?"

No, it's... "I have to get to the Stone. It's..." I'm about to sound like a lunatic. "It's calling me or something, and it hurts when I stop."

Her eyes widen as her hands fall away from my face. "Oh."

Oh? Just, 'oh,' like this is normal? It's not normal.

"I'm going crazy." I run a gloved hand through my hair and lick at the sweat trickling from my scalp down to the corners of my mouth. But my body aches with the need to go, to leave the others behind if they won't come. The Stone doesn't belong to them anyway. Just me.

"Is he all right?" Mineshka calls.

"Relax, soldier. He's getting over a panic attack." I start at the closeness of Xijure's voice. He's only a foot or so away, peering over Ilea, at me. His dark eyes seem to read me. "What's your decision on your court coming with you, Leader Two?"

Ilea picks my headgear back up, pushing it into my shaking hands. She waits...for my command?

"Uh..." I can't see beyond Xijure now. His big body hides Mineshka and Loniad, Loniad who's stuck in the narrow hall. Licking my lips again, I make the decision. One deep breath, two deep breaths, then, "Ilea and Mineshka will come with me. Loniad, go back to the beginning. Xijure, do what you want to do, man, but I don't think you'll be much help if this space doesn't open up soon."

Xijure nods. I can't tell if he's proud I manned up and made a choice—oh crap. I made a choice, didn't I? Is this one of the decisions that'll affect the world? Damn, I hate this! I hear muffled voices. Xijure traverses backward. A minute later, he's gone and Mineshka's in his place, walking to Ilea and me.

Both women watch me, ready for me to do something. What? Rave, rant, go crazy?

"You know the way," Ilea says after a beat, eyes never leaving my face. "Lead us."

Mineshka nods. "We're behind you, *babila*."

I should be tired of her calling me 'darling,' especially now, but it's all right. I think my head needs it as much as my body needs the Stone. The word grounds me a little, brings me back to them, my court.

"Okay." I turn my body around, so that I'm facing unexplored territory. "Come on."

Deeper into the maze we go.

We walk through more hallways so tight I have to turn sideways and some wide enough for us to travel side-by-side. Mineshka hums a happy tune, though her bright eyes remain alert. I bet she'll kill anything that isn't us moving through the dark. She catches me glancing at her and smiles.

"My brother is probably complaining about missing out on the adventure," she says, her tone amused. "He loves missions like these. He wanted to join an exploration party, before he was chosen for you. There are a few headed out to several new planets the Silver Allegiance wants to terraform, if possible. Being a part of your team was the more interesting job."

I blink. I don't know what 'terraform' means. There are a lot of big words I don't understand, and, unlike Lawrie, I don't keep a dictionary in my brain.

"Uh, cool," I say, because if Loniad had wanted to 'terraform' it must be fun. "That's nice of him, and you, to want to come with me." But who were they before this? I do want to know more. "Before, on the ship, you said you were trained fighters. Even though that was kind of what you were brought up to be, did you have choice to be something else?" I mean, yeah, on Earth you can be anything if you have the money, but these people seem so different.

Mineshka snaps, "Watch your step!"

I skip over a rock in my path and get back to the subject. "Didn't you want to go exploring and be something besides a soldier?"

"Well, I don't know. I rather like beating people up."

I laugh, think about it some more and laugh again. "It's fun?"

"Very satisfying, but only in true combat. In tournaments, not so much. You have to hold back, and there is nothing at stake, aside from a championship title."

"I love winning titles and championships." My football and basketball teams have state titles. I miss them.

"What's wrong? You're sad, now. I thought you said winning makes you happy."

"It does." I shrug it off. "So, when you're not beating people up, what do you like to do?"

Mineshka sighs and a light smile crosses her lips. "I like to spin tebils."

"What're tebils?"

She looks as confused as I am.

"What do you mean 'what're tebils?'" Mineshka asks. "Tebils! They are the hooded cups, the ones that hold the menkere baes!"

Her face, when I continue to stare at her, is hilarious. It's a mix of frustration, disbelief, and determination as she tries to describe what she's talking about using additional foreign words and hand gestures. My laughter doesn't make it better.

Behind us, Ilea clears her throat. "Sorry to interrupt your good time, but we are on a mission."

I jump, turning around to look at her, and trip over my own feet. Mineshka halts to catch me, which makes Ilea have to stop. An awkward silence passes between us. Ilea huffs, rolling her eyes, and we all start walking again.

"Thanks." I grin at Mineshka. She feels like a partner-in-crime now.

"I think we're both in trouble with teacher now," Mineshka whispers.

"I'm never not in trouble with teacher," I mutter, but I'm still grinning. I bump Mineshka's shoulder with mine and Mineshka bumps back. A warm blanket of camaraderie settles over bad nerves and fear of failure.

Sudden, intense pain in my ribs doubles me over.

"Devon!" Arms wrap around me and slowly my knees meet stone. Someone is lowering me.

"Are you all right? Can you talk?" Mineshka and Ilea ask the same questions, or maybe they aren't. I can't distinguish individual voices over the pain in my chest.

My heart hammers then flutters, like it's going to stop, then pounds, and falls into its regular rhythm. Struggling for air, I clutch my chest, reflexive tears streaming from eyes, making my faceplate blurry. I fumble for the release on the side of my headgear and the plate snaps to the side. Moldy air seeps into my lungs. This place smells like a Chuck E. Cheese ball pit.

"Devon?"

My vision blurs for a second as an invisible hand grabs my heart, pulling. I crawl forward until I stagger to my feet. If I don't move fast enough, whatever this is will rip my heart out of my chest. I panic, breathing in but not out. I can't breathe out. The world loses color, my head swims. Hands on either side of me hold me up, keep me from falling down.

"...a trance?" a voice hisses.

"...but he's in pain!" another says.

"...keep him up and moving."

"...looks like he's going to die!"

"...keep him up and moving."

An eternity passes. My lungs burn, can't think right, can't really see. Everything's gray matter. The voices around me bark and snarl at each other, but I can't make out the words. Only feel their strong hands.

The grip on my heart loosens, the pain receding. I let out a full breath and blackness takes me. When my eyes open again, I'm staring up at a gold-flecked ceiling. Hard rock presses under my body. Two faces hover into view—Mineshka and Ilea. They peer down at me.

"Are you awake?" Ilea asks. Her mouth doesn't move with her words. A lag in translation?

"Are you okay?" Mineshka sounds scared.

In here. In here. In here.

Foreign thoughts flood my brain. *In here.* The mental voice won't stop. Is this how Lyle feels?

I sit up, struggling to get my headgear off. Tiny hands push at mine, and the annoying helmet clicks and comes off, so I can hold my head. Rubbing the balls of my hands into my ears doesn't help, the voice is inside me.

Here. Tug in my chest. *Here.* Tug. *Here.*

I look around, desperate, seeing nothing but more yellow walls. No doors, no windows, and nothing pulling me forward. I'm in the right place. I just don't—

Here.

I scoot back, staring at the spot my butt had been on. There's no 'X' or anything extra to indicate that this area is special, but...

"Devon?" Mineshka's voice.

I punch through the floor, breaking a fist-sized hole through the rock. I hear feet moving away as I continue to strike the ground, plowing deeper into the earth.

Here.

I stop, wheezing, lungs fighting for air, hands throbbing, arms bleeding, eyes burning from dribbling sweat, gazing down at a bright, red glow through a zig-zag crack. My body trembles.

It's here.

Using one hand, I break through the final layer and gape at a palm-sized ruby.

My Stone.

I pick it up and sit back on my heels as it warms my palm through the glove. My vision blurs again, then splits: on one side, I see the ruby in my hand, on the other, I see it in Jain's. Tepid energy drips from the Stone, seeping into my skin. Fear, claustrophobia, and bad nerves are soothed away completely.

I'm not afraid anymore. What's there to be scared of? I can kick anything's ass. I can outrun, outjump, and outthrow anyone. Power. My body feels like it's made of titanium. I stand up, squeezing the Stone, about to tuck it in a pocket, somewhere safe.

"*That*'s it?"

I start at the sound of Ilea's voice behind me. I whirl around to find both her and Mineshka staring at me, their eyes trailing down to the Stone. They don't look impressed. How can they not be impressed? Do they not feel the power coming off this thing? Confidence and strength radiate through me.

"It's pretty," Mineshka says. "May I?" She steps

back, eyes going wide. "Sorry." Her hands come up in a defensive position.

I check myself. I'd stepped toward her, my free hand balled in a fist. Holy shit. "I…" I unclench my hand, staring at Mineshka, then at the brilliant glow of the ruby.

"How are you feeling?" Ilea asks, voice curt. "Are you all right?"

"Better than all right," I say. My voice is deep and steady, no cracks or squeaks. I sound like somebody other people should listen to. "I feel good. Stronger." So much stronger. I look around, my eyesight sharper, seeing farther than I could before. I don't need headlamps or glow-in-the-dark walls. "I have to test this out!"

"When we get to the surface," Ilea says.

"You can't tell me what to do." I crack my knuckles. I turn around, stalking forward, going deeper into the maze, the heat of the Stone stoking a hidden furnace inside me. I reach a dead end, and grin, hands meeting the cold, thick rock. I'll make a new door here.

"Stop!"

Something that feels like a huge, gropey hand grabs me around the middle, crushing my arms to my sides.

"You don't know what's on the other side of that! You could let in water!"

"We've got suits on!" I yell.

"You're not wearing yours correctly." Ilea's starting to sound like Mom. Nag, nag…

"Let me go!" I flex my muscles, trying to break out of…of…whatever the hell this is! I don't see anything holding me, but I can't move.

"The more you fight, the tighter that grip is going to get." Ilea's voice comes closer. "You think I haven't dealt with your type before? I'm pulling energy right out of the ground. It won't run out."

I roar, trying to kick out. The vice grip squeezes, my body feels ready to burst. I can't... "I can't breathe."

"Calm down, and it'll loosen," Ilea says.

I turn my head. She stands next to me, eyes glistening with purpose. "Give me the Stone."

Give her my Stone? I didn't hear her right. My fingers go numb, as I grip my Stone. Power pulses in my blood, but the more I push...

"Ilea! Ilea, he's going to pass out." Mineshka's voice.

"Good," Ilea says. "That'll make this easier. Keep fighting it, Devon. Go on."

"Y-y-you're...f-fired."

"You never contracted me."

"Min..." knock her out. Take her down. Can't talk.

"Ilea, you must release him."

"He's gone power mad," Ilea says. "Devon, try to think. Remember why we're here, and what you have in your hand. That Stone is a gift from a goddess. The divine like to manipulate us with things beyond our comprehension."

Too many words. Vision's going black. Lungs burn, body hurts.

"Just a minute more," Ilea says.

"What if you strangle him and he dies?" Mineshka yells.

"Have it your way then," Ilea says after a beat.

Release? Is she going to—pain blasts through the back of my skull. My vision goes white. Stars, like in cartoons, float around my head, then it all goes black.

"Did you have to hit him so hard?"

"He was so *wiffed* I didn't have the luxury of being

gentle."

"Let me look at it again!"

"No, I'm sealing it!"

"But…"

Broken conversations from so many voices. I think I know them all, male and female. I crack open an eye, flinching at the dim light and shutting it back.

"Oh-ho, he's coming to." A guy's baritone voice. Loniad.

"Keep still." Ilea. Small fingers touch the throbbing ache at the back of my head. A rush of coldness frosts the area and reaches in to inspire my cells to start repairing what's broken inside. I breathe out a sigh of relief and open my eyes as the pain abates. Four faces swim around in a circle before stopping: Xijure, Loniad, Mineshka… and Ilea.

"You…"

"Stopped you from trying to kill us all?" Ilea asks. "Yes, I did. You were under alien influence. I had to treat you as a threat to yourself and the team."

Under alien influence. But they're the aliens! I can't—the Stone. My Stone. "Where's…"

"Relax, little leader. I've got it."

"Give it back!"

"Whoa!" Hands hold me down. Xijure scowls at me. "Calm down. Now. No one is keeping your weapon from you."

Like hell they're not. Ilea knocked me out. She almost killed me, so that she could take my Stone. What cause did she have? "I wasn't trying to kill anybody!"

"Oh? You weren't going to break through a wall that could have flooded the cavern we were in? You didn't even stop to think about it when I warned you."

No, I wasn't going to....

Oh god. Horror creeps in.

I was. I wanted to.

I really didn't think about it. I didn't care. I just wanted to use my power, see what I could do. The Stone kept me from being afraid, kept me from thinking about consequences, because they would scare me.

Oh hell.

I could have... Oh god.

"Keep it away from me," I murmur. I shut my eyes, shame filling me. I don't want to see their expressions.

The strength. I loved that feeling. I could do anything, save the world or destroy it. My stomach twists, the nerves the Stone had calmed freaking out again.

"I won't keep it away from you," Ilea says. "I'm just warding it, so you won't be tempted to pull on its power until you need it. And now, you'll truly think about when you need it and when you don't."

So matter of fact. She sounds satisfied.

I open my eyes again. Ilea's out of sight, only Xijure, Mineshka and Loniad hover, but none of them seem angry.

"It looks so boring," Loniad says. "Like a regular rock, not even a big one!"

"It was a clear, red ruby when he carried it," Mineshka says. "Beautiful. No noble has anything finer. But his eyes when he held it, they reflected the red."

"Like a *mamu*?" Loniad asks.

"No, you *snitter fop*."

Xijure chuckles and meets my eyes. "Can you sit up now?"

Should I? What if I go psycho again?

"We can't stay down here. The Disi will think we

drowned," Ilea says. She comes back into view. She's holding a brown pouch the size of a Crown Royal bag. It bulges like it's full of money, or diamonds. Or the Stone.

"Is it magic?" I ask, eyes on the bag.

"You must've seen one before." Ilea looks as unimpressed as when she'd laid eyes on the Stone. "Yes, it's a damper. You won't feel the Stone's presence as much, unless you open the bag. You can strap it on your belt or loop it around your neck." She lowers the pouch onto my chest. I recoil, but the light weight settles on me. I grit my teeth, waiting for the insane rush of power.

This is crazy. Who doesn't want to feel invincible?

My big-little brother doesn't.

And I don't, not like that.

"Do you feel the Stone?" Xijure asks.

I don't want to, but I realize I'm trying to. A weak current of energy trickles through the chest of my wetsuit, like holding a battery against my tongue, but nothing else. The last of my headache disappears. I touch the back of my head, feeling damp stickiness on my hand, and a small lump that smooths under my fingers. Shit. Is that me healing? I heal fast, but not this fast. I sit up, marveling at the fact that the room doesn't spin. "Are we in the first chamber?"

"Yes," Loniad says. "We waited here for you."

"But nobody was expecting these two to come back in here carrying you," Xijure says, shaking his head. "Thought you were dead for a *wisp* there."

I rub the back of my head and peer at the blood on my glove. "What did you hit me with?"

"A *barash*," Ilea says.

Barash...my translator whirs, spitting out random words until it settles on: magical karate chop. Really?

That's the best you got?

"And that thing that grabbed me?" I ask.

"That was a *clissp.*"

Clissp...magical straight jacket.

"Ah." I watch Ilea as she stretches her arms over her head, until her shoulders crack. Never thought I'd get taken out by a Cabbage Patch Kid, and I don't intend to share this story with Lyle or anybody else not currently present.

Lyle. Worry makes my throat tight. Has he found his Stone yet? And if so, what would it do to him? Would he go nuts like I did? He'd lost it on Earth. He was barely keeping it together off Earth. I wrap my hand around the pouch on my chest and struggle to my feet.

"We have what we came for. Let's go." The sooner we leave here, the sooner I can get to my brother.

"Are you sure you're ready to go back out there?" Xijure scans me carefully. "You were out for a while, and you don't seem very steady right now."

"I'm steady. I'm good." I let the pouch dangle. Its cord is probably a half foot long. I sling it around my neck, the pouch hitting me in the solar plexus. It's luke-warm and comforting. This is better. I can manage it this way, by just taking a little, letting it help me calm down.

Going back out into the water won't be so bad. This time we'll be floating back up to the surface. The adventure's done. I breathe in and realize... "Uh, where's my headgear?"

"I have it," Mineshka says. The tall woman comes to me, holding out my underwater helmet. I reach to take it from her, but she shakes her head, moving to put it on for me. I stand still, studying the serious expression on her face that turns soft when she steps back, smiling at me. "There you go, leader. Please secure it, now."

I press a button on the neck of the gear, hearing the head and neck section attach to the rest of the suit. Recycled air filters in, blowing over my sweat and blood matted hair. I grab her hand. "Thank you. Ah, back there, I uh…."

"Lost your way," she finishes. She clears her throat. "I'm glad we got you back." There's no fear in her eyes, no anger.

"I don't get why you guys aren't pissed." I crack my knuckles, waiting for anxiety to creep up on me, but it stays at bay. The Stone is like Valium. I don't want to run screaming, I don't want to puke, but I do feel sorry.

"You weren't yourself," Mineshka says. "This is you, and I like you. I never feared for myself."

"And I didn't either." Ilea appears at Mineshka's side, a hand on one hip. "You wouldn't have hurt us."

"You don't know that." *I* don't know that.

"You would have snapped out of it, while we were drowning, and tried to save us," Ilea says. "You've got that kind of heart."

I blink at her. "You just met me a few hours ago."

"Hate to break it to you, but you're not deep," Ilea says. "You wear everything you're about on the outside."

"Huh?"

"It's endearing," Ilea says, "and helps me out a lot. It tells me what you need."

I think she's calling me shallow, but claiming it's a good thing. Shallow is *not* a good thing.

Ilea punches my shoulder. "What you're thinking is all over your face again. You see it, Min? Look, Loni."

What?

Mineshka and Loniad crowd me on either side,

ogling my face and laughing with Ilea. "Yes, yes, I see it!" Loniad laughs full-out. "Like a guilty *pooshka*!"

"No one's ever told you this, *babila*?" Mineshka asks.

"That I'm shallow?" I'm so confused...and embarrassed. These guys are laughing hard, at me.

"No." Ilea snorts. "All right, obviously 'not deep' means something else where you come from. I meant that your facial expressions and body language are open. I read your honesty in your motions. You're sweet. So, no, I did not think you would intentionally hurt us. But I know you'd have felt guilty if you accidentally did, so I bound you and knocked you out. No harm done, and mission accomplished."

Loniad squeezes one of my shoulders, while Mineshka pats the other.

I feel patronized. Is that the right word? No, I think 'patronized' means something negative. I don't feel insulted. The twins and Ilea wear amused smiles. A funny sensation ripples through me as I randomly think about Lawrie. He's annoying, loud, and frustrating, but also hilarious and smart. I don't know what to do with him half the time, and I bet I used the same expressions as Loniad, Mineshka and Ilea had when dealing with him.

Are they giving me a 'little brother' look?

"I hate to break up this warm moment between you all." Xijure's voice makes me turn. He stands under the closed door that had let us in here. "But the mission is not completely accomplished until we're back on our ship, heading to Lenore."

Right. Right. Back to my brothers, Lenore, and being coronated.

"Should we flip the lever again, and let the water

back in?" Mineshka asks.

"It'd make the door easier to open," Xijure says. "Though, Devon probably won't need it to be easier." He grins at me and I grimace, hating the attention.

"Our bodies will need it to be easier," Ilea says. "A drastic change in pressure isn't good for us. Devon, pull the lever."

"Oh, okay."

"Secure your headgear, everyone," Xijure says.

"What if the water comes crashing back in here, though?" I'm scared and not. The Stone's still working. My voice stays level.

"Remember," Ilea drawls, "Order actually wants you to get that thing and wants you to use it. You can't do that if you die in the retrieval process. There shouldn't be anything down here that you can't withstand."

"We've been through this, *babila*," Mineshka says. "You know what we feel." She taps the top of my headgear. "Pull the lever."

I go to the joystick in the wall, wrapping my fingers around it, looking at my group, waiting for one of them to yell, *"Never mind!"*

No one does, so I pull.

The ground shudders and rumbles, and water bubbles from the floor, filling the chamber like a bathtub. It's a slow crawl, water rising to my waist then up to my chest. I pat my headgear, double and triple-checking that it's on right. I breathe in, expecting my heart rate to speed up. It doesn't.

As the water completely envelops me, I stay focused. The soles of my wetsuit keep me from floating upward. My team stands near me; they're fine. We're fine. The ground lightly quakes as the water touches the ceiling. My insides are tight and heavy as the suit adjusts to the returned water pressure. This can't be healthy. Don't deep sea divers get weird disorders from doing this stuff too much?

Whatever.

And suddenly, I'm not that worried about it anymore. The Stone hums in the bag, still playing the part of a tranquilizer. Can I break this thing into tiny pieces and sell it to shrinks back home?

"Devon." A voice shakes me from my thoughts. Xijure. "Try the door now."

"Yeah." I flip a switch on the ankle of my shoes, body floating as the suction is released. I swim up to the double doors, splaying my hands on each one. Pushing is going to be harder than pulling. Should I go back down and try to ram it open? I push. Nothing gives way.

"You need a springing start," Loniad says. "Come down to the floor."

I click the ankle-switch again and sink back to my group.

"Concentrate all of your strength in your legs," Loniad says. "That will give you the force you need to break through."

Jump with my arms out like Superman? I can't keep from smiling. Superman, the alien, that's me. "I can try it." Might even look cool, unless I bust my head open or something. But I'm not worried about that either. I stroke the pouch and nod to myself.

"Okay, move guys." I wave the group away and crouch low, readying my leg muscles for a jump. No, not just a jump, a single-bound leap. I turn off the suction one more time and unleash my coiled muscles. My arms shoot up as my body hurtles toward the ceiling.

The world flashes by so fast and—impact. My arms scream, muscles protest as I meet solid metal. It gives way with a deep moan. Double doors smash open as I launch through, a bullet in the ocean, heading toward the surface.

I am friggin' Superman!

Then…my insides bubble and my heart quivers painfully in my chest. I'm going up too fast. I'm going to implode like those divers that surface too quickly. I try to throw myself down and end up sending myself into somersaults. The water grows lighter as I move toward the surface, the sun breaking through layers of murkiness. My heart is in my throat. My innards burn, my throat and chest closing. I gulp air, hearing the hiss of extra oxygen being fed into my helmet. I think the suit senses I'm not taking in enough air. The dense fabric melds to my body, coolness leaking from its threads, trying to regulate my body temperature. It's trying to save me.

Voices yell at me through my helmet: Xijure, Ilea, Loniad, Mineshka. They sound freaked. A hard, invisible fist the size of my body slams into me, almost stopping my ascent, slowing it until…until…

I stop, hanging in the water. Everything in me throbs and aches. My vision goes black and white every few seconds. I can't catch my breath. A jumble of voices call to me.

I don't know how long I float in place, before hands grip my shoulders. I open eyes I didn't know I'd closed, and gaze at Xijure. He looks rattled. "Are you all right?" he demands.

That's a good question. I do a mental check: I have feeling back in my limbs and my heart's not trying to escape out of my mouth anymore. The Stone resting on my chest hums. Had it ever worried? Could it worry?

"I think so," I murmur. I straighten out, shaky, but fine. "What stopped me?"

"Ilea used a water wheel. She wasn't sure if it'd be strong enough to stop you, but you helped by making yourself flip around. You slowed your momentum enough for the spell to be effective."

I did something right, on my own, instinctively. That makes me feel good. "Yeah? I didn't think it helped anything. I kept going, but…"

"You don't give yourself enough credit," Xijure says. "Which is good. Means you'll stay humble." He pats my shoulder. "I'm glad you're all right. I didn't want to have to tell your older brother I'd lost you."

I chuckle. "Really?"

"That *gak mopi*'s scary," Xijure says. "Don't tell him I said that."

"Where are the others?" I peer down, my eyes sharper than normal. I can't make out my team, though.

"They have to come up slower than I did," Xijure says. He raises a brow. "Us Champions are a bit hardier."

"Yeah, I guess." I shake out my limbs. I almost died, and I'm not freaking out. I laugh, enjoying the pressure it releases from my neck, shoulders and chest. Is this as cool as winning a football or basketball game? Yeah. Is it better? Hell yeah. My laughter's contagious. I hear Xijure join in, his hand squeezing my shoulder, and I give him a light punch in return.

A minute passes, and three suits come into view beneath us.

Loniad and Mineshka barrel into me, hugging and patting me down like parents checking their kid for injuries. Ilea slaps me over the head. They all pelt me with health questions, and I assure them twelve different times that I'm okay, before they believe me.

Xijure shakes his head and presses a button on his suit belt. "The boat is north." He points one way and begins to swim forward, slowly ascending as he does. The rest of us follow his lead, the twins swimming on either side of me while Ilea takes rear guard.

Loniad sings a song that translates badly—seems to be about a girl mermaid with a thick beard that wants a prince with gills and a nice boat. Mineshka comes in with the harmony. They actually sound kind of good, so good that Ilea doesn't tell them to shut up until we've almost reached the surface.

I see the shadow of a large boat, our boat. We made it.

I float the last few meters to the surface, breaking through the waves and smiling at my team as we all bob, tread water and swim to the ship, treasure in tow. As I'm helped onto the deck of the ship, where I can throw my headgear to the side and breathe fresh air, I lean my head back and stare at the blue sky.

Victory.

I touch the pouch around my neck, humming with the Stone. I win.

"Is that the Stone?"

I jerk toward the voice. Owelu's assistant, goldfish orange and wide-mouthed, holds out his hands, like he thinks I'm going to let him take my Stone. I step back.

"Yes." I stare him down, aware I'm being rude, but who does he think he is? It's not his merchandise, it's mine.

I shake my head, wondering if the pouch's dampener spell is wearing off.

"Ah," the man says. He smiles, round teeth white, his eyes glittering with something that turns my stomach.

What the hell does that look mean? I can't take it to heart. Most of the people I've met have been very human in appearance, this guy isn't. So, I can't judge his expressions fairly, but still....

A hand on my arm. I meet Ilea's eyes. "I'm changing out of this suit. It's cold."

I nod. Yeah. Getting back into my own clothes will be nice. I pat the Stone, wondering if my body's going to look more defined in my uniform now that I have this new power and all. Looking more jacked won't be a bad thing. I could go for a goatee too.

Leader Two of Rema's going to look like the cool one.

The Stone pulses, the small amount of energy that seeps through the bag warming me.

I follow my team and Xijure into the ship's cabin, forgetting all about Owelu's man, though I feel his eyes on me until the cabin door shuts.

14
LYLE

THE NEW COLD GEAR STRETCHES tight over my standard uniform. The blue, long-sleeved coveralls are insulated with material that seals out cold and moisture. The straps in back make sucking sounds as they snap together, and the suit adjusts to my measurements. Someone secures my headgear, the fabric wrapping around my face and neck like a ski mask, only my eyes are uncovered.

Shreti-Hak stands back, watching Caea, our team of soldiers and me getting dressed. The chamber room is gun-metal-gray and as sterile as a surgery ward. White pod-chairs line the walls. Soldiers sit, shoving their boots into ice-covers. A man had helped me with mine, saying he didn't trust a novice to put the sole protectors on right. He'd watched too many *wetlings* break their necks on black ice.

"There." The person working on my headgear pats the top of my head and comes into view—a tall female soldier also dressed in cold gear. Her grey eyes scan me, as if checking for imperfections. She hums and steps back, handing me a pair of blue goggles with dark lenses. "You almost pass, *adaji*."

Adaji? I frown. Her tone was condescending. I graze her mind, skimming the surface for…ah. *Adaji*: spoiled child, brat. It's strange how the translators don't quite translate everything, tossing in foreign words with their English. I can usually figure them out based on context, but when I can't, I don't care enough to search the person for an answer. Today's different though. I need to know what these people think.

On the rover-ride to the site, Caea insisted on having an open mind-link between us. She wasn't sure if we should trust the Kupi and told me to probe everyone we come in contact with. So far, every mind I've touched is horrified by the thought of Order being underground, and they want to 'save the children.' They look at me with judgment. They all think I'll die below. Some think it won't be a loss. Some fear my death will mean their way of living will be crushed by Su or Nazflit occupation. But none of the people who are afraid want to die for me. Not like Falun, Orion and Sensuen.

My stomach and head ache in tandem. The female soldier offers me water. I shake my head. My throat is so dry I feel the burn in my ears when I swallow, but anything I ingest right now will end up on the floor. A huddle forms in the middle of the room with Shreti-Hak at its center. Her voice is low as she talks to her people.

A shoulder brushes mine, and I look at Caea, dressed in a black snowsuit, her brown eyes grave. She nods to Shreti-Hak's circle and I focus. Shreti-Hak's shields are sound as I spread my awareness over them like mayonnaise, a thin coat that bleeds into the bread. Careful not to let her feel me, I open myself to her emotions. There's no fear. The woman is made of steel, but there's an undercurrent of apprehension. She doesn't want the Allegiance to blame her for my failure. I sink deeper, under her top layer, and sense her fear for Kupiku. The Allegiance will forget about the frozen planet if I die here. She can't let that happen. Her soldiers...

I pull away, turning. Caea brushes my shoulder again. *What is it?*

/She's telling them to save us at all cost./ I shake my head. /If things go bad down there, she wants them to sacrifice themselves./

Caea blinks. *I wasn't expecting that.*

/And those people.../ They're not my court. They don't want to die for me or Shreti-Hak. They want to go home to their families, but they're loyal to Kupiku. They'll die if they have to. I thicken my barriers, cutting myself off from all outside thought and emotion. I don't care what Caea wants. I can't take anymore. /We can trust them. They think helping us helps Kupiku./

You're sure?

My heart thuds. I don't know. I only know what they feel right now. Who knows what they might actually do down there. /I.../

Can you keep your mind open to their thoughts and feelings?

I stare at her.

How are you doing? If you can't handle being connected to them all, it's fine. We'll make do. She pats her belt with its double sheaths for her daggers that she'd put on over the coveralls. *How is your offense?*

/My.../ Telekinesis. /It's okay./ It's not the weapons she has. My training on the Ievisara focused on shielding and telempathic control.

If there's trouble down there, you push as hard and as wide as you can with that gift, and I'll take care of the rest. She pats my shoulder and touches my chin, gaze boring into mine. *And when we come back up, you and I are going to work on your offensive powers...and we'll resume your art lessons.*

If anything, my heart beats faster at the warmth in her eyes. Without needing to skim her aura, I know she means what she says. I give a sharp nod, breaking eye contact with her and moving away. /Thanks./ I mean that, and I want her to know I mean that, but damn. I pat her shoulder twice and pull back again. Girls on Earth were easy—kisses, hugs, exchanging empty words. But Caea's not like them.

She chuckles, the sound making some of the soldiers around Shreti-Hak jump. Caea shakes her head at them. *When we get in that tunnel, you stay one step behind me the entire time, until I tell you to do otherwise. Understand?*

/Yes./

I'm not in your court, but I won't let anything happen to you either.

I gulp, wishing I could say the same. But I can't count on my busted powers, and without them, I don't know how to fight. I might not be able to protect her.

Shreti-Hak's football huddle breaks, each soldier bowing before leaving Shreti-Hak and filing around us. They're ready to leave the chamber and enter the lift that will lower us into the pit, down to the tunnel. A heavy metal door squeals before it opens to reveal the interior of a white elevator cabin. I feel like bait being put in a trap before it's dropped into the ocean for sharks.

Ten soldiers squeeze around me and Caea. Ten strangers breathing hard and murmuring prayers to gods I've never heard of. No one prays to Order, which should be strange since She's who we're fighting for and who we're about to meet.

No one says *Order-va*...or *Kahanna-va*—the expression for 'oh my: insert patron god.' I wonder why. The cabin shudders to life. The interior lights are a warm yellow that makes everyone look sallow and sick as the floor seems to drop away.

The ride is like Disney World's Tower of Terror. Something built into the compartment keeps my feet rooted to the floor, but doesn't stop my ears from popping as we hurtle downward. The sound of the cabin scraping against the tubing that lines the rocky walls of the pit competes with the tough metal cable rattling against the roof, meant to halt us before we smash to the ground. No one screams. A random image of Devon pops into my brain. I fight the urge to laugh at the memory of him screaming like a four-year-old when I'd tricked him onto a rollercoaster. I miss my brother.

Please be okay. Please don't be doing something like this. Please end up back wherever we're supposed to be, safe and not guilty or sad over whatever happened to me. I shut my eyes, counting backward from one hundred. The cart shrieks to a halt when I reach twenty-six. My neck jerks, my legs tremble, and the magnetic field on the floor releases my feet. I stagger into the soldier behind me and almost fall as that person stumbles too. Caea catches my arm.

The doors open, pale exterior lights break through the gloom of the tunnel stretched out in front of us. The cave walls are pitch black. The first people to step out of the cabin cry out as they windmill and fall flat on their asses. Black ice.

"I thought the boot covers..." I start.

"They help, but don't work miracles," a soldier behind me says. "Mind your steps, Leader Three."

People file out around me, leaving Caea and me last inside the cabin. I gaze out at the tunnel, or cavern. The Kupi had drilled until they cut a hole into this gap between the frozen mantel and core. I'm in the bowels of a planet. Lawrie would bounce off the walls, knocking me over to get out and go slipping and sliding over that damn ice. I, instead, wait for Caea. She places a careful foot down on the ice, then the other. After taking two steps, she looks over her shoulder. "One step behind, Lyle. Come on."

I look at the small prints her boots leave in the grit covering the ice and travel in her footsteps, a team of soldiers with liquid light-sticks, torches with lava lamps in place of fire, leading the way. The sound of our feet slushing through ice and snow echoes through the tunnel. No one speaks and the sound of other people's breathing is muffled by the masks. I hear my own breath loud and clear. After walking for what seems like miles down a slippery incline, I sound like I'm about to expire as I struggle to keep up. I'm ready to fall over, but I won't ask for a break if no one else needs one.

My empty stomach growls, and I wonder how long we've been walking. It could be hours based on how hungry I am. I reach out to tap Caea, and stop, freezing in place. A tuning fork vibrates between my ears. My head spins, the walls close in. I drop to my knees, pressing my hands against my temples, trying to relieve the pressure behind my eyes.

A hand on my shoulder. The feeling of someone kneeling in front of me. "Lyle? Lyle, what's wrong?"

The white noise between my ears screams. My throat runs dry and raw. Am I screaming too? Two hands on my shoulders, shaking me. "Lyle?"

The ground rumbles. Muffled curses. I sink lower, head cushioned on the frosted-over fabric of someone else's cold suit. The contact snaps me out of the pain loop for a moment. I suck in air, but the screaming starts again. Millions of nails on chalkboards. My head is going to explode. It has to stop. It needs to stop.

Hands push my head toward the floor, and a slim body covers my back. More curses. The cavern continues to quake. Sounds of rock crashing against ice.

"Cave in!" someone shouts.

"Retreat?"

"Lights, go first!" Caea barks. "No! Halt!"

Silence. The screaming stops. I let out a shaky breath as the person shielding me from falling rocks shifts away. I remove my hands from my face. My ears feel wet. I taste snot and blood on my lips. The ground is still.

"*Bawenthis*-va!" someone yells over dozens of other curses.

"The entranceway is completely sealed. We're trapped down here," a high voice announces.

"Bring a light here." Caea. Behind my eyelids, I sense the glow of a light-stick. When had I closed my eyes? "*Fip*. Lyle, can you hear me?"

"Yeah." My throat hurts.

My goggles and ski mask are removed. Cloth touches my face, scrubbing under my ears, nose and eyes. "Where does it hurt?" Caea asks. "Lyle, where do you feel pain?"

There is no pain. I'm just heavy. My head falls forward, and gloved hands hold my cheeks. A finger peels back an eyelid, and I flinch. Bright. The light is too bright. A hot poker stabs through my brain; then small toothpicks dipped in acid pierce my temples, traveling down my jawline on both sides. "My head, my head…" I keep moaning after I stop making words.

I'm going to die. My brain is hemorrhaging. I feel goopy masses trickling through my ears again.

"I'm getting you out of here," Caea whispers. "Who here works underground? Who can tell when the rocks are stable after a shift?" Her voice resounds. She talks to the room as she dabs at my ear lobes, moving the cloth from one ear to the other. *Lyle, does this hurt?*

Her mental communication is a scouring pad on bath tiles. I cringe.

"Okay, your powers are overloaded." She sounds relieved. "I thought something hit you." She tenses, and I feel the sensation of the towel falling away from my face. "*Krevai-va.* Is it Her?"

Her. The screeching. Recollection of walking in the memories of Evan's past life. Order, shark-toothed and black eyed. Her voice. The sound is familiar. It was how She spoke when She used Her voice.

My insides lurch, the hollow pit of my stomach suddenly full of acid. I retch, pushing away from Caea and spitting up on the ice. My head throbs. She rubs my back as the emotions of the soldiers around me hum against my shields: disgust, pity, doom. They think we're all dead down here, that even Caea is useless. The thought makes me angry. Caea hasn't faltered once. The only person they should look down on is me.

"Sh-sh-she…" I spit sour saliva off to the side. "She's here. Her voice, I heard it. But I couldn't understand what She said. I think She just..." wants our attention and to make sure we can't leave.

My teeth chatter as my stomach gets itself back under control. I half-gag at the lingering taste on my tongue. Straightening my back, I sit up, though my head is a raw wound. "I'm going to try something."

"Don't do anything." Caea's voice is sharp, but I ignore her.

I reach out with my mind, tears rolling down my face as pain vibrates down my brain stem. Each stretch seems to tear something inside, like I'm ripping through fresh stitches. Something waits just beyond my grasp. I sense it and, steeling myself, I grab on.

I'm aware I'm falling, but I never feel myself connect with anything. Static creeps into my head. White noise, bright lights, then grayness…and a mass, a shape, at the end of a hall. It shifts, turning, becoming a body with black eyes bulging from a stone face, eyes that swirl with stars, galaxies, a vast expanse of endless space.

Come forward, My Champions.

The words slice into my being. /You're…/

Only My Champions. Leave the rest.

A mental slap. My mind spirals backward, my body feels like it's tumbling.

I finally feel my face connect with cold fabric again. Caea's gloved hands grip my suit; she's talking. "Someone else hold him upright. I'm going to try to make an opening."

"No," I say.

"What?"

I sit up straight. The skin of my face is slick. I wipe

at it, while cautiously shaking my head. It aches, but I can think. I catch Caea's worried brown eyes. "She wants us to keep going forward. Only us."

"You spoke with Her? Just now?"

"Yes," I say. I chance a glance at the soldiers around us. Some stare without shame, others look uncomfortable, feet shifting.

"Orders, ma'am?" someone asks.

I flinch at the word 'order.' Caea notices.

"Stay here. Try to make an opening, if you can," Caea says. She looks at me, mouth a grim line. "Leader Three and I will go on. If there is a means for evacuation further down, we will come back to lead you through. But for now, only us."

"Majesty, we cannot—"

"You *can* do whatever I tell you," Caea says. "Once you exited that lift, I became your queen. I appreciate that you feel responsible for our safety, but we also have a mission to complete. Remain stationed here, or escape if an opening becomes available, but you will not follow us unless we call."

I blink at her. Shit.

Emotions around me vary, from insulted, to awed, to wary. Caea needs these people on her side. I tense, letting my power pass through my barrier and touch foreign emotions. I need the Kupi soldiers to feel as if Caea is right, as if Caea is Shreti-Hak. /This will save Kupiku and your families./ I push false feelings of loyalty, obedience, and purpose through them, and associate those feelings with mental images of Caea, beautiful and fierce, short black curls against a perfect face. A warrior queen who can't be questioned. Their emotional tides sway.

My head hurts and I pull back inside my barrier, squeezing my eyes shut. I can't do anymore. If that didn't work, I don't know how else I can help. But why should it work? I've only done that once, on one person—silver eyes, heart-shaped face. Go away, Nisse. Not now.

The soldiers tense, straighten and stand at attention. "Yes, ma'am," a few say. They march, some moving toward the walls, others head for the cave-in, running their gloves along the rocks. One gives Caea a light-stick.

I sigh. It worked.

"Did you do that?" Caea asks.

I watch the soldiers a moment longer, before answering, "Yeah."

"Can you stand?"

We'll find out. She gets to her feet and reaches down to help me. I wobble and shake, but steady my body against her before righting myself.

Caea studies me. "You ready?"

"I might pass out," I warn her. "But let's go."

The angle gets sharper the deeper we descend. I count the seconds, converting them into minutes to keep time: three thousand, six hundred and twenty-two. An hour, we've walked for more than an hour. I'm running on fumes, stumbling into Caea every few minutes. She puts a hand behind her to steady me each time. After another thirty minutes, she gives up being the leader and shield and slows to walk at my side, snaking an anchoring arm around my waist. I swear I will not fall and bring this woman down with me.

The slope levels on a patch of black ice. My feet slide out from under me and I push Caea away so I can fall alone. My knees strike the ground, the sensation hammers through my kneecaps. I touch gloved hands to the floor, panting. Caea's boots shuffle, moving past me. The light-stick casts a dull glow a few feet in front of us.

"Stay down," Caea says. I look up, watching her cautious movements. She stops, holding the light-stick out and taking a hesitant step back.

"What?"

"The tunnel is done. There's a drop in the floor," Caea says. "We don't have climbing equipment."

I grimace. "Dead end, but—"

Caea puts out a silencing hand. "We're here!" Her voice echoes. A few pebbles sprinkle down on me from the ceiling.

Come down.

I grit my teeth at the burn of the words. "Did you hear?"

"Yes," Caea says, sounding irritated. "How do we come down? We have no gear and can't tell how deep this pit is."

I sit back on my heels, staring at Caea and the way she's talking to a monster goddess. She sounds in control, as if she and Order are on the same level.

Trust and let yourselves fall.

The only thing worse than that idea was coming down here in the first place.

"Caea, we should go back," I say.

"We have come too far to go back," Caea says. Her shoulders square and I blink at her.

"I'm going to do as She says." Caea turns and tosses the light-stick at me. I fumble the catch. The stick clatters to the ground. Its light winks out. For a moment, we are in total darkness.

I pat the floor until I find it, picking the stick up and shaking it until it glows again. Caea's looking at me.

"Come over here," she says.

Get up and move? With what energy? If she had been anybody else, I would have said: Not today. I want to give Caea more than that. She's been giving me more all day. But what does *"I'm going to do as She says"* mean?

I struggle to my feet, taking small steps until I reach her. Up close, I make out the tight press of her lips and a gleam of uncertainty in her eyes.

"I'm going to do as She says," repeats in my head.

"You're going to jump?" My breath catches in my throat. My head spins as I reach for her mind, brushing over its surface for any hope that I'm wrong.

"I need you to lift me." Caea grabs the arm holding the light-stick. The light steadies and I realize I'm shaking.

"What?"

"Lift me, just a bit, off the ground here. I want to see if your power can hold me." Her grip tightens and she invades my space, her nose touches mine, her eyes bore into my soul. "I need you, Lyle. I trust that you can do this, because you don't want me to fall. Now, pick me up."

I breathe through my nose, trying to keep myself from hyperventilating. The light dims, and I feel myself wobble.

"You're breathing too fast and too shallow," Caea says. "Calm down. It will be all right. We're just going to test this out. If you can't do it, we'll come up with something else. But remember, Orion, Sensuen and Falun are waiting for us to rescue them. They trust you. Coming up with another plan may take too much time. Who knows if they're warm enough down there."

Pressure builds in my chest. What if they're dead already? What if it's all just a trap? And if they're dead, did I kill them? Would it be considered murder because I sent them here?

I close my eyes. Something strange swells inside me, the feeling I get when family is in danger. Orion, Sensuen and Falun aren't family. I don't know them at all, but that goes both ways, and they jumped into this pit for my sake.

Does that make them people I can trust to look out for me? Are they friends now? I don't have friends. I have brothers, parents, blood relations who care about me unconditionally, even when I'm an asshole. Which is all the time.

A flash of silver eyes and a heart-shaped face. The taste of gritty water back in the club and the harsh cold as I'm led outside and left to freeze. Nisse working with Order. Order punishing my court for trying to help me. Everyone needing me to do what's right for someone who's not a brother or me.

I suck as a person. I suck as a leader.

These people can't seem to realize that. They trust me, need me.

My eyes open, meeting Caea's. "Step back and let go of my arms."

She moves back and I almost sigh at the loss of her close presence. I'd liked having her in my personal bubble and not wanting to kiss or grab her and feeling she didn't want that from me either. We're more than that.

A grin cracks across my face and Caea tilts her head. "What's wrong?" she asks.

"Nothing." Because, for once, nothing's wrong. "Tell me if anything feels weird." The only person I've ever lifted was Devon. My stomach flutters. I'd almost strangled him to death. But I'd been out of control then.

I think about my injections, and how long it's been since I've had one. Would they make this mission easier? My head wouldn't hurt as much, maybe I'd be clearer. But they're not here now, and no one likes me using them anyway. This is all me.

I focus on Caea. The waist or under the shoulders might be the best way to do it. I picture myself going to Caea and placing my hands on either side of her waist. Tendrils of force leave me, they touch Caea and, for a second, I sense the fabric of her coveralls as if I'm touching them with my own hands. I lift, and feel like I'm picking up my little sister, ready to spin her in circles as Devon sometimes did. Caea is light in the grip of my power. I can hold three more Caea's; I can hold a boulder. This power is strong where I'm weak.

Caea yelps, then lets out a laugh. "All right! This is high enough, Lyle!"

I blink, raising my head to see her several feet off the ground. She spreads her arms wide and does a high, roundhouse kick. My hold wavers as the strain from her moving breaks my focus. I grip her tight and her movements stop. My head throbs. The invisible hands, my extra super-powered set, go slack. Caea starts to fall, but I thrust out, catching her and lowering her to the floor, before my knees buckle and I'm back on the ground.

She rubs my neck. "Rest, and then we'll try it over the pit."

"I almost dropped you!"

"Because you were lifting me. Next time, you'll just be slowing my descent. It's much easier to lower things at a controlled pace than to pull them up. And, if our goddess keeps Her word, I won't be in danger of actually falling."

"So, you trust Her?"

"Of course not," Caea says. She touches the top of my head. "But I trust you. Lie down and close your eyes for a bit. We'll try again when your head feels better."

She guides my head onto her lap and pulls off her goggles and ski mask. "You threw your equipment away back there." She spreads her mask over my face, tugging it down over my hair, being so gentle it hardly hurts. "Never do that again. I didn't even think to look for them."

"They'd be gross anyway," I mutter. "I bled all over the mask."

She hums and massages my temples. "I don't feel Her Godliness rushing us along."

"Because She knows your plan." For some reason, I'm sure of it. "She knows we're not running."

We sit in silence. She strokes the side of my face, while I try to get it together. My skull aches like I've been smashed in the head with a two-by-four, but the brain inside it is shaking itself off. I bring a hand up to touch Caea's.

"I think I'm ready."

"You're sure?"

"No, but this is probably as good as it gets. It's not like…" I'm waiting for medication to kick in and ease my pain or clear my head. I sit up slowly, peeling off Caea's mask. It's warm against my cold-burned face, but it's also suffocating. I pass it back to her. "You wear it better."

"Oh, really?" She takes it, pulling it back on and snapping the goggles into place as I stand up. She gets to her feet in one motion and moves to the edge of the pit. I join her, shining the light-stick down into the deep hole. Vertigo makes my senses swim. I don't see a bottom.

"Are you sure you want to?"

"Yes. You won't drop me, and I won't fall. I want to feel your power grip me before I step off." She takes the light-stick from me.

I nod. Here goes. I extend my telekinesis, grabbing her around the waist again and picking her up as she steps out, one foot suspended over an endless void. I push until her entire body hangs above the pit. She's not heavy, but the pull of gravity is hard. I let her drop, but keep a hold on her, like lowering a bucket into a well, only the bucket's already full of water. Inch by inch, she descends.

"I don't see anything," Caea calls up.

"How far do you want to go down?" We can't do this forever. "We need to figure out a point of no return, because I might have to pull you back up." And what if I'm too tired to do it?

"Tell me when…" she trails off.

"What? What is it?" I kneel and peer over the edge. I only see her light and the outline of her body. "Caea?"

A rough yank on my power. I scream, hands clapping over my ears, trying to hold my brain in as something tries to rip it out through them. I stagger, rocking forward, empty space prickles my senses. Oh shit! I'm gonna fall over the—

Free fall. It's fast and endless. Ohshitshitshitshit! Caea! I'm not holding her. "Caea!" I don't hear any voice but mine. Did she hit the bottom already? Is she dead?

I'mgonnadieI'mgonnadieI'mgonnadie!

Everything stops. I flail my arms and legs, nothingness surrounds me. The world is black. What the hell happened? ... "Caea?"

A bright light snaps on, illuminating the space around me. Cool pavement meets my backside. My hands clutch gravel, and sharp pieces slice through my gloves, almost cutting my finger. I hiss, snatching my hands back, and gaze around. There's nothing to see, just dull-colored rock walls that match the ones above. "C-Caea?"

Horrible screeching, the shriek of monster nails on a massive chalkboard, the screams of a thousand angry babies, the roar of a million people cursing in too many languages to translate, the maddening sound of a billion indecipherable whispers. I grind my teeth, whole body shuddering. The noise, it's in my head. I claw at my temples, wanting it out. Warm liquid pours from my ears and nose. I'm going to die of blood loss before my brain completely bursts.

"I-I thought You wanted me alive." I cough, blood leaking down the back of my throat from my nose. Is She trying to kill me? I can't take more.

This is your world, eternally noisy and uncontrolled, with trillions of untrained thoughts and emotions that will torture you until you die.

/No, it's not. This is what You're doing to me./

This is what your world does to you. As your power grows, your barriers will continue to wither.

/And I'll fix them./

Temporary solutions. They will not suffice. Your mind will always be too much for you alone.

/That's not what.../

The cacophony increases. I'm flat on my face. Whimpers that don't sound like me echo from the walls.

/Do you want me to die? Is that what this is? What about your war?/ My thoughts corkscrew out of control. The outside world makes less sense. I know I'm lying on the ground, but I don't feel it anymore. I might as well be falling.

Let Me help you.

A hot sword cuts through the mental wall of crushing sound, a single aisle of silence stretches out in front of me, taking physical shape. It's a passageway. I drag myself to my hands and knees, but can't push up from there. My arms tremble as I crawl forward, down the quiet path.

What's at the end of this trail? Caea? Order? My court?

I mop blood off my face. If I pass out here, the path might close with me in it. I crawl faster, losing my balance, landing on my face, spitting out blood, and starting over again. The other side. I have to get to the other side. Desperation fuels me. 'The other side' becomes a mantra.

I flop into a small chamber with smooth marble-like floors. The walls are polished mirrors, throwing back broken reflections of a guy covered in blood. He looks like a car crash victim, clothes ripped and dirty, dark bronze skin gray, eyes fever bright.

Is that me?

That's no airbrushed actor. That's what I really look like. But through whose eyes? These are mirrors, reflections. The eyes have to be mine. I see me. Broken. Bloody. Pathetic. Weak. Alone.

Caea. Orion. Falun. Sensuen.

Gone. I'd let them go.

I rub the back of a crusty hand across my bleary

eyes. Horror and self-hate fill me. Do I hate myself? I...
No. I'm an awful guy, but I...

No. That black feeling inside...that's loathing.

Because I can't fix this. I need to fix this. I need...

Let Me help you.

I whip my head around, crying out as my neck pops and muscles strain. My ears ring. "Wh-where are You?"

A shadowy figure emerges from a mirror several feet away from me. The chamber is suddenly small, the reflective walls too close. My eyes rise from clawed, bare feet, and travel up a set of blue-white robes to reach a stone-like face, features sharp enough to cut, but oddly beautiful. Black eyes like holes in space glower down at me. The wide mouth opens, jagged predator teeth flashing in a hungry smile.

Hands with nails as long as butter knives reach down to touch my cheek. The skin is cool but soft as satin sheets. The other hand rakes its nails gently through my hair, as the massive goddess kneels.

Let Me protect you, My Champion.

Not me. There are...

I forget who I'm here for.

Let Me give you what you need.

Her fingers soothe away all of the pain. In Her hands, there is quiet, peace, and I can think. Caea. Sensuen. Falun. Orion. I came here for them, for my court. I lost Caea. There was a cave-in. There are people trapped. Clarity floods me.

Focus.

My body settles. The panic abates, my mind stays clear. I raise my eyes, peering into the face of Goddess Order. /Are You doing this for me?/

Of course I am. You need My protection, My

strength, to do what must be done.

/And what is that?/

Save your court, the Zaran queen, and your family.

/How can I save them?/

With My power guiding yours, sharpening it, strengthening you.

Her eyes are bottomless. She speaks in riddles. The prophecy still doesn't make any sense.

/What does the prophecy mean?/

The endgame curse?

My stomach clenches. /Curse?/

A spell that gifts My Four of Rema with the power of probability. It was a fortune spell, but the only means I have to control it is you.

/A spell?/

I am a goddess of magical creatures. I am magic, but magic is unpredictable at best. Winning this war ensures the survival of many. Losing means everything I have built is gone. I need you.

/I don't trust You./

Which is why I love you.

/Like You loved Corin Peredil?/

I loved Jain Peredil more.

I sit back on my heels. Her hands slide from my face. /Tell me about him./ People don't talk about him like they talk about Corin. They mention his amazing powers, but nothing else.

He spoke to me, told me to *"take care."* In that vision of the past, he'd cried for his dead brothers. I'm dizzy and weak again. I don't want to cry for my dead brothers.

He wanted to save them all.

/His people, the Remasians?/

A shark-toothed grin, a screeching laugh that makes me clutch my head.

Do you care about the Remasian people?

/I'm not from Rema./ I don't know those people.

Jain cared for his own: his brothers, his lover, no one more. His precious ones I would have saved. I always had plans for My Maidens and My Child of Magic. But for Jain Peredil, I made plans for all of My Four.

/What?/ My chest is heavy, my head hurts again, but not from psychic strain. I don't understand what She's telling me. /The war wins us our worlds—Rema, Zare, Lenore, Earth, the other planets with us. It means the bad god can't take over./

Another horrible laugh. I grit my teeth.

I am afraid it does not work that way, My Champion. My Maidens understand. Your Councilors understand. Jain Peredil understood.

Maidens. Hellene's cold features flash into my mind along with Nialiah's sultry glances and Imari's shifty discomfort. Councilors: hawk-nosed Theorne with his glacier blue eyes and Viveen with her pointy vulture face. I never felt right around any of them. The Maidens were too weird, the councilors too slimy. What do they know that Jain Peredil also knew? Because they were around in those days. They knew Jain. The Maidens met Order. Had the Remasian Council met Her as well?

Cold fingers on my chin, sharp nails grazing my throat. I jerk away, toppling backward and scrambling onto my knees. I try to stand again and can't. My legs don't work.

Allow Me to share a vision with you.

No. /I don't.../

She grabs me again, my face an egg between Her thumb and index finger as She squeezes. **So soft and fragile this skull of yours. Nothing I Create would be as breakable. Nothing I have made is this weak. I offer you a way to survive this shell, to survive this power that is ill-suited to such a frail form, to survive the death of an empire and the rise of a new world, to save what you love. Yet, you cannot allow Me a moment of your time?**

The pressure increases.

Devon is in danger.

/What?/

Lawrence will die.

Her being radiates truth.

Do you want to see?

Grief suffocates me. Tears and snot gush over the dried rivulets of blood on my face.

See what I see.

I lean into Her touch.

15

LAWRENCE

IT TAKES HOURS TO FIND our way out of the jungle. When we reach the first dirt road that leads to the small village in question, Nialiah makes us pause so she can work an identity spell. She murmurs a few words under her breath and a slight wave of vertigo rocks me onto my heels. I gaze at my group, disappointed everyone still looks the same to me, only wearier.

"Did it work?" I ask, confused.

"On outside eyes," Nialiah says. "The spell was not cast to make *us* see each other as strangers."

We approach an old-fashioned sign on a wooden post with scrawled letters carved into it. A welcome? I tap Evan's shoulder and nod my head at the sign.

"Says you better have money, because you're about to experience the best shopping on the East side."

I make a face. Evan can't lie, but I get a strong feeling he's loosely interpreting. Just how far can Evan stretch the truth before whatever magic in him that keeps him from lying kicks in?

Evan beams at me, like he knows what I'm thinking. "It actually says welcome to the East Shopping District."

"Thanks." I elbow him in the side, something I'd do to Dev or Ly when they're being douche bags. He catches my elbow, sending a spark through my skin that hits the ticklish spot under my armpit. I laugh and punch him in the shoulder. He takes the hit, pulling me to him briefly for a slight one-armed hug.

"You're doing well, little brother." He lets me go.

I cheer inside, feeling warm and proud, as if Mom or Dad said 'good job' even when I thought I was screwing up. I shrug, biting my lip on a smile as we continue to walk. I miss the shade of the jungle. The high sun bakes my skin and the growing humidity makes me want to strip out of my hot gear.

The village comes into sight a few minutes later: a strip mall, surrounded by treetop apartments. Storefronts made of dark wood line the main street, carrying clothing, jewelry, supplies and food. Brown and copper-skinned humanoid people move about inside the stores, some spilling out on the sidewalk and road. Some glance at us, but no one asks questions. Either Nialiah's spell is working, or these people are used to travelers.

The doughy smell of baking bread and melting cheese wafts through the air, making me homesick for malls and pretzel stands. My stomach grumbles. The chewy jerky mixture of protein, fiber, vitamins, and disgustingness we have for food is only satisfying for so long. A girl shifts her yellow eyes from her group of friends and grins at me. She looks away before I can smile back. I walk backwards, gazing at the side of her deeply tanned face and perfect thick lips. Chasyn grabs me by the collar.

"Not now, *gikak*," he says. "There'll be other missions where you'll get to do *that*."

I flush, shrugging him off and scowling at his chuckle.

Nialiah works her way around the group to put herself at the head. "This way."

We follow her to the end of the street where a medium-sized wooden tavern sits. Its large front window is frosted glass with loopy print in the center.

Nialiah turns to us. "I need to talk to someone in private. Make nice with the locals, until I am through."

Imari looks troubled, but says nothing, and I'm surprised no one else does either. Evan shrugs like he doesn't care, and everyone seems to follow his lead. Okay, I guess if he's not worried...and then, Nialiah swings open the wooden door to the tavern and a blast of cold air that smells like nacho cheese has me running past her to get inside. Everything else is temporarily forgotten in the face of air conditioning.

Centralized air is god. Forget Order and Pandemonium. I peel off the uniform jacket, ignoring my own funk in favor of plopping down on a wooden stool at the long bar near the rear of the establishment. My legs sigh at being given a break. I tie the jacket around my waist as I gaze around the place. A stupid smile cracks my face. I'm in a seedy bar, just like in an old movie, with smoke hazing the air, sticky surfaces, wooden tables, and chairs and stools that look older than Grandma. I want to order a beer, nah, a whiskey, and sample the bar nuts. There's a bowl of round yellow things a few inches away from my knuckles.

The rest of my group trudges in, Chasyn crossing over to me, while the others stake the place out, breaking into smaller factions. Evan and Adonis go to a far corner, looking for all the world like a couple of guys waiting for buddies who were supposed to meet them here. Desiri goes to the other side of the bar. Is she ordering a drink?

Jalee and Ramesis grab hands, leaning into one another like lovers. Imari goes to a table and starts a conversation with the quartet of ladies sitting there. Nialiah drifts through the room, heading toward the rear of the bar where there's a door that looks like it's for staff use only. She knocks twice, it opens, and she disappears.

I wonder if this is really okay. Should I really just be sitting here. Should the others be mingling? Do they have an unspoken plan they didn't share, because they're all badass soldiers that don't need to talk to send messages?

Something thumps the bar in front of me, and I look up into dark red eyes shadowed by black hedge brows. Thickly muscled arms rest folded over each other on the table, as the man/woman leans forward, sizing me up.

Uh…eep?

I clear my throat, wishing we'd had more time to get my translator installed. Chasyn speaks for me, the language lilting and light, almost Gaelic.

Hedge-brow grunts and turns to the rusty taps against the wall.

"Ordered the house brew," Chasyn whispers to me. "Maybe don't drink it."

I feel like an undercover operative. My first drink, and Chasyn says not to try it. Is he crazy? Two dark cups without handles smack down on the table. Hedge-brow grunts again and Chasyn says something else in that language.

"He wants money?" I ask.

"She, and no," Chasyn says. "It's free. She says you need hair on your chin."

I blink. Maybe I won't drink the house brew after all. I pull the cup toward me, staring into the pale green liquid. Smells like red licorice. I dip a finger in, brush it over my tongue and stifle the urge to puke. Licorice, lemon, and hot sauce. Hearty laughter from Hedge-brow. She sounds like my grandpa cracking up in the afternoon over bad soap opera acting.

I glare at Hedge-brow and take a sip. It's worse this way, but this lady isn't gonna laugh at me all night. Chasyn gawks at me, eyes wide with a mixture of horror and awe. "*Oi...oi...*you..." But he doesn't stop me, as I chug the rest and slap the empty cup down, wiping my upper lip with my arm.

Belching and ignoring the cloying burn in my throat and belly, I look around. "That wasn't so bad." My voice is a squeak. I cover my mouth as Hedge-brow howls with laughter, a few other people crowd the bar and join in on the fun.

Chasyn slaps me on the back, a broad grin on his face. "You're something else, you know that. How are you feeling?"

"I think I'm good. But, uh, you were right. Don't drink that."

Hedge-brow plunks down a big clear glass of water and I guzzle it like Mountain Dew. Damn, I miss Mountain Dew.

I clear my throat a few times and cast a glance around the tavern. Evan and Adonis sit with a group of men and women, laughing and chatting. Well, Evan's laughing and chatting, while Adonis makes eyes at the person across from him. He's not so creepy when he's into somebody. I can see some girl or guy falling for him. Desiri's still on the other side of the bar, doing a good job of pretending she's drunk and hitting it off with a couple of greasy-looking guys in gray coveralls. I can't find Jalee, Ramesis or Imari.

"They're really good at blending in," Chasyn says under his breath. "Bet they're getting all kinds of intel."

I nod, wondering how long Nialiah is going to take.

A room temperature brown cup presses into my hand. "Here you go," Hedge-brow says without accent.

I take it, peering down into dark blue liquid and tilt my head.

"It's just berry juice, on the house."

"You have a translator."

"It'd be bad for business if I didn't have a talk-box, boy." Those brows snuggle together as red eyes analyze me. "Don't always turn it on, though. Especially when I'm talking to people who look like they're from around here. But you ain't, 'cause you talk funny. Where ya from?"

Shizz. Nobody came up with a backstory for me to use. Uh...

"Amsree. We're on a break from school," Chasyn says.

Hedge-brow hmphs, looking Chasyn over too. "You came *here* on a break?"

"It's cheap. This guy," he gestures to me, "can't even afford a translator. And we wanted to visit that temple that's supposed to be around here. But..."

Hedge-brow growls deep in her chest, lips turning down, face going cold.

My stomach flips. I chance a look at Chasyn, about to shove him back and yell, "Run everybody!" There's a flash of worry in Chasyn's eyes, but he stays cool as my pulse jumps. Are we gonna have to fight our way out of this place? My hands clench around the cup, already thinking of what I might be able to do with the juice inside.

"Don't bother with that temple," Hedge-brow says. "S'not even on holy ground anymore. Duke Hasal moved it over to Trinah, 'cause it's more of a tourist spot. Unless you two are looking for pretty trinket shops, shade, and lounging wear?"

I shake my head and Chasyn rolls his eyes. "No," he says. "We're studying theology. We want to visit the sacred grounds. I thought the temple placement seemed odd. Our books gave other coordinates to the site than what we were told when we got here."

Hedge-brow clears her throat and leans in. "If'n you ask me, I think that duke found something under that place and didn't want nobody to know he dug it up, so he moved everything. The real grounds are all gated in now."

"What do you think the duke dug up? A temple relic?" I ask.

Evan's Stone looks like a piece of finely cut concrete when he's not near it. There's a good chance the duke wouldn't have thought anything of it, unless it was sealed up all fancy. Evan's Stone had been at the bottom of a shallow pond, and if he hadn't been there, it wouldn't have transformed into anything someone would notice. Unless they knew what to look for.

"Some rock."

I turn my head to the light voice that had spoken. A tall, young guy with short blond hair puts his elbow on the counter next to mine. "Heard it got sold to that army settling into the West."

"When?" I ask.

A shrug. "Couple *jewels* ago. Hey, Tip, can I get a brew?"

"You got brew credit, Cybre?"

"I got all kinds of credit now, Tippy. Duke Hasal pays good."

My eyes widen. "You work for Duke Hasal? Did you actually see the 'rock'?" Not that it'd look like anything special when it's not around me. How would anybody know what it was?

Cybre raises an eyebrow that's almost as white as his skin. His eyes are a pale blue. "Who wants to know?"

"Uh…" Theology students?

I look over at the sound of tiny thunks hitting the bar counter and see four flat crystals cut into squares skidding across the wood toward Tip. Silicone and oxygen atoms flicker under my radar—quartz. I turn my head, cheek brushing rough cloth, and look up to see Evan standing between Chasyn's and my barstools. His keen gaze is on Tip as he smiles.

"I'm paying for these three. Does this cover it?"

Tip takes the money, her gaze fixed on something over Evan's shoulder. Cybre is looking in the same direction. I follow his gaze, and, in a heartbeat, I swear the whole bar goes quiet.

A tall, green-skinned man strides toward us, Nialiah at his side. Another Lenoran, here? He closes the distance between himself and Cybre, grabbing the pale man by the collar.

"I don't want no trouble," Cybre blurts.

"I thought I expressed to you the last time how unwelcome you are in this place." The Lenoran man's solid black eyes are cold. A harsh line wrinkles his brow. "Anyone assisting with temple desecration is unclean company."

"Come on, Sayan. You know I had to!" Cybre's face reddens by the second.

Shizz, I don't think he can breathe. My stomach lurches. I start to complain, but Evan places a hand on my shoulder. "Sayan's with us."

I bite my lip, reassessing things. He'd come to the bar with Nialiah. He's undoubtedly Lenoran. Nialiah walked into this place like she owned it. Huh. "Her brother?"

"Husband."

I jerk my head back to gawk at Sayan and his wife, Nialiah, the lady who'd come onto Lyle like a thirsty cougar. Hell, is Hellene married too? Imari? I thought The Maidens were celibate, like priests.

"You had nothing to do but be honorable, and you could not," Sayan growls. He lets Cybre go, and reaches into his pockets, pulling out a handful of quartz squares like the ones Evan gave to Tip.

"Take this money and go away from here. Dig up anymore artifacts or sell anymore secrets and I will know about it."

Sayan throws the crystals at Cybre, several of them hitting the floor and scattering under the bar. I hate watching the guy drop to his knees to scour for every last piece of quartz. He must really need it.

I get down on the floor with him, finding a couple pieces myself and passing them to him. There's no reason to humiliate the man, the whole bar's watching. Cybre snatches the squares from my hand, glaring at me like I'm the one who threw his money.

"Hey, I'm sorry."

"Save it," Cybre grumbles. He clambers to his feet and rushes out of the tavern without a backwards glance. Two large men with dark red skin and the builds of pro-basketball players sidle up beside Sayan.

"Follow him home," Sayan says, smooth as the Godfather. The men nod and walk to the door. I doubt they'll be discrete in following Cybre to wherever he's going, and that would be the point. Sayan wants Cybre to know he's watching him. Is Cybre that much of a snake? He didn't seem that bad to me. Aside from temple desecration, which to Sayan must be an insanely serious crime, what had he done?

"Wha—" I start.

"Lesson one, don't talk to anybody about anything when you haven't been briefed or trained. Lesson two, don't drink alcohol." Evan studies me, expression so intense my damn anxiety locusts wake back up.

"You didn't give me any directions! You walked off. How was I supposed to know?"

"I didn't think I needed to tell you not to draw attention to yourself."

"Look, you guys were all working the room," Chasyn says. "We were too."

Evan narrows his eyes at Chasyn. "You haven't had enough field experience. You shouldn't have been chosen for my brother. Get up."

Chasyn blanches and gets to his feet. I'm still on the floor, like there's more crystal- money to be found down here. "Hey," I say, "he's doing great! You can't talk to him like that."

I stand up and enjoy the fact that I'm taller than Evan. Hard for him to look down on me now, but his eyes cut me to his level.

"Oh?" Evan stares at me, looking just like Mom when she knows I'm full of shizz. A weird pang of homesickness twinges in my chest, before it dies and I'm left glaring at my brother.

"Yeah. You said it earlier. He's not one of your people. He's one of mine. And I...take care of my own."

Evan continues to watch me.

"Let us leave now," Sayan says.

I notice the rest of our group's joined us now. How inconspicuous is this? "Should we...?"

"You are with me," Sayan says. "This township is mine, and now that you are my guests, no one here would dare mention your presence."

I think about those big men trailing Cybre and crack my knuckles. Yeah, I bet they won't. This guy *is* the Godfather. He moves past us, Nialiah's hand in his, and exits the tavern, the others following, leaving Evan, Chasyn and me behind.

"Um..." I say, because my brother's still looking at me. "I'll catch up, Chasyn. You go."

"Are you...?"

Evan breaks his gaze on me to glare at Chasyn and Chasyn salutes, and leaves.

I watch Evan looking after Chasyn's retreating form before his eyes come back to me. His mouth's a straight line. I can't read him, until he smiles, eyes crinkling. "Good."

"What?" Isn't he gonna yell at me or punch me or something? Devon would, but no, Evan looks ready to burst out laughing. He claps me on the back.

"I hate that you almost compromised the mission. I'm going to have Desiri drill you on blending in. That won't be fun, but…" He nods. "You stood up for your soldier. No matter how wrong you both were, you didn't let me threaten him. You did that instinctively. So, good."

"Thanks?" I don't know what to do now. Hit him on the back too? I mean, it still seems like I should be getting yelled at.

"Now, get away from me, before I set your hair on fire. I can't believe how stupid you are!" He smacks the back of my head with an open-hand and storms past me out the door.

I rub my scalp and look back at the bar. People are still watching us, but they awkwardly go back to their business when they meet my gaze. I make eye contact with Tip and she gives me a nod, stopping a pour to raise a partially filled mug in my direction.

Approval? Does she know who I am now, since I'm with Sayan? Who knows what these people think. I wave, feeling an overwhelming need to get out of here, and jog to catch up with my brother.

SAYAN'S HOUSE IS A MEDIUM-SIZED stone mansion, nestled in a cleared-out lot of woods, a few miles outside of the town. The sprawling foyer is a manicured green garden with five-foot trees. The branches are face-smacking low and long, making the trees seem like they're holding hands. Gold bobbles of fruit the size of my head dangle from vines wrapped around tree arms. It looks like a bit of Lenore in a box. I frown at Sayan as the tall man drifts through his garden, gesturing at his trees and fruit and gazing at Nialiah, like he wants acknowledgment for it all.

"Why'd you leave Lenore?" tumbles out of my mouth before I think about it. Shizz, but oh well. I do want to know. It's obvious he's homesick.

Sayan's eyes follow Nialiah as she cups a bobble in her hand. She waves like the Queen of England. Sayan utters an oath as he gazes at me and the others again. "Ah, so this is what you all look like without the glamor. Wonderful spell, Nia."

Nialiah's features soften and her dark eyes sparkle. I see why Sayan probably thinks she's gorgeous. I clear my throat to get his attention.

Without looking at me, he says, "I had no choice, but to leave Lenore."

A small hand touches my shoulder—Imari. She shakes her head at me. I blink, not wanting to leave it at that. There's a story here. Sayan moves to Nialiah, arms going around her waist from behind. He attempts to kiss her cheek, but she breaks free of his hold and glares at him.

Sayan stares at her. "We should go upstairs to discuss business matters. I am afraid I have information that will make your task more difficult, if not impossible."

"Not liking the sound of impossible." Chasyn seems to materialize beside me. He'd kept his distance from me on the walk here. I'm glad Evan didn't scare him away from talking to me.

Sayan leads us toward a wooden, moss-covered staircase that corkscrews through the ceiling. Green-skinned people, men and women—more Lenorans— bow deep as Nialiah and Imari pass and greet Sayan as 'sir.' They keep their bodies bowed as we all pass by.

My leg muscles cramp climbing the steep stairs and I'm reminded of everything I've done today. Shizz, it feels like it's been two days, not just half of one. Though, my perception of time is all messed up with the different hours in the day on various planets. Earth people complain about jet lag, but jet lag has nothing on space-lag. I'm second to last to reach the next floor and am disappointed to see that it's normal compared to downstairs. Wood floor, beige stone walls, massive windows shrouded by heavy purple drapes and a large round table in the middle of the room surrounded by high-backed armchairs. It's the home office of a corporate boss. Sayan goes to the table, running his palm along the edge. The table glows a warm silver and images project from its center. A 3-D display of a building. Its walls fall away, revealing a skeleton plan of its insides.

"Though these reels were *snared* a *jewel* ago, the images captured are still useful in learning the lay of the land. This building is where your Stone is being kept," Sayan says, taking a seat in one of the chairs and nodding for us to join him. Evan and Ramesis sit on either side of Sayan, Imari beside Ramesis, Adonis next to Evan, and so on. I end up sitting the farthest away from Sayan, shoulders brushing against Chasyn's and Nialiah's.

"That's a big building." I ogle the schematics. I should feel amazed, relieved, but ugh. "Do you have an exact location inside it, like a room number or something?"

"No," Sayan says. "As you know, your Stone does not emit signals or radiate any type of energy." His eyes are on Nialiah.

Evan leans forward. "Do you have any plans for getting us into this facility? These are layouts, but can you see where there are sentries, soldiers, weapons?"

"Yes." Sayan stretches his hand toward the building skeleton. The picture expands. Cubes of various colors appear, populating halls, rooms and doorways.

"The small golden palles are soldiers. My sensory tech detects the frequency of their translation and communication devices, the red overlays depict whether the soldier is carrying an energy weapon, the green indicates that the person may be a type of magic user."

"Roughly half of them use magic, then," Ramesis says. "The other half are undoubtedly specialists trained to complement magical attacks."

"Some greens are darker than others," Evan says. "Is that an indication of strength or magic type?"

"Strength. The darker the stronger," Sayan says.

Evan hums, gaze thoughtful. "Can you run your sensory tech on us?" He waves his hand toward Adonis, Jalee and Desiri. "I want to compare our magical strengths against theirs."

Sayan nods and waves his hand at the building projection. The image scoots over to make room for another glimmering construct. Four gold cubes, or palles, the size of baby shoeboxes, revolve in a small circle.

"Hold still," Sayan says, running his index finger across the table's surface like he's signing a contract.

Green mists over the gold cubes, starting out neon then darkening to army green. The middle cubes practically turn black they're so dark. Sayan rises to study them, then turns his attention to Evan and Adonis, his posture rigid like he opened a cabinet and found a nest of roaches inside.

"You have active Breed blood inside of you," Sayan shouts.

"That's common knowledge," Evan says.

"Not…" Sayan shakes his head. "I did not know this. Nialiah, you did not inform me."

"I thought you knew," Nialiah says, her tone haughty. "As Leader One said, it is common knowledge, and with you being the governor of this district, one would assume—"

"The governor?" I bust in. Well, now the house and deference make more sense. Governors on this planet are the equivalent of dukes in monarchies. People pay them taxes and celebrate their birthdays with fireworks. Or mini explosions that looked like fireworks in the file I read.

"Yes, meet Governor Chiastraiyn of the East Ipirot District," Nialiah says flatly. "He was our original point of contact before our first sojourn was deterred. We trust him more than most since he is a native son of Lenore *and* my former consort."

"I was never your consort!" Sayan's nostrils flare.

"You were given the title. You chose not to accept it."

"I was your husband! You fled from me and chose this," he nods at Imari, "and that witch woman, Hellene. You let them take you. I could have saved you."

Nialiah glares. "I have an obligation to Lenore. The honor was bestowed upon me and you do not turn away from such things. You could not understand that, and so you are here."

And shizz just got real. I don't hear anybody else breathing, but Sayan and Nialiah. They look angry enough to kill each other, but under all that I think I see something else. Nialiah's hands tremble. Sayan's lips quiver. They're either going to commit double homicide...or smash.

A shrill whistle cuts through the air. Everyone grabs their ears, eyes going to Evan who's standing on one of the chairs.

"You can go and have all the sex you want later. Right now, tell me why you're so bothered by my magic."

I bite my lip. Don't laugh. Don't laugh.

Snorting from Imari tells me she lost the battle. Nialiah shifts her glare to her sister. Ramesis covers the lower half of his face with his hands, but his eyes gleam. I'm pretty sure he thinks this is funny.

Sayan huffs and moves away from Nialiah, coming to stand in front of Evan as he hops down from the chair. Sayan sizes Evan up. "Elanyd, fire affinity, Ember Sprite. Your power signature would indicate that you are probably a half-Breed, but I know you are not."

"It doesn't matter what he is," Ramesis says. "His advanced magic is to our advantage. However, with the way you're acting, we won't be able to use it, will we?"

I blink. Go Ramesis. I hope I get more of a chance to hang out with him after all this.

"No," Sayan says. He clears his throat, attention still on Evan, then on Adonis. "You may not be half-Breeds, but are you affected by halif?"

"Halif?" Evan asks.

Imari moans. "It can be called titchum, or crania, or dotira sikle in various regions."

"Dotira sikle." Evan's shoulders slump.

"The grounds for the false temple may not be sacred," Sayan says, "but apparently, they were chosen for other reasons. The land is known for its halif trees. The blossoms are full this time of year, the pollen plentiful.

The grass is white with the dustings."

"Could a shield spell or protective covering help?" Ramesis asks. "You won't have to touch it or breathe it in."

"No." Evan shakes his head. "It nullifies our connection to nature magic. Anything it coats, we can't reach. And just being near it makes me nauseous."

"So, we're down two powerful members," Ramesis says. He looks to the image of the building skeleton and the colorful palles depicting soldiers. "Do you have anyone we can take in with us, Sayan?"

"Um, excuse me, Majesty Harliel." Chasyn's cheeks flush as Ramesis's brown eyes rest on him. "Aren't you enough to take down a force as small as that one? I saw what you and your brother and sister did on Lenore."

"Yes," Ramesis says, sitting back in his chair. "That was on an open field. I'm not skilled in close-quarter combat. If Caea was here in place of me, this situation wouldn't seem so bleak."

"It's not bleak," Desiri says. "My magic's stronger than most of the people in that building, and one of my specialties is stealth. Jalee's too. We could slip in and get the Stone. We just need to confirm at least two or three definite spots the Stone could be kept in."

"We could plot paths from here," Evan says. He pulls his braid out of the man-bun and tugs it over one shoulder, fingering the woven strands, a habit of his when he's thinking something over. "Are you sure about this, Des, Lee?"

Desiri's gaze is steady and Jalee raises her chin.

"We have to try," Jalee says. "But obviously, we will need more resources than what we have. Sayan, are any of your personal guards trained in infiltration?"

"Why would I have guards trained to steal things? I have people who…" Sayan trails off.

"What?" Nialiah asks. "Did you get an alert?"

Sayan's green complexion goes waxy as he nods, hand going to his ear. "My perimeter guards are under attack."

Chairs scuff across the floor as Evan, Ramesis, Desiri, Adonis and Jalee get to their feet. My thoughts flash to Cybre storming out of the bar with those guys following him. Did he…?

"Nikand is leading them." Sayan rubs his temples.

"Who is Nikand?" Nialiah demands.

"One of the men I sent after Cybre. I should have gotten rid of Nikand a long time ago."

"Is Cybre with them?" I don't know why I'm so worried about the guy. He didn't like me.

The others talk over me as Sayan changes the image on the table to show his outer grounds. People in black and gray uniforms march the lawn, led by one of the big guys that had been with Sayan in the bar. Knocking on a door to my left. Sayan snaps out a loud command and a troop of men and women in white and gold tunics enter, lining up by Sayan's seat.

"What's being done out there?" Sayan asks.

"Pacht and Uniz are engaged on the outer walls and left inner wall, but Nikand knows our layouts," a woman says. "We've lost twenty of our staff."

"Those uniforms," Ramesis says, "they're Su officials. The woman nearest Nikand has an icon on her breast pocket."

"Are you thinking that's our Champion?" Evan asks.

Grim looks around the table.

Sayan lets out a loud breath. "They are requesting an open line of communication."

"Put them on," Evan says.

Annoyance flickers over Sayan's face, before he nods, and suddenly there's sound to go along with the footage of the front lawn. The woman with the golden icon of wings and squiggly tentacles on her right breast pocket puts herself in front of Nikand. She doesn't smile. Her skin is light blue, and her irises are so pale they almost blend with the whites of her sclerae. She talks through a long mouth that stretches from pointy ear to pointy ear, revealing four rows of flat silvery teeth.

Her voice is a croak that Sayan's system translates with a stutter.

"Greetings Maidens Nialiah Ac'kor Mayaistri and Imari Ac'anastia Distilyani, Majesty Ramesis Harliel and Leaders One and Four of Rema. I am General Gy'ri Uferg of Kanchetep, Honored of Kahine. I have come to extend to you a second offer. The first was made to Leader One and rudely refused. However, this time I assure you we have the advantage, and now that more reasonable parties are present, perhaps you will reconsider our generous offer to forsake Kahanna and unite under Kahine."

Evan rolls his eyes, but Ramesis's glare keeps him quiet.

"What is your offer?" Nialiah asks. She and Imari rise, and I jerk my head at the new arrangement. Evan and Ramesis are shoulder to shoulder, and Imari and Nialiah join them. They've created their own group on one side of the table.

Should I be over there too? Evan motions me over, and I get up, touching Chasyn's shoulder as I go over to stand with my brother and the other Champions of Order. Wild energy whirs through my body as I squeeze between Evan and Imari. No one's overlooking me now.

"Surrender," Gy'ri says. "Renounce your gifts and your goddess. You owe Her no true loyalty, and Kahine will ensure your safety and comfort. He does not even require you to serve."

"But that safety only extends to us, right?" Evan asks. "Not our nations or planets, or families?"

"That may not be entirely correct," Gy'ri says. "I am sure Our Most Exalted Kahine will grant you an audience for further bargaining, but you must accept his initial offer. He feels a demonstration of mercy could end this war more peaceably, unlike your Kahanna. However, this offer will not be given again. I believe some of you to be wise. Take your time to consider. We will give you an *airmark* to decide."

"A single *airmark* is not sufficient time to—" Ramesis starts.

"An *airmark* is all you will have," Gy'ri says. "I urge you to use your host's enhanced viewing technology to observe the latest Silver and Gold Allegiance reels. You may disconnect this comm, so that you may watch in private."

Sayan waves a hand, cutting communications with Gy'ri. Another swipe of his hand makes several cubes displaying black space spring up from the table. Scribbles in Common run across cues superimposed on images of soldiers and civilians, bloody and wounded; some standing in ruined cities, some on open fields. The people featured are of all colors: bronze, purple, blue, pink, yellow, tan, white, copper. Some seem as human as I do, others remind me of Star Wars, but they all wear similar expressions of pain, fear and defeat. Some of the cubes cut to reels of men and women in official robes, pantsuits, and unblemished, shiny military uniforms. All officials in every cube hold their heads high, shoulders back—a universal stance of pride.

Words run across the screen as each leader, some in Common, some in other languages, all with a slight delay in translation, say: "We will not submit." The words seem to echo. The reels cut to people being shot down, cut down, dropping to their knees as fires rage behind them. The screens split to show the cities and fields being destroyed, and leaders standing stone-faced, but bright-eyed. A tear runs down the cheek of a female official with long blue hair and small horns on either side of her forehead.

Sayan makes a choking sound, four more cubes rise from the table, each displaying swirling stellar systems of color and light. I love looking at images of space, had spent some of my time on the Ievisara between training, lessons, and studying, staring out windows, wanting to space-walk like an astronaut. I blink as one of the stellar systems trapped in a cube darkens, like a god didn't pay the light bill. The blackness billows out like smoke. An implosion?

"What the *fip*?" Evan yells, reaching out, hand going through the cube. Jalee and Ramesis cover their mouths, Adonis's dark skin grays, Desiri's jaw goes slack. The only people who don't look affected are Nialiah and Imari. They stare like scientists watching a simulated project fail as they prepare a second crash dummy.

"That was the Hylt Formation, in Sector Seven," Chasyn breathes. The cube that had displayed a ruined city and the one that showed the crying woman are completely black.

I stare at Jalee, remembering her goddess story. "They lost and didn't agree to go to Pan, Kahine, whatever the hell you want to call him, and...I thought only one planet died." Along with whatever people were still on it. Because that happened in seconds. How could anyone escape? Shizz.

"The Hylt Formation is a smaller star system," Jalee says, words slow. "They had a single sovereign—Juliss Ama-Niyad."

"She was *fipping* amazing." Desiri's voice is subdued in a way I've never heard from her. "Are those reels verified?"

Sayan nods, expression grave and terrified. "What are we witnessing?"

The other stellar systems in cubes stay bright, but then the focus narrows on single planets. Their atmospheres, some blue and green, some pink, one looking way too much like Earth, swarmed by dark clouds, before their images gray, the space around them rippling.

"Good gods," Ramesis murmurs. "This..."

"It is what happens in wars between gods," Nialiah speaks up. "It is why we fight, Champions. You have never experienced these horrors. My sister and I have. I shielded you, Sayan, perhaps too much."

A lot of cold eyes are on Nialiah. Imari looks at her hands.

"It would've been nice if you Maidens had opted to share this with your fellow Champions rather than having us 'go through the motions,'" Ramesis says. "Not one of my relatives believes in 'gods.' We follow the mandates of Parliament and hope to be released from duty before we're too old to pursue occupations we actually enjoy.

However, we do love our people, and if we knew this was at stake... That woman outside, she says if we surrender and lose to Kahine, He won't let this happen to Zare, or Rema, or—"

"Earth," I croak. "What about Earth? I don't..." I look at Evan. "I don't care about Rema." I've never been there. I don't know those people. I don't know my father, and according to the Council, Rema was attacked, and good old Devrik Lauduethe was evacuated. So, he's not even there. Wait, Rema was attacked. "Were any of those..." I look at the cubes. They're all black.

"No," Evan says, tone hard as granite, "but it easily could have been. The rest of the Remasian Council was evacuated when our father was. So, if the council was to say, 'We won't surrender,' they wouldn't have died with Rema, but they still would have made a dramatic public stand against the enemy."

I taste bile at the back of my throat. "They wouldn't do that, though? Because there are still people left on Rema, right? Everyone wasn't evacuated. The council wouldn't let all those people die like that. Kahine's giving them a choice, like us. If they decide to surrender, they'd just...pay tithe to Kahine?" I look to Jalee.

Jalee frowns at me. "I told you a story, Lawrie." She nods to The Maidens. "Only they know the truth. I think they should answer your question."

"I do too," Evan says. "Because maybe I'm up for accepting the deal that woman is offering."

Nialiah looks furious.

Imari's eyes widen, her face alarmed. "You cannot!"

"Tell me why I shouldn't." Evan sits down and puts his feet up on the table.

"Because you cannot trust Kahine," Nialiah says

through her teeth.

"But we can trust Order?" Desiri asks.

"Gy'ri mentioned there was an initial proposal, Leader One." Nialiah waves a dismissive hand in Desiri's direction. Desiri snarls, but Evan gives her a look and she stays in place.

"Yes," Evan says.

"Did that deal involve saving anyone but yourselves?" Nialiah asks.

"No, and so I ignored it, but I did not ignore the part where one of Pan's Champions told me that I'm missing pieces you have." Evan focuses on Imari. "If you were me, would you accept the offer given just now?"

Imari shakes her head. "No, no god..." She stops, taking a breath. "The woman did not say Kahine would re-negotiate the terms of your asylum. She simply said He *might*. And though your truth-seeking ears heard no lies, it simply means she is unsure. If someone does not know an outcome, they can say whatever they want."

Evan gives a grim nod, glancing back at Adonis who looks stone-faced in response.

"I do not know what stories you have been told," Imari says, "but gods do gain strength when they take another god's realm and tithe. The atrocities we just witnessed may have been prevented by complete surrender, but the people would be forced to submit to a new government and they would have to worship Pan. In our years, we have seen few successful conversions of power. Most planets and small solar systems were annihilated during the First Sector Wars. There are histories you will never know." Her gaze is sad, her voice solemn. "But know this: I do not believe any god would spare the people of another god's Champion. It is enough for Them to steal the loyalty of the Champion, but an example, a show of strength, must be displayed for the greater universes to see. Too much mercy is weakness; too generous a deal is folly. Kahine will not save your Remasian people." She looks at me. "And He certainly would not save your Earth, or any other planets that hold your dear ones."

"What do we do, then?" Locusts beat against my ribcage. "Because that can't happen to Earth, or any more places."

"But it's what will happen to Su and Nazflit regions," Jalee says.

I close my mouth. Right, the 'evil' places, filled with people who might be biting their nails like I want to right now.

"We're just choosing ourselves over other people," Jalee says.

"So, what?" Desiri snaps. "That's what they're doing too. We win or they win. There's no compromise. I prefer for us to win. The benefits are better. But how do we do that from in here?"

"Pull up a layout of the perimeter," Ramesis says. "Let's see where they all are."

Sayan's hands shake as he wipes away the black cubes and new screens open, displaying the grounds around his house. The small army with Gy'ri stands on the lawn. Gy'ri seems to be giving a speech. Her lips move as the soldiers stand at attention. Surrounding screens show smaller gatherings of soldiers holding bazooka-like weapons on their shoulders.

"I'm enough to take out the rear yard," Ramesis says. "There are only about twenty soldiers there."

"And we'll take the front." Evan gestures to himself, Jalee, Adonis and Desiri. "When you're all done in the rear, come and join us, Ram."

"What about me?" I ask. "I've been practicing. Chasyn and I can take the flanks to help out."

Everyone stares at me.

"You can't do it unsupervised," Evan says. "You need back-up that can't be spared."

I seethe. "But..."

"The plan is flawed," Nialiah says.

"You got better, hag?" Desiri glares at Nialiah whose hands spark with black magic.

"Mage-child, I have lost my patience with you." Nialiah's voice is low and silky. If murder has a sound, this is it.

"We need Lawrence's Stone to win this fight." Imari places her hand on Nialiah's arm, holding her sister's wrist until the black flames around her fingers die. "We cannot let them drive us from this place without it. That is our main goal."

"Who here doesn't know that?" Desiri tosses her hands up in the air. "I'm still waiting for—"

"Evan, come to me," Imari says, as if Desiri never spoke. She doesn't wait for Evan to move. She walks, slipping between my brother and me, touching his shoulder. Evan starts at the contact, eyes going wide. He looks ready to take a step back as she invades his space.

"Remove your jacket and tunic. I need to see your Mark."

Evan tilts his head, then frowns, unzipping his outer jacket and shrugging out of it. The tunic rolls over his head next, until he's naked from the waist up. It's not time to be jealous, but Ev's pretty ripped to be so skinny. Am I the only Leader Lauduethe without a pack?

Evan turns, showing Imari the awesome scrawl

down the length of his spine that starts at the base of his skull.

"This might be unpleasant." Imari's body sways as her lips mouth words. I flashback to the Mark-reading session Devon, Lyle and me had on Lenore. We'd had to sit down. The world had spun and Lyle popped a brain vessel.

"Wait. You can't just—" I start, but nothing stops her hand running down Evan's Mark. Evan spasms, doubling over as she holds on, hand resting on the small of his back.

Adonis, Desiri and Jalee are alert, inching toward Evan, eyes glinting. Desiri pulls the blade from her belt again.

"He is fine." Nialiah sounds preoccupied. She watches Imari and Evan, her face unreadable. "The letters, Imari, the coordinates. Could you decipher them?"

Imari pulls back, looking at the group, sweat dotting her brow. Evan moans clutching his stomach as he straightens, face pale. "What did you get out of that?"

"What I suspected," Imari says. She clasps her hands in front of her. "Leader One's Mark does not contain a map that would have taken him anywhere near Onkurus. Your Stone should have been buried on Bruhje."

"So, why was it on Onkurus?" Evan asks.

Nialiah smiles as something seems to dawn her. Her black eyes gleam. "Oh."

"Oh, what?" Evan looks like he might puke, even his lips are pale. Sweat mats a few curls to his forehead.

"You think you died on Onkurus, but the Stone saved you." Nialiah laughs. "Oh, Imari, you genius girl."

Unspoken conversation passes between Imari and Nialiah, as Evan gags and claps a hand over his mouth.

Sayan yips like a teacup dog and motions to a door and Evan does a runner. Okay, war outside, and Sayan is worried about barf on his rugs? Really? I take a step after my brother, but stop as I feel eyes on me.

Right. I need to be processing what no one's saying. Evan should have died but didn't on account of his Stone appearing in a new place, because he needed it.

Holy shizz.

"Lawrence," Imari says softly.

"I have to die, right? If I die, my Stone will try to save me?"

No one speaks.

"At least that's what you think, or hope, I mean. That if I die, it'll come here." I'm rambling. I'm crazy. I tempt death all the time, leaping off stuff that's way too high, diving into ditches too shallow, but there's always a chance I'll make it. That's what makes it fun. This isn't just tempting fate. Are they plotting to kill me and see what happens?

"No," Chasyn says. "There's another way. We can fight our way out and come back with a full-on militia to get that Stone."

"We have to get it now," Nialiah says. "There is no fighting our way out of this and returning for what is ours. If we leave, we lose the Stone. We lose the war. We all die."

"Or maybe we don't," Chasyn says. "And Lawrie doesn't die at all."

"Oh, come off it, child. We are not planning on simply murdering him and seeing what happens!" Nialiah shouts and I stare. Did she read my mind?

Evan returns, still looking like Texas roadkill. He comes to my side, putting his hand on my shoulder. "It's up to you, Lawrie. We can escape, if we need to."

But nothing will be won, and everything might be lost. If we lose… I see those black cubes and imagine Earth inside of one. I picture Mom, Dad, Nikki, Jeremy, Galeo and Saphera going on about their normal lives. Off to work, school, banquets, oblivious to the end. Would I be in another room like this one, watching the Orion Arm of the Milky Way Galaxy go dark, knowing I could have done something and didn't.

I can't.

I remember Stop the Hate Texas, and that poor You-Tube kid I couldn't do anything for. I think of Stringy Reggie being beat up in Kemah, and the mess I made trying to help him out. I see Quent, crazy ass Zeke and purple lightning. Helpless. I'd been helpless.

But I'm not anymore.

I saved eighty people on a ship with my brain and awesome powers. I'm learning, doing things, but to be stronger, to win this, to help, I need….

"What do I have to do? I mean, what do *you* have to do? I mean, will it hurt?" Because, holy friggin' shizz, I am asking the people in this room to kill me and/or watch me die.

"I know a spell," Nialiah says. "There will be no pain, and if our plan does not work, I believe I can reverse it."

"You believe?" Evan's voice is loud.

"I can," Nialiah says firmly. "But you have to ensure that I am not disturbed. I will have to stay here with Lawrence. I will need a circle of protection and two people to remain so that I can draw life force from them. One shall have to be my sister, the other…" She looks to Ramesis. "Only the strength of Champions can return life to another Champion."

"How will we hold off what's outside without Ramesis?" Jalee asks. "We need his brute force. The army will invade these walls."

"No," Evan says. "No, they won't."

"What are you talking about?" Adonis asks. It's always weird to hear him talk, when he's quiet for so long.

"We have an attack that can render that army useless for five minutes, maybe longer if I..." He touches the warded pouch on his belt where his Stone is kept.

Adonis pales, Jalee shuts her eyes, and Desiri looks anxious.

"Entropy?" Jalee asks. "You want to use that spell with the Stone?"

"How much time do you need?" Evan asks, ignoring Jalee.

"I will need half an *airmark* to prepare," Nialiah says. "The ritual itself will only take a minute to perform."

"Gy'ri gave us a full *airmark*," Evan says. "We'll wait until time is nearly up, and then we'll go out. When you're ready to begin your spell, I'll initiate Entropy."

"Evan, that spell drained almost everything in you the last time you used it!" Jalee shouts.

"But this time is different." Evan pulls the Stone out of the pouch; the bright green glow casts shadows on the walls around us. "And it doesn't want me to die. Nialiah said as much."

Jalee's mouth opens and closes, she turns away from him. Desiri licks her lips and Adonis brushes a lock of hair behind his ear. A nervous tick? Adonis has nerves?

I have nerves. Evan may be going out to kill himself, while I am definitely killing myself. No, Nialiah is killing me. I blink at the woman as she nears me. We're the same height, but right now she seems taller. Her hands are soft as they brush my face.

"Do not worry, young one," she purrs. "I know what I am doing."

I sure as shiggity hope so.

"Is there a smaller more secure room we can use for this?" Nialiah asks Sayan. "And we will need access to a bath chamber as well."

"Y-yes," Sayan says. "My underground chambers were built to accommodate me should I need to…disappear. I can conjure images of the outside from any room, and there are tunnels below that lead to the outer grounds."

Sayan leads the way, Nialiah holding my arm and urging me to walk beside her, close behind Sayan.

"You will live to see the end of this war, Lawrence Lauduethe," Nialiah says in my ear, her breath tangy like exotic fruit. "Trust in the goddess, and She will reward you."

But something tells me I shouldn't trust gods, especially not ones that let whole planets die to serve as examples to us.

I think about Devon and Lyle, so far away. Will they know I died today? Of course not. How would they? I don't even know if they…if they're alive. One of them, both of them, could be dying or in trouble.

Just like me.

The journey to the basement is a blur of color and random darkness as 'gotta do something' chants 'oh shizz, oh shizz…' and my locusts hum a funeral dirge.

A hand on my back and the sweet smell of some kind of mint. I look over to see Evan.

Is he gonna tell me that everything's going to be fine? I wait for him to speak, but he doesn't. Maybe because he can't lie.

I can't call my Mom, or Dad, or…. Wet warmth prickles the corners of my eyes and I scrub it away, but nothing takes away the aching pit spreading through my gut.

Today, I die.

16
EVAN

THE LAVATORY HAS THREE CHAMBERS—one for waiting, one for washing, one for privacy. I lean against a cold wall in the waiting chamber, counting the swirls in its rocky, white and gray surface. Vines drape the wall across from me like curtains, red buds of a dormant plant shift in my direction. I trudge to them while grazing soft, closed petals with my fingers. Tiny drips of life energy seep into my pores. The tension in my neck eases, though my stomach's still a little queasy from Imari's flash-reading.

I give a soft whistle of thanks and more energy dribbles under my skin. I pull away, going back to my original position, and knock on the door to the toilet chamber. "Almost done in there?"

"Y-yeah." Lawrie's voice is small. "Just give me another minute."

I don't laugh. He's scared as *pidge*. I know how it is to want to hide that from people, especially ones who would hold it against me later. However, we only have an *airmark*, and we're wasting time. I hear the sound of running water; then the door opens and my brother's bright green eyes meet mine. His skin is ashen, his posture slumped.

"Sorry. Uh, let's do this?"

It sounds more like a question.

I nod. The waiting room connects both the privacy and bathing chamber. Lawrie's behind me as I open the door and step down onto a sunken beige floor. A large bathing pool shimmers in the center of the room, and I close my eyes, flashing back to a shallow pool of glittering green water. It had been warm, the water soft and smooth. It'd been a decent place to die. The Stone of Magic feels heavy in its pouch. My fingers brush the cloth and I shake my head, dragging my hands over my face, rubbing.

Stop it.

I turn to Lawrie, watching him strip off his uniform. He's lean with no muscle built from strength or endurance conditioning. The more defined muscles in his legs tell me that maybe he rides...bicycles, that's right, or something of that nature, something for recreation. He pulls off his shirt, revealing the long expanse of his Mark, similar to mine, but with longer vertical shapes.

"Can I keep my shorts on?" Lawrie asks.

I start at the sound of his voice. "No, but I promise I won't look at anything."

He snorts. "Whatever. I don't care. Just don't get jealous of my amazingness or anything."

"Shut up and get in the water, *gak mopi*."

His bare feet slap against the floor as he walks by me and leaps into the pool headfirst. I blink as he splashes and bobs to the surface, treading water. He throws water at me, laughing as I jump back, and then sobers all at once, frowning. "So, uh, do you come in, or do you sit on the side?"

"My coming in would dilute the magic," I say. I also hate deep water. "Swim around, do what you want, while I purify the pool." Jalee gave me the herbs and crystals she carries to cleanse dark energy. The council loves sending us onto hallowed grounds for product deliveries and exchanges with other government leaders. Allegiance surveillance isn't allowed to survey activities held in religious territories, and a lot of political 'understandings' happen behind temple doors. Jalee thinks negative energy follows us from those meetings.

I suddenly want to step into the shallow end of the pool and wash the dirt from some of my missions off. To keep Rema strong and influential, the councilors say certain unspoken alliances have to be made, like they expect more territory wars after the end of the Second Sector War. My first missions were envoys to planets in Cold Zones. I smiled and took back signed treaties that allowed Rema to exhaust resources from those planets in return for military aid we were always too busy to send. I wipe my cheek, recalling the glob of saliva a little girl had spat at me during a tour of a dead forest.

"Hey, you okay?" Lawrie calls.

I want to tell him I'm fine, but I can't. I sigh. "Still not over the reading. Don't worry about it."

"But you're going out to fight after we do this," Lawrie says. "I heard what Jalee said about the spell you want to cast. She said it hurts you."

"It doesn't matter if it does. If you're going through with this, the only way to give it time to work is that spell." Entropy, the chaos plague. I feel my insides bleed every time I work it. The longer I hold it, the darker my world becomes. A few heartbeats are usually long enough to get the effect I want, but this time...

"If this works, but you die, then it's—"

"Tell me something about you I don't know." I kneel on the gold border around the pool and unclip Jalee's pouches from my belt. I open a bag full of fresh camise sprigs, their clean scent relaxing me. I gaze out at Lawrie, he's still frowning.

"There's a lot you don't know," he says finally. "Where do I start?"

Sprinkling sprigs into the water and watching their white and yellow stalks fan across the surface before sinking, I wonder where he should start. Our travels together have been too short. He probably knows me about as well as he knows Adonis. I'm failing my brother. I should have taken him aside long before now to talk. But when had there been time?

"Tell me about your friends," I say. "I learn a lot about people from the company they keep." I pour the second pouch of rounded pink quartz into my palm and blow on the crystals, weaving magic through them.

Lawrie snorts again. "Maybe, but what can I learn about you from your friends? Let's see, you've got a crazy warrior girl who can take down the Rock. You've got a guy who's like a living statue, and a really pretty, proper girl who grew up in a temple. They don't fit each other, or anything I can tell about you, but you all get along. I think that even if it wasn't their job, they'd die for you, man."

I take in a sharp breath. Yes, they would. "I'd do the same."

"And that's the kind of guy you are," Lawrie says.

"Loyal, protective, a little scary, sort of intense, but, you know, people can take you at your word. I mean, even if you could lie, you probably wouldn't, not much anyway, and not to people you care about."

I stir the water with my hand and gaze at him. He stares at me, eyes shining.

"My friends can't tell you all that about me," Lawrie says slowly. "Because they don't have to. We ride skateboards and four-wheelers and throw firecrackers into pools like this. I've got this one friend who'd do anything for me…but I don't think he'd throw himself on a grenade."

"Would you for him?" I ask.

Lawrie shrugs. "After all this? Yeah. I mean, I want to help people. I have all this energy inside, always have. And I can't keep it in. It makes me want to do all kinds of crazy shizz that pisses Mom off. My friend Galeo says it's because of my power, that's all it is. But I don't think he's right. I mean, do your powers tell you who you are?"

I blink at him. "Yes…and no. Why do you think he believes your powers define you?"

"I don't know," Lawrie says. "If I wasn't so hyper, I might not do half the things I do or am willing to do, I guess. But I think I'd still want to. I'm nowhere near as electric as I used to be, now that I'm working with my power and all, but I'm still me. At least, I think I'm still me."

Dipping both hands into the warm water, I shuffle notes in its melody, urging small currents to circulate the herbs and crystals around the pool. The atmosphere in the room lightens, a minty scent perfuming the air. The cramping and churning in my stomach slow as I breathe deeply. "And just who is that?" I keep my eyes on Law-

E. ARDELL

rie.

He grins and slicks wet curls off his face. "I'm still figuring it out, but I want to learn as much as I can about anything. I want to understand people and languages and cultures. I want to build tech that makes things better and faster. I want to assure people that things will be fine, and really mean it, because I can make those kinds of promises. I want power, but..."

"You don't want to lead?" I ask.

"No." He shakes his head. "I think I do want to lead. Maybe not a planet, but the idea of being in charge of something good excites me. Ev, I'm scared as shizz, but I have to do this. I think about family and friends back on Earth and how they could end up like those people we just saw. It makes me sick. I can't stand by, if I can do something, because...I gotta do something."

I stand, not needing to touch the water anymore to keep the cleansing elements moving. I hum a song, swaying to the rhythms of air, earth and water. The melody whispers itself to me without words, embracing me, and for a moment I'm not aware of Lawrie anymore, just the power he doesn't want defining him. Magic makes me who I am. It's a part of everything I do. It's everything I hear, breathe, taste and touch. It even takes my mind at times.

If I lose control, it can do what it wants with my hands and voice. I shut my eyes, remembering Onkurus again, and the fire spell—Immolate. The Stone had amplified it, and there had been a minute where I tried to stop it from burning and I couldn't. It scared me.

The whispers stop. The water glistens a milky white hue.

"Ev?" Lawrie's at the edge of the pool, long arm

outstretched, hand on my ankle. "Are you sure you're all right?"

I kick his hand away and kneel in one motion, scooting to the edge and leaning toward him. "I'll tell you something about me."

He lifts his chin.

"I scare myself. Sometimes, there's too much power in here." I pat my abdomen where my inner fire burns. "And you heard them up there. You've seen the fear when someone brings up the active fae magic in me. It does affect who I am, my reactions, my instincts. I own them all, but it means I'm wild. Do you know what I mostly remember about Earth?"

He rests his arms on the ledge, setting his chin on them. "What?"

"Mom and Dad not knowing if they could put me in school with other kids," I say softly, those memories resurfacing, fuzzy yet solid. Mom's face, younger than the face I had met on our recent journey. Dad looking exactly the same, ageless. Mom saying *"yes,"* Dad saying *"no."* He was afraid I'd hurt the other kids, burn them. Mom wanted to try. She thought I was better than Dad believed. My eyes sting over that.

I see her again, older, staring at me on the Ievisara. Her eyes glimmered with unshed tears and she'd looked so *fipping* guilty. She'd hugged me like she never wanted to let go, like she'd carry me out with her. Does she still believe I was better, am better, than a creature that hurts people to get what it wants?

How wrong she is.

"I remember," Lawrie touches my arm, "playing. I remember you helping me build Lego towers that looked just like the picture on the box. You knew how important it was to me to do it right. I also remember scamming Lyle and Devon. They were some dumb ass kids. I wish you'd been with us longer and I'd been older, because, after about four, my memories are perfect. I missed remembering you clearly by a year."

"You don't remember bad things about me?" A flash of a burning bedspread, bright with goofy-looking characters, turning brown and black. Dad yelling and Mom rushing in with a large red canister. Horrible smelling fizz coated the bed. The twins screamed while I clutched a plastic toy, a car or something, to my chest. Phantom feelings of rage, maybe even jealousy, boiled inside me, as I glared at the twins sitting in my toy box, mine, howling, faces red, noses snotty. Dad picked them up and stared at me like I was a monster.

I blink, willing the memory away, because it hurts that every now and again, the few times we're in the same space, Dad still looks at me that way.

Lawrie suddenly laughs and I look out at him as he shakes water out of his eyes. "I just remember laughing, a lot, with you."

I sigh and wonder again what I could have been like had I been with Lawrie and Mom and my other brothers longer. I'd undoubtedly be a lot more hesitant to fight, but I'd probably be like Lawrie in wanting to help people. I like protecting what's mine: family, friends, soldiers. The Remasian people look to me to save them, and so they're mine as well.

"You're a better person than you think you are, bro," Lawrie says out of nowhere. He lets go of my arm.

"How did you know I was questioning that?"

Lawrie smiles. "Look, we may not know each other well, but I pay attention. You heard me before. I wanna learn everything. That look in your eyes just now, that's the look you get when..." he bites his lip, "you think you're letting someone down, because of things out of your control. You don't do it when too many other people are around, but you do it around your court, and now me. I've seen it a few times."

I raise my other brow. "Guess I'll have to work on that." From somewhere in the room, a timekeeping bell chimes. Time is precious. "Submerge yourself for..." what's a time-keeping measure he knows? "...thirty seconds."

He gives me a worried glance, before he audibly inhales and slips under the water. I sit back on my heels, counting and pondering his concern. I have control issues. Most people know it, but not many worry about it because it means I handle business.

Soft ripples in the water get my attention. Lawrie bobs an armlength away from me, head fully surfaced. "I'm getting cold."

"Good," I say. "It's working. You'll be ready soon enough."

He floats on his back. "A lot of old people used to ask me what I wanted to be when I grow up. You know, college was a must, but jobs? I thought maybe a surgeon. I could cut open brains and find cures to diseases and disorders. Then I thought about being an engineer. I could work for NASA and get into a program to travel through Allegiance Space."

I smile at his need to talk. This brother's only quiet when something's wrong.

"So..." Lawrie drawls. "If you weren't leader, or let's say, we win this, and you quit being leader, what would you be? Because you're considered grown-up, right? Would you go to some kind of college?"

"I'm not considered an adult, but I'm done with primary schooling. So, perhaps I'd continue my education." I attended sessions at various magic-user collegiums, learning foreign casting techniques and brewing styles. There are so many different ways to cast the same spell, but they all work if the user has skill. Accessing magic comes out in multiple forms—mage-craft, sorcery, enchantment, channeling, weaving, composition—and most magic-users are limited to one form of craft-play. I'm not.

"I like going to school," I say. "We have an uncle who owns half a university on Bruhje, so I've got an open invitation for enrollment there. I'd study magic." I think about my gardens outside of the flat I share with Adonis on Rema. "And botany."

I feel a pang of loss for the spare room I converted into an animal shelter for strays. I placed my last rescue, an adolescent teglu, with a local conservation a month before I'd left for Onkurus. "And zoology too."

"Hold on, we have an uncle who owns a college, and *you* want to triple-major? I have fellow nerds in my family!" Lawrie kicks his feet, propelling by me. "I was really excited to meet you. I still am."

"What do you mean 'still am?' You've met me."

"No," Lawrie says. "I've met Leader Lauduethe, Leader One of Rema. I've only met my brother a few times, and none of those times were long enough for me to get to know you."

I nod. "Hmm, I'll give you that."

"And I want to meet you," Lawrie says. "Devon and Lyle, they have that twin thing. They lock me out. I want to be locked in, and I think you and I could have that. I think we did when we were little."

I wish my childhood memories could be as positive as his.

A knock on the bathing chamber door, then a voice. Imari's. "A few moments more, leaders. Is the cleansing almost complete?"

My stomach clenches, but the nausea is gone. "How do you feel, Lawrie?"

"Colder."

"We're almost done," I tell Imari. I tilt my head back, staring at the moss-covered ceiling. The same red buds from the waiting room wave back at me.

"So, what do you think?" Lawrie asks.

I tear my gaze away from the ceiling, looking back to him. He's treading water again, inches from the pool's border, staring at me.

"About?"

"Us being close," he says. "Do you want that? I mean, Lyle, Dev and me kinda crashed your party. Did you forget about us? Think about us? Want us?"

I feel as cold as Lawrie says he is.

I don't want to tell him about my anger and resentment, or that I'd forgotten them as Evan Lauduethe replaced Evan Ladreth. Ladreth...that was the Earth name, wasn't it? Looking back at my life, I see with clarity my time with Adonis, Jalee and Desiri. Learning magic and control, training instincts and honing them to enhance hand-to-hand combat skills and weapons mastery. Practicing with soldiers two and three times my age, telling them what to do and making them listen. Bowing down to the council, pretending to respect the purposes of my missions. Between all of that, there was time for laughing, dancing, playing, making friends, growing, meeting new family.

Wet fingers on my arm bring me back to reality. I peer at Lawrie, frowning at his sad face.

"It's a 'no,' then?"

I blink. "A 'no' to what?"

"Thinking about us? Wanting to be close, maybe?"

"I didn't think about you after being on Rema for a few *revs*," and maybe I wouldn't have ever thought about them again, if they hadn't come to me. But that's not how Fate would have it, and I'm with Lawrie now, a little brother who makes me smile, when I want to be sick, and who talks because he's bored. A brother who wants to be brave and help others, who doesn't necessarily want to lead, but will if he has to.

"You know," I say. "I do remember Legos and crunchy cheese things. And sharing them with a curly-headed boy I liked because he was shorter than me, unlike those other two."

I recall him, blurry, curls in his eyes, shoving crispy orange snacks in his face after offering me a powdery handful. Cheese on the white rugs, on toys I know weren't mine or Lawrie's—misleading evidence. An uncontrollable urge to laugh doubles me over. My forehead touches Lawrie's outstretched arm, his fingers still on my wrist. I laugh until my chest hurts. Lawrie squeezes my wrist and I look at him through runny eyes.

Niobe-va. It felt good to laugh that hard. I straighten up, wiping my damp cheeks and grinning at him. "Yes, Lawrie. Let's be close."

He grins back.

The knock comes again.

We stare at each other. "But it can't happen, if you don't make it," I say. "If you choose not to do this, I promise I'll get you out of here and we'll figure something else out."

"I'm doing this." His eyes are clear, grip firm.

"Then, it has to work. You have to make it work. I don't have advice. I didn't do anything, didn't know anything, except that I didn't want to die. Keep that in your mind, Lawrie. Say it while you're going under. I don't know if it'll help, but it's something."

Lawrie nods, serious. "Okay. And you, you have to do the same. You have to make it too."

"Don't worry. You pull through, and so will I," I say, choking a little on the last clause, because I'm not really sure about it. Lawrie frowns, then squeezes my wrist again and releases me.

"I'm ready!" he yells, voice reverberating around the room.

The door opens and Imari, Nialiah and Ramesis shuffle in. Nialiah holds a large cloth bag. "You are needed outside, Leader One. Remember, you must wait for at least ten minutes, before you begin."

I rise to my feet, giving Lawrie one last look. I can't hug him, or he'll have to be cleansed again. Touching hands is the most we can do, and we already did that. I let out a shaky breath. "Good luck, brother. I'll see you outside."

Lawrie offers me a grin. "Yeah. To you too, bro."

His words have a funny pitch to them, not a lie, but truths he can't promise. Hope always sounds flat to me, but today it's sharp, desperate. I want to be desperate too, but I can't, not with a job to do. Desperation clouds focus, so I will it away. I'm not desperate, I'm determined. This has to work on both ends, and I will put everything I am into its success.

That's a promise.

I move past Ramesis and Nialiah, slowing before passing Imari. I grab her elbow and we make eye contact. "I trust you," I say, and realize that I do or I wouldn't have been able to get it out. Why would I trust her?

A ghost of a memory brushes over me. Corin.

"The spell will be worked perfectly, Evan. I promise," she whispers.

She pulls away from me and I watch her walk to the pool where her sister constructs a ring of fat white candles. Ramesis speaks to Lawrie who's still in the water. I'm an afterthought in this room. I leave it, heading to the tunnel Sayan says leads to the surface where Desiri, Adonis and Jalee should be waiting for me.

17

LAWRENCE

THIS IS NOT WHAT I ever imagined hero-work would be like. My newly returned, and blessed, boxer-briefs and I lie in a wet puddle, surrounded by a ring of candles. My teeth chatter so hard I swear my jaw's coming loose. My skin prickles, still freezing from the water and whatever Evan put in it. Light footsteps and bare, green, human-like feet come into view. Ugh. I scrunch my nose. I hate feet. A whoosh gusts over my ears as the person sits behind my head. Another pair of green feet, then brown ones, step into the circle. It's so weird how I can only see the floor. The air above me shimmers with what Nialiah calls *eschones*—air spirits summoned to bind souls to objects or bodies. Instead of looking up and seeing the others, I see me...and feet.

Damn. My last view of the world will be full of feet. Yeah, Murphy loves me.

A slender green hand hovers over my face, the fingers slathered with white gook. A hot dab of it goes on the middle of my forehead, and a smear of the toothpaste-y crap covers my chest like vapor rub. A smaller green hand replaces the more elegant one, holding a stick that looks like a mechanical pencil without lead, and carves shapes into the paste. The skinny tip tickles my pecs and nicks a nipple. I chuckle. I'm ticklish. A light laugh comes from my right, Imari. A masculine sigh from my left, Ramesis.

"All right." Nialiah sounds breathy. "This spell must be worked sky-clad."

Sky-clad? Doesn't that mean...

"I have respected your modesty for as long as I could, but now it is time to lose the shorts."

Aw shizz. Had Imari let me put them back on just so Nialiah could get the pleasure of telling me to strip?

"Try not to upset the runes as you move," Nialiah says.

Imari and Ramesis stifle their laughter.

Are they naked too? Convenient how everybody can see me and I can't see anybody. I'd be less self-conscious if I knew everyone was naked. I groan and shimmy out of my briefs, hissing at how cold the floor is under my butt. Small green hands help work my undies the rest of the way off and they get tossed over the candles and disappear from my range of sight. And now, I can die. It's completely okay with me.

Except that it isn't.

My heartbeat rockets. I feel it in my throat. I take deep breaths, trying to calm down. Nialiah is good at what she does, or she wouldn't be a Maiden. Imari's here too, she can help. And Ramesis...Ramesis can cut Nialiah's head off if this doesn't go right.

The slender hand returns, covering my eyes, closing them with wet fingertips. Moisture dribbles under my lids, but it doesn't burn. The lukewarm liquid seems to pool behind my eyes and seep into my brainstem. My heartbeat slows and my lungs expand and deflate at the same pace. The fingers leave, but I can't open my eyes. My skin warms and...

Am I falling asleep?

"Let it take you, Lawrence" Nialiah's smooth voice. "It will be easier for you, if you just go to sleep."

No. I want to be awake. I try to take deeper breaths, try to open my eyes. I can't. My limbs don't respond when I want them to move. Nialiah says words, fast, in a language with a Celtic lilt. My chest burns. The paste sizzles, searing my flesh, branding my skin. I can't scream. I want to...

Suffocating.

My lungs won't.

Breathe.

A shallow breath I can't exhale.

Oh my God.

Heartbeats dull from a heavy stick on a metal drum to a soft mallet on a plastic table. Slower.

Waiting for the next beat.

Waiting for a new breath.

I can't.

"Let go, Lawrence." A whisper.

I don't want...

"Let go."

...to die.

The voice fades. The sizzling stops.

Quick breath in.

A soft beat.

Quiet.

Waiting for another beat.

Another breath.
Waiting.

18
EVAN

THE TUNNEL TO THE SURFACE is cold and narrow. Moss coats the ceiling and walls. The dirt floor is crisp under my boots. I stop at the wooden trapdoor, pressing a palm against it and listening hard. Voices on the other side: Desiri and Jalee. The sounds of stretching leather and blades on whetting cloths sing in the trembling air. I whistle and the trapdoor creaks open. Jalee leans her head in, a frown on her lips.

"You look awful," she says then pulls her head back.

I crouch and spring up, landing on the grass between the girls. We're behind the great house. Around the corner, gruff voices bark nonsense phrases at each other, like: "Wild dogs fly easterly." "Raptors dive deep." Has to be some sort of field code. The night around us shimmers, a cloak spell, one of Jalee's specialties.

"Adonis is staking the field," Desiri says. "The enemy has soldiers at every entrance. Sayan's people are going to help us cut them down, until you're ready for the spell."

"Do you have communication with him?" I ask.

"I do." Jalee taps her ear. "I wired his channels into my compal net."

"Make sure he knows his people need to clear off the field before I throw Entropy."

"I told him that before we came out here," Desiri says. "Told him anybody slow enough to still be out in the open when that spell hits is fodder."

I nod. It's the way it goes. I can only shield so many people from infection when the spell starts: Adonis, Jalee and Desiri. "How much time is left?"

"Not much," Desiri says. "You ready to make your entrance?"

. My mind goes to Lawrie, feeling his hand on my arm, asking me about myself. Is he...? I shut my eyes. Doubt I'd even feel it if he was. There's no reason for his Stone or Order or whatever it had been that had sent out my distress signal to blast one out for Lawrie. His help is here.

"Evan, I think you'd better..." Jalee begins.

"I would have your answer now, Champions of Kahanna." Gy'ri's voice booms across the field, amplified by some type of tech. Her words have a metallic undertone.

I square my shoulders and throw a glance at Jalee and Desiri. Adonis materializes from the darkness to stand at my side.

"She's center field," Adonis says, "and wearing no weapons, but she's surrounded by men who are heavily armed."

"Hm." I stride forward, stepping through the curtain of Jalee's cloak spell and around the corner of the house, planting myself in front of six very tall men with large canon-type guns on their shoulders. One starts, another places two of his four fingers to his chest, a religious warding.

"Oh." I open my eyes wide in mock regret. "Did I scare you?"

They curse and growl.

"Our leader waits." The spokesman has a smooth baritone voice that flows easily over all four rows of his pointed teeth. *Fip.* These people don't need guns. They can rip us to shreds with their teeth, if they're fast enough. Maybe they're slow.

I smile at him, then at the rest of his group. They stand still. "So, are you going to escort us, or are you going to move, so we don't keep your boss waiting?"

The spokesman snorts like a tamed steed. The other five part down the middle, making a way for me and my court. I walk through them, Adonis and Jalee at my shoulders with Desiri holding the rear, straight across the field, through Sayan's trampled flower beds and scorched shrubbery. Men and women in the uniform of Sayan's house lie stretched over the ground, dead eyes watching the sky. I murmur condolences to them as I maneuver around their corpses. The copper stench of blood and burned ozone hangs heavy in the air.

Several *ka* away, I see Gy'ri with a guard of ten around her. Her head whips in our direction and her soldiers fall back, leaving her exposed. Her wide mouth opens. "Greetings, Evan Lauduethe! Where are your fellow Champions?"

"Inside," I say. I stop a body-length away from her. My court fans out behind me, ready.

"You are the only one to accept this offer?" Gy'ri asks.

"I'm the only one to come outside." I look over my shoulder as if searching for The Maidens and Ramesis.

Gy'ri has ridges for eyebrows. She raises both. "You reek of *Breed* blood. Do not insult me with subterfuges. I know you cannot speak lies."

I stare into gray eyes so pale they're almost white. "Then I won't speak anymore."

Jalee touches my shoulder, and I spare a brief look at her. She mouths, 'The *airmark* is up.'

I reach for air, twining three threads together, then breathe a spool of flame, weaving it into the invisible braid of wind. I whip the fiery cord at Gy'ri as Desiri shrieks a battle cry. Magic thunders around me as Desiri, Jalee and Adonis unleash their weapons. Adonis calls water from the air and earth, throwing blankets of liquid around advancing enemies, drowning them on land. We move as a unit, Jalee uttering spells that cast glamours and shields over our team. Desiri's daggers spark with electricity as they slice through the air and throats of the men running to Gy'ri's defense.

In my peripheral vision, Sayan's bodyguards storm the field, fighting, roaring. I can almost taste their anger as they try to avoid running over the fallen bodies of their friends. I leap back as a wall of needles flies at me. Gy'ri holds a shield of spikes as long as her body is tall. She'd pulled it from nowhere, a *sutir*. She can rip things from other dimensions or store them there for later usage. *Fipping pidge*, I hate *sutirs*. I duck another shield-thrust and channel energy into my palms, shoving it outward, a blast of pure magic.

Gy'ri shouts, bringing up her shield, and screams as she's blown back, spikes vibrating until they shatter. She tosses the shield aside and plucks a long thin sword from empty air. The black blade glistens as she charges forward. The hilt of a pronged dagger is pressed into my hand by Desiri as she runs past. Twirling one of her long swords, she leaps onto her next opponent.

My fingers grasp my new blade, and I catch Gy'ri's sword in a dagger prong, thrusting upward with everything I have. My left shoulder screams at the force of Gy'ri's blow. *Niobe-va*, she's strong. Maybe stronger than me. I bare my teeth and push and hear a crystalline ping. A crack spreads across the metal of her sword and the black blade bends. I bring my knee up into Gy'ri's stomach, and the woman huffs, stumbling, bent blade held tight. She spin-kicks, but I drop into a low spin-kick of my own. She jumps over my leg, stabbing down with her crooked sword. I flip backward, landing on my feet, and spring into a new stance.

Blasts from behind. I duck and turn. More soldiers. A red laser blast hits the air in front of me, shimmering before it dissipates.

Thank you, Jalee.

"*Fip!*" I dodge a swing at my head and go after the nameless soldier that'd taken Gy'ri's place. I slam my fist into his gut, then jaw, and watch him fall. I take the next one down with a hard kick in the ribs that sends the man sprawling across the grass, momentum stopped by a corpse.

"Enough," Gy'ri roars. White energy grows between her palms and explodes toward me, taking out her own man instead. He screams, his blood spattering my face as I dive to the ground, rolling. I snatch at the wind, plucking four note chords to create warm and cold air currents that meet and rotate. Increasing the tempo of the song rushes the maturation of the cyclone. The funnel drops toward Gy'ri, storm building to devour her. She runs with animalistic speed, evading the storm spell.

I breathe, finding my center and reaching for my inner flame. Plumes of fire bloom in my open palms as I weave wild magic around them, then take an archer's stance, sending out a volley of fury hails at Gy'ri and her soldiers. Her people aren't strong, but we could lose to their sheer numbers if we misstep. My hands shake as I continue to blast. Gy'ri, though on the defense, doesn't seem tired at all. Her movements are graceful, her face unmoved.

I chance a quick scan of the battlefield. Jalee, Adonis and Desiri are holding their own. More of Sayan's guards lay in bloody heaps on the ground. *Niobe-va*, the man should have kept all of his people inside. They're no match for this army. In the distance, I see more soldiers march onto Sayan's property, all in enemy colors.

I hope that Nialiah isn't full of *pidge*. I'm trusting she really doesn't need more time. That…that Lawrie's… that it's done, because it's time for something drastic. I breathe a spire of flame straight into the air and fracture the light around it, so that it burns green—my signal. Jalee's voice buzzes in my ear, "Sayan's given the retreat order to his men. One minute, Evan."

I countdown, exhaling a green spire of flame in a roar, smoking four soldiers headed my way. Four down; forty more rise to take their places. Waterspouts and electric blades cut down more bodies. Jalee's corrosive potions smash into soldiers, degradable phials disintegrating upon impact, eating through their leathers and destroying flesh.

Not enough.

My hand touches the cloth damper-bag on my belt.

My heart skips a beat. I fumble with the buttons and strings keeping the bag closed. It seems to take forever for the lips of the pouch to open. Green light sparkles up at me, and the Stone sings to me: *Entropy.*

It knows what I want to do. Like it can read my mind or had listened to our plans. Like it's alive. I reach in, sparks shooting up my fingertips as they make contact. Magma hot power floods my veins, boiling beneath my skin.

"Time, Evan." Jalee in my ear.

I look beyond the elements, beyond the particles of matter, until the space around me is a jumbled mass of color and sound. Millions of symphonies play at difference speeds in multiple time signatures, some loud and somber, some soft and lively. A horrible mess to someone trying to listen to it all as one song, but I dissect the cacophony into solo sets. One of the softer songs: the growth of the purple grass. A somber tune, deep and throaty: the earth being soaked in blood. Furious, fast melodies spiral around jittering blobs: the enemy soldiers. Familiar riffs, as important to me as my own life song, glitter around three perfect spheres: Jalee, Adonis, and Desiri.

I feel my new power.

Entropy, it sings.

Stretching out my hands, I pull at the unmarked, rushed melodies of my enemies, scattering the notes, tangling their scores. Gritting my teeth at the awful noise, I yank more chords, throwing in extra rhythms while cutting others short. I'm a conductor in control of one-hundred orchestras gone wild. Play what you want, play as fast as you want, change it up. There's no order here.

Power blazes from me, fracturing harmonies with

a vengeance I've never felt before. One minute is my usual limit before I pass out. But now? There is no limit. I keep going, expanding the chaos, reaching beyond the soldiers on the lawn...

Wait, wait...

Entropy spreads like a disease.

No.

I pull back, covering my eyes, falling, tumbling. I'm on my knees, staring at a field of enemy soldiers hacking each other to pieces.

"Report," I breathe, accessing my compal connection. A crackle.

"*Oi vati fipping pidge*, Ev." Desiri's voice is soft.

"You can stop," Jalee says.

"Look straight!" Adonis.

I shake my head, bringing my eyes forward instead of letting them roam the field. A hand with spikes over the knuckles rushes at my face. I drop flat on my back and kick up, smashing the hand with my boots. I don't hear bones crunch. I spring to my feet. Gy'ri stands spaces in front of me, shoulders heaving. Her face drips with gray and yellow matter that stinks like gutter rot. Her pale eyes glint, her sharp teeth bared in a snarl.

"You..." she gurgles.

The Stone's power burns through me. My ears ring, my head swims, but I'm not weak. The chaos spell pulls at my core, but each time my flame sputters, the Stone feeds it.

"Evan, stop!" Jalee again.

Stop.

I can't look away from Gy'ri as she grows black lightning between her palms. I cut the energy-flow to Entropy.

Stop.

The horrible symphony slows as I grip the power, bringing it up into a shield to block Gy'ri's lightning. Black waves smash into my invisible barrier, breaking and rebounding in all directions.

"Guard-up!" I shout.

"Under cover." Jalee.

"On standby." Adonis.

"Waiting." Desiri.

I blow fire in Gy'ri's face, fanning it to generate smoke, wanting to put distance between us. A sudden sharp pain in my ribcage. I stagger, catching Gy'ri's foot and throwing the sharp booted toe back. She whirls, arms grabbing for my throat. I gather energy, weaving a light spell used for entertainment at parties, but when supercharged...

"Gah!" Gy'ri howls as white light flares in her face. I back it up with a pure energy blast, and a chop to her throat. My hand screams as her teeth bite into my flesh. I feel bones yield. *Fip.* I snatch the hand back, going for a roundhouse that connects with something soft. Gy'ri grunts and I follow with a high kick to the chin, weaving wind behind it for more force.

Gy'ri jumps back, reaching for one of her leather sleeves. Using a clawed nail, she rips the material. A golden band gleams around her wrist. Her body shimmers and seems to grow.

No, not seems to. She's bigger, broader, taller, her teeth longer. *Pidge.* I draw more power from the Stone, throwing up two shield spells as black light strikes fast, pushing me across the dirt, shields struggling to hold.

E*ntropy*, the Stone sings.

Her soldiers are all dead. I can't use them anymore.

My boots crunch over corpses as I give ground.

Who said they must live?

The dead have no music.

Then, an awful chorus that drills holes in my guts and sends splinters of ice up my spine moans from the bodies on the ground. The Stone hums a song my brain catalogs. What is this score? It's unlike anything I know.

The bodies twitch.

Hades and Ether.

Necrotic Arts.

Gy'ri's black power drives me back, beams fracturing, sending her lightning everywhere. It's going to hit somebody, kill somebody. I have to take her out. I don't need the help of dead soldiers. Give me more power.

I harden my shields, coating them in fire and air, and shove out, pummeling Gy'ri. She growls and bludgeons me, lightning flaring. Why is she so much stronger than me?

The song of the dead plays in my mind again.

If I sing it, can they hold her down? I just need her to quit moving.

One shield shatters; the other trembles. The lightning's heat cooks my exposed skin. I let the last shield go, rolling, using a dead body as temporary protection. Lightning cuts through the cooling flesh like soft cheese. Getting to my feet, I try another volley of fury hails, bleeding the Stone's energy into them. They tear through the air, thick and forceful enough to rip several bodies apart with one bolt. Gy'ri bats them away, one arm elongating toward me—a sword hand. I whirl out of the way, losing my balance as her knife slices into my thigh. I fall to my left knee, as my right leg throbs, hot blood oozing under cargo fabric, pasting it to my skin.

Gy'ri stalks toward me, knife hand out.

Vati fip. I'm going to lose. I can't lose.

Then sing.

I open my mouth.

The notes have a wrongness to them that make my insides writhe. Several *ka* away from me, the air shudders and fractures, like glass. Blackness pours through the fissures, creating a void that makes Gy'ri stumble back.

Terror grips me in a vice. I let go of the song and the black hole vanishes. Twitching bodies slump back to the earth.

I can't.

Gy'ri bellows, lunging at me again. Her teeth glisten as she opens her mouth wide, showing me all four rows. I struggle to my feet, realizing I'm still on my knees. My right leg gives way and I'm staring at the point of a knife. *Fip.*

The knife wobbles, as Gy'ri screams. The flaming end of a blade protrudes through her middle. Desiri plants herself in front of me, whipping out a pair of small, double staffs, blades dangling from short chains. A wall of water surrounds me, and Adonis appears. He kneels beside me, hands reaching for my leg.

"Ad..."

He gives me a hard look; then rips my pants' leg away.

Gy'ri struggles to rip the sword out of her belly.

Desiri springs forward, taking advantage of Gy'ri's distraction.

"Desiri, no!" Gy'ri is stronger than her.

Sing.

Desiri shrieks, falling backward. Adonis lets her

pass through the water barrier. He catches her, laying her down beside me, briefly immobilized by the sight of blood spilling from a long slash across her midriff. His dark eyes dart from my wound to Desiri's. I follow his gaze—Desiri on the ground, lips pale, eyes blinking.

She grits her teeth and curses under her breath. "Get pressure on it!" she hisses. Adonis pushes down on her stomach and she groans, bringing up a knee. "Tape it up. I need to get back out there!"

"No," I whisper. Behind Gy'ri is a shape I know too well. Jalee. She aims a stolen canon-rifle at Gyri's neck. *Sing.*

Gy'ri's knife-hand turns. The world seems to move in slow motion.

I throw my head back, opening my throat and howling the notes. Desiri and Adonis jump. Magic quivers; the earth moans. I sing bar after bar, weaving the spell, opening a new void. Corpses convulse, rising, staggering, then speeding toward Gy'ri. Gy'ri screams, eyes going wide as she uses her knife-hand to slash at her dead allies. Jalee disappears in the undead rush. My mouth closes, song over, yet the void remains, the dead still fighting for us.

Desiri coughs out a laugh. *"Vati fip, Ev."*

"Shut up," Adonis snaps at her. He rips her uniform tunic, making a bandage.

"Hades and Ether!" Jalee passes through the water barrier covered in the same gray and yellow matter Gy'ri had been.

I huff a breath of relief. I don't know how she made it to us, but thank gods she's okay. Jalee drops beside me, setting down the dirty canon-rifle, and staring. Black spots flicker across my line of sight, my vision dimming as dizziness crashes down on me. The Stone's power threads across the field, pulling undead soldier-strings like marionettes as they battle Gy'ri. I flinch every time Gy'ri cuts a thread and an undead soldier falls. The pain is like long sharp needles piercing my body.

"You can't keep this up," Jalee says.

I sway, wheezing as her slender arms fold around me. Her body's warm, the fabric of her clothes soaked through with sweat and enemy blood. I watch the battle through the blurry water barrier. Gy'ri vanishes in the flock of corpses and a flash-bomb of orange light sends body parts flailing through the air, thick globs of gray and yellow matter and dark purple blood strike the water barrier and run off. More bodies trudge toward Gy'ri, ready to fight, but not able to win.

"I can't get her down," I murmur. My eyes feel sticky. My fingers and toes tingle with numbness. The Stone sears, its presence beating in place of my heart.

Sing again, sing louder.

White noise screams in my ears. I think...

"Evan, she's coming." Jalee's tense. She holds me, but her head is turned. I squint at Gy'ri's lumbering form moving forward. The water's color shifts from clear to crystalline blue. The temperature inside our protective shell drops.

"My barrier won't hold for much longer." Adonis's voice is muffled, like there's something in his mouth.

Desiri curses. "Let me out then."

"You'll die that much sooner," Adonis says.

No. No one in here dies.

I breathe in, borrowing steel from the earth, life from the air, power from the Stone. I pull away from Jalee, missing her warmth, ignoring the blooming panic on her face, and sing again.

This time there are words.

Just as I didn't know the song, I don't know this language. The words come fast, sharp; they crescendo. Jalee covers her ears. The water barrier wrinkles. Gy'ri freezes as the void behind her doubles in size and something inside it lumbers toward the opening.

Terror twists inside me as large, black hands stretch from beyond the Veil, grabbing the reanimated corpses and pulling them through. Hands grab for Gy'ri as she slashes at them, trying to run. The dark fingers hook around her ankles, arms, waist, and throat. She yowls like a strangling beast as she's dragged into the void. Cold wind blows, the hole widening.

I stop singing.

It's over. I'm done, but the hole remains, the large hands still reaching.

I have to close it.

What do I sing to close it? Tell me what to do.

The Stone is quiet, power cooling. My heartbeat is my own again. I sense the Stone's presence, but the voice is gone.

Is this my purpose? To take out one of Pan's minions and that's it for me? Is this one of my destined choices?

"Evan." Jalee's voice trembles.

"Close it," Adonis says.

I can't look at any of them. My eyes fix on the billowing void in front of us, a rip in the Veil, a gateway to an *ether* world, to death. *Fip. Fip. Fip.* I'm sorry. "I…"

My friends. I reach out, grabbing a slender arm. Jalee? "I'm sorry," I murmur.

The water barrier turns navy blue. Adonis' hand touches my back.

A wet cough. "Vanishing spell?" Desiri.

"No power," I whisper.

The dirt beneath us feels soft, muddy, the water barrier leaking, making a pool. Adonis can't hold it anymore.

The void gapes, the fingernails on the black hands lengthening; only a *ka* away now. The *ether* realm beyond the Veil hums the song of the dead, as a large hooked fingernail touches the water barrier.

My heart beats in my ears, saliva catching in my throat. Huge black eyes materialize within the rip, peering at me, humming to me now.

I let go of Jalee's arm and move away from Adonis, finding strength from somewhere, knees knocking together as I stand. Jalee grabs at me, scratching my wrists as I bat her away. I lean against the water-wall, staring into the black hole, meeting those dark eyes.

Just take me.

Only me.

The finger passes through the water, touching my chest, and a bolt of stinging numbness runs through my body.

19

LYLE

SOFT FULL LIPS PULL AWAY from mine. I put a hand to my warm swollen mouth, and then run my tongue over it. My lips taste sour and flat, like the time Mom let me take a sip of her wine. The presence of the woman who kissed me hovers near my face. Her cool breath smells like rotten grapes.

Where am I?

Faces flit through my mind—Heather, a cheerleader back home; Gabby, a volleyball player; Nisse…shit. My eyes snap open and I topple sideways off the chair. Maiden Nialiah steps back, smirking as I scramble up.

"I find your neurosis charming, Jain," Nialiah says, voice light. "However, it would be wise for you to settle down before we join the circle."

Jain. I look around the room. The walls are coated with green moss; the floors are leafy and soft. We seem to be in The Maiden's palace on Lenore again.

My mouth moves on its own. "I apologize, it's just a bit overwhelming."

My voice spoke to Nialiah, but *I* didn't say that. This is a memory I'm seeing through Jain Peredil's eyes. I dig, trying to get a sense of his emotions, but I can't feel anything. There's a solid barrier between us. I can't interfere.

"You agreed to this. You said you would take part." Nialiah's voice is sharp, her beautiful face lean and cold. She's no longer the woman who kissed me, er, Jain. "If you renege, I will look a fool!"

"I'm not backing out." I'm on my feet, closing the distance between us. I take her hands. "I don't know how I'll be accepted is all. You know I'm not the one She hopes you'll bring."

"Do not be stupid," Nialiah says, caressing my fingers. "She knows your brother would never join us willingly. She has other plans for his inclusion."

My brother. Could we be talking about Corin Peredil?

Nialiah tilts her head, as if listening to something in the distance, then smiles. "They are ready for you, my love. Come."

She twirls like a ballerina, still holding one of my hands as she turns, putting her back to me. I'm pulled forward as she walks to a moss-covered wall and parts it like a drape. My ears pop as I step over the threshold, the temperature going from warm to cool. The bold blue lighting makes the room glow like a nightclub. A long black table sits in the center of the room, surrounded by six, backless saucer chairs. Two are empty, the others are occupied.

Councilors Theorne and Viveen spin their chairs in unison to stare at me. Neither seems welcoming. Theorne's glacier eyes scan me as Viveen's glare dissects me. Do they not like Jain Peredil? Or maybe they just hate everybody. I've never seen either one of them act pleased to see anyone. Across the table from them are Maidens Hellene and Imari. Hellene wears a smile that could be interpreted in two ways: borderline amused or borderline surprised. Whichever it is, she appears to be happier to see me than Imari who bows her head as soon as I meet her eyes.

I recall her mental voice saying that she'd protect me this time around. I want to talk to her, but Jain isn't looking her way anymore.

"Greetings, sisters," Nialiah says, "councilors. I have brought our guest of honor. He sits with us now as a New Believer. He will be beside us when we become the First."

Hellene nods her head. "Very well." She frowns at me. "You are prepared for what is to come? There are no questions in your heart? Because once I summon Her, there is no returning to your original state of ignorance. We can make you forget ever coming here, if you choose to change your mind now."

I don't like this. /Jain, I don't like this./

But he either can't hear me or isn't listening. This is the past. This is what happened. Inside of Jain, I tremble.

"I've made my choice," Jain says. "Summon Kahanna."

Hellene smiles and fingers a chain around her neck, pulling at it until the pendant appears. A miniature silver dagger catches the light. She slices into her palm and holds her hand over the table, letting the blood trickle onto the white surface. I stare as the blood moves, on its own, forming symbols and shapes that look familiar. Holy shit! If I had control of my hands, I would touch my back. Some of the symbols look like the ones in my Mark.

The Mark on the table catches fire. The flames leap into the air then burn low, like the dying end of a cigarette. The room feels heavy, gravity tugging at my arms and legs, making me want to sit. Nialiah takes my arm and leads me to a chair beside Imari's. She sits on the other side of me.

The table rumbles as the Mark spreads, the bloody letters taking over the table. I want to push my chair back, to jump away, but Jain is motionless. Nialiah holds his arm, grip strong. This is like that dream with Evan, the memory walk, when Order first appeared. Black space billows up through the symbols, creating a curtain, a veil that rips like cheap fabric, so a monster can come through. She seems taller than She had been in the Kupi tunnels. Her eyes deeper, teeth sharper.

Everyone around the table bows a head, murmuring prayers or greetings. I stare at the goddess. I don't know how many times Jain had seen Her before now. Is this his second time? I feel my hands clench in my lap. My teeth grind as my body starts shaking to match my quivering insides. Now, Jain is scared too. What was he thinking? Why would he come here?

Nialiah pushes my head down. My forehead nearly smacks the table. I stare at the crispy blood trails that reek like charred veggie bacon.

You are not the brother I want, Jain Peredil.

My head comes up. "He would never accept Your true offer. I'll do what needs to be done."

And you know what it is I truly offer? Order sounds amused.

"A place in Your new world for myself and my

brothers, as well as for those sitting around this table. We are the ones who accept You for what You are—a goddess with a desire to become one of the greater gods."

You do not feel betrayed? Her questions don't seem like questions. She's leading Jain's answers. Will She barbeque the shit out of him if he answers wrong? If that happens, will it barbeque the shit out of me too?

"I'm not betrayed, because I never trusted Your first offer," I say. "It made no sense to me. Why would a goddess be concerned about planets She didn't create? Why do You care about Pandemonium wreaking havoc in places You aren't invested in? Gods don't feel shame. Gods only feel the need for blood, because blood is power. Wars bring blood. Your proposal continued a war that might have been over in a few Years-in-Common."

Years-in-Common? Standardized years. I don't hear many people use that terminology. But then, the majority of the people I've hung out with have been Remasian soldiers. All time to them is based on Remasian revolutions.

A horrible laugh that scratches my brain with ragged fingernails. The others around the table wince. **Why did you accept My initial offer then, Jain Peredil?**

"I wanted to see the power You said You'd give to me. Your Stone eases the pain in my head and allows me to think clearly. I don't worry so much about my brothers' safety when they go off to battle, because the Stones give them more power. I was satisfied."

And now?

"I am honored You'd give me more, when You hadn't planned to. The destiny You handed to my brothers and myself—"

—is but a spell I cast. You are familiar with For-

tune Magic?

Jain's breath catches in my throat, forcing my nails to bite into my callused palms. This is Jain's reaction. Is he surprised? He doesn't know about that endgame curse she'd started to tell me about?

"You cursed the Stones."

Your choices will determine if I am victorious, and so I must ensure all of your choices are in My favor. You are not My creatures, so I cannot control your actions. I can only guide and persuade. However, with you a part of My circle...

"I can get my brothers to choose what You need," I say, "and You'll win. This reality will fade, and You'll Create a new one to Your liking."

Jain's tone is steady, like he understands everything going on, but that can't be right. What I get out of this is that Earth and everything else is going to disappear. All that will be left will be the people here, and Jain's brothers.

The Maidens and Theorne and Viveen are okay with this?

"Lenore will live on in the new world, as the crown jewel of Lady Kahanna's new society," Hellene says, her voice smooth and clear. Her gaze is even. "Everyone at the table, and your brothers of course, will have a have place on our council."

"Why are You saving all of Lenore?" Jain asks.

"Because of our magic," Hellene says. "Every person born on Lenore has access to its magical core. We are models of the beings Great Kahanna would like to Create."

"And She needs living models." Jain nods. "Is this why Corin is favored?"

Order smiles. **Your bloodline is ideal. It is one infused with the blood of My creatures. However, your brother is the only one with both active magic and a sound mind. I want to make more such as him. A child of Mine with access to all of life's magics and the intellect to reign.**

Jain laughs. Is he crazy? I thought Corin was the crazy one. I brace myself for lightning, holy fire and intense pain.

Everyone around the table sucks in an audible breath. Order's smile widens to show more teeth.

"Your Magic Breeds are feeble-minded and You *are* embarrassed. Do the other gods gossip about Your creatures?"

I swear Viveen and Theorne look ready to dive for cover.

Order's screechy mental laugh makes me want to scream. Wetness seeps from my ears. How am I still alive?

How could I have overlooked you, Jain Peredil?

A pulse of soothing energy wraps my brain in a warm blanket. I moan in relief. It feels so good.

Sit beside Me, My Jain.

My legs move. I scoot back from the table, gliding to Hellene's seat in front of Order. I say nothing as Order glares and Hellene practically jumps out of the chair, going to stand by Nialiah. I sit, shoulders loosening as Order's clawed hand strokes my cheek.

You are now My favored leader. Serve Me without question and you will have your place.

"I'll serve," I whisper. "You'll win, and I'll sit beside You. My brothers and I will sit beside You, always. So long as You save them, You can have me."

But She's still lying. They all died. They all died, but came back.

My stomach flutters as it does right before a fall. She didn't lie, but She didn't give him exactly what he wanted.

Because he did not serve without question in the end.

Her claws still caress my cheek, grazing the stubble I hadn't gotten rid of this morning.

Wait.

I blink around the empty room. What happened to everybody else?

"Where...?" My mouth, I moved it. That was my voice just then.

You have now seen all you needed from that memory. Corin was no longer an acceptable vassal, favored or not. I could not bring the diseased, withered shell of what he had become into My new world, and Jain proved to be weaker than I thought.

"You killed his brother. That wasn't part of the deal You made with him!"

He had no faith, but I did hold true to Our agreement. I could use none of them as they were, and so, here you are before Me. You, who contain the essence of Jain, and your brothers, who were once My other Champions. If you take up Jain's part in the design, you will attain all that he wanted with more inclusions.

"More inclusions?"

You have more loved ones than he did. Your mother and second father, a sister. Your court...and perhaps a lover who is not Nialiah.

A lover? Flashes of Nisse. No. A vision of Caea

falling. Where is she? "Where is…?"

I will bring her.

"To Your crazy new world? To sit around on Lenore, knowing everything around us is dead?"

But not for long. You will see creation at its beginning. Who else can offer you such a beautiful opportunity?

"And Pan?" I clear my throat. "That other god, Your kid, right? Is this what He's giving the people on His side? Do they know?"

I will not pretend to know what My Son does. I would not be surprised if He offers the same, or if He offers nothing.

Nothing. To fight and still die.

Are all gods assholes?

If I was Jain, which I am, would I ask that out loud? The guy was psycho, but he had balls that I don't. He chose to screw everybody and trust this monster. Had there been a better choice? It was a cold decision to make, to save his own, while helping Order mislead entire populations into thinking She was going to save them too. The idea is horrible, but at the same time, Order and Pan wanted to wipe out everything and start fresh. Everyone would die. Jain's choice could have saved a few, and if those few happened to be people he loved, it was a win. Then, he failed, and lost his brothers.

Fear hurts worse than brain-bleeds as it clenches my guts in a knot. "You said Lawrie's dying. You said Devon was in trouble."

They do not have to be.

"What?"

Images knock me out of the chair. I flop on the floor, muscles contorting, pain gnawing every inch of my body as I seize.

Lawrie lying on a damp floor, limp and lifeless.

Devon drowning in black water.

Evan standing on a grass field littered with bodies, leg wound gushing, a demon just about to punch a hole through his chest.

We can stop this.

/But…is all of that happening now? I'm here! You're here! What…?/

Not just these occurrences. These are inevitable fates of your brothers, if you do not choose to save them now.

More images.

Mom, in her office at work, door closed, blinds drawn, head in her hands as her shoulders shake. I want to reach out to her. I'm right here.

Dad, in his SUV, parked outside of Nikki's school. Nikki in pink overalls and bows, running to the car as he gets out. Their hug lasts a little too long, both seeming to need something that isn't there. But I'm here. I could bring them here.

Caea falling.

Sensuen, Falun and Orion assuring me they would take care of everything before they left the compound.

What do you choose, Lyle Lauduethe? Will you fulfill the role Jain Peredil could not?

…

…

…

The convulsions stop. I lie on the hard floor, eyes open. I'm back in the cave on Kupiku. My face and chin are crusty with dried blood. My cold gear is stiff but warm. My head pounds so bad my vision pulsates. The room blurs and sharpens in waves.

Choose, Lyle Lauduethe.

...

...

...

My ears ring as my nose runs. I taste salty copper on my lips. Will She let me die here, if I just don't answer?

...

...

...

I swallow blood. A hand helps me sit up, rubs my back. The soothing blanket that had helped Jain helps me, swaddling my brain. Feels so good, don't stop.

...

...

...

"I choose You."

A sudden bright light makes me cringe. I squeeze my eyes shut, waiting for it to dim to a pale shimmer behind my lids. I open my eyes slowly, staring at the beautiful sapphire Stone in my lap. It's perfect, square cut with no rough edges, its deep blue the purest I've ever seen. I cradle it in between my dirty hands, channeling its healing power.

The headache fades, my mind clears. Energy rushes through my veins, massaging my muscles, giving me the strength to stand. I run the Stone over my lips, loving its comfortable heat. I close my eyes as its power merges with mine, working its way across my mental barriers, seeping into the cracks and filling them in with cement and then coating the entire wall with unbreakable steel. The wall shifts from impermeable to semi-permeable, allowing sensory input from the outside world in, but keeping it at a dull roar.

This is what Sensuen does for me. It's what all the drugs do. But better.

I'm better.

I touch my head with both hands, rumpling my hair, laughing.

I look around. Order is gone, and so is the back wall. The cave's expanded and... I laugh again. A group of people lay on the ground in a neat circle, all wearing Kupi cold gear. I run to them, sliding on my knees beside Caea. I kiss the Stone, before tucking it in my pocket, where I can still feel it. Oh yes, it's there. I fight down another laugh. Maybe I'm delirious, but who the hell cares?

"Caea?" I pull down the wrap over the lower half of her face and touch her brown cheek. "Caea?"

Her eyes flutter open, her lips part, then her fist flies at my face. I barely miss the punch. "It's me!"

"Wha-wha? Lyle?"

"I'm here."

"*Krevai-va*! What the...where is this? What happened?" She bypasses sitting up and springs straight to her feet, weapons out. She pivots and spots the others lying on the ground. "Are these...?"

I reach out with my telekinesis, giving each sleeping person a shake, wanting to avoid another violent awakening. Yelps and groans. Sensuen, Orion and Falun sit up, rub at their eyes and stare at Caea and me, before bolting to their feet almost in unison. They pull lasics that look like pistols from belt holsters and surround me, backs to my body as they hold their lasics steady.

"What happened?" Orion croaks. "How are you here?"

"You've been hurt," Sensuen says.

"At ease." Caea sheathes her daggers and waits for my court to break their protective formation. They hesitate, each turning their head a bit to peer at me.

I see through their eyes that I look like hell.

"I'm fine. It's fine. We're all fine." I raise my hands. "You can put your weapons up."

"Lyle, what happened?" Caea asks. "Last I remember, something grabbed me and pulled me down. Did you fall too?"

I nod.

"What are you two talking about?" Orion asks. "And why can't I remember what happened here?"

"I can't either." Falun shakes her head.

"Shreti-Hak's people came back to the compound," Caea says, "without the three of you. They told us Order took you and would only talk to Lyle and me about letting you go. We came in after you, but there was a cave-in and then..." She looks to me. "What happened, Lyle?"

"I..." I stop. I can't tell them what happened. Not all of it, not even if it's going to help them all.

They will not understand.

I mentally start at the new voice in my head. It hadn't come from outside the barrier. It came from inside it.

They will not accept our choices. We have to guide them instead. It is the only way they will be safe.

Yeah.

"I don't know. I remember falling too," I say. "I... uh...I dropped you."

I *did* drop Caea. Guilt wracks me. I can't do right by anyone. But I want to, and I can now.

"Stop being stupid," Caea says. "Something

grabbed me, and you ended up getting dragged down too, because you didn't let go."

But I had, or maybe I hadn't.

Go with it.

"If you say so." I rub the back of my neck through the thick fabric of the cold gear. "I woke up here, with you guys." I take a deep breath. "And this." I dig the Stone out of my pocket, trying not to smile as it casts blue light against the gray walls of the cave and makes my friends look like campers listening to a ghost story.

Sensuen falls to her knees, wailing in a language her translator can't offer meaning to. Is she praying?

"*Fip*," Orion says. "So, *that's* it then?" He studies it, not seeming awed. I don't think he can feel its power, my power.

Falun reaches for the Stone, and I clutch it to my chest.

She blinks, looking startled, and then frowns at me. "And you're sure you're okay, Lyle?"

I nod. "Yeah, I'm good. Better than good. I mean, this is what we came for, and we got it. We just need to find a way out of here."

"But how did you get it?" Caea asks, her eyes scanning the Stone too, and like Orion, she doesn't seem impressed. But she's seen Gifts from Order all her life; carried and fought with those same Gifts for years. "Order wanted to talk to us face-to-face. Where is She?"

"I don't know."

"And that's okay with you?" Caea asks. "We're missing time. All of us are. Who knows what She did to us. And look at you, holding that thing like a damn baby. Put it away."

I blink at her. She's angry? I run my thumb over the

Stone and it hums in my mind, a lulling white noise. It's okay if Caea's mad, because she isn't questioning what I know. The fault is on Order, not me.

"Why don't we worry about getting out of here now?" I say. "We can go over what happened later. These guys have been down here a long time. How are you on water and food?"

Orion honestly seems surprised that I'm taking over. "My water is almost out, but we can share if you all have a fresh supply."

"The supplies won't stretch for long." Falun turns her attention away from the Stone, looking at me. "We need to scout around, you're right."

Caea narrows her eyes at me, mouth thinning, before she rolls her face-wrap back up, hiding any new expressions. "Fine. We scout as a group, though. No splitting up. There's a light source, obviously, because we can see each other just fine. We'll walk toward it...after someone shuts her up."

I turn to look at Sensuen still on her knees, praising the gods. I touch the top of her head. /Sensuen, we have to go./

You are the Goddess's tool, Sensuen's mental voice is a husky whisper.

/Uh...yes?/

You are my leader.

/Yeah./

You will save us all.

My heart staggers. /I.../ I will save her.

Sensuen gets to her feet and hugs me. I sputter as she squeezes, then plants herself in front of me. *I will protect you with my life.*

I hope it won't come to that. But if it does, I won't

be like Jain. I'll save as many as I can, instead of letting everyone go down.

Go forward favored. I have great plans for you, and a seat for you to fill.

I squeeze the Stone one more time before putting it away, then follow Sensuen and the rest of the group toward the light.

20
LAWRENCE

"*IT BURNS.*"

I jump, spilling hot laokei all over my book. "Ah kraet, *Corin! Make some noise next time!*" *I get to my feet, my head butting against the lowest branches of the tree I'm under. The empty mug dangles from my fingers as I shake out the pages of my ruined book. There goes another antique, courtesy of a Peredil. But* Hades *and* Ether, *no one ever expects us to bring anything back intact, so why give us antiques? In my opinion, people lend to us at their own risk.*

Corin drops from the middle branches and lands beside me. "*Where's the fun in giving you a warning, Aman?*"

I toss the mug aside and snap the damp book closed, swatting at him. He dodges and catches my arm. His amusement fades. The large leaves above cast long shadows over the planes and angles of his face, sharper now than they'd been last month. He holds his body rigid, forever ready for a fight. His voice has lost its music, even in teasing.

I swallow saliva thick with concern and force a smile, because Corin hates pity and worry. He's always fine, even when he's not.

"Why are you stalking me?" I ask. "What burns?" I let the book drop, and it hits the grass with a soft clump.

Corin tilts his head, green eyes taking on that hazy faraway look he's adopted as of late. He nods as if carrying on a conversation with someone just beyond my line of sight. I stay still, waiting for him to come back to me.

"The Mark," he finally says, his voice soft. "It hurts."

I touch the hand he keeps on my arm and he starts, releasing me.

"What mark?" I press.

"She's punishing me." Corin scratches the back of his neck and pulls his braid over one shoulder. "I asked too many questions." He shakes his head, the hazy expression gone. "What was I saying?"

"You made me ruin Maistre Dosefa's rune book, so you could tell me your mark burns, and that someone said you ask stupid questions?" I deadpan. I study him for any signs of recognition and groan in frustration at his blank look.

"Cor." I stop. I don't want to say it. No one does, but I'm sure he knows. He has to. "You're scaring us. Let me take you to a healer."

"A mind *healer?" Corin's voice has a sharp edge. His eyes glitter. "I'm not insane." His left hand pats the back pocket of his trousers, where he usually keeps his Stone.*

Energy charges the air, causing the ends of my hair to crackle. I reach for the cool trickle of power from my

Stone, my control of the wind warring with Corin's magical influence over it. The energy calms and the air goes flat, dead, a stalemate between us.

"You haven't been right since you went off to meet with Imari," I say. "I told you to leave her alone. There's something wrong with those women."

"Leave her out of this." *His body sags. He seems tired.*

"If she did something to you..." *A mark that burns. Sounds like magic to me.*

"She didn't do anything." *He scratches the nape of his neck again.* "You just don't understand her."

I snort. "Nobody understands Lenorans! They don't feel things as normal people do. I don't think they acknowledge anyone other than their own kin. That woman can't love you. Maybe she wants to, but she can't."

Corin flinches, and a glimmer of hope flickers inside me. Do I have him? He's been following Imari around like a faithful servant, watching her like some kind of rare treasure. I don't ask what they do behind closed doors, but Corin used to leave each visit smiling and whistling.

Gods. How long has it been since he's truly smiled, or whistled, or even sung?

"Is she what's bothering you?" *Corin's been in love before, but this is something else. I just want him to open up, maybe even to step down.*

The Remasian Council's vote days ago made him our general. Before that, we'd all been equal leaders. Maybe a cycle ago, hells, a rev ago, I would have been okay with the decision. But now that Corin's being eaten alive from the inside out by this sickness, I don't know that I can trust him to make the right decisions for us all.

One bad choice and it's over. Strangely, it seems Viveen and Theorne trust him more. Then again, he also doesn't question them, not anymore. With his illness comes a strange obedience.

"Corin?" I push.

"Aman." He opens his eyes and my heart sinks at the tears brimming. "I... I..." He stutters, like he's being made to eat his words. I move toward him, to pat his back, but he stumbles away from me, rubbing his neck. "I should not have come to you. I have maps to approve." He turns, tossing his braid over his shoulder, so that it drapes down his back.

I blink. The thick rope doesn't quite cover the edge of a dark shape at the base of his hairline. I surge forward and snag the braid, pulling Corin toward me, and then raising it up to stare at the inked symbols trailing from the nape of his neck down into his collar.

"When did you do this?" I ask. Corin's never shown any interest in inkings.

"Do what?" Corin tries to move, but I grab his shoulder and hold him in place. I run an index finger down the length of the inking, and peel back his collar to see that the design continues past his shoulder blades.

"Did you ink your entire spine?" I ask.

"What are you talking about?" Corin breaks my grasp and spins around. He's iuts shorter than me, always has been, but the authority around him has always made him seem taller. That authority's gone as he stares at me, horror darkening his eyes. "What's on my...?" He touches his neck again, and winces.

"It must be new, if it's still tender," I say.

"I didn't..." His eyes glaze over. "Niobe-va." He looks like he's going to throw up. "I have to go."

"Where?"

He stalks away from me, and I chase him. Corin is fast, but I breathe in, calling on the wind to make me faster. I plant myself in front of him, catching him as he crashes into me.

"Brother?" I hold his arms as he shivers, like he's coming down with a fever. "What's wrong with you?"

He takes a deep shuddering breath, eyes locking onto mine. "Aman. I think... I think I..." He seems to struggle to speak, before he spits out the words, "She used a spell!"

"Who? Imari?" I'll kill her. The violence in the thought shocks me, but no one hurts my brothers.

"Not..." Corin's eyes fog over again, but before he's truly gone, he murmurs, "I found a way out."

"Out of what?" I shake him, willing him not to give into sickness when he might tell me something, anything, that might be able to help him.

Corin smiles mistily. "Out of destiny, brother."

I blink at him as the last vestiges of sanity leaves his eyes. I've lost him and there's nothing I can do to get him back. I wrap my arms around him. Maybe if I hold on, he'll fight to come back, to stay.

He shifts in my hold, so that he's gazing up at me and I start. His green eyes are bright with tears, not insanity. "But I think..."

"You think what?" I whisper.

"...that I've been cursed."

IN A DIM HALLWAY LIT by cloth torches in sconces, I sit up, heart racing, and call for Corin. For anyone. My voice echoes through the empty corridor.

I'm all by myself, but I wasn't before. Corin was just… I shake my head, tangling my fingers in my hair, confused by its longer length.

Holy shizz. Holy friggin' shizz.

The world comes back to me. I'm Lawrence Ladreth. Lawrie. But I had been someone else. Aman Peredil. Did I just have a flashback?

Excitement makes me laugh; the sound echoes down the hallway. I stare at my surroundings. Where the hell am I? What happened?

It's important to remember. There's something I need to do.

Artic air whistles around me, and I shiver. It's as cold as a morgue in here.

A morgue.

I think I'm dead.

I jump to my feet, whirling around, staring down the abyss of the hallway. The air behind me is dense with fog, the air in front of me is thick and practically tangible. It wraps wispy tentacles around my wrists, pulling me forward. There's a door at the end of the hall, one I feel like I need to open to pass through.

Wonder if there's a light behind it, like in that 80's movie *Poltergeist*. If that's the case, then I'm not dead yet, just caught in an in-between. Like Evan had been on Onkurus.

Good going, Nialiah.

Maybe she knows what she's doing after all. Never doubted her—much. Though maybe I should. Unease shifts in my stomach, becoming food for hungry locusts.

Aman Peredil didn't like Imari, didn't trust her, and maybe didn't trust any of The Maidens. I don't trust them, but I think I like Imari. Though, Evan says she knows something. Whatever Corin was trying to tell Aman, Imari probably knows. Corin had the Mark and said he was cursed for asking questions, and maybe finding a way out of destiny.

Holy shizz.

My heart thuds in my chest.

Corin died bat-shizz crazy and told Evan to trust no god. And here I am killing myself to retrieve a Stone a goddess wants me to have.

Maybe I should try to turn back and forget about it. But if I do, then I'll probably really die.

My head spins. Confusion sets in. The desire to travel to the end of the hall, open the door and pass through grabs me again, its airy tentacles pulling me. It wants me to come and find rest.

…find rest? Die?

No. That's not what I want.

I'm not tired. And I definitely don't want to die.

A sharp pain, like a fishhook in my chest, buries itself in my heart, tugging me backward, keeping me from moving down the hall, though my legs fight it. I hear chanting. The voices are familiar, but the words are foreign.

I see a flash of bare feet.

Nialiah, Imari and Ramesis. They must be working the second spell that holds me here, in between life and death.

The allure at the end of the hall pulls at me again, but the hook keeps me anchored in a game of tug-o-war. Something's gonna rip and I'm scared it'll be my ribcage. I want to scream at the others to stop, to remove the hook. Don't pull me back, it hurts.

But if I go forward, it's over, completely.

My head swims and I fall to my knees, sprawling on my face as my body seizes in pain.

Nialiah should have told me this would hurt.

I can't even cry out. Can't breathe. My face is wet, drool dribbles down my chin.

My heart shudders, ready to give out. Am I going to die without going through the door? Is it possible to die in the in-between? What happens if I do?

...I want to go home. I want to go home. I want...

There's a hand on my face, cold and rough. My eyes flutter open, staring up into...my own worried face, but my features are older, my hair shorter.

Aman Peredil?

I can't say his name. Can't speak.

"Is death what you want, young one?" he asks.

I can't manage to say, 'No.'

He touches his forehead to mine. "Value your brothers. Make your destined choices for them." His breath is cold and without scent. "Save them, Lawrence."

And then he's gone, and I'm alone again. There's no desire to pass through a door, no cold, no fear.

I hear nothing but chanting.

...until I don't.

...

...

SEARING HEAT, THEN SOMETHING COOL presses against my body.

Wake up now.

A voice, familiar and not.

But I don't want to wake up.

The pain is gone. I'm in the best bed made of memory foam, buried under warm, soft blankets. I can sleep here forever, except for the strange chanting nearby. It's annoying and keeping me from slipping into the deeper sleep I want.

It's louder now.

I recognize the voices.

Nialiah. Imari. Ramesis.

The scent of mint fills my nostrils. My eyes flutter open and I look up to see my own face peering back at me from a mirror-like barrier of air—the *eschones.* Full awareness returns. I'm on a damp floor in an underground chamber surrounded by candles and feet. The ritual. Nialiah and the others worked a spell. It was supposed to....

I sense something the size of a fist, warm and solid, perching on the center of my chest.

"*Krevai-va,*" a low voice whispers. Ramesis.

"It worked." Imari.

"Lawrence? Can you hear me?" Nialiah. She sounds urgent, maybe even worried.

I try to talk. A squeak. A croak. Then, "Yeah."

I stare at my reflection and at the square-cut quartz on my breastbone—the Stone.

It glows, and a strange power flows through my body. I feel the air currents, the sturdiness of earth, the calm nature of water, the crackle of fire, gentle tickles from minerals and combinations of atoms. I breathe in power as I sit up, letting the Stone fall onto my thigh. I pick it up, holding it in one hand.

It's beautiful, clear as pure water, catching and fracturing the light.

"Lawrence?"

I rock back and forth, loving the swirl of energy currents around me. I can take the building blocks of life and rearrange them, engineer new elements.

"Lawrence!"

Someone grabs my shoulder, clenches down and shakes it. I blink and look beyond my power, slowly focusing on Imari. Her black eyes are wet.

She sighs. "Are you all right?"

I think about it, assessing my body: no fatigue or weakness. I feel good, great even. "Y-yeah. I'm fine."

"You are sure?" Her black eyes drift from me to my Stone as I nod. "It has not changed at all."

"Did you think it would?" I ask, not liking her eyes on my prize. I cover it with my hand. I remember Aman and Corin talking about her, about the spell and curse. I don't want her looking at my Stone. I don't trust her.

"If you are well, you need to get up now." Nialiah's voice is crispy. "I gave your brother a set time period for this spell to be worked. That time has passed. Get dressed."

Clothes are shoved in my face. I almost drop the Stone to catch them in both hands. I don't want to put it down to pull my clothes on. I don't want anyone else to touch it, take it. It's mine.

I dress one-handed.

"I'm going topside now," Ramesis says. "Sayan isn't responding to my comp-hails and there's no word from outside."

My heart pounds. The Stone pulses. I grip it tight as our power latches onto a current of air that travels outside and pushes itself around obstacles, bringing back the scent of oil and something rank and rusty—blood. The sturdy earth above feels wet with liquid made up of iron, carbon, nitrogen, oxygen, hydrogen and some unknown elements. Shizz. That's a lot of blood. "Wait for me!"

I struggle into my boots, watching Ramesis's back as he rushes to the door.

"Halt, Ramesis! We go together," Nialiah says. "It is better to emerge as a unit."

My boots are on. We run through the door of the bathing chamber, out into the foyer and up a tunnel. I keep a steady pace beside Ramesis, running like the trained athlete I'm not, as the Stone fuels the long and short muscles in my legs.

This is awesome sauce. It's awesome sauce with cheese and pepperoni and whatever other corny topping I can add to this feeling. Why does Evan not want his Stone? Why were we all so afraid to have them?

Ramesis holds out an arm, stopping me before we reach the end of the tunnel. The door is closed. He whips his battle axe from its sheath. "We come out with caution. Get behind me. Have an attack in mind that does a lot of damage. Are you ready?"

I'm breathing so fast I don't think I'm really taking in much air. My head spins, but I don't stumble, because I'm strong. The Stone vibrates in my palm. I can't just hold this thing, though. I unbutton one of my cargo pockets and tuck it inside. Its power heats the side of my thigh.

I can do more than I know. I can fight battles. I can—a hand on my arm almost makes me scream. I turn to see a pale face surrounded by bushy red curls.

"Chasyn?"

"I've been waiting."

"Where did you…?"

"I was outside the chamber, in the tunnel. You ran right by me," Chasyn says, his eyes going to the pocket I'd just put the Stone in. "I fell in line and you didn't notice."

Ramesis shoots us a glare. "Are you ready?"

"Y-yeah. Yes." I look at Chasyn. "Are you?"

"I'm with you."

"Then stay behind me," I say in the same tone Ramesis had. It's so weird. I'm responsible for this guy, a guy who waits in the dark for me to come back from the dead, who follows me without a word, literally.

Ramesis pushes the door open, and we step out onto the battlefield, as soldiers. The strength of the Stone pumps its way into my veins as I connect to the world around me. No, we're not soldiers. We step onto this battlefield as Champions.

Ramesis growls, breaking into a run and I trail, eyes locking onto a scene about twenty feet away that makes my blood run cold.

A black hole stretches across the horizon, the black hand of a monster reaching for my brother who stands proud, ready to take it. The ground around him is littered with corpses, gore and blood. Dark blue water makes a cocoon around him and his court. Jalee and Adonis are on their knees, someone's sprawled on the ground, not moving.

"What in *Nth Hell* is that thing?" Ramesis yells as

he skids to a stop.

"It is a rupture," Imari shouts. "An *ether* plane has been opened!"

"Can you close it?" I yell.

"Yes." Nialiah stands beside me, huffing like a couch-potato gamer. "We can do it. It will just take time. Hold it at bay for as long as you can!"

"By doing what?" Ramesis shouts. "*Krevai-va*, it's got him!"

He aims his axe like a spear and hurls it Hercules-style in the direction of the monster punching its battering ram sized finger into my brother's chest. The axe strikes the demon. A flash of obsidian lightning from the axe zig-zags straight up into the sky. The black hand jerks back like it's been spanked and hovers in front of Evan who just stands there.

"Run!" I yell at him. Why is he not running?

A spark of energy zaps my thigh. The Stone.

The air.

I stiffen at the whisper. Another spark against my thigh. Fear and excitement squeeze my heart and lungs into a nasty organ sandwich. I hiccup, patting my chest, then freeze as my senses reach out on their own, like someone pushed 'play' on my remote. I strangle a yelp as the dry feel of the atmosphere hits me in the face.

Dry? It had been humid as hell only a few hours ago. How the...I feel it. Like I'm being bled in some medieval doctor's office, something's draining vapor from the air. My eyes lock on Adonis's water barrier, but no. That's not what's doing it.

It's that other thing, the rippling black hole. The more vapor it draws, the larger and more solid the emerging monster becomes.

Can I take the vapor back?

The Stone vibrates. My body heats. Sweat trickles into my eyes. "Ramesis, I'm gonna try something." His weapon had stopped it, for a minute, but he'd thrown the axe. "Do you have anything else?"

Ramesis nods, holding out a hand. And damn! His axe comes whirring back, like Mjolnir. He throws it again, another zig-zag flash of lightning explodes from it as it strikes the monster's hand. The monster flinches back, but doesn't retreat. More water rips from the air as the void spreads across the horizon, maybe twelve to fourteen feet wide, putting us in its trajectory.

Aw shizz.

"Keep doing that!" Imari yells at Ramesis. She and Nialiah stand across from each other, linking hands like they're about to play 'London Bridge.' All of their formations look like nursey rhyme set-ups.

Ramesis hurls his axe, eyes flitting over to me. "Do what you're going to do!"

I throw my awareness back into the dry air, seeking hydrogen and oxygen, pulling the atoms together. The closer to the void my awareness gets, the harder it is to draw the elements out. My real muscles strain as I meet resistance. It's like trying to save a cement truck from going over a cliff. The elements are too heavy, the void's pull too strong. Stars burst behind my eyes. I have to let go.

No. That voice again.

A shock rod to my thigh sends a current through my entire being. Gritting my teeth as neurons fry, then fire, my power surges out into the air, wrapping around water molecules and sucking them out of the void with the strength of a hundred elephant trunks. The black hole shrinks a foot or so, but it's not enough. The atmosphere dampens, slowly warming as humidity returns.

More.

Power rockets through my system, becoming the boss of all industrial strength vacuums. The black hole shudders, struggling to keep its gained ground. Ramesis's axe strikes the monster again and it flails, stumbling back into the shrinking void. It disappears, but I'm guessing not for long, because the hole remains, still fighting me.

I tear my eyes away from it to look at my brother. He sways and crumples to the ground. The water barrier protecting him thickens, turning purple, before it bursts. A mini-tidal wave crashes around Evan and his court, flooding through the void that drinks the water and pulses with new life, regaining what I took from it. The tip of a finger traces the edges of the hole, the monster poised to come for my brother again.

Adonis, soaking wet, gets to his feet, but he staggers. He reaches for Evan, trying to pull him up, but falls on his ass. He tries to get up again and can't. Jalee wraps her arms around Evan, pulling him toward her. She looks to Adonis and speaks to him. Adonis shakes his head. They both turn to Desiri who's not moving.

Shizz.

They need a shield. I need to keep fighting that thing. I need more power.

A massive surge of energy from the Stone hits me like lightning. Someone screams. Is that me? My nerves burn, overloading from too much energy. Everything inside is pins and needles. I cry out again. What's happening? Did I do something wrong?

"Krevai-va," I hear Ramesis whisper. I turn my

head to see him backing away from me.

I stretch an arm toward him and gape. My arm. Crispy sparks of static jump from my fingertips. I raise my other hand, staring at the white electricity cracking all the way up to my shoulder. I follow the current as it travels across my body. I'm a living lightning rod. The sky's gone pitch black as dark clouds gather, the ones above my head charged with white-hot electricity. They circle me like vultures over carrion.

My heart beats in my ears, a drum so rapid it thrums in place of pounding. WhatdidIdoWhatdidIDOWHAT-DIDI—

Multiple lightning strikes flash toward me. I try to dive, run, but my body won't move. It remains stiff, still crackling, the sensation of pins and needles increasing. Is this it? Is this really it? I don't want—

Searing nails of fire stab me in a thousand places, but instead of being deep fried, my senses go on hyper alert. I hear my lungs dragging in breath, feel my heart staggering, smell the soil moist with tangy blood. Ramesis is shouting. He sounds like he thinks I'm dying.

Imari and Nialiah scream, but they don't sound afraid or worried. They move closer to me and pass me on either side, arms raised to the sky, chanting at the top of their lungs.

The black hole in front of my brother wavers, shudders, shrinks to porthole size, then expands out again to the size of a city bus. The monster takes a step, digging its nails into the dirt of our world, trying to drag itself out.

Now.

The lightning in my body blazes out, leap-frogging over Imari and Nialiah, and barreling toward the monster. I throw my arm over my eyes as it explodes in a blinding flare of white and black light. My retinas burn. I see white behind my eyelids. My feet leave the ground as the force of the blast blows me backward. Wind gathers behind me, catching and lowering me to the ground. I lie on my back, panting, not sure if my eyes are open or closed. I only see white.

"Lawrie!"

That's Chasyn's voice. He sounds far away, but, as he continues to call, his voice gets closer. I think someone's touching me. I can't tell. I'm so bone tired I can't feel much. My limbs don't even tingle anymore, and the burning is gone. The Stone's quiet against my thigh.

The Stone. Did it save us? I wish I could see.

There's light pressure against one of my wrists, then my throat—fingers probing for a pulse.

"Lawrie? Lawrie, can you talk to me? Are you all right?" Chasyn again. I sense gentle pats on my flanks, arms and legs as the feeling in my body slowly comes back to normal. Is he checking me over?

I blink, nothing but white. I open my mouth. "Ah…"

"What?" Chasyn shakes me, and shizz, it hurts.

My muscles wake up one by one. I think I pulled everything in my body, even crap I didn't know I had, and that's a task because I memorized every muscle in the human body when I was five. There's gotta be some made-up muscles in here cussing me out.

And holy friggin' shizz, why can't I see anything?

"M-m-my eyes, Chas. Are they open?"

Hope against hope.

"What? Can you see me?" Chasyn sounds confused at first, then scared. "Lawrie? Your eyes are open right now, but I need you to close them. Okay?"

They're open?

Widespread panic. "Oh God."

"Lawrie, it's all right. That lightning was too bright. You were too close."

He uses his fingers to close my eyes, but there's no difference. It doesn't get darker. Everything's still white.

"Hold on."

I hear fabric ripping, feel something soft covering my eyes, touching the bridge of my nose. It stinks like armpit. The cloth tightens.

"I just covered your eyes. It's what a medic would do. Would it be all right if I sat you up, or do you hurt anywhere?"

I hurt everywhere, and I can't see. My lungs struggle. I can't get in enough air.

"Easy," Chasyn says. "You'll be fine. You'll be more than fine. You are amazing."

The awe in his voice. I take a deep breath, then another, trying to calm down. *"[I'm] amazing,"* he said. The void, the monster, my brother... "What's going on, Chas? Tell me," because I can't see.

I hear shouting and pounding feet coming toward us.

"Leader One and his court are down, except for Jalee. She's helping Majesty Harliel and The Maidens do field triage on Leader One and Desiri. Sayan's house guard just came back out. They're coming toward us. Maybe they have medics."

He stops talking as other voices take over, barking things I don't understand. They must not be wearing translators. Chasyn talks back to them, his voice hoarse, but firm.

Triage on Leader One, on Evan. An image of him

crumpled on the ground flickers in my mind. "Chas? Chas?"

A hand on my shoulder. "Yes?"

"My brother?"

"Some of the guards are over there now. They're making a stretcher. They'll take care of Leader One."

Oh. Good. Exhaustion rolls through me. Blackness wanting to replace the white. "Is it over?"

Chasyn lets out a breath, then chuckles. "Is it—" He laughs. "Yes, yes, it's over. The Maidens closed the rupture. You killed the monster. Your brother got rid of one of Pan's Champions. And you have your Stone. It's over."

It's over...for today.

I hear more foreign language from so many different voices it makes my head hurt. Blackness seeps into my consciousness.

I'm so tired. And this time, I do want to rest.

"Lawrie, we're going to get you on a stretcher," Chasyn says.

"Whatever, man," I murmur.

So long as everyone I came in with is alive, I'm good.

"*Ayo*, it's okay to pass out now," Chasyn says. "You've more than earned it, Leader Four."

Leader Four. That's me now. Leader Four of a planet I've never set foot on. Champion of Order. Killer of shadow hands. Possessor of one of Order's Gifts. And destined to save a lot of people.

I'm hit with a flashback of stellar systems on a map going dark, because they were on the losing side of a war. People who lose to me, people not part of the Allegiances, will have that happen to them. Meaning, I might help save a lot of people, I can protect Earth, but to do that, other worlds will end up like those places on the map.

The real curse of the Mark, in my opinion.

But suffering the curse is worth it to save what I love.

My hold on consciousness slips. I can't stay awake. The last thing I'm aware of is Chasyn squeezing my hand and saying, "You'll be all right, *gikak*."

And I will.

The other side will do what they can to save what they love, not caring about me and mine. So, my choice, one that will decide how this war ends, is a good one, right?

Nothing answers me.

But I sleep anyway.

21

DEVON

I STUFFED MY FACE AND loved every bite of the dinner Owelu's staff served. My stomach was an empty pit by the time we were escorted to Owelu's big house and let inside. We'd been congratulated, fed and set free to roam. Owelu's home, a multistory high rise that's probably about two-hundred feet above sea level, is sweet.

The top floor is for political guests. The outer rooms have floor-to-ceiling windows for walls, sprawling beige couches facing the awesome view of a sun setting over a darkening ocean. The blue sky turns purple as stars make themselves known. It's pretty, something my parents would enjoy, and maybe Monica too. I rub my chest, thinking about her and wondering if she's waiting for me. I mean, it hasn't been all that long, but she's missing out on sitting around looking at stuff like this with me, or somebody else.

I sigh. I'd wait. I am waiting.

"What are you thinking about, *babila*?" Mineshka. She sits beside me on one of Owelu's large couches facing a window-wall. She passes me a long-stemmed wine glass half full of pale- colored liquid.

Along with the banquet, served in an inner room with red-curtained walls and black crystal flooring, Owelu had supplied alcohol. He'd called it *aranga*. The others had waved it away, but I had some, and it was disgusting. I scowl at Mineshka, and she laughs.

"Relax, Dev. It's juice, freshly squeezed I hear."

I take the glass and sniff it. Smells like Minute Maid. Tastes like Minute Maid, only less sweet. "Are Owelu and Xijure still talking business?"

Xijure told me to go explore the place with the others and let him deal with the rest of the talking stuff. He thinks I'm tired and need a break. My muscles mold to the soft cottony feel of the couch as I finish off my drink and let my head roll back. I think he's right.

"He came out a *wisp* ago, went back to the buffet for more dessert," Mineshka says. "Our king can eat."

"I know you're from Zare, but is he still your king if I'm your leader? Isn't it weird?"

Mineshka shrugs. "It means we bow to him, but your orders come first. It'll be easier once we've settled on Rema. Housing is low on the priority list right now, but once we are Remasian, our bowing will only be out of respect, not duty."

Settled on Rema. "You all are going to live on Rema? Just like that? What if you don't like it there?" Hell, I've never been and I'm sure I don't like it there.

"It's a nice place," Mineshka says. "Very clean and silvery. Lots of good food, shopping, and the nightlife is fun."

Nightlife? "You've been there?"

Mineshka nods. "Several times, on training tours.

The Remasian military is very well organized. Its generals are *feratz*."

Feratz: superb, excellent, topnotch.

"Just the generals. The Remasian Council doesn't have anything to do with how good the military is?" I ask.

She quirks a brow at me. "Why would you think that? The councilors give us our tasks. The military leaders figure out how to achieve them. The worst military moves are made when politicians disregard the expertise of their generals and push things forward. Though, no one, but us, would ever admit anything like that."

"Us?"

"The pawns, Devon," Mineshka says. "We are nothing but figurines on a grand *minatche* to be laureled or sacrificed."

Minatche: game table, game board.

Xijure pretty much said the same thing earlier. We're nothing but boardgame pieces.

"Does it scare you?" I ask. She seems so fearless.

Mineshka's eyes skim my face, her expression serene. She sighs and produces a second wine glass from the side of the couch. She must have had it on the floor. "Of course it scares me, *babila*." She swirls her pale drink and takes a sip. "Loniad as well. Does that answer please you? You're smiling."

I chuckle. "I like when you call me that."

"What? *Babila*? My brother hates it when I call him that."

"I should hate it too," I say. "But it's nice. Kind of reminds me of my mom a bit."

"And you miss her," Mineshka says. "I miss mine as well. Loniad and I do not see our parents often. Once our training took us off-world, we truly only saw our parents when we were on leave. So, maybe three or four times a Common *rev*. You will probably get to see your mother as much as we do. After this, I mean."

I nod. After this, I'll see my family three or four times a Common Year—which is about fourteen months on Earth. Nikki might be seven before I visit her next. My little sister will grow up without me. I won't be her favorite brother anymore, just some stranger Mom will tell her to hug.

Mineshka rests an arm around me. "It will be all right, *babila*. You have family with you here, as well."

Smiling at her, I toast her glass with my empty one. "Thanks."

She nods, and we gaze out the window, watching the sun disappear below the horizon.

I WAKE UP WITH MY head on Mineshka's shoulder and Loniad sitting on the other side of me. Ilea sits on the floor in front of a window, polishing a set of short white knives. Xijure paces, stopping in front of me as I rub my eyes.

"How are you feeling?" he asks.

Yawning, I give a nod. I'm good. "We leaving?"

"Our flight crew has run through all the safety measures and Owelu had gifts that needed to be weighed and secured."

"Weighed?"

"All ships have take-off weights they can't exceed,"

Ilea says. "Don't Earth ships have this?"

"Uh, yeah, but I thought, you know, that..."

"Us aliens would have stuff like that all worked out?" Ilea rolls her eyes. She tosses the towel she's using to clean her weapons at me. I catch it on reflex.

"I didn't mean..."

"Relax, leader. I'm joking. Now, throw that back. I'm not done."

I glance down at the dirty blue cloth in my hand and flip it back to her. Oil stains the pads of my fingers, and I wipe it on my pants.

"Should we eat again, before we get on the ship?" I get to my feet, stretching with a moan as my back and shoulders pop. That feels good. Absently, my hand goes to the pouch resting against my chest. The Stone purrs like a kitten.

"There's food on board," Ilea says. "I'm beyond ready to get out of this place. We should have refused the gifts. We'd be just out of orbit by now."

"Why are you so ready to go?" I ask.

"We've done our job. We have what we came here for. I finished the barrier spell. All of this celebration and taking time to rest and enjoy the view feels like—"

"Stalling?" Xijure asks. I notice he's still pacing.

"Are you all nervous about something?" I ask. I look to Loniad and Mineshka, who are so chill you'd think they were at home. Neither looks bothered: Loniad's reclined with his feet on the couch; Mineshka's got another glass of juice.

"I think you two are the ones who need a little rest," Loniad says. "We're victorious, the locals are pleased, the food is good, and the lodging is comfy. We could stay the night and see what the bedding is like. Ship beds leave much to be desired."

"This isn't a luxury vacation," Ilea says. "And we're not victorious, as you say. Victory means we've won a battle. We are simply on our way to battle and taking too long to get there. There are no good stories about warriors who wait when they should move."

I blink at her as she tucks away her knives and folds her cloth. She's on her feet, pacing with Xijure now. She says something to him and he nods.

"We should go check on the crew. They'll probably be glad to have us on board, even if we're not leaving yet," Xijure says.

"These Disi presents to the Allegiance Councils better be good," Ilea mutters.

Loniad groans. "Must we really?" He looks at me, as does Mineshka. If I say no, these guys will probably stay put.

I glance over at Xijure and Ilea who give me imploring stares. They really want to get going. Personally, I don't see what staying here and enjoying the view and some more juice can hurt, but I don't want to make Xijure and Ilea mad when I don't have to.

We're going to have to pack up anyway, might as well do it now. It's not like the ship is awful. It's just not this.

"Come on, guys." I reach out to Loniad with both hands. "I'll pull you up." He laughs, loud, and sticks out his arms, letting me pull. Loniad bounces to his feet and reaches out to tug his sister up.

"Lead the way, Xijure." Because he's probably trooped around this whole floor and knows the way better than any of us.

The king does an about-face and marches out of the

room, the rest of the group falling into step. He leads us around the outer room, me taking in as much of the beach, ocean, and sky as I can, before we head into the inner rooms with opaque walls. The house is strangely quiet for it to be full of staff. Owelu had people in the kitchen running in and out to re-stock the food table. Did they go home for the night?

One man stands in front of a door at the end of the hall, tall and orange, in a plain black suit with gold trim. We stop.

"We're going up to our ship," Xijure says. Our ship is on the roof. Coming in, we'd landed on top of the multistoried trade center tower. The pilot moved to this roof at Owelu's request, so that we could leave directly after our reception.

"I'm afraid Honorable Owelu has not given you clearance to leave the building yet."

"That's all right. We don't need his clearance to board our ship." Xijure tries to move forward, but the man blocks the door.

"He wishes for you to stay the night," the man says. "He will come to extend the invitation soon, if you would return to your previous location."

"We decline the invitation," Xijure says. "Send him that message and stand aside."

There's clicking and chattering from the man, as he relays something on a communication device near his mouth. After a moment, the man bows his head slightly and moves away from the door.

"Thank you." Xijure doesn't sound like he means it. He takes the stairs slowly. The door closes behind us as we climb.

"That was strange." Mineshka frowns.

"Weapons out." Xijure's voice is low.

"Why?" I ask.

"Something's off." Ilea whips out those tiny, white knives.

Xijure pulls out Haribu. Loniad and Mineshka stand in front of me, closing the gap so that I can't see what's ahead of us. They get out their lasics.

"Should I take the Stone out of the pouch?" I don't have weapons, not yet.

A heartbeat, then Xijure says, "Yes."

"Just open the pouch," Ilea says. "You don't have to pull it out. The spell circle becomes incomplete when the bag's unsealed."

I nod, pulling at the pouch strings, and feel the cool flood of confidence and power flow through me. My hands and feet are my weapons. If something's wrong, I'm ready for it.

As we reach the top floor, I hear voices outside. One's Owelu, but the others are weird, and they speak a different language than the one spoken by the Disi. The sounds are throaty, guttural, and too far away for the translator to pick up.

What good are super ears if I can't understand what anyone's saying?

"The plan is to make for the ship. If there's a fight, you engage with the objective of getting aboard. If the crew is compromised, our objective is still to get aboard."

"And pray they haven't damaged the ship," Mineshka says. "I can pilot big spacecrafts. I'll make for the pit. Loniad can back me. He can also pilot."

Loniad salutes.

"Devon, stick to the middle. Only fight when you're exposed, otherwise..." Xijure trails off.

Stay out of the way, kid? Yeah, like I'm really going to do that when I'm packing all this juice.

Xijure pushes open the door and bounds onto the rooftop with Ilea, Loniad, Mineshka and me behind him. Owelu stands with a group of soldiers in red and black uniforms. The soldiers are pale skinned with eyes like snakes and long hair tied back at the napes of their necks—clearly not Disi.

One man near Owelu grins with sharp, shark teeth. Like Order's.

"*Fip*," Xijure mutters. "*Fip*. Let them talk first."

Talk? I thought we were supposed to fight? My eyes go to our ship. It looks fine, no damage.

"Greetings, Leader Two of Rema. Majesty Harliel." The smiling, sharp-toothed man steps forward. "I am here to offer you a ride, as it seems your ship's crew can no longer accommodate you."

"What's that supposed to—" Xijure begins, then cuts himself off as the door to our ship opens.

Oh God.

More snake-eyed soldiers come out of the ship, each holding a body: the captain and the rest of the small crew that made sure I had food and water while I'd holed myself up in my cabin on the way here. The bodies are thrown on the ground, making a pile, as the soldiers dust their hands together like they'd just been cleaning up.

They killed—I growl deep in my throat. I count about thirty soldiers on the roof. I can take them. A shot rings out.

My ears scream louder than Mineshka. Wetness splashes against my cheek, touching the corner of my eye. A chunky thud and a weight on my boot.

I look down, mouth falling open, then turn to the

side, spewing dinner.

Loniad. Laughing, singing, grinning, overwhelmingly friendly, and slightly claustrophobic, Loniad is on the ground. I look down at him. His body jerks and shakes as blood spurts from a hole in his neck. Mineshka drops to her knees beside her brother, hands going to his neck, putting pressure on the wound as Loniad chokes on his own blood.

Xijure and Ilea close in, making a body-barrier between the soldiers, and the twins and me.

"We do not wish to fight," the same man speaks again. "But you must know that we will not tolerate resistance. The only people we need here are His Majesty and the leader. Come quietly, and we will not make another mess."

"Do you think they've incapacitated the ship?" Ilea asks. "Do we risk it?"

Do we friggin' risk it?

I watch Loniad shake once, twice, then still. His eyes go sightless and Mineshka closes them with bloody fingers. She touches her forehead to his, before gazing up at me.

At me. Her brother is dead, murdered, right here, by those things, and she's looking at me. The Stone pulses. I can fight these monsters, and I can win. I know I can. But what's the plan after that?

We take another ship. These monsters had to have come in somehow. But what if they brought more soldiers?

Mineshka jumps to her feet, bringing up her gun faster than any draw I've seen on TV. She fires, taking out five guys before a reaction kickstarts. Violence erupts with a roar as guns blast and magic flies. Ilea sends out volleys of red, magical fire. Xijure whirls and kicks, wielding Haribu in deadly circles.

What were these guys thinking? They don't stand a chance!

I surge in, my fists bullets as I pummel snake-eyed bastards, howling as I think of Loniad on the ground and Mineshka's scream. Owelu's disappeared. Where'd he go? I want to kill him. I want him dead.

The sky quakes, the floor beneath us unsteady. My knees give way as vertigo makes me sick and dizzy. The air turns sour and my head spins. I squint, making out a large black ship billowing above us. Is it real or a mirage? It flickers in and out of being. It's there and it's not.

"Take the leader and the king!" A bellow from somewhere near.

I grab my head and focus on the roof, the soldiers, my court, Xijure. Bodies everywhere, soldiers in black and red lay on the ground like Loniad. "Mineshka! Ilea! Xijure!" I yell.

Arms grab me and I kick out, feeling for the Stone. My hands close around nothing. The pouch. When did I lose it?

My mind whirls as I feel myself being dragged. Scorching air that stinks like roadside tar hits my face. I struggle to keep my eyes open. What's going on? What happened?

A figure stands on a ramp leading down from the black ship. It's solid now. Something silver glints on his wrist. Blackness rushes forward. The figure stalks toward me, his presence twisting my stomach in knots. Tweezers pick through my brain, pulling apart the grey matter. I can't fight it.

Where's my Stone?

"It was too easy to take, little leader." The figure's voice is young, but deep. A man, then? "You would benefit from training. Too bad you will not get the time."

I'm flying through the air. No, being thrown. My body hits metal and rolls into another person. "Mineshka...Xijure...Ilea..."

"I'm here."

Xijure? I can't see him.

"Your petition to the Nazflit has been approved, Honorable Owelu. Disiez will be welcomed into the Coalition." The young man is talking. Owelu's voice cuts in, praising the man and thanking him.

"We helped you!" I sit up, ignoring the urge to throw up.

I'm onboard a ship, the loading door is open. Owelu stands, talking to the man with the silver thing on his wrist, a thick band.

Owelu's head moves, he looks in my direction. "You helped yourself, and I helped my people."

"The deal from your Allegiances came too late," the other man says. "A regrettable trend."

"I'll drown your city for this." Ilea's voice comes from somewhere behind me. "I'll drown your people."

In my peripheral vision, I see her. She raises her arms and steps forward, head falling back as she chants. A blast of light rips through her middle. The impact throws her body backward. She sails through the air, hitting the ground and skidding.

"I-I-I..." I stammer.

The image of spurting blood and ropey innards exploding from Ilea's back as her body flies through the air burns into my retinas. A permanent scar. I struggle to replace the carnage with memories of her teasing me, bright blue eyes gleaming and alert. Body, whole and compact, always ready to fight. To protect me.

Oh God.

Owelu hollers something about his city, and the other man glares at him. "Our mage can repair the spell." Owelu hollers again, frantic, and the man shoves him off the ship, onto the ramp. The metal door slams closed. Fists pound on the exterior, but the man turns. He studies me, snake-eyes narrowed as he stalks over. He sneers and his boots slip in Ilea's blood.

Mineshka. "Mineshka?"

A hand grabs me by the chin, my neck cracks as I'm made to face the monster.

"Champion of Kahanna." His breath smells like ashes. "I am a Champion of Kahine. You may call me Shiham."

"Asshole. Th-that's what I'll call you."

He laughs. "'Asshole.' I like this term. But..." he punches me across the jaw. The explosion of pain has me seeing cartoon stars, "you will call me Shiham."

I spit at him.

He's going to kill me. I'm going to die like Loniad and Ilea, people who are dead because of me. My stomach gives a lurch.

"This did not have to happen," Shiham says. "You thought you could fight. You thought you could win. You were stupid, and now, all of your soldiers are dead, and this planet will drown. Courtesy of your dead mage. Death all around."

The planet will drown. Owelu betrayed us. He killed Loniad, Mineshka and Ilea by bringing these people. He deserves it. Let him drown. But he won't be the only one who drowns. There are people here.

"You said you had mages," I say.

"Yes," Shiham agrees. "I do. So?"

"Save them?" My suggestion sounds like a question. Owelu did this to us, so that these people, this guy, would help them. Said the Allegiances were too late. Serves him right that this man doesn't care, but the people don't deserve this.

Shiham laughs. "This planet holds no value. Not good barter. Only good for bringing us leaders. Are you awake, Majesty?"

Xijure growls something and Shiham laughs.

"You like my Gift, no?" Shiham pats the silver bracelet on his wrist. "Makes you sick. Makes you see things. Lets me in your heads."

"If you're going to kill us—" Xijure begins.

Shiham laughs, almost sounding hysterical. He wipes at his snake-eyes after a moment. "If we wanted to kill you, we would have after you brought the Stone from the water."

"Then, what do you want?" Xijure demands.

"I do not want anything," Shiham says.

My head throbs and my jaw aches. I taste blood in my mouth. Shiham releases my face and steps back, studying me.

"It is Kahine who wants you," Shiham says. "I hear He tried to speak to your brother, twice." He looks at me again. "But that one is uncooperative. You, on the other hand, are unspoiled by the Allegiances."

Kahine? Who the hell is that? It sounds familiar.

"You're taking us to Pan?" Xijure asks.

Pan, Order's kid, the other god we're going against. My heart jack hammers. It's going to explode. And...all I can think of is how I want my Stone to calm me down.

I'm not scared when I have it.

Give it back.

"What makes you think we're going to listen to Pan any better than Leader One did?" Xijure asks.

"Hm," Shiham says, breathing his ash breath in my face again. "Did I say we killed *all* of your soldiers?"

"Yes," I croak.

"Maybe I lied." He moves away from me.

I can't turn my head. I'm too dizzy, but he's going somewhere. I hear moaning, a girl's voice. My heart leaps. Mineshka's voice.

A muffled cry, and Shiham's back, holding Mineshka by the hair.

"You will behave better now, yes?" Shiham says. "See, I am nice. I said I killed them all, but I know it is better if we keep someone."

"We don't negotiate with—" Xijure starts, but I cut him off.

"I do! I negotiate. Let her go!"

"Devon!"

"She's not yours. She's mine. Loniad, he…" I stop as my voice quavers and take a quick breath. "I'll listen to Kahine."

Xijure snarls at me. But I don't care. I said I'd listen to Kahine, not do what he says. Not agree to hurt other people. I can listen, if it means Shiham won't blow a hole through Mineshka's stomach like he'd done to Ilea.

"Devon, no," Mineshka says, blood running down one side of her face, masking one eye.

"Very good," Shiham says, his grin sharp. "I knew you could be reasoned with. You are better than the other."

The other. Evan. God, what would Evan do right

now? I don't know, and don't care, because I can't do it anyway. Magic, why couldn't I have gotten magic? Evan could probably knock this guy out, so he wouldn't feel sick anymore, and then he'd be able to fight. What good is super strength, if you can't move?

Kahine will find out I'm the worst of the group, and He'll kill me so that Order can't win. What will Lyle do without me? And Lawrie? What will happen to Mom and Dad when someone tells them? Nikki won't understand. And then there's Evan. He'd shed a tear, right?

I don't want to die. I don't.

A great quiver and the roar of an engine announce the ship's launch. Pressure builds as I feel the ship shooting upward at a speed so fast my ear drums are ready to burst. I double over, throwing up again and again. Shiham doesn't seem to care. No one touches me until the motions stop.

A rough cloth mops my face and I open my eyes to see Shiham. He's dropped Mineshka on the floor. "Now that we have an agreement, we can move you. We cannot have Champions sleeping on the ground, can we?"

I swallow air and spit up more bile. He wipes it away. "We will have you changed and bathed as well. But first, we will need you to send a message."

"I'm not making any threats or ransom demands."

Who am I kidding? I will, if it means they won't throw Mineshka out of an airlock. I'll do what he wants.

Shiham laughs. "No threats, no ransom. We just need you to tell your people that you are fine. This will give us time to complete our travels before your Allegiances realize you are with us."

I blink. I'm not fine. Nothing about this is fine. From the other side of me, I hear crying. Mineshka. Still alive.

I'll keep her alive.

"All right."

I'm pulled to my feet. The room rotates and I hurl again, before Shiham binds my hands behind my back and marches me toward another door to go deeper into the ship. Xijure yells my name, and Mineshka...

Her hoarse sobs break my heart.

"Clean his face and find a clear path for the signal," Shiham's saying to someone I can't see or hear. The hallway we travel down is black with silver flooring. Nothing remarkable, but I remember every step as if it'll save me or someone else.

As ordered, a man shoves me in a chair, and scrubs my face with another rough towel soaked in freezing water. He leaves me alone in the small room, hands behind my back, legs like jelly. I want to lie down, I want a blanket, Lyle, aspirin.

God, Loniad's face. Ilea's.

A bright light from the front of the room nearly blinds me as heavy footsteps approach. Shiham is back. He stops beside me and clenches my shoulder. "Remember, you are fine. You were successful. You will join them soon."

Wh-what?

"After this, we will bring you to Kahine. You should be honored, leader. Your first audience with a god is upon you."

I'm going to throw up again.

"Speak now!" Shiham says.

What? I look around. Speak to who? There's no camera or anything for me to focus on, no receiver, no...

"Dev? That you?" A familiar voice filters into the

room.

Lyle. It's Lyle, and he sounds so…normal.

"Lyle?"

"Yeah, can you see me?"

No. But I wish to hell I could. Can he see me? I…I… Shiham digs his nails into my shoulder, a warning to behave. I shut my eyes: Mineshka, Loniad, Ilea. Mineshka crying.

"Yeah, yeah, I can see. You look good, bro." I wish I knew that was true.

"You look tired. Everything go okay?"

Did everything go okay? Did it? Is it? Hysteria bubbles within me. I hold it in, because I don't know what will come out. I might scream or start laughing like a crazy person until I cry. If I cry, I won't stop.

The nails dig deeper.

I let out a breath and smile. "Yeah. Everything's okay."

"You didn't end up having to fight or anything? What's your court like? Is it weird being with them? Do you…"

I bite my lip, blinking back startled tears. Lyle seems so elated to talk to me. He asks so many questions, curious about me in a way he hasn't been in a very long time.

"Dev?"

I'm not answering fast enough, probably missed a few things. But just listening to his voice, recognizing the relief in it, is breaking me in half. "I'm glad you're okay, Lyle."

"I didn't tell you I was."

"You sound okay." I let out a careful chuckle, cutting it off before it mutates into something I can't control.

"And you sound weird." His voice is laced with

suspicion. "You can tell me if you ran into trouble. Did you...have you used your Stone?"

A sob tries to escape my throat. I swallow hard. "Yeah. I did. There was a fight, but...we won. It was just..."

Shiham's nails draw blood. Maybe I'm saying too much for him, but Lyle needs me to say more. My next exhale is shaky, but my voice is firm. "I just don't want to talk about it now. We can talk when I get back to Lenore."

Silence from Lyle again. Does he know something's wrong? Please let him know something's wrong. *Lyle, help.* I try to push the thought across Sectors.

"When will you be back? Did anyone give you an ETA?" His tone is normal again, the skepticism gone.

My heart crashes and I forget to breathe. He believed me. Holy shit, he's letting it go.

A prod from Shiham. Lyle's waiting for my next answer. "A week or so. Maybe a little longer. The ship was...damaged." I shut my eyes, shoving memories of my murdered crew out of mind. I'm sure I'll have nightmares for the rest of my life. My head spins as I force a smile into my voice and onto my face. "Hey, is Lawrie back yet? How'd he do on his mission?" Lyle wouldn't sound this upbeat, if Lawrie wasn't with him, right? Though, I'm not with him and he's... I shake my head. No. This isn't Lyle's fault. "Tell me about Lawrie. And your court and Caea." And I won't tell you about Xijure.

Lyle fills me in that Evan went with Lawrie to retrieve his Stone, and they got back before he did. They're recovering and giving the Lenoran healers hell. But when I ask what they are recovering from he says, "Don't worry, Dev. They're fine." After that, he changes the subject and I know something's up. I need to stop him, press him for what he's not saying. But he's talking so fast. Going on about his court and Caea in a voice I've never heard him use when discussing other people. His words are light, almost tentative, as he compliments them. Did Lyle make friends?

God, Lyle, do you even need me? I'm simultaneously devasted and hopeful. My brother might be healing in a healthy way, but without me there to foster it. He hit a major milestone on his own. Shiham's grip is the only thing keeping my brain focused for the duration of the conversation. I "mmhmm" and "oh" in the right places, until finally, Lyle's voice fades away.

I slump out of the chair, hitting my head on the floor. The last words I hear before I pass out are: "You will be favored by Lord Kahine."

SHIHAM DIDN'T LIE. I WAKE up in a softly lit, small room in a fresh jumpsuit that feels like cotton. The bed beneath me is thin and hard with no blankets or pillows. My hair is damp, and my body feels clean. Clammy feelings of revulsion make me shudder. Someone stripped me and gave me a wash off, while I was unconscious.

Who knows what else they did or could have done while I was out? My body continues to shake. Revulsion escalating into anger. I leap off the bed, bare feet hitting the warm floor, and punch out. My fists strike the door in front of me, the sound of flesh meeting steel the only thing louder than my panting.

Faster. More force. If I hit hard enough, I can break down the door. I can run, find Mineshka and Xijure. And we can…

The floor vibrates beneath my feet. Large engines groan. I stop punching, listening to voices outside my door. They laugh as they discuss how easy it was to win today. How pretty the enemy woman in the cell is, and how she doesn't fight. That it's fun to make a king eat crumbs. And how pathetic the little leader of Rema is. Could they all really be that weak?

I fall forward against the door, letting it support me as I struggle to catch my breath. I punch at the steel again, and it doesn't bend. My knuckles throb, as I stare at the bloody fist prints staining the metal.

"*Ayo*, shut up in there!"

One of the voices is closer. Bet whoever it is wouldn't talk like that if this door was open. If I could reach them, I'd grab them by the neck and…

My stomach aches as the rage dulls. I wanted to slaughter the people who hurt Loniad and my crew. Wanted to kill Owelu. I fought so hard with my Stone, pummeling bodies until they went down. I don't remember seeing them get back up. I didn't check. My pulse rockets as my body slides down the length of the door. The floor is hard and unforgiving, but it doesn't stop me from lying on it.

If I hurt anyone, I was right. They murdered my people. But my actions didn't help anybody in the end. Ilea and Loniad are dead. I pound the floor with one bloody hand. Mineshka is a hostage with perverts guarding at her. I pound again. Xijure is somewhere, like me. Helpless. Lost. About to be dragged to meet Pan.

Or maybe I'll be the only one delivered to the god.

Xijure said he didn't want to hear Pan out. But after I listen to Him, what happens? Will He kill me, because I won't go against the people who trust me to end the war? Those people will go on about their normal lives when this over. But what about my life, and Mineshka's, and Xijure's?

Hopelessness smothers me. The last words I said to my brother were lies about joining him soon. No one knows I'm missing, that Xijure and Mineshka are missing. That Loniad and Ilea are dead.

Oh God.

Why didn't I yell out to Lyle? Blurt out what happened, that I love him. That I... don't want to die. Save me. But maybe I would have died then. Mineshka certainly would have. Tears burn my eyes, and I don't care if the laughing soldiers hear me. Don't give a damn how weak or pathetic they think I am.

A knock on the door doesn't interrupt my breakdown. Come in and kick me. I don't care.

"Landing soon," the person outside grunts.

The sound of heavy footsteps moves away. The laughter grows distant.

Oh G—wait. Why do I keep thinking 'Oh God?' It's an expression for frustration, fear. I was never actually calling out to anyone, because I didn't believe there was anyone. Now I know there is. And I've been calling the wrong name.

It's hard to breathe through my clogged throat and runny nose. Hard to think as my heart threatens to explode and my body shakes so hard my brain rattles. But prayers, real prayers. I've heard them. How do I rephrase them to speak to Her? She owes me. I came here on a mission for Her. This is Her fault. She has to send somebody to get us out of this. She'll broadcast a message, like She did for Evan, because this can't be the end for me.

Time ticks by, and eventually things quiet. No more taunting voices from the outside. No marching boots. My body exhausts itself. I don't have the energy to tremble and my heart's too tired to race. I sigh, lungs sluggish, heavy from overwork, and shut my eyes.

Religious people claim that prayers to gods need to be said aloud for them to work. I lick dry lips, tasting blood and salt, and crack my healing knuckles. I block out pain and every other pitiful emotion I feel, and pray to Order, because it's the only thing I haven't tried.

I wait for Her answer.

But, if anything, it's quieter in here.

The ship shudders. Engines coming back to life with hearty groans. My stomach does a familiar dance. The one that lets me know a plane or spacecraft is preparing to land. I feel the odd sensation of a slow descent in the middle of my gut.

I roll over, waiting to be sick. And waiting for Her voice. An announcement from overhead comes instead. It drifts from the ceiling, throaty and firm. "Secure yourselves for landing."

There's probably a chair somewhere in here with straps. The previous ships I've been on had them in every room. I don't get up to find it, as we continue to sink into the atmosphere of whatever planet we've reached.

"Order?" I speak to the air or the *ether* others go on about.

Nothing. I feel nothing from Her or the Stone.

I mentally reach for Lyle again. But I know he can't hear me.

Know it's over.

No one's coming to save me.

I pray Pan is better than Order. I need Him to be, if I'm going to get myself, Mineshka and Xijure home. I wonder what He'll offer and what He'll want in exchange.

Because screw Order.

22
LYLE

"YOU KNOW, PEOPLE ARE GOING to start think-ing you were the brother sent to the tundra planet," I say, chuckling as Evan blows a smoke ring at me. I fan away the smoke, and the breeze makes him shiver, even through two layers of clothing over a thermal suit.

"You let an *ether* beast put its claws through your chest and see how well you do afterward." Evan stum-bles on his bad leg, and I reach out to support him until he rights himself. He rubs at the partially healed wound in his thigh. Behind us, Healer Palyani utters a curse and Evan growls. I don't have to read either of their minds to know that they think the same thing about one another: *idiot*. Healer Palyani can't get over how stubborn Evan is about resting, and Evan thinks she's holding him back from getting into shape.

I've been on Lenore for a week, keeping to the pal-ace to avoid the common people who enjoy staring at one of the Four. Can't say I mind hanging out with Law-rie and Evan on the healing floor, but that comes with its own set of groupies. A few of the palace-hands have taken to bowing to me, like I'm one of their Maidens or a Harliel. Caea laughs every time I cringe or refuse to leave the great house for dinner with her in the city. She's used to being royal. I think it sucks.

"Ev, maybe we should rest." I glance over my shoulder at Healer Palyani. The tall, green woman looks annoyed, her long arms folded over her chest. "We've walked around the pond trails three times already."

On Earth, the distance would have been a few miles, and I can tell my brother is tired. "Let's sit there." I nod to a bench carved into a tree a few paces away.

The healing floor's atrium is an indoor forest of green grass, vines, electric-blue ponds and rainbow-colored bodibices, hopping from fat red and yellow flowers. Tall trees that reach through the ceiling to the floors above are hollowed at ground-level to make bench seats. Some have curled roots, large and flat enough to be tables, circling their trunks. Two healers and an apprentice sit on a bench, white crackers and colorful jams spread out on the table in front of them. They wave in our direction and I nod.

Evan doesn't fight me as I steer him to an unoccupied tree. Healer Palyani smiles at me, scowls at my brother, and joins the people who waved.

"*Hades and Ether*," Evan says with a long sigh. "I'm starting to hate that lady." He shrugs off my help and lowers himself onto the bench. His eyes squeeze shut as he grips his leg with both hands.

Worry has me crouching next to him. "Are you okay?"

"Back off," he says through his teeth. I raise my hands in defeat. My brother's impossible.

He and Lawrie had portaled back to Lenore with their group days before me and mine and had spent those days in recovery chambers. Neither had been at the mini-parade that greeted my team when we first landed. I'd seen them later that night, Evan stuck in a mobile chair and Lawrie wearing a pair of goggles with dark blue lenses that hid his eyes.

"I should be running by now, and warmer." Evan lets go of his leg. "My rhythms are so off." He gives a full-body shudder. "Never should have worked that magic."

He keeps saying that, hating his choice, so I offer a little positive reinforcement. "But you killed one of Pan's Champions with it. If you practice—"

"No." Evan shoots me a dark look and blows into his steepled hands. "It was wrong. If I had cleared my head and thought about it for a *wisp* longer, I could have come up with something else." He winces, hand going to his leg again. "That *fipping* Stone, it made it seem like that particular spell was my only option."

"Maybe because it was the only thing that would have worked," I say.

Order wants us all to live. Of course Her power would help Evan do what needed to be done.

"Yeah." Evan sounds bitter. "Look how well it worked out. A lot of people are dead, Desiri's still in a healing chamber, and Lawrie's blind."

My chest tightens. "The blindness is temporary."

That's what the healers think anyway. With all the magic and science in the Allegiances, someone can fix Lawrie's eyes. I've seen them re-attach arms and legs that would have been lost causes on Earth.

"I could have summoned a wind sphere," Evan

says. "That didn't even occur to me and it should have. I made choices that dug me deeper into the grave. It's not right, Ly."

"So, we'll fix it with training. We've all got our Stones, and we're ready to move on with Silver and Gold Allegiance plans."

Evan's forehead furrows as he shakes his head. "You're almost like a new person, little brother. Stones and Allegiance plans? You typically don't care about that kind of stuff."

I shrug. "It's what we have to do. Being trapped in a cave, scared shitless, with a bunch of people counting on me to save them was a wake-up call. Ask Caea. I stepped up."

Evan puffs another smoke ring. "I *did* ask Caea."

My heart skips. "What?"

"I wanted to know how it was for you over there with head trauma and without Dev. I wasn't sure you'd be comfortable talking to me about it. She said you had a rough time, but in the end, you did what needed to be done."

"Yeah, yeah, we did," I say.

"Yeah, *you* did." Evan smiles at me. "You, Lawrie and Dev are amazing, you know. I don't know that I could have just stepped into this, without real training, and won."

I roll my eyes. "Of course you would have."

I'm pretty sure of it. It hadn't taken more than a week for me to learn that my big brother will find a way to do anything or die trying. "But it does mean a lot to me that you think I did something good." I'm so used to Devon looking at me like I'm losing it, and Lawrie straight up thinking I don't give a shit about anything.

"So, the Stone, how does it make you feel?"

I blink, suddenly aware of the warm sapphire hanging from a fancy silver chain against my chest. All of us have to remember to send a thank you note to the city-smith who turned each of our Stones into a pendant. So convenient, but it's tacky as hell to wear with a T-shirt, so I keep it tucked in.

"What do you mean how does it make me feel?"

"You have it on you," Evan says. "I sense it."

"Yeah, so?" I ask.

His greens eyes, shadowed with purple bags, analyze me. "The only way I can sense your Stone is if you're using it. Are you taking power from it now?"

The Stone's energy seeps through the skin of my chest, flowing through my heart, pumping into my brain, keeping my shields strong. "Yes."

"And it doesn't bother you to borrow power from Her, when you don't need it?"

"No."

"Liar."

"I haven't had a migraine in days," I say. "Haven't blacked out, haven't had to take any medicine, or get treatment." It *would* bother me if I was borrowing power from Order that I don't need, but I do need it.

"That Stone isn't medicine, Lyle. You haven't made any new appointments with the mind-healer since you've been back. You can't stop going."

"I'll..." I can't say I'll make new appointments, not to Evan. So, I say, "Fine." The word by itself isn't a lie Evan can pick up on.

He quirks a brow at me in a very Mom-like manner. "A call came through from Earth this morning."

My heart speeds up. "Mom?" I ask, before I realize

it couldn't be.

Evan shakes his head. "Ambassador SeCaeta's son—Lawrie's friend. He used his dad's codes. The call almost got all the way to Lawrie, but Viveen intercepted it."

"I don't get why they won't let us call home or let home call us now that we all have our Stones," I say. "We should talk to them about it."

Evan tosses his head back and cackles. "I like this new Lyle very much, but *he* still needs to make sure his head is screwed on right. See the mind healer and take that rock off every once in a while." He pokes the Stone under my shirt. "It's not good for you."

The Stone pulses gently, my heart palpitates.

"I get it, little brother. My Stone makes me feel powerful too." Evan pulls his finger away. "Too powerful. After it's done, I look at the destruction we caused together. And yeah, we won, but…" He gazes past me, and I follow his eyes. Two bodibices fight over a yellow flower. The thick petals, large as palm leaves, break off, and the fleshy center disintegrates. The bodibices jump apart, hovering over the flower's carcass.

"It didn't have to happen that way," Evan says slowly. "Better choices, better outcomes."

"The Stones help us. Offer us answers. I mean, you can give or take them, but in the end, here we are. I don't see anything wrong with what we've done."

Evan hums, attention still on the bugs. "No, you really don't. And maybe that's okay. I don't know. Listen, we've learned some things about Order and Pandemonium. I'm going to question Imari about it. She had a relationship with Corin Peredil."

Panic. I slap the table to get his eyes back on me.

"You should keep away from Imari."

His eyes sparkle with amusement. "Why? Scared she'll start eye-stripping me the way Nialiah eye-strips you, when you're not looking. You better watch yourself in dark corners."

Ugh. Just ugh. I shudder, thinking about Nialiah's openly thirsty looks in my direction.

"Shut up," I say. "But look, we know The Maidens are hiding something. Research can be good, but let's keep it between us: Lawrie, Dev, your court, you, and me. Okay? The last thing we want is for them to get defensive."

I won't let my brother end up like Corin Peredil. I can't let anybody in Order's circle think Evan is going to cause the same problems his predecessor did.

Evan practically glows as he chuckles, and then crinkles his eyes in pain, between breaths. "Okay, you're scared of The Maidens. So, fine. We'll keep our investigation a 'family affair,' for now. That all right with you, Leader Three?"

I really don't see what's so funny, and I won't try to get into his head to figure it out. "You're nuts, bro."

He grimaces. "Are you going to see Lawrie after his session?"

"Yeah, why? You want to come?"

"No, I'll see him for dinner. I want to lie down for a bit."

I get up, ready to help him up too. It's not every day Evan admits to fatigue. "I can drop you off at your room."

"I'm not sleeping in there." Evan smacks my hands away.

I watch him limp over to the pond. He lowers himself carefully and lies on the grass.

I follow him. "You'll be okay here?"

"Please. What do you think can happen in the middle of a healing ward?" He shuts his eyes and it takes only seconds before exhaustion slows his breathing.

I hover over him a minute longer, and a surge of emotion cramps my stomach. He's thinner. His dark brown skin pale, his braided hair lackluster as it rests over his shoulder. Seeing him this way sends me back to the time he was half-dead in limbo. I'd been frantic to rescue him because he was my brother, even before I actually knew him.

Healer Palyani's still at the table with her friends. She'll take care of Evan. I plant the suggestion for her to cover him with a thermal throw, and I relax as it takes root. I don't wave goodbye as I pass them and travel through the atrium into a hallway that leads me to the recovery corridor.

The recovery wing is broken into two sections: therapy and resting. Evan has been on the resting side since his surgeries. The rooms are small and private, access limited to healers and Maidens. I heard Imari was in and out of Evan's room while he was recovering from anesthesia, when even his court was denied entrance. She stopped visiting after he woke up completely, and I'm glad.

I head to the therapy section to see Lawrie, going down another hallway with moss-covered wooden walls. What made Lenorans decide they needed walls and roofs? They seem to do everything in their power to bring nature indoors. Why not just stay out there with it?

Privacy maybe. But they could rope off places. Make magical fences that curse people who walk on their grass. Damn, that would be a nightmare on Earth. I imagine kids slung halfway across the world after jumping a magic fence to retrieve a soccer ball. The lawsuits would be ridiculous. Mom's legal services would be worth millions.

A pang of homesickness lances my chest. I want to call Mom, talk to her and Dad, and even Nikki, for a minute. What would Mom think about my choice? Would she say I'm doing the right thing?

She's a dealmaker. She would have taken it. At least, I think she would. But...

I pass five doors, pausing at a sixth before knocking. I'm still thinking about that 'but.' But what? Uncertainty makes me want to take the medicine I'd thrown out. I finger the chain around my neck instead, comforted it's there. A soft blue glow traces the edges of the Stone under my gray shirt. The light fades, and I reach out with my power, probing the room. The swirl of Lawrie's rambling thoughts behind a thin barrier meets my mental touch. His mind is the only one I sense.

/It's me. You decent?/

Whoa...uh...gimme a minute.

The door hums and slides open after a few seconds. I enter the dim room, lit by a single lamp that casts my shadow across the floor and walls. Two yellow armchairs sit in the center of the space. Lawrie is sprawled in one, head tilted toward the vaulted ceiling, dark goggles positioned over his forehead like a sweatband. A skinny strip of white cloth protects his eyes.

"Hey, Ly. Evan not coming?"

"He said he'll see you at dinner."

"He okay?" Lawrie straightens. The cloth doesn't slip off his face. It's stuck on like a superhero mask.

"He's tired. And his leg hurts."

"He's still feeling that phantom shadow," Lawrie says. "Imari told me it's like frostbite on the soul, but it fades. It'll just take a while for him to shake it."

"Imari's not a healer."

"No, but she knows things."

An understatement.

All the furniture in the room's been taken out, aside from the two chairs. Last time I was in here, there had been tables laden with smoking bowls and wind chime-things hanging from the light fixtures. "What'd y'all do today?"

"Meditation and visualization stuff." Lawrie leans forward to put his hands on his knees. "What do you have against Imari?"

"Huh?" That had come from nowhere.

"When you talk about her, or any of The Maidens, your voice changes," Lawrie says. "You sound colder."

"Oh?"

Lawrie smiles, seeming pleased with himself. I don't like it, though. People say that when you lose one sense your others get stronger. I think it just makes you pay attention to senses you downplayed in the past.

"I don't like The Maidens," I say. Not a lie at all.

"I think you used to hide it better. Nialiah sounds all wounded when you talk to her." His voice lowers, tone teasing. "Better be careful, or she'll quit crushing on you."

I flop down in the other armchair, across from him. "Shut up. Both you and Evan are stupid."

Lawrie grins. "Weak comeback, bro."

I kick his knee with the heel of my sneaker, letting him find my leg with his hand and smack it away. His grin widens.

"You know what else I notice?"

"What?"

"The way your voice changes when Caea Harliel's around. What's that about?"

I'm glad half his face is covered by that rag so I can't see his eyebrows doing that dumb dance. "Thought I told you to shut up."

"Seriously, though." Lawrie's wild smile calms into a regular one. "You like her, or something?"

I shrug but realize he can't see it. Poor kid. Sadness envelopes me, but somebody's going to fix it.

"Yeah, I like Caea."

Whatever. I'm not going to hide it from anybody. And hell, she asks me out all the time. Well, to dinner, and it's with her brother too, but still.

It makes me feel good to see Lawrie beam. He reaches over, missing once before finding my shoulder. He squeezes it. "Good for you. I think she's cool. Do you? I mean, she's not like those other girls, you know, back home."

Shame fills me as my long roster of high school girl-friends and hookups revolve around my brain, stopping on a silver sheened, heart-shaped face. No, Caea would never be Nisse—or Heather, or Gabby, or anyone else. She'd never let me hurt her. I'd never let myself hurt her.

It never has to come to that again.

I rub the Stone through my shirt. "No, Caea's different."

"Your voice changed."

"Because I'm talking about Caea?" How funny.

"No." Lawrie's grin is gone, expression troubled. "It went distant and kinda flat."

I touch his hand. "Are you okay?"

"Are you wearing it?"

"Wearing what?" I ask.

"Your Stone," Lawrie says. "You get this faraway tone sometimes, and Evan says you talk like that when you're touching it. He says you wear the necklace a lot. And...I sense it. You're using it."

"And?" I ask. "Are you going to tell me you feel the same way Evan does?"

Lawrie laughs. "Look, I get it. I felt like Shazam with my Stone. I didn't understand why Evan hated his so much, but when I took it off and put it in a damper pouch, like he does, I felt different. Not bad different, not OMG I was brain-jacked, but without it, I realized that maybe it's not such a great idea to feel like I can do anything all the time. Evan feels like he makes bad decisions under his Stone's influence. We might end up feeling that way too. I think we should only wear the Stones when we need them."

"I don't feel like my decisions are impaired, Lawrie."

"All right, Smeagol. Whatever you say, but now you know what I think, and what Evan thinks. Wait till Dev is here to weigh in on it. Let's see, you talked to him two days ago, and he told you he'd be here in about week." Lawrie hums, probably checking off calendar days in his head.

My body goes cold at the thought of Devon looking at me like I'm some hopeless mental patient. He would probably see me using the Stone the same way as he'd seen me using Aderyn's drugs. His judgement would hurt.

"Ly?"

"Huh? Oh, yeah. He'll be here next week." After we disconnected, Dev's team had gone back on radio silence.

"Must have been an insane party on Disiez, huh?" Lawrie said. "Did he talk much about his Stone?"

I shake my head. Dammit, he can't see me. "No, he didn't." He hadn't talked much about himself at all. He wanted to know how I was doing, and I rambled because he sounded like he needed to hear my voice. Worry stirs deep inside me. Devon said he fought, and I think someone close to him died. It's the only way to explain why he seemed so reticent to share his mission experiences. We hadn't seen each other in weeks, yet I was the only one who seemed eager to reconnect. It hurt. But if he's grieving over someone and blaming himself—because that's a Devon thing to do—then, I understand. I just wish he were here, so I could do a real assessment of his mental state. He'd looked so tired.

Lawrie touches his face, fingers trailing over the cloth. "He's gonna crap a brick over this. It was a good idea not to tell him."

Crap a brick and guilt himself for not insisting that he go with Lawrie. But that hadn't been a choice he could make. We were separated. He should be glad that Evan was with Lawrie, but Dev doesn't take well to answers like that.

"Maybe we'll have you all cured, before he gets here," I say. "How'd therapy go?"

Lawrie leans back. "Same old, same old. I still can't see, Ly. No shapes, no shadows, no changes in light. My head hurts when my eyes aren't covered though. The healers think it's a sign that something in there is still working and light sensitive. They're gonna try some magic tomorrow."

"Why haven't they been trying magic?" I can't keep frustration out of my tone.

"They used it to heal the burns, but they don't want to overload my synapses. They claim it could burn me all over again, and cause spell damage. So, it's gotta be slow. They even…"

"They even what?" I ask, as his words register within me. Spell damage and burns. They could hurt him more.

"They want to send me to a medical center on another planet. They've got people there who specialize in restoring senses and working around spell damage, if it happens."

"Travel's dangerous. We need to limit unnecessary comings and goings," I say. "Can't they come here?"

"They don't leave Bruhje," Lawrie says. "Can't. I hear they draw their magic from the planet's core."

Magic users and their stupid limitations. "Where is Bruhje?"

"In Sector Five," Lawrie says, as if I've memorized the same star maps he has.

I don't know where the hell that is, but it sounds far from here. Something's off about him. He's not bouncing in his chair. Even in this horrible situation, Lawrie should be a little excited about going to a brand-new planet.

"What's wrong?" I ask.

Lawrie sighs, a half-smile forming on his lips. "One of our uncles lives on Bruhje. Devrik has two brothers, you know. The one on Amphora who helped us, and this guy. Apparently, he's Devrik's favorite."

"And you don't want to meet him?" That's weird.

"Nah, it's just..." Lawrie slouches lower in his chair. "He's Devrik's favorite, so Devrik stays with him when things go south."

Devrik Lauduethe. I honestly forgot about him. He's just a guy that was important a long time ago, because he and Mom made us, but who cares about him? Has he made any attempt to call? No. And he's the parent who's actually allowed to contact us. There's no ban on his presence in our lives at the moment. He'd been safe on Rema, while I was on Kupiku, almost dying. Now, he's hanging with his favorite brother on a planet that has to be as well-guarded as Lenore. If it wasn't, they wouldn't be considering sending Lawrie there without us.

"So, guess who's on Bruhje with Uncle Aeric?"

The air turns heavy, literally. It's so dense each breath feels like it comes with a glass of water.

"Lawrie..." is he doing this? "I think you need to calm down."

"Huh?"

"You just made the—never mind." I check him over, looking for bulges in the pockets of his sweatpants or a shape under his white 'GOT CHOCOLATE MILK?' T-shirt. "You're not wearing your Stone. When did you start having problems with your powers like that?"

Lawrie shrugs and the air pressure eases, the moisture returns to normal. "It's not a problem. I'm just *on* now. You know, once I started exercising what I can do, my powers feel free to come out and just connect, without me having to actively think about them. Chasyn says that it should have always been like this. Earth cramped my style. Now, I just have to practice not letting my power give away my moods."

"So, *that* was nerves about meeting Devrik?"

Lawrie shakes his head. "No, it's…" He waves his hands over his face. "I'm blind. This trip to Bruhje is it. If they can't fix it, well, then, this is me."

"The healers said that?"

"They didn't have to," Lawrie says. "And the person I get to be with, if things don't work out, is Devrik. I don't want him."

"I'll go with you." My response is automatic, but my feelings about it aren't. I don't want to be exposed to Lawrie's devastation, if his blindness is permanent. I'm not equipped to comfort people. It's not my forte. I… "Or Devon will go. You know he'll want to."

Lawrie pops his neck. "The war, Ly. None of you guys can come with me. It'll be all they can do to sneak me out and keep it quiet that I'm not here. And who knows how long the treatment might take, before it either works or doesn't. It's just gonna be me, and my court probably. Gotta have the bodyguards, huh? But Chasyn's mad cool. If he's coming, then it'll be okay." He scratches the back of his head. "But, you know, I always thought that we'd meet Devrik together."

"Yeah." It really isn't fair to make Lawrie meet our father alone.

"Evan says it'll be fine, though." Lawrie stands up, stretching his legs like a runner. "Shizz, I feel like I've been in that chair all day. My butt's asleep, man. But, yeah, Ev says *Ricky* is chill, won't push me or anything. He'll even leave me alone, if I end up feeling really weird about him being around me."

Ricky. Mom's name for Devrik back when they'd been married. "Maybe he'll be happier if you don't act like you want him there for you."

Lawrie's back cracks as he twists from side to side. "Yeah, I get that feeling too. But he's our friggin' dad. I don't want more from him, and I kind of do. I guess I want to feel some connection even though he won't be like Dad. I don't even think he's like Dad for Evan."

True. When Evan talks about Devrik, it's almost like he's discussing a roommate he'd had once—messy, quirky, and ultimately not around enough to ever really hate. How had that guy raised a little kid on his own? But then again, I don't think he did. Evan belonged to the Remasian Council and the Silver Allegiance from the time he set foot on Remasian soil.

I should ask Evan more about his childhood. With so much shit flying around, I forget I don't know more about Evan than he what tells us. He's lived a whole life I don't know about, doing more than just 'leader' stuff. He's a guy who never got to dream about college and senior prom night and a birthday car for his sixteenth. Not that I dreamed about that stuff either, but still... What does Evan want after this?

I smile, remembering Caea's wants and starting to think about mine. Because there will be an 'after' for us. And...

Will they hate me, when they find out what I agreed to? In the end, they'll watch other worlds die, knowing that I knew it would happen, and despise me.

And 'after' those feelings pass, they will be glad they are not dead as well, that there is new life to do whatever it is they so choose. Because of you.

I rub the Stone. "You'll be fine, Lawrie. No matter what."

"Even blind forever?" His voice is soft.

I glance up, realizing I'd been staring at the blue

glow emanating through my shirt. When had it started doing that again? In the dim light of the room, I catch wetness on one of Lawrie's cheeks. My stomach twists. "Lawrie?"

"I'm okay." He puts his back to me. "But, uh, let me catch a shower and maybe a nap too. Dinner in the atrium?"

An image of Caea in a sleeveless red tunic and black slacks smiling up at me from an art book pops into my head. I feel a knock on my mental barrier, and I open the gate.

/Yes, Majesty?/

Dinner in the city tonight? Come on, you need to get out.

I want to eat with her, share with her, know her more, like I want to know Evan, but I also want to cheer Lawrie up.

"We should do dinner outside of here, Lawrie. We can go to a place with music and lots of accents."

/Pick someplace interesting...and loud./ I think to Caea.

Lawrie doesn't face me. He's quiet, and I stand up. I'm not the hugger, not the nice one, but I take a few steps in his direction, touching his shoulder. He spins around, hugging me quick, then letting go.

"Not tonight, Ly. But you sound like you want to go out, and you should. I think I'm going to eat with Chasyn and my court. I'm still getting to know all of them. Better we do it alone. Take Evan out with you."

"Are you sure?" It doesn't feel right. His face is still wet.

"When do you ever have fun, Ly? Like ever? In fact, don't take Ev, ask your girl Caea."

I blink at him and he continues on as if he can see my blank expression. "Brah, let the queen take you on a date. Who knows how many chances you'll get? Once Dev gets here, things are really gonna start blowing up, literally."

They already have. Reports of border skirmishes have multiplied, and hundreds of previously unsigned planets are flocking to join planetary allegiances as more Cold Zones are seized.

My body trembles, the Stone hums.

"All right then. But Lawrie," I pat his shoulder again, "I want dinner in the city with you, before things really blow up. When Dev gets here, we'll all go out."

Lawrie smiles and wipes at his face, tears gone, but he looks so tired. "Okay."

He clears his throat and touches my hand on his shoulder, then flicks it off. "Now stop being weird and get out of here! You're giving me the creeps."

I leave the room to the sound of his laughter. Silly little brother. But I don't think I'd have him any other way.

/Hey, Majesty?/

It's about time.

/Will it be dinner for two, or are you bringing Ramesis?/

Her mental image in my mind grins. *I'm sensing that you'd rather it be two, and I'm sure Ram won't mind at all. But you better keep me entertained.*

/Yes, ma'am./

WE TOOK A CART INTO the small city about thirty minutes away from the palace and ate in an outdoor restaurant. Red and purple bulbs as big as birthday balloons floated around the tables, keeping the wooden patio area lit. All of the food had a strange grass-like after taste to it that neither of us liked, so we grabbed dessert from a booth on a silver-cobbled street. The custard-like cream was delicious, and we took it with us into an open art gallery.

I'd never really gone to any art exhibits to enjoy paintings and sculptures. I saw artwork on museum trips with schools or my family, and none of them were inclined to stop and study technique. It was always, 'oh that's pretty,' 'that's hideous,' 'a toddler did it,' 'move it, let's go!' Just strolling around, listening to Caea analyzing styles and colors and trying to see the same thing she saw was perfect. She's perfect.

Walking, instead of taking a cart back to the palace, side-by-side, I relive every minute of our time together. I jump when the large entrance is opened for us and she grabs me, pulling me toward a staircase. Her lips are soft on mine, a gentle tease that she breaks almost immediately. I reach for her, wanting to pull her against me, to try that kiss again, deeper. But she laughs and shakes her head.

"I can tell you have plenty of experience with other women," she says, "but you've got much to learn when it comes to me."

We hold hands, ignoring stares from nosy Lenorans pretending to clean and be into their own business. I walk her halfway up a staircase and stop.

"You're not going to bed?" Caea asks, frowning at

me not coming with her the rest of the way.

I shake my head. "I need to check in with Viveen and Theorne."

"Hm." Caea's eyes are warm. "They're starting to see something in you, aren't they?"

I shrug and jump when she pulls me close, not caring that we might fall down the stairs. She smells like outside, flowery and sweet. I take in her beautiful face, millimeters from mine. What does she want? I know what I want.

Our lips meet again and this time she doesn't pull away. I wrap my arms around her, feeling her hands slide into my hair as the kiss deepens and lasts, until I need to breathe.

She laughs full out, ruffling my hair and kissing my cheek. "Goodnight, Lyle."

"Uh…yeah…'night." I sound like a dumb kid who has never been kissed, and maybe I haven't been, if that's what it's supposed to be like.

I want more, and not for the sake of pain-numbing pleasure, or brain-healing silence. I'd felt none of that while I'd kissed her. I just felt. Felt her smooth lips, warm mouth, firm hands. I hadn't tapped into her mind for emotions. I didn't need them, didn't want them. Instead, I just felt my own.

Caea continues up the stairs without looking back.

Romantic love is a useless concept made up by sappy idealists without a clue about what really goes on inside of a person's brain. It isn't real, not like most people think it is.

But…maybe I'm wrong.

Caea's form vanishes and I glare at a few Lenorans not even pretending to be doing something else anymore.

I shake my head, hand on my lips, as I venture into the back halls.

The deeper under the palace I travel, the colder it is. The dungeon, where the Ruj prisoners had been, is down here somewhere, but the Stone leads me beyond that. I pull it out of my shirt, letting it light the way as the torches against the walls become fewer and farther apart. Cobwebs stretch across rough black rock. My feet crunch over carcasses of dead insects. I chance a look down, grimacing at multitudes of legs and antennae. Guess Lenore has roaches too.

I shake off a chill and reach double doors that look like the entrance to a medieval vault. Two huge black rungs hang where doorknobs would be. The Stone pulses once, and I grip a rung, hissing at the rusty grit that crusts my palms. I pull and the doors yawn, low and long. Five heads around a table turn. They're too far away for me to make out their expressions, but I feel their shock.

Go on.

Right. Steeling my shoulders, I walk in, struck by déjà vu. I've been here before. I recognize the mossy walls, milky floor, and the long table surrounded by chairs. This is the room Nialiah had brought Jain to all those years ago.

Nialiah sits beside Hellene, her dark eyes curious as I come closer. Theorne's face is slack and pale. Viveen seems angry, or maybe that's just her natural facial expression. Even smiling, the woman looks evil. Imari clenches her hands on the table, her small fists shaking.

"Ja—Lyle," Nialiah breathes.

I make myself smile.

Tell them.

I take a deep breath and go to stand beside Hellene who might be ready to strangle me. If Viveen is angry, Hellene is furious. Jealousy echoes off her body in waves. Her shields are rock- solid, but the Stone lets me read her emotions anyway.

Too bad, Hellene.

"I spoke with Order on Kupiku. We have an understanding, and I'm going to be joining you down here from now on." I hold the eyes of everyone around the table.

Hellene growls, rising from her seat. "She cannot trust *you*. She cannot trust any of you. This will be like last time! You were the reason—"

The Stone's light flares, the brightness hurting my eyes. Hellene cries out. I've never heard her scream. She falls to the ground, her green cheeks pink, raw, scorched. Her hands go to her face.

Viveen gapes at Hellene. Theorne, Nialiah and Imari stare at me. I hope my expression is calm, because I'm not. Shit. I didn't want the Stone to burn Hellene. Just knocking her over would have been enough to scare her.

It would not have been enough.

I can't settle my unease at those words, but I have to trust the Stone is wiser. It channels its knowledge from a goddess. I focus on Theorne, Nialiah and Imari, still gaping at me. Do they want me to say something else?

"You know about the New World and what must happen to achieve it?" Theorne asks.

"I made a deal with Order, just like you. I help Her, She saves the people I care about."

"And you know that Jain Peredil struck a similar bargain, and was unable to fulfill his role?" Nialiah places her hands on the table. "Lyle Lauduethe, we make many decisions at this table that bring bloodshed and ruin to people who trust us. Many sacrifices must be made to bring about our goddess's victory."

She's talking about screwing over planets and people. I think of strategy games where I sacrificed pieces of lesser importance in a desperate attempt to defeat my opponent. Anything to win. Only, we're not talking about pawns and knights on a chessboard.

"I see doubt in your eyes." Hellen picks herself off the floor.

"You don't." Because I know all the people being used are going to die anyway. I just… I hate that so many will perish not knowing that what they fought for was a lie. I'd want to know. "I don't doubt my choice. I just don't like it."

Hellene looks like she wants to say something, but Nialiah speaks instead. "None of us likes it, but you seem to understand that there is no other way for survival."

I frown at her. She and the other Maidens are saving their entire planet. They have less to feel guilty about. But Theorne and Viveen and the handful of other officials from the Allegiances who made bargains with Order? They're evil, because as far I know, the only people they're saving are themselves. For hundreds of years, they shaped and manipulated governments and populations into living tools to be thrown away. Did any of them argue for additional lives?

Theorne and Viveen's eyes are cold. Were they always like this?

Hellene moves to reclaim her chair and cries out again, stumbling backward as if struck. The Stone glows.

That is no longer her seat. Kahanna favors you.

Hellene recovers, and stands still, looking from the

chair to me. All eyes are on me again.

Take your seat, Leader.

I try to seem steady as I cross Hellene's path to steal her place. I sit, waiting for magical bells to chime, but there's nothing special about this chair other than its position. I'm at the head of the table watching Hellene take the empty seat beside Imari.

"It seems the goddess wishes you to lead our circle tonight, Lyle." Nialiah's face is impassive. She's no longer the woman who wanted to make sure I understood what I was getting into.

Lead Order's Circle? My hands sweat as my pulse races. Order said follow Her. She would give me tasks and tell me what to do. Ancient eyes continue to watch me. The councilors and The Maidens wait for my next move.

You told me to come down here. Now, what do I do?

Silence from the Stone. I don't know what's next. I'm ready to tell Order's Circle to go back to what they were doing before I interrupted. What were they talking about? I should be listening, taking notes, learning how to work with the people I'm betraying without feeling sick.

Or do they feel sick sometimes?

But I'm doing what's best, right? This isn't a mistake because there's no other way. I'm here because I'm the only one of my brothers who can make this cold choice. This is right.

I am right.

Warm energy thrums through my veins.

And now that you are ready, repeat after me.

I wait for instruction.

Look to Maiden Hellene and speak the words…
"Summon Kahanna."
It's time to discuss how we end the war.

ACKNOWLEDGMENTS

I know acknowledgments are supposed to be eloquent, but all I have to say is "Wow, Book 2!" Getting here has been a literal rollercoaster of events. Some parts of the process were steep hills to carefully climb while other parts were fast and exciting. This is a story that has been with me since I was in middle school. I know my characters inside and out, but I have never been this far in their actual plot before. This series is an expanding adventure, and I'm a thrill-seeker.

However, I would not be this far along in my writing journey without the support of my village. I will forever be grateful to my sister, Candice Harris, who might love the Lauduethes more than I do. I am also grateful to my best friend, and fellow writer, Kathleen Andrea-Liner who keeps me on my toes and who will read anything for me. I also want to thank Jason Jurinsky, Andrew Stillman, Kathy Nielson, Phoebe Pagano, Cindy Bird, Janice Blaze Rocke, Galia Baron, Colin Campbell, Beth Haymond, and Cherie Rowe for offering excellent feedback and critique through the many stages and versions of this novel.

To my parents, Dale and Teresa Harris, my godmother Joyce Sanders, who believed I could do anything (may she rest in peace) and her sister Tommie Lee Burley, the funniest person I know, thank you for your love and patience.

Finally, I want to say thank you to the 48fourteen Publishing family. Thank you, Denise DeSio, for being a fabulous editor who leaves copious notes, and much thanks and gratitude to Juanita Samborski who continues to give the Lauduethes their time to shine while offering guidance every step of the way.

It is now time to return to my previous state of ineloquence. Wow, Book 2! We're here, and I couldn't be here without everyone mentioned above and then some. To you all, my most heartfelt thanks!

THE AUTHOR

E. Ardell spent her childhood in Houston, Texas, obsessed with anything science fiction, fantastic, paranormal or just plain weird. She loves to write stories that feature young people with extraordinary talents thrown into strange and dangerous situations. She took her obsession to the next level, earning a Master of Fine Arts from the University of Southern Maine where she specialized in young adult genre fiction. She's a big kid at heart and loves her job as a teen services librarian. When she's not working, she's reading, writing, running writers critique groups, filming comedy sketches for social media, directing Zoom plays and even writing fan fiction as her guilty pleasure. Her first YA science fiction novel, *The Fourth Piece*, was released by 48fourteen Publishing in July of 2016. *The Fourth Piece* went on to win the bronze medal for YA Science Fiction in The Readers' Favorite Book Awards 2017, Most Promising Series in the Red City Review Book Awards 2017, and to be a finalist for the 2017 RONE Awards for YA Science Fiction/Paranormal.

For more about E. Ardell,
visit her at:
http://www.eardell.com/

Like her Facebook page:
https://www.facebook.com/eardell

YouTube Channel:
https://www.Youtube.com/EArdell

Instagram:
https://www.Instagram.com/E.Ardell_author

Made in the USA
Middletown, DE
26 March 2022